SCOURGE

OF GODS

Book 1

Born in Darkness

-by-

Thomas A Farmer

ISBN-13: 978-0-9987679-2-5

ISBN-10: 0-9987679-2-1

Published by: Black Knight Books, 2019

For my Parents, John and Susan.

It's all your fault I became a writer anyway.

Chapter 1

In the darkness, letters blinked into existence wreathed in a bloody red light.

FINAL MEMORY DOWNLOAD COMPLETE

As though dredged up by the words, the dreams flooded back into her mind. Monsters without faces clawed at her from the darkness, tearing and ripping with claws and knives caked with blood. At least, they tried to.

This time, when the dreams came, she reacted and moved. Arms and legs and weapons darted around, moving her this way and that. Knives and other weapons sailed harmlessly through the air as she gracefully sidestepped every blow. The monsters grew larger and more distinct with every attack, until burning green eyes glared death into her mind.

Now, when she struck, it was with a weapon. She kept the monsters at bay, piercing them through the face or the throat. Her weapon never sought their chest, where she knew her own heart lay. Instead, every thrust penetrated deep into the impossible darkness behind their masks.

And then the dream faded, as they had all done, with the feeling of her life ebbing away in a pool of blood and pain.

NEURAL ARCHITECTURE AND SELFHOOD ANALYSIS

Something electric ran through her body. The movements and limbs of her dreams were now real. The passage of seconds and the sound of her beating heart filled her ears. She took a deep breath, savoring the sensation of her lungs filling with fluid as though for the first time. A thousand cold needles rushed into her fingers and toes and they flexed, stretched.

Her heart sped up at the new sensation, something the dreams never showed her. It passed in moments as the bloody light around her cooled into a gentle blue. The feeling in her limbs warmed as the chill pinpricks faded away.

COMPLETE

Experimentally, she flexed the fingers of one hand. To her surprise, and perhaps even fear, they moved. The rush of endorphins that accompanied the discovery of motion ensured that the sensation coded itself into her brain as "pleasant." She moved her other hand, turning her head to watch her fingers dance in the dim, blue light of the overhead screen.

The murky biofluid surrounding her body and filling her lungs slowed her movements. Some part of her brain knew that moving in air would be faster and easier. She had been moving through air, not fluid, in her dreams.

DECANTING PROCEDURE ACTIVE

A timer accompanied the message now, counting down. The numbers grew smaller as her heart beat, but this was another thing the dreams never prepared her for. Logically, she assumed that somehow this procedure was a necessary step between her life as it had been and the cold terror of her dreams.

Despite that, she felt no fear. If anything, the emotion lording itself over her thoughts was anticipation. She wanted to be out there—where or whatever "there" was—as quickly as possible.

The countdown continued and she exhaled, eyes following the minute ripples in the current of the fluid as it caught the blue light from above.

She watched the countdown. As each number grew less, additional numbers added themselves to the end, each moving faster than the ones before it. Now, it read: "00:00:30:597." She watched with strange fascination as they seemed to grow faster as her newly-awakened brain grasped the passage of time. The fastest numbers hit zero, and the next set of numbers over clicked to "29" followed by "28" and "27" at an ever-increasing rate.

The countdown finally stopped with a zero in every spot and she heard a faint hiss. It came from the thick biofluid around her. The blue light shimmered as the liquid curled and twisted slowly toward her feet. In moments, it dropped below her head, eliciting an unfamiliar cold chill as air touched her skin for the first time.

An involuntary muscle spasm emptied her nasal cavities and lungs. Instinctively, she took her first deep breath. Air rushed into her lungs, chilling them even colder than her skin. The cold made her shiver, but she was amazed at how quickly her body moved now that it was free of the thick biofluid.

The last of the murky fluid vanished through the drain between her feet as her skin started to adjust to the air. A faint current warmed her, blowing through the interior of her birthplace-turned-prison. After a few moments, she no longer felt cold and her heart started to slow down again. The shock of new sensations was over for the moment.

Now that the opaque fluid no longer shrouded her eyes, she could see past the glowing display of numbers and information. As her eyes adjusted, she noticed the display held more than she first realized. In small print, backwards, were little lines that said her health was good, that her reactions were the way they should be, and a dozen other minor things that she had taken for granted in the moments between oblivion and now.

All of that brought to her mind one question: if the words on her shell were written backward, then for whom were they written? She could read them well enough, but if they were intended for her, they would have been printed in the proper order and direction.

She scanned the room outside her shell and found scant detail, only darkness and vague, shifting shadows. The wall opposite her little window was black tile, lit by the blue-green glow of a single computer screen. Her mind filed those details away as the shadows shifted and moved and a clawing sound scraped through the shell around her, sending a chill down her spine.

The blue light abruptly burned a bright, angry red again. She could not tell if the color was brighter because the biofluid was gone or if this was a different shade of red. At the moment, however, the exact color of the message was not her concern. It appeared backward, designed to be read by who or whatever the small messages were for. Again, reading it proved easy enough for her.

ERROR

MANUAL RELEASE REQUIRED

With no real way to measure the passage of time, and indeed the passage of time itself still being a new concept, she could not be sure how long she stood there. It might have been seconds, or it might have been hours. However much time actually passed, it quickly exceeded her patience and she began to search the inside of the shell for some type of release.

A voice that was not her own, speaking to her in the back of her mind, told her that this was no test. No such problem had ever been encountered by any of the lives in her dreams. Whatever this was, it was unique to her and her alone.

She scraped and pressed on the smooth inside of the shell, failing to find any seam or gap that she could conceivably use to open it. As she searched, her stomach rumbled. Seemingly the last of her organs to function fully, it now tightened upon itself and demanded that she find something to eat.

Angry and frustrated, she sank back against the back wall of the shell as another dream played itself out in front of her eyes. This was different, new. Before, the dreams had taken her entire attention, sight and sound as real as what she was experiencing right at that moment. This dream played itself out in front of her eyes, superimposed on the real world, and she fought to differentiate between the two.

In front of her eyes, hands that were not her own hid a bag made of black fabric. The dream gave her no other information beyond the bag's location. She knew she could find it again if she needed it. When her stomach rumbled again, she assumed she would be needing it very soon.

The scratching on the exterior of the shell grew louder, more regular, and she raised her own hands to beat on the inside. If she could hear sounds from outside, then whatever was out there should be able to hear her.

She struck with the heels of her hands as memories and dreams of lives she had never lived told her how dangerous it would be to use her knuckles to hit something hard and unyielding like the inner surface of the shell. The dull thuds reverberated around the small space, but otherwise went unanswered for some time.

Eventually, the scratching sounds from outside returned. This time they were accompanied by a featureless black visage at her window. Her first reaction was relief, and it washed over her before the more rational parts of her brain could catch up. A mixture of anger and fear replaced it in moments as she remembered other, similar, faces like that from her dreams. The glossy black visor that regarded her from the other side of the window belonged to one of the things that always tried to kill her in her dreams.

The head tilted this way and that, regarding her with what felt almost like curiosity. A long-fingered hand scratched at the window next to the head, then vanished. A moment later, the helmet-shrouded face vanished as well.

Her heart thundered and she struck out at the inside of the shell. Again, the only answer to her attack was a dull thud.

A minute passed before the shell itself groaned and shifted. In front of her, it cracked open and slid apart. One half went to her left, the other to her right, and a small part at the bottom folded several times to create a step down to the floor. Cold, dry air assailed her skin, and she shivered at the sudden sensation.

Smells assaulted her nostrils. Inside the shell, the only thing she could smell was the lack of biofluid. Even that did not have a scent she could describe, only the lack of one. In the time since it drained away and when the shell opened, she became aware of her own body's scent, but that was subtle compared to the complex smells washing over her now.

Even without moving from her spot inside the shell, the scents were strong. The room beyond smelled like dirt and blood. The terms came to her unbidden a moment later. Around her, everything smelled of decomposition and decay. Subtle, buried under those smells was the scent of oil and machines.

As though that had been the missing piece, the smells assailing her awakened the past parts of her brain. They were the smells not only of life, but also of death. The air carried a strong tang of blood, bright and metallic. She had dreamed of that scent. It filled the air when the monsters died. A similar smell, one darker and more faint tickled at the edge of her memory, brought out only in dreams where the monsters killed *her* instead.

Instinctively, She balled her hands into fists at her side as the smell of blood awakened one of the most primal sensations the human body possessed: adrenaline.

Yes, she thought, this is good.

Her adrenaline spiked again as her brain finished parsing the scents around her. Under the dirt and blood, even more faint than the machine smell of oil, were chemical smells. Ozone hung in the air, heavy from the destruction of some computer component or electrical relay. She had no idea what those things were, nor any context for why they might smell like that, but the terms layered themselves in her mind anyway.

Even more faint came a whiff of antiseptic that evoked another memory. This one was dim, barely remembered. Everything about it was fuzzy, from the sights to the sounds and even the smells. The other memories, the dreams especially, all felt real. The featureless blobs of primary color that flitted around at the edges of her vision did not feel like events that ever actually happened.

Despite that, it made her angry. The very feeling of unreality that memory conveyed angered her not because of what it was, but because of what it was not. Her mind tried to tell her that it was just as real as anything else, but she could not reconcile the bright lights and clean scents with the dirt and darkness around her.

Her brain processed all of that in under a second, the memories coming more as flashes and sensations than actual images. Sounds came an instant later, loud and high-pitched. Through the biofluid, everything had a muffled, low quality. With that gone, dim buzzes, pops, and crackles all came as one wall of noise.

She flinched, trying to make sense of it. The shell's once-comforting hum was gone and its absence only intensified the sensation of adrenaline coursing through her body. Even her own breath sounded strange as it echoed in her chest with every inhalation. Like the smells of cleaning chemicals, something else lurked behind those louder noises.

Whatever it was, the sound warned her of danger as a quiet scraping noise slowly climbed above her. It rose by centimeters until it sat directly above her, then quieted again.

Quieting her own breathing, she took stock of her surroundings. The cold feeling in the air was gone as her skin cooled with exposure. She made a fist and the muscles on her arm stood out like steel cables beneath olive skin. She kept that hand in front of her, ready to strike, and raised the other above her head. The sound might have ceased, but the gut-deep warning of danger persisted.

Simply assuming a more guarded position with her arms triggered more snippets of memory as pieces of her dreams coalesced into reality. Her hands may not have experienced violence yet, but her mind had, and connecting the two was proving to be a very simple process.

Walking, however, was more difficult. The first time she tried to move her legs, she wobbled. One leg came up before the other was ready and her balance struggled to adapt for a moment before that foot slammed back down on the floor of the shell. The second time she tried it, her brain was ready. She raised one leg, shifted forward and set it down on the first step outside the shell. A second step followed it, then a third, and she was out of the shell and standing on the cold tile of the floor. The grayish-white tile felt cold and dry, everything that the interior of the shell was not.

She turned, but before she could take in much of the room, a thin shout from above took the entirety of her attention. She pivoted in place, hands already where they needed to be in order to deflect the attack and send the black-suited figure over her shoulder and to the floor. Before it could right itself, instinct took over her limbs and she pivoted on her heels, crouching into a secure ready stance.

Her assailant wore a black bodysuit and helmet that obscured its features. She remembered the suit and helmet from her dreams. This was one of the monsters that she hunted—and that hunted her—in a life before this one. It stood shorter than her, with disproportionately long arms and fingers that darted around in a chaotic swirl that made them hard to follow. In one of the thing's hands, she caught sight of the glint of steel—a knife.

It lunged, arms outstretched. She shifted backward in a move that was not quite a hop and the attacker fell short. It stumbled, overbalanced, and she stepped back in. She remembered shattering the faceplate, but as she raised a hand, a memory flashed across her vision.

In her mind's eye, she struck one of the creatures in the face with her fist. The visor shattered, but the pieces cut deep into a hand that was not hers. That hand bled, sending searing agony through her real hand. The pain only grew worse as she remembered more. The wounds grew infected, swelled, and turned black. Eventually the rot spread, black tendrils along the arm that led to an agonizing, drawn-out death in the darkness.

A violent kick to her ribs brought her back to reality. She sprawled on the floor as her attacker shuffled forward to kick her again. It raised the knife, keeping it pointed at her eyes the entire time.

When the monster raised its leg to stomp, her hands shot out and seized it by the foot. She rose, twisting, and it fell. The knife clattered out of its hands, skidding two full meters across the cold tile floor.

It came to its feet, ready to attack with its hands, but she was faster. In one smooth movement, her rear leg came up, around, and her heel slammed into her attacker's head. The impact sent a shock of pain through her foot, but this was the pain of impact, not the pain of being cut.

The creature fell to the floor, shattering the black plexiglass faceplate. When it rose again, she could see the fishbelly-pale face underneath. Three green eyes rimmed in red stared hatefully back at her. Blood ran from its small nose.

Her attacker uttered something that might have been a curse and lunged again. This time, its attack was much more controlled. The three-eyed thing threw several quick punches, a kick, and then another series of punches. She dodged each of the attacks easily enough, then spared a moment to glance at her surroundings.

That told her two things. First, she was being backed into a corner. Second, she should not have taken her eyes off of the monster right then. A black-gloved fist struck her in the side of the head, sending her stumbling backward. It lunged forward, throwing a punch with its other hand. She stepped into this one, taking it just under her collarbone, and used the momentary interruption of the thing's rhythm to grab that same arm and sling it around.

She threw the creature head first into a nearby table. The impact made a hollow thud and the massive black topped table slid away on hidden wheels. It kicked off the table, pushing it further away and took a moment to claw at its face. Shards of black plexiglass fell to the tile and it glared at her with its three lurid eyes.

She stepped forward, ready to strike, but had to drop into a deep crouch in order to evade a head-level kick. The monster kicked with its other foot and she struck out with the heel of her hand against the side of its knee. It buckled and nearly lost balance, then twisted in order to bring its foot down on her face.

She rose with her hands in motion, grabbed its extended foot, and flipped it onto the floor. Her foot shot out between its legs once—not that such a strike would hard these monsters, the voice in her head warned—then she twisted them to one side, dropped down against the side of its knees, and pinned the monster to the floor.

Instincts and movements she remembered but had never performed led her into an effective pin and she held one hand against its collar, choking her would-be assassin. It bucked and thrashed, but could not throw her off. Realizing that, it resorted to hammering the bare skin of her back with its gloved hands.

She barely noticed the pain being drummed into her ribs, but knew that being hit over and over was bad. Shifting slightly, she pinned its arms to the tile with her knees and opened her mouth to speak.

Her voice cracked as muscles she never used tried to form words she never remembered learning. She inhaled again, conscious of her breathing having deepened and quickened during the short encounter, and tried to speak a second time. "Who are you?"

Her attacker raised its head and smiled, if the twisting motion its fishbelly face made could be considered a smile. Its teeth were needle sharp. "Kill humans, we."

"Why?"

"No talk, us!"

Using her momentary distraction to free an arm, the monster struck out at the side of her head. She released its collar to block the blow, shifted forward, and slammed the monster's helmet against the tile with her other hand. It bounced with a dull thunk.

It bucked again, and she seized its head with both hands, twisting until the helmet ripped free. Its hairless skin seemed to glisten in the faint light and its three eyes regarded her with a mixture of amusement and hate. Capitalizing on her shift of position, the monster struck her in the shoulder with one hand.

With a ferocity that felt like reflex, she bashed the back of the creature's skull into the floor. The tile cracked as she did it a second time. By the fourth impact, the creature stopped moving. The fifth and sixth impacts splattered bright blood onto the dark, dirty floor.

Finally, she took a deep breath and pushed herself to her feet. She swayed unsteadily as adrenaline had its way with her muscles. As her heartbeat calmed, she examined the creature that had tried to kill her. It was smaller than she was, thinner. Even without any way to see a reflection or image of herself, she could compare their arms and legs. She was taller. Her arms were longer and stronger. Even with its black suit adding bulk, she was larger as well.

So why, she asked herself, did it try to kill her?

With no one around to ask and the monster's dead body not revealing any useful information, she returned to her shell and climbed inside. It was cold now, and dry, but the confines were familiar. They gave her a place to think, to catch her breath. She dreamed about these monsters, but facing one in reality was very different. Worse, if her dreams were accurate, this thing was the smallest kind.

She told herself she would move again once her limbs and lungs stopped trembling and burning.

***

She rose to her feet no more than five minutes later. Her steps remained shaky and her fingers tight, things that lingering memories told her were normal when adrenaline faded from her system. The places where the green-eyed monster hit her were sore, but not damaged. She dreamed about enough wounds to tell that much.

Other than the damage from their fight, and the monster's corpse itself, the room outside her shell was exactly like it was when she first stepped out. No new creatures moved around, no subtle shifts in scent or sound that might hint of danger.

Now that she could look around without worry, she could take stock of the room and, perhaps more important, herself. None of the surfaces around were reflective, but she was obviously not one of the green-eyed monsters. What she could see of her skin was much darker and even without seeing her face, she knew she would only find two eyes there.

Still, curiosity ate at her, and she ran her hands over her face, feeling the bones of her skull and trying to picture it in her mind. Under her fingers, her cheekbones stood out most of all, high and sharp. The top of her head was as smooth as anything else, letting her feel the subtle contours of the bone though the thin skin.

Her ribs were tender where the monster struck her, but nothing felt swollen or broken. It was too early for bruising, as well. She remembered such basic injuries from her dreams along with injuries far worse. By comparison to the things she remembered, her current state was almost pleasant.

Near where the monster fell, she found its knife. The thing was small and dirty, very much like the weapons she dreamed about using. Testing the edge against her fingertip almost drew a laugh from her lips. Even if the creature managed to slash her with it, she doubted it would have done very much. However, an overhand stab would be useful enough, and so she turned it over in her hand.

Content for the moment with her own state, she finally turned her attention toward something more than her immediate surroundings. She, and her shell, stood at one end of a long, narrow room. Other shells like hers sat in a double row that ended where she stood and stretched several hundred meters in the other direction. Hers was, if she stared down the line of empty shells, the last one in the leftmost row. Her shell now looked like all of the others: dark, empty, cold.

Above, the high ceiling was flanked by a catwalk that spanned the room from end to end. A half-dozen doors studded the walls at the catwalk level, but she saw none on her level. Nor did she see any any way to get up there.

Above, lights had been torn from the ceiling or smashed. Parts of the wall suffered similar damage, like something had torn out specific sections or pieces. Wires dangled from most of those holes, but there her knowledge ended. Nothing in her dreams explained how to understand wiring or computers, and the broken equipment yielded nothing useful.

She scoured the area, looking for anything that might be useful. So far, her only possession was the dull knife taken from the small monster. Memories told her of other useful tools, more effective weapons, or even food. All of those memories showed her other places than this room. In fact, to her growing annoyance, she had *no* memories of the room around her. Her fight with the monster had been all instinct and memory of other fights in other places.

She scowled. The long wall opposite her shell looked like it once displayed a series of computers—but what, she asked, *were* computers?—but all that remained now were smashed pieces. The only intact piece of furniture remaining was the heavy table with its thick, black top and busted cabinets underneath. Despite the growing hunger pains in her stomach, she went through drawer after drawer. Her instincts told her that before she moved on, she needed to examine everything around her. Too many dreams ended with an ambush or some other danger coming out of the shadows.

So she searched diligently, pushing down the feeling of hunger for a little longer still. She vividly remembered another pair of hands hiding food and water not far from where she awakened.

A cold pit opened in her stomach as she connected the obvious logic there. She had been treating the memories and dreams as though they really happened. Her instincts and reactions came automatically, and, until she truly woke up, the dreams had been as real as anything else. Now, she wondered where those memories came from.

Perhaps one of the previous lives of which she dreamed went out of their way to prepare a bag of supplies for the next one. Perhaps, those thoughts continued, it knew it was going to die and wanted to make sure she did not suffer the same fate.

She found talking easier now, and her voice echoed in the empty room. "How many times has this played out?"

No useful tools or weapons presented themselves, no matter how long she searched. Signs that tools or weaponry once filled many of the drawers and cabinets were obvious. Markings, ones she recognized somehow as being made by human hands, could still be made out underneath all of the dirt and grime.

She wanted to curse, but did not know how.

She briefly contemplated stepping back into her shell to rest again. That urge lasted only a few moments but her attention lingered on her shell. Instead of the inside, now what fascinated her was the outside. Screens she had never seen from inside dotted the shell's exterior, but every one of them were black. The only identifying markings on the outside were four blocks of red letters, each in a different font.

"VI:C:T – O.R.I. – A."

The string of characters had no meaning for her as they were printed. Unlike her other surroundings, nothing in her memory or instincts gave any context to what she was seeing. The letters could have any one of a billion meanings, assuming they were part of an acronym at all. The periods between some of the letters made it seem that way, but she had no way to be sure without context.

The A was clearly the oldest. It had faded somewhat, like it had been subjected to time and weather. The block of characters in front of it was newer, though its colors had darkened over time as well. The first block was the newest; it showed no sign of fading or discoloration.

Unfortunately, without any idea how quickly the environment outside the shell affected the paint, she had no way of knowing how long even that newest marking had been there. Ten minutes before, she had barely been aware of herself. She had not been aware that the world beyond her shell existed except in ideas and thoughts only half-glimpsed in a lifetime of dreaming. None of that told her how long her shell had sat there or why it had been painted with that particular string of symbols.

She focused on the first and last symbols. The A was ornate, with a small circle over the point and a larger, filled-in circle at the base. Her mind told her it was some sort of logo, which meant it was more than a letter. It meant something, even if she had no idea what. She filed that information away in her mind and looked at the first symbols. They were newest, possibly something that directly identified her shell.

Curious, she took a few steps toward the next shell, examined it, and went on to read the markings on a third one. What she found there confirmed her suspicions. They each had the same second and third blocks that all looked to have been printed at the same time. What differed was the first block of characters. The next shell over was marked "VI:XCIX:T." The one after that was labeled with "VI:XCVIII:T."

As she walked, she passed dozens of empty shells like the one from which she originally came.

The lettering system on the shells ran all the way down to the first pair, labeled "VI:I:T" and "VI:II:T" respectively. The labels had gone past "VI:VI:T" a few rows back, and she felt a sick fascination as she wondered if the first pair of symbols indicated that somewhere five entire other sets of shells sat empty. The paint on the first two empty shells looked older than it had on hers, and the first block of symbols were nearly as faded as the ornate "A" logo.

So, she thought, returning to stare at her empty shell again, they were a numbering system. There are, or were, others that came before her.

"How many others?" she whispered, finding her voice again.

Eventually, she came back to her shell and reread the markings there. The entire scheme might have been a simple catalog, but the symbols on her shell were hers specifically. She touched the cold outside, running her fingers along the smooth metal there.

She read the markings aloud as though they were a single word. She nodded, satisfied. Something about that sounded proper. It gave her a sense of identity where before there had only been an empty spot upon which she was writing her experiences.

"Victoria."

Chapter 2

First Lord Tritogenes, Hexarch of Limani, adjusted the hem of his robe for what had to be the tenth time since getting dressed that morning. This one was new, and the bright purple satin currently in fashion among the Hexarchs hung in a stiff curtain around his feet.

He made a general sweep across the symbols embroidered on his robe. A handful of them had to do with the Project, but with most of the details still classified, there was only so much he could pull from. Others related to more recent, and positive, achievements such as the recent financial success of one of his media corporations. That design snaked its way down one arm in a twisted maze of pictographs that showed not how much the company made, but how much of a bonus it was able to provide for its employees.

Tritogenes turned. He supposed he was rather proud of the glittering hawk stitched across his shoulders in gold and red. Under its wings were a series of names rendered as single glyphs, patrons on one side and star performers on the other. He was proud enough of his holofilm company, but in his mind it was simply that: a company. The Golden Hawk, however, was an *opera house*, the design and construction of which had been Tritogenes's passion for years, decades even.

17

The final choice that morning had been between this newest robe and an older one. When Project Titan began, he designed and commissioned a garment to celebrate the occasion. Unlike the robe he wore at the moment, that one had been hand-designed using old-fashioned pencil and paper. Each stitch had been individually programmed into the machine, resulting in a process that took the better part of a year to complete.

He much preferred that robe. It was older and soft, but it was growing threadbare in places and was in dire need of repair. For any other visit, he would not have cared, but rank had its demands as well as its privileges. From the moment he stepped off the shuttle until he entered his private room in the facility director's suite, he was there for Official Business.

Fortunately, at least, he had very little to do directly. The Project handled itself rather well these days, especially now that things were officially winding down.

Tritogenes frowned. That was the problem.

The agreed-upon deadline for the end of Project Titan loomed. He hoped this visit provided some useful information or assurances he could pass along to the other Council-members. If not, he was going to be in a rather unenviable position. Either he presented them with nothing or he rushed an eleventh hour solution. Neither option appealed to him.

His thoughts returned to the same place they frequented when he came here: if it had to do it all again, he would...

This time, he stopped that chain of thoughts, offering assurances to himself that the Project was in good hands. It was certainly in better hands than his, and had been so for four years now.

More to the point, he was about to get an update on things, so worrying himself about it would do no good.

He did, however, allow himself to get somewhat cross at the slow speed at which the dock staff seemed to be operating. Under ideal conditions, his ship should have been through decontamination the better part of an hour before. Tritogenes sighed. It *had* been nearly six months since his last visit and the station did not get very many other visitors, so he supposed he could cut the ground crew a little slack. Their skills did not get very much polish.

Of all the times he wanted to abuse his rank and just push his way through the system...

The indicator light on the table next to his prep mirror interrupted that thought. Simple, unobtrusive, it told him directly that the shuttle's airlock was ready for him. He had no use for underlings—servants, if he was being honest about the way they were usually treated—whose only purpose was to relay messages to him in person.

The last check was his makeup, yet another piece of formality Tritogenes would have preferred to do without. Still, it was expected that he present himself with all the proverbial bells and whistles of his rank, and the wing-like stripes across the sides of his face and underlining his eyes were the least he could do.

At the shuttle's airlock, he met with the two staffers that took the trip with him, a pair of blue-clad Second Lords. Like Tritogenes, they had donned their best robes and spent more time than usual on their appearance.

Well, thought Tritogenes, one of them spent more time than usual on his appearance. Second Lord Amalia was the sort to wake up early in order to present the best visage possible. In a way Tritogenes envied her—he certainly never bothered to care that much.

Tritogenes greeted the two Second Lords in turn, offering his hand first as was customary for the one of senior rank. They clasped arms just above the wrist and exchanged a curt head nod of acknowledgment.

"Good Morning, First Lord," Amalia said.

"Good Morning, Second Lord Amalia, Second Lord Isodorus."

"What are our orders?"

Tritogenes chuckled. "For the moment? We're going to walk in there and look impressive. After that, the two of you have the next few days off."

"As you say, First Lord."

"First Lord?"

Tritogenes raised an eyebrow. "Yes, Second Lord Isodorus?"

"If I may, why did you bring both of us. The shuttle can be crewed by a single person."

"Speak to Second Lord Glaukos when we arrive. I suspect he will be able to give you more information."

Isodorus's excitement was barely concealable. "Yes, First Lord. Thank you."

"First, Lord, if I may?"

Tritogenes turned slightly. Amalia regarded him with stiff formality. As much as he appreciated her attention to detail and constant proper presentation, he found her to be a tad inflexible. Of course, he reminded himself, he could use that sort of inflexibility from time to time to help keep himself on track.

"Yes?"

"Does this mean Project Titan is completed?"

He waited a moment before replying. Amalia had been here before and was one of the few people other than the facility's staff who knew the full extent of his branch of Project Titan and what he intended to accomplish.

Despite that, he smiled and clapped her lightly on the shoulder. "That's the exciting thing, Second Lord. We're about to find out."

She nodded. "As you say, First Lord."

Tritogenes laughed. "Alright, shall we disembark?"

Amalia nodded. "Of course. Isodorus?"

"The shuttle's systems have been completely shut down, First Lord."

"Good, good." Tritogenes smiled. He raised his right forearm and waved his left hand over it, activating his computer's holographic interface. Smart sensors in the device knew they were still in the shuttle, and the first menu to appear highlighted several of the ship's key functions.

Finding the airlock controls were easy enough, and the door began its short cycle.

"First Lord?"

"Yes, Second Lord Isodorus?"

"We're just here to make you look good, aren't we?"

Tritogenes laughed. "That's not the *only* reason."

Second Lord Isodorus smiled in amusement as the airlock opened.

A tall, red-haired Third Lord with hair braided into a complex, three-helix pattern waited on the other side. She waited until Tritogenes offered his hand, then clasped the First Lord's wrist in greeting.

"Welcome to Aphelion, Hexarch Tritogenes."

Tritogenes strode out of the ship a few paces ahead of his ostensible escort. "Thank you, Third Lord Stasia. How have things been in my absence?"

"I was instructed by Facility Director Pallasophia to tell you that things have been going excellently without you, sir. My apologies."

He laughed. "Of course she did."

"Shall I inform the Facility Director of your arrival?"

Tritogenes shook his head. "Don't bother her, I'm sure whatever she's doing is more important than entertaining me. Leave her a text or something."

Stasia nodded. "As you say, First Lord. Where would you like to inspect first?"

He looked over his shoulder, offering an inquisitive grin. "Isodorus? Amalia?"

Neither responded for a moment. Then Isodorus said, "I believe I have business with Second Lord Glaukos, sir."

Tritogenes nodded. "Of course. You may leave."

Isodorus nodded. "Thank you, First Lord."

21

"Amalia?"

"I will go where my Hexarch commands."

"Then I command that we take a brief detour for lunch."

Amalia nodded, fighting to keep a smile off her face. "As you say, First Lord."

He turned back to Third Lord Stasia, their apparent escort for the day. "Have you eaten?"

She shook her head. "Not since breakfast."

Tritogenes nodded firmly. "Then my first command for the day is that you bring Second Lord Amalia and myself to the dining hall, and that you join us for lunch. Will that conflict with your existing orders?"

"It will not, First Lord."

Tritogenes smiled. "Good, good. Now, while we walk, tell me how things have really been around here."

"There's been little news lately, but I overheard Pallasophia and Glaukos talking..."

At its core, Aphelion station was built around a massive complex once designed to house Tritogenes's branch of Project Titan. Since the Incident, it remained largely unpopulated beyond the scientific and engineering staff monitoring the area through the few remaining systems.

The only people that ever went quite this far were Facility Director Pallasophia and Tritogenes himself.

After lunch, he went on a short inspection tour of the more regular parts of the station. Even Aphelion had functions beyond Project Titan, and the other areas had projects and experiments of their own. With that done, he took a short break to change into a more comfortable robe and remove most of his makeup. This was a personal meeting, not a professional one.

He raised a hand and knocked on the simple metal door, waited a moment, and opened it by hand. It swung silently on its hinges—the machinery to operate the automatic door might have been damaged in the Incident, but what remained was well-maintained.

A young woman in a blue robe waited on the other side of the door, occupying one of two chairs in the small room. She looked up when the door opened, greeting the First Lord with a bright smile and a wave toward the other chair.

"Hey, Boss. I didn't see you come in."

Tritogenes grinned, taking the seat she offered. For the moment, he decided to ignore the subject of the cameras and personnel sensors in the hallway outside. If she somehow had not been notified of Tritogenes's arrival by the facility staff, then the facility itself would inform her as he approached.

It was a game, and he played along. Now that Tritogenes was back in more comfortable clothing, settling into the old, worn chair was easy. He crossed his legs at the knee, ignoring the room's large window for the moment. If anything of interest was happening out there, Pallasophia truly never would have noticed him.

"How long have you been down here?"

Pallasophia shrugged. "Not long. The hard lines connected to Number One-Hundred's pod activated this morning. I came down to see, well," she shrugged. "I don't know."

"None of them have ever made it to the arena in a single day."

Pallasophia waved dismissively. "I know."

"So?"

Pallasophia leaned back in her chair and ran her hands through her short, plain hair. It hung in stark contrast to the complex design braided into Tritogenes's hair, but she preferred it that way. Were her position less important, it might have mattered more, but Second Lord Pallasophia, head of Aphelion Facility and Director of this branch of Project Titan, had enough social clout to flaunt tradition almost any way she saw fit.

Tritogenes knew the expression on her face. At the moment, even if she needed to conform more closely to convention, she would not have cared.

She sighed, more a single, long exhalation of breath. "So. I don't know. She's the last one, Tritogenes."

"You can monitor her progress from the main workroom better than you can from here."

"That's not the issue. What if she fails?"

"You know better than I do how unlikely that is."

She turned back to the window, gesturing to it. "The others shouldn't have failed, either."

"I *understand* that, but what can we do about it?"

"You mean what can *I* do about it, Tritogenes."

"Pallasophia, Aphelion Station belongs to..." He stopped himself. Despite the steady level of improvement, he took the Project's continual failure personally. The other Hexarchs and their projects were all

24

producing glamorous, and sometimes quite public, results. By contrast, Aphelion station remained so secret that even its name was not spoken outside the facility itself.

Finally, he took a deep breath, correcting himself, "us. It belongs to us."

"And *I* am the Facility Director."

"Pallasophia, I... I'm sorry. I didn't mean to snap at you. I reviewed the data you forwarded and I admit that it doesn't look good. That's part of why I came out here myself."

"To see how the Project was going or to make sure you won't lose face in front of the Council?"

He started to snap again, opened his mouth to curse, and shut it with a subvocal growl. "Let's not talk about this right now."

Her face pinched in for a moment. "Then when?"

"Later, I promise. The lack of results are bothering me, that's all."

She sank back into her chair with a curt nod. She knew—he knew she knew—that she was one of the only people, and perhaps the only non-Hexarch, that Tritogenes would be that candid with.

"It's alright, Tritogenes. You're usually not here so soon after one of them wakes up, so you don't see me like this either."

He nodded, saying nothing.

Her eyebrows lowered, hardening her face into an angry mask. "To answer your question, if she fails, then we break the lower levels open and kill every mastigas down there."

"That option has always been on the table, Second Lord. The reason it's never been done is manpower, pure and simple. If we assault the lower levels with conventional soldiers, if we attack that *monster*, we stand to loose all of them. If One-Hundred fails," he hit the table with the side of his fist, *"then we* evacuate the station and destroy it."

Pallasophia finally turned to face Tritogenes. "Then it's good that she won't fail. One-Hundred has every scrap of information we could distill from previous iterations."

"What's the plan if," he stopped himself, "*when* she succeeds?"

Her face twisted into a grin. "We break open the lower levels and kill every mastigas down there."

Tritogenes sat in silence for a minute. He turned to the window for a moment, but the sand far below remained empty and still. "I'm surprised to see you've not commissioned a new robe."

Pallasophia laughed. "You're wearing one that's nearly eight years old, yourself."

"I'm off duty at the moment."

"I am, too."

Tritogenes shook his head. "Do you ever rest?"

Her laugh might have been angry, but Tritogenes was not sure exactly who it was directed at. "Not when one of them is alive down there."

"Do you know when she'll get to the arena?"

Pallasophia shrugged. "A week, maybe less."

Another moment of silence passed before Pallasophia said, "when was your newest one done?"

Tritogenes took a moment to parse the subject of her question, then realized she was talking about his robe, deflecting from the subject at hand. "Six months or so? It's the one I arrived wearing."

"The one for your opera house, yes. I saw it."

He grinned. "I thought you didn't see me come in?"

"I see everything that happens here, *First Lord*."

"Of course you do."

Yet another quiet moment fell. This time Tritogenes pushed his chair away from the table a little and propped his feet on it in a breach of social protocol he never would have allowed anyone else but her to see. Unfortunately, the motion trapped his long braid between his shoulders and the chair, robbing the pose of any remaining dignity it might have had.

He sighed. "I can't thank you enough, Pallasophia. The work you've done here is incomparable."

She frowned for just a moment before smiling. To anyone else, the smile would have looked genuine, but Tritogenes had known Pallasophia long enough that he could tell how fake the expression actually was.

She had been an ardent supporter of Project Titan since he first brought it to the other Hexarchs. The other five First Lords had been hesitant, but he was able to sway many of the Second and Third lords who, in turn, persuaded the other First Lords to go along with the plan.

Out of the direct light from the window, her blue robe appeared nearly black. "Thank you, Tritogenes. I have done everything possible to ensure its success."

"Why do I feel like there's a 'but' coming?" He paused, raised his eyebrows and opened his expression. "Second Lord?"

She sank back into her chair, relaxing visibly. Tritogenes knew what she was doing—the same thing Pallasophia always did. Formality only added to his stress, so she would ignore it whenever possible. He had to admit it helped. "I've got more faith in each passing generation."

He interlaced his fingers in his lap. With practiced calmness that was, slowly, having an effect on his tension, he asked, "will it be enough?"

"At this point, it will have to be. Otherwise," she shrugged, "we'll be far behind the other branches of the Project. I'll have my data, but without physical results, that won't mean much."

That did nothing but bring him back to the original problem. Tritogenes knew he was allowing too much of his emotion into his voice, but at the moment, that was a secondary concern. "What if she fails? We won't have time."

She interrupted him with a voice like a knife edge. "I will go myself."

He sat up in his chair in a single movement that slammed his shoes on the floor, and he shot to his feet. "You will... No. I forbid it. As your Hexarch, I would forbid your volunteering."

The edge in her voice persisted and she glared at him from her seat. "Tritogenes. My Hexarch, and my friend, if you think you could stop me, you are mistaken. If One-Hundred fails, I will go before the Council as Limani's Titan."

"No."

"Who else, Tritogenes? *Who else?*"

A long, very long, tense silence grew between them before Tritogenes gingerly returned to his seat. In a quiet voice, he asked, "how long since ninety-nine made it to the arena?"

Pallasophia's voice was distant, and completely formal, when she said, "nearly a month." When he had no reply to that, she asked, "Why did you really come here today, First Lord?"

"As I said, I wanted to verify the status of the Project." He narrowed his eyes slightly in a gesture that was a touch angrier than a frown. "And, yes, I wanted to have something I could take to the Council. Some shred of good news to make it seem like my insane idea was finally going to work."

Pallasophia watched him for a long minute, brown eyes boring deep into his soul. In the dim, room, backlit by the bright arena lights, her gaze might as well have been black. Finally, she said, "no. Why did you come here, to this room, today?"

"Because I knew you'd be here."

"Did you know One-Hundred was awake?"

He shook his head.

"Then how?"

The ghost of a smile crossed his lips. "Where else would you be if you were too busy to greet me at the landing pad?"

She watched him for a second longer before an answering smile opened her face and she laughed. "I suppose I do have somewhat predictable habits. You could have called me, you know."

He nodded. "I know, but I wanted to go over the footage from the most recent trials."

She gestured to the holoprojector that occupied the center of their shared table. While it theoretically had access to any computer system in the Facility, provided the user had the right passwords, the two of them only ever used this particular holo for a single purpose.

While she navigated through holographic menus on her computer, Tritogenes stood and looked out the window. From there, he looked out over the arena. For the moment, it was empty. No one or thing prowled the sandy ground. The bloodstains remained. They always would, he reflected, at least until they were able to re-open the lower levels.

He sighed, but only barely. The motion and noise were scarcely larger than a normal breath. The bloodstains served as a reminder of the cost of his Project.

He felt her eyes watching him from behind.

When he did not turn, she said, "only two have made it this far since your last visit, First Lord."

He winced at the sudden formality in her tone. "Two? This time last year you had reports of seven or eight in a similar time frame."

She nodded. Her voice returned to level formality for a moment. "Those trials ended rather quickly. Each generation is more skillful than the last."

"And the network?"

She frowned. "The mastigas rip out any sensors they uncover, making it difficult to distill data. I can only use visual information from the arena anymore. Everything else is conjecture and simulation pieces together from atmospheric data. The chemical detectors are sturdier than the others and the mastigas have a harder time destroying them."

"Are you not worried about losing data?"

She shook her head once, firmly. He knew, despite her never admitting it to him, that Pallasophia felt the cost of the Project as much as, if not more than, he did. He also knew the pain involved in even contemplating an answer to his question. "No. The goal is to pass on the

29

most useful data possible, and if that means synthesizing data using simulations built by spotty sensor data, then that's what we do."

"How much does One-Hundred know?"

"All of it," Pallasophia replied. "Or she should. It is a time consuming process, especially with the mastigas sabotaging everything and no one down there to actually work the systems. And, as you so eloquently put it at the last Council session, time is something we have little of."

For a moment, Tritogenes places his head in his hands and leaned his elbows on the table. "How far have the recent trials gotten?"

She sat straight again, once more stiff and formal, projecting a wall between herself and her work. "Subject ninety-seven made it to the arena, as I said, as did number ninety-nine. Ninety-eight was killed seven levels down. I believe too much of ninety-seven's bravado made it into his memory."

"But you have no way to be sure."

"Not directly, no," she answered. Her voice went beyond cool formality, and the icy edge sent a shiver down Tritogenes's spine. "We de-emphasized ninety-nine's focus on personal accomplishment, because, as you will see in a moment, it was pride that killed ninety-seven. Ninety-nine made it to the arena, and lasted longer than any others have so far, but in the end not even he could finish the task.

"Come," the Second Lord said, gesturing toward the holo. "I'll show you."

She pressed a final button and the details of the floating menu faded out. They were replaced by a perfect representation of the arena from ground level.

From there, the size of the arena was obvious. Nothing but the sand, lit from above by powerful lights, showed on the screen for several seconds. Then, one of the large doors opened, and through it strode a man. He was naked save for strips of fabric wrapped around his feet like rudimentary shoes. His toned, nearly hairless body instantly started to sweat under the intense lights as he scanned the arena with his eyes. In one hand he held a long spear that was barely more than a sharpened wooden pole, but the reddish-brown stain on the pointed end spoke to its efficacy as a weapon.

"Come out!" he called. His voice was a rich baritone that echoed off of the bloody, metal walls of the arena. "I have killed hundreds of you by now. Come out!"

The other large door opened and the ground shook. The creature on the other side was the same every time, and so the camera remained fixed on the ninety-seventh challenger. It zoomed in on his face, watching for little muscle ticks or changes in his expression that would indicate the emotions and thoughts running through his head. All of that was be cataloged and analyzed, then distilled down to component emotions and passed on to the Project's future generations.

A shadow fell across the arena, and number Ninety-Seven sprang into action.

***

By the time Tritogenes returned to his suite, night had fallen. Rather, the arbitrary point on the station's clock, synced to Limani's Day/Night cycle, which indicated "night" had arrived. The station's interior lights dimmed slightly, but that was all. The effect fooled no one into thinking it was actually "night," but the existence of the cycle helped the human mind cope with living inside a windowless asteroid.

A *nearly* windowless asteroid, Tritogenes corrected himself. The suite where he stayed had a few small windows in the upper rooms, as it was one of the only structures to poke above the surface. The other, the landing bay for small shuttles like the one he arrived in, sat directly above his roof.

Four years ago, the entire suite belonged to him. Tritogenes designed and built it to his specifications to provide a comfortable place to stay when he came to inspect Project Titan. After handing the reins to Second

Lord Pallasophia, she moved in full time and had since extensively modified the area.

Tritogenes smiled. In a way, he was pleased that the suite barely resembled his original dwelling. It made coming and going easier if he thought of himself as a guest in someone else's home. As a Hexarch, Aphelion was one of the few places that engendered that feeling.

Now, through the window in his room, he stared out at the distant suns. Aphelion, as its name suggested, sat at the outer edge of the system, far away from any inhabited planets. Espionage was a way of life for the Technocrat civilization, but the real reason he located Aphelion where he did was that its current location put his secret research station as far as possible from the mastigas battleship lurking on the other side of the system.

He composed a pair of messages before checking to see what, if anything, required his attention. To First Lord Hyperion, the ostensible leader of the Council, he relayed a short dictation indicating that he had full faith that, come the next session, he would have good news to tell the Council. The second, slightly longer, went to First Lord Enyalios, requesting permission to visit Katarraktes before the Council session.

With that out of the way, he checked his own messages. Most were the usual sort of things a Hexarch got on a daily basis. This was a task for which he did employ staff, which meant that the hundred or so messages hovering in the air above his desk had been pared down from ten or twenty times that many. Most of them were easy enough to reply to, a short dictation or holorecording and he was done.

Here and there, however, lurked notes that he actually needed to pay attention to. First among them, was a message from Second Lord Philip.

Tritogenes selected that message, and the menu vanished, replaced with the holographic visage of a man who might have been Tritogenes's younger brother. Philip smiled a greeting, saying, "I would shake your hand, but the distance might prove prohibitive."

He waited a moment, likely to give Tritogenes a chance to laugh at the attempted joke, which the Hexarch did. Continuing, Philip said, "First Lord, when you return to Limani, I would ask you to visit me in person. There are some troubling rumors coming out of Dasos concerning Pteryga. It seems First Lord Aegesander believes First Lord Hyperion to be ill and may be planning to call for his abdication."

Tritogenes frowned. Under his breath, he muttered, "bullshit. I spoke to Hyperion last week."

Philip's message continued despite Tritogenes's interruption. "On a positive note, the information publicly available from the other Hexarchs points to overall success with their branches of the Project. I know you don't like to talk about yours, but that's one of the things I would like to discuss with you in person."

Tritogenes raised an eyebrow. "Why?"

As though anticipating the question, Philip's message said, "I believe I have uncovered information in First Lord Ophion and First Lord Adrasta's records that will be of personal interest to you. I will not trust this information to any encryption.

"Selene's light guide you," said Philip's hologram moments before it vanished. For someone in his position, Philip had an oddly religious streak.

Tritogenes sat in thought for a moment. Philip never left Limani, and his position as Tritogenes's personal information gatherer more than adequately explained his distrust of electronic security. Those two things meant any information he had was kept under better security than even Aphelion Station, but it necessitated a trip to Limani to speak in person, which often took more time than Tritogenes really had to spare.

Still, if he had information that would help Project Titan, the Hexarch could cut short his visit here, go to Limani, and then go to Katarraktes.

He sighed. One of these days, he was going to finish decorating his shuttle. If this sort of schedule continued, he might find himself doing so very soon.

The last thing that caught his attention was actually a note from First Lord Hyperion. Like everything the elder Hexarch did, it was brief, and to the point.

"Do not forget our conversation. Remember Diomedes. Consider doing the same. I am. Do not speak of this to anyone."

Tritogenes deleted the message immediately. It contained no incriminating information, but if Hyperion had a reason for keeping the meat of the message secret, that was enough for Tritogenes. He might have been referring to a few different things—their conversations had a way of wandering, after all—but Tritogenes was sure he knew what Hyperion meant.

Normally, Hexarchs were elected from the Second Lords, meaning that only six First Lords existed at any time. However, a legal precedent existed where a Hexarch could name a successor directly. It was almost never done that way, however, because the uproar from the Seconds was often proved difficult to deal with.

Stars knew Rivka had more than her share of problems in her early years as Hexarch, Tritogenes reflected. People, First and Second Lords alike, eventually came around, but it took considerable effort on her part to sway the majority.

The last time they spoke, Hyperion indicated his desire to name a successor and suggested that Tritogenes do the same. While he did not share Hyperion's outlook—in recent years, especially after an assassination attempt, the old Hexarch had gotten somewhat paranoid—Tritogenes failed to shake off his suggestion.

Finding it at the forefront of his mind again, Tritogenes mulled over his options while he disrobed for bed.

First on the list was Pallasophia herself. She certainly had the skill and the qualifications. There were days that he wanted to turn his entire empire over to her and be done with it all. She could run things far better than he could.

With a chuckle came the thought that dashed that idea. Pallasophia would kill him for even suggesting she become a Hexarch. He raised the subject with her once, ironically when they discussed Hyperion's age, and her distaste was palpable.

Tritogenes had not mentioned it again.

Glaukos would also make a good Hexarch, but like Pallasophia, he would hate the job. Plus, with Enyalios still in power, the Seconds were unlikely to accept another military mind on the Council, mastigas or no mastigas.

He never got to a third option, because Tritogenes fell asleep within moments of his head hitting the pillow.

Chapter 3

A crash rousted Victoria from her attempts at sleep. She found her knife, still her only possession, in her hand before consciously thinking about it. A moment after that, she was on her feet, crouched low, and moving away from the semi-secluded corner she found.

Around the corner was another large room, smaller than the one in which she woke but less crowded by equipment. The crash came from that direction, and so it was in that direction that instinct drove her. Many of the times she died in her dreams were because she ran from the green-eyed monsters. When she pursued them, her chances of surviving the encounter increased substantially.

At least, that was what happened to the others in her dreams.

Three hulking, black-suited figured struggled with one another at the far end of the room. Caught between them was the remnants of something humanoid. Victoria was thankful for its damaged state. She could not tell if it was a person, like her, or if one of the green-eyes fell victim to its own brethren.

At her approach, the three monsters stopped their struggle. One raised its head, making motions as though it were sniffing the air. Perhaps it was, Victoria realized a moment later as it bellowed and pointed her direction. As one, they threw the corpse away from them and picked up metal weapons from the ground.

A notion, barely even a voice, told her that the trio was an easy fifteen or twenty meters away. She growled at the intrusion on her thoughts, but then stifled that as she realized exactly how useful that information was. The distance between herself and the three creatures was too far for them to cross without her reacting, which gave Victoria a moment to think.

The nearest of the trio bellowed again and struck out with the metal object in its hand, smashing what remained of a nearby table. The action also let Victoria judge the weapon in its hand, little more than a small spike. The one behind it did likewise, reducing the already destroyed table to splinters.

The third, not to be shown up by its brethren, kicked at the smashed pieces, sending them scattering.

More important, knowing the distance allowed her to more accurately judge their size. That realization told her why they were making no attempts to be stealthy. The little monster that attacked her outside her shell was much smaller than she was, but these were easily much larger. Victoria suspected her eyes would come level with the creatures' chests, but it was their massive bulk that told her how much danger they posed.

It helped that she remembered fighting similar creatures and knew that her eyes were not playing tricks on her. They really were as massive, and as strong, as they seemed.

Two memories flashed across her mind at the same time, fighting with reality. She stumbled as three different things presented themselves in front of her eyes. For a moment, reality lost out as she again remembered how easily the faceplates on the monsters' helmets shattered. The other memory was a motion which brought only a little visual memory with it.

Victoria stumbled again as the second memory fought with her real muscles. It replayed itself, feelings of her arm raising and uncurling, propelling something in her hand with the powerful muscles in her stomach.

Her eyes widened as she understood. When the memory replayed for the third time, she raised her real arm in mimicry of the dream and threw the knife across the room. It rotated once, twice, and then smashed into the faceplate of the nearest of the giant monsters.

It bellowed, screaming as it fell, and clawing at its face. The small knife sank past the rim of the thing's visor, and its attempts to remove it only drove the weapon deeper and tore the wound wider. Brilliant red blood streamed from its face, visible even from ten meters away.

Victoria stood on guard, watching them come closer. Their ponderous, self-assured gait gave her several long moments to formulate a plan. She waited, not wanting to move too soon lest she discover firsthand exactly how much reality matched the losing fights she remembered. Though they looked small in the hands of the giants, vivid memories of ribs and bones snapping under strikes from the "little" spikes told her how much damage they could do to the human body.

She adjusted her feet, subtle little variations in posture and stance as the next few seconds ticked by. The one she downed thrashed and flailed, forcing the third in the group to step around it to avoid being struck. Victoria watched as they maneuvered; the first one was now a step closer than his only still-living comrade.

They took one more step before she sprang into action. She lunged at the nearer of the two, but turned her motion into a tight roll along the floor that passed under its counterattack.

For a moment, she was surrounded, but she took another step, moving toward the other giant. It struck out and she shifted to the side. She seized its massive wrist with her right hand, and, in the same movement, lunged forward and pulled. The giant lost its balance for a fraction of a second, but that was all she needed to shift her posture again, slither around it, and propel it into the other giant with a shove.

Her muscles protested with the exertion, but as memories and reality meshed, she knew the second time she executed that technique it would be smoother.

The giants fell into one another in a tangle of limbs, and the one she threw crashed to the ground as the second swatted it aside. She made a mental note of that; her dreams had not prepared her for how poorly they coordinated their attacks. That piece of information would keep her alive, she knew.

Victoria sprang forward. She threw a kick that intentionally fell far short and used that momentum to drive a second kick. Her heel, despite throwing the kick as high as her body would allow, only connected with the giant's throat. It coughed and growled, but remained on its feet.

The prone giant struggled to its feet, bellowing rage. Its attempts to stand failed when the other giant, the one whose windpipe she should have crushed, twisted and grabbed the other's leg. With a grunt of exertion and rage, the nearer of the two hurled the other one over its shoulder like a club.

Victoria lunged to the side, leaping out of the way of the falling giant. It hit the floor with a thud that echoed on the room's metal walls. Instinctively, she moved forward, intending to straddle it and snap the thing's neck. Instinct told her that was the wrong plan before she could move very far. A flash of moment out of the corner of her eye told her the other giant was maneuvering behind her in a surprising display of tactics.

The still-standing giant swung its massive fist at her, leading with the metal spike. She jumped backward, out of the way, and it stepped over its fallen companion without any apparent care for the fallen one's wellbeing.

It lashed out again and she retreated. It was only for a moment, Victoria promised herself, but she had to put some distance between herself and the giants. The first one had gone down easily enough, but without another weapon or some way to separate them, her list of potential options was growing shorter by the moment.

The giant lashed out again, barely missing Victoria's bare skin with the end of the spike in its fist. A surge of adrenaline rushed through her blood as the proximity of the weapon drove home how much damage it would do to her.

She maneuvered more, finding a heavy table similar to the one in the room where she woke up. The black-topped table had been pushed against one wall of the large room, lost in shadow. Hoping it was built the same way, Victoria grasped one edge and jerked it away from the wall. It rolled a meter on hidden wheels, but stopped abruptly as it caught some unseen piece of debris in the dark.

She moved to the other side of the table and shoved again, this time with her shoulder. It slid another few meters as the other end rotated, but then it too stopped. The side that had been facing the wall was full of cabinets and drawers like the other table had been, but she ignored them. If the first table held nothing that could help her, this one would not be worth the moments it would take to search.

The giant regarded her from behind its black facemask for a moment as the other struggled, again, to its feet. The featureless mask tilted left and right, examining her. Without eyes or any expression, it sent a chill down her spine.

Victoria started to act when the nearer giant jumped flat footed onto the table. Instinctively, she jumped as well, using her hands to propel herself onto the black top. It slammed into the wall a heartbeat after her feet cleared the edge, knocking dust and dirt loose.

She briefly considered diving between its feet, but the possibility of it bringing that spike down on her spine stopped her. That instinct, she noted, had been her own. The thought that followed it was hers as well.

Victoria sprang backward, kicked against the wall, and propelled herself against the giant. It struck out at her, but did not expect her to move as quickly as she did. Its blow went wide and she slammed its chest with her shoulder.

The giant rocked backward and the table went with it, sliding away from the wall slightly. That sudden movement gave her the instant she needed to get away, and Victoria backed to the edge of the table and dropped lightly to the floor.

Unfortunately, the giant regained its footing in that instant and stepped toward her. Its legs were long enough to take it to the edge of the table with that step. One more step and it would be within range to kick or stomp.

She sprang forward. It raised its foot, prepared to bring it down on her head, but she again moved too quickly. She never could have blocked that blow, but it never came. Instead, she stepped, lunged, and then kicked at the table. Unlike the faceplate of the first assailant which cracked and yielded under her attack, the hard black tabletop held firm and sent a spike of pain up through her bare foot.

Victoria winced, but there was no time to pay her foot any attention. The table moved backward, then shot away as the giant toppled off of the end. It hit the ground with a hard thump. She dove for the giant before it could stand. Instinct told her where to put her arms and legs, even on something so much larger than she was. It was disoriented by the fall, but even so she only had a few seconds to act, and she pinned the thing's arms with violent twists. She placed one hand on the back of the giant's head and the other on its chin and wrenched its head to one side.

The giant continued to struggle, fighting to free itself. It tried to bring the thrusting spike down on her back, but Victoria kept most of her weight on the arm holding that weapon and the attempt was only partially successful. The tip struck Victoria's ribs anyway, sending a shock through them that eclipsed the feeling in her foot.

She yelped involuntarily, but suppressed any other noises of pain or discomfort as she twisted the giant's head sharply to the other side, then back the other direction one last time. The third attempt was met with a wet snapping sound and the giant instantly went limp.

She pushed herself away and stood panting over its corpse. She felt of her ribs. The skin was torn, and bled freely. She probed the wound and the area around it, gritting her teeth against the pain. None of the sensations matched her dreams of broken bones.

A chair crashed into the table, bounced over the top, and skidded to a stop next to where Victoria stood. She looked up, then dove to the side as another chair crashed down where she had just been. It landed on top of the giant she just killed, bounced, and clattered to a stop a few meters behind her. It hit something and rattled and Victoria spun in place. She knew nothing had been there before; even in the dim light she had been able to tell that much.

When the second giant died, it dropped its rod and she lunged for it. Her lunge turned into a roll and she tucked the cold metal against her chest. Victoria rose and turned toward the last giant. It stood on the far side of the table, which itself now sat in the middle of the room at a sharp angle. Having seen what happened to the other one, or perhaps simply being smarter, it avoided the table altogether.

With nothing between it and Victoria, their arena shrank to a scant five meter triangle. The corner of the room was only a short distance behind her back, and the table sat blocking the rest of the space from easy access.

She hefted the rod. The whole weapon was longer than her forearm, but the blunt thrusting spike on the end fit into her hand well enough. The end that had been the giant's grip served as her striking surface, turning the weapon from a small spike to a heavy baton.

Victoria watched the giant, using the baton as though it were a sight. Something about the weapon in her hand felt right. It moved easily, and seemed to float rather than drag. She had no real time to appreciate it, however, as the problem of the last giant remained. If its bearing was any indicator of whatever was going on inside its black suit and mask, being slammed into the floor only served to make it angry.

It lunged for her, intending to strike with the spike in its fist. Victoria sidestepped with one foot, pivoting off the other, and let the giant's arm sail harmlessly through the air where she had just been standing. She lashed out with her own weapon, thrusting it into the monster's belly.

It stumbled, bellowed, and swung again. This time, it aimed for her legs. Victoria completed her turn, brought her weapon close to her body with the point down, and intercepted the giant's swing. Against an enemy closer to her size and strength, that would have worked. Instead, its wrist slammed into her baton like a sledgehammer. She was able to deflect the spike away from her ribs, but only barely. The impact still wrenched her wrist in a painful circle.

Victoria moved, coming forward and toward the giant rather than away from it. Its arms were long, but getting inside the first giant's reach had been the only thing to disrupt its strikes.

The giant hammered on her again, going for her head, and she raised the baton to protect herself. The thing's weapon skidded off of hers and she used the force of the impact to twirl her wrist around and slam the baton into the side of the giant's helmet. The hard strike sent a jarring stab of pain through her wrist. The voice of her memories told Victoria the pain was only from where it had been twisted moments before.

The faceplate shattered like the little one she first fought. Beneath, the features were different. Its face was flatter, squarer, and with only two eyes. Its skin was still the same oily white beneath. The same unnaturally green eyes ringed in red skin glared out at her.

It swung downward again. This strike came with more force, but less precision than the first two. Victoria seized upon the opportunity, pivoting on both feet. She turned her body halfway around, shifted her weight onto her rear foot. She brought her baton up in an arc that struck the side of the giant's forearm, deflecting the attack. As the spike on the end of its rod slammed into the tile at her feet, she thrust out at its face with her own weapon. The baton crunched the bones on the receiving end of the attack, and it recoiled with a roar that shook her insides.

Victoria shifted her balance again, grabbed the thing's knee, and flipped it onto its back. It hit the floor hard, harder than it had when its former compatriot threw it. As it fell, it struck out with its weapon. The move looked instinctual, rather than planned, but the metal rod aiming for her knees would do the same damage either way. She slipped backward; the blunt spike slashed across her thigh just above the knee, sending another jolt of pain through her body. It was forgotten a moment later as she moved forward again, toward the fallen giant.

By the time she got back to it, the giant was already starting to rise. She planted her foot as it came to a sitting position, pivoted, and drove her other heel into the giant's forehead. It dropped back to the tile, immediately struggling to rise again.

Victoria darted forward, mounting and pinning this one. Its neck was easier to snap than the other's had been. She knew now how much force was required to do the job. Her mind was a frustrating patchwork of ideas she had no context for, and memories she could not possibly have formed.

She took out that frustration on the giant. Her hands found the ideal positions on the giant's head and she gave a single sharp twist that severed the spinal cord instantly. It twitched, went limp, and she dropped the head with a heavy thud. Just to make sure, Victoria jerked its helmet off and drove the heels of her hands against its face several times.

She stood and took stock of herself. The wound on her ribs dripped blood. The giants' blunt weapons failed to pierce her skin with every other strike, but she could already feel the deep ache of bruised tissue. Her leg showed a bright red streak across the front, but no blood.

It was the wound in her side that worried her. Her exertion in fighting the last giant had opened the hole wider and, while it was still a rather shallow wound, it bled heavily. Her entire left side from there down was covered in wet, red streaks. She knew had to stop the bleeding before shock set in.

Victoria knelt, examining the giant's suit. Underneath the armored plates the suit itself seemed to be a tightly woven fabric, the same fabric that made the bag she dreamed about hiding. Her mind then went back to the first black-suited enemy—the smaller, unarmored attacker—that she fought. She remembered breaking its nose, but no blood ever leaked beyond his helmet. Either the fabric was water-tight or very absorbent. She moved the giant's arms around, searching for an unarmored spot, and spat on it. Her saliva instantly soaked into the fabric. The dark wet spot was gone a moment later and she felt of it, finding it dry to the touch. That gave her the answer she needed.

None of the giants' suits would fit her. She stared at the fallen giant, contemplating for a moment the idea of simply taking a weapon and continuing as she was. A quick glance at her skin, already showing signs of bruising and cuts from the first few hellish minutes of her life told her how bad of an idea that was.

Another memory, another body, flashed through her mind, bare skin torn apart by unseen teeth and claws.

She stood and crossed the room to where the first of the giants fell. The handle of her knife jutted from its face. She withdrew it, returned to the body of her first attacker, and set to work cutting its suit apart into pieces large enough for her to wear.

Underneath the heavy black fabric, she found the giants' skin to be the same shiny white as their faces. She was momentarily repulsed by the idea of wearing the same fabric that had been in contact with those corpses, but she saw little other option if she wanted to wear anything at all.

She considered trying to disassemble the giants' armor, but her only tool was a knife. She found it profoundly unsuited to the task of cutting through the armor plates and left them alone.

Every noise from her environment made Victoria jump, and each time she jumped like that, brandishing her baton at nothing, she lost her place among the growing pile of fabric. After the third random creak from the walls, she sped up her efforts. She knew she needed to finish, but each passing second made it harder to calm her heart rate enough to concentrate properly.

Rather than try to cut form-fitting pieces, she hurried through the simple process of cutting long strips, which she wound around her body as best she could. Victoria left her hands, head, elbows and knees bare. The fabric strips bunched too much there and interfered with her movements.

Again the memory from before surfaced. Infected hands from cuts that went unwashed for too long grew black and bloated in her mind, the pain translating onto reality as hideous cramps along the bones of her hand. She took some of the thinner fabric from the back of the giants' suits and cut long strips, winding them around her wrist and between her fingers in a pattern she never remembered learning.

Two of the giants' helmets were intact, but they were far too large. Even stuffed full of padding, they would have been dangerously heavy and bulky. Frustrated, and growing ever more nervous as time passed, she tossed them away from her.

The closest she came to any sort of head covering was a long piece of the black fabric wrapped around her forehead to keep sweat out of her eyes. Where ever she was now, the air hung warm and wet around her, and sweat threatened to be a problem during her fight with the giants.

Another few minutes of nervous searching turned up nothing of use in the room or on the corpses of the giants. A vague sense of remembered exploration pointed her in a direction she could only call forward, and with the metal baton raised high to defend or strike, Victoria slowly moved that way.

She tried several doors as she passed, finding most of them locked. When she finally came upon a door she could open, Victoria did so with the baton high over head head, ready to smash anything on the other side.

The room beyond was so dark that the dim area she was leaving seemed bright by comparison. She opened the door as far as it would go, but the light spilling into the darkness only went a short distance before the absolute blackness of the room beyond took over.

She stepped inside, led by that feeling of direction. Above her, something creaked, and the door behind her shut. In an instant, the room plunged into total darkness. Something else hit the floor a few meters ahead of her with a dull thud.

It growled.

***

Nothing tried to kill her for more than a day as Victoria moved through the facility, aided by memories of the noises the green-eyes made as they prowled. Her guiding beacon, at least in her mind, was the memory of a previous pair of hands hiding that bag of food. The closer she came, the more she remembered, including that the room contained a source of water that did not kill those who drank from it.

She found a different source of water that morning, but another vivid memory kept her away from it and the strange white creatures that swam in it. A slow end brought about by vomiting herself to death was not ideal.

As she grew closer, she followed the scent of iron. The water she drank in her dreams smelled like metal and nothing lived in it. Except for one dream that ended with an ambush and her death, she always survived the experience.

Unfortunately, this time seemed to be more like the one bad dream. When Victoria found the water, she also found a group of the small creatures, like the first one to attack her. They had no weapons of their own, but they fought so well as a team that they overwhelmed and tried to drown her.

Her lungs began to burn as one of the creatures held her head underwater. Others held her arms and legs as well, and despite her thrashing, she was unable to free herself. As the burning in her lungs grew worse, her head began to throb. Her vision started to fade as well, first going gray at the edges. This death was different than the one she remembered. That one had been hands on her head, submersion, a quick turn, and then nothing. This was going to be drawn out, long, and quiet. The hands holding her head did not possess the strength to snap her neck.

In her struggling, she took a deep gulp of the iron-rich water. The sudden influx of cold fluid rejuvenated her dehydrated and nearly asphyxiated brain, giving her enough of a momentary surge of energy to break free of their grip.

She spun and twisted in the air, pulling one of them into the water with her. She knelt atop that one, subjecting it to the same end she nearly met.

Another grabbed at her head and, with the help of the other two, started to force her face back down underwater. She slammed its faceplate into the edge of the basin, shattering its visor. It stepped away as she rose from the water, slinging great sprays of the life-giving liquid around the room as she attacked and killed the remaining green eyed creatures.

Victoria spent the rest of that day in that room, steadily drinking more of the water as its gentle flow carried away the dirt and grit she left in it. A flash of memory, of drinking contaminated water followed by an agonizing death where her stomach seemed to be consuming itself from the inside, prompted her to remove the corpse of the green-eye as well. In that room, exactly where it was supposed to be, she found the bag made of green-eye fabric. Inside, she found nothing but crumbs and broken tools.

Two small pieces of meat so dry that they could barely be called food sat at the bottom. Victoria tore at the hard meat voraciously, eating both in only a few seconds. The sudden influx of food only made the ache in her stomach worse.

With hunger gnawing at her stomach, she crawled into the darkest corner of the room, under the tank of water, and closed her eyes.

Even that proved to be too much for her nerves, and she awoke no more than a few minutes later. The water left puddled in the floor from her fight had yet to dry.

Awake again, she took several long drinks from the fresh water flowing through the trough. Dirt and grime flowed away from her hands when she plunged them under the water's surface, and Victoria was careful to let it drift away before taking each subsequent drink.

Her stomach cramped with the painful twists of hunger and she sat with her back against the cool metal of the water tank. That gave her a few minutes to inventory her personal possessions.

Strapped to her shins were two long daggers, firmly secured in their scabbards. They came from the monsters that attacked in the dark after her fight with the giants. Six of them descended on her, but, like the giants, they failed at fighting as a team. She found them by their squabbling and the noises they made. They all died quickly, and Victoria claimed all six of their knives for herself.

In the time that followed, she went back to the giants and used the knives to carve their armor into pieces she could use. She blunted two of the daggers and broke a third one by the time she had finished, but it was a day's effort well spent.

At the bottom of her new bag, she found the remnants of a small box made from the green-eyes' armor. Seeing it, she remembered a dream where she used long needles to actually sew pieces of fabric together. That memory was fuzzy, coming out of a dream from a very long time ago.

This box had been made for a different, unknown, purpose, but it would do. Flashes of memory and dream, all fuzzy and old, showed her hands that were much more patient and calm than some of the clearer memories had been. Those hands worked methodically, shaping tools out of trash. With that knowledge, Victoria used her fourth knife to whittle green-eye bones into new needles. For thread, she carefully unraveled long strips of green-eye fabric. She spent another day in the room with the water, cutting and sewing new clothing.

The entire process was surreal. Even while making the needles, she remembered knowledge that she could never have gained on her own. Other pairs of hands all blurred together in her mind, but those strange hands had felt like her own as their memory guided her through the process of whittling the needles and sewing a suit of properly fitting clothing.

None of their helmets fit her, and so she stitched together a rudimentary covering made of small pieces of armor sewn to a tight cap. It was uncomfortable, but so was death from head trauma.

The water also solved her food issues, at least indirectly. The next morning, Victoria awoke to find several rats gnawing on the green-eye corpses. With difficulty, she was able to trap and kill many of them and, guided by events experienced in her dreams, she built a small fire to dry the meat. Another memory brought out the terrible pain caused by eating contaminated meat, and so she cooked the meat until it was dry and leathery.

Another dream told her not use use their skin to hold water. She awoke from that memory cold and sweating, haunted by a painful, protracted demise that she felt as vividly as if it had been her own.

What she needed, if she was going to survive, was a way to transport water. The green-eye fabric was too absorbent, which ruled out the only material she could work easily. Whatever her decision, she needed to leave soon. The green-eyes would likely come looking for water and, perhaps more importantly, she needed no mysterious memories to tell her that sharing a room with rotting corpses was a short route to a bad end.

Victoria paced the little room, hoping the physical activity would stimulate her brain. The water stayed clean, with none of the murky rust she found from other, less safe sources. Hoping it had something to do with the trough itself, Victoria reached into the chilly water, feeling of the inside surface of the metal.

She scratched at the slick coating on the inside, peeling some away with only minimal effort. The material that came away was pliable and grew softer the more she worked it with her fingers.

Wax, said the voice in her head, and images flashed through her mind of candles and waterproof coatings. With her knife, Victoria scraped as much of it from the inside of the trough as possible. It would likely start rusting now, ruining the only clean water she had yet found, but if she could carry it with her, the effort would be worth the risk.

She spent another day cutting and sewing bottles from the green-eye fabric, melting the wax to make them as waterproof as she could manage. They went into her bag with as much dried rat meat as she could save, and she hoisted the bag onto her shoulders, finally ready to move on.

***

An internal sense of time Victoria could never explain told her five days had passed since she woke. In that time, she never slept for more than fifteen minutes at a time or ate more than a few bites of food at once. Hunger became such a constant that, so long as she had *something* to eat when it became painful, she could ignore it. Thirst was the same way, and she only drank from her dwindling supply of clean water when she absolutely had to.

Over those five days, she and the green-eyes fought constantly. Most of the time, they attacked her, lunging from the shadows or from overhead. When Victoria was lucky, she could ambush them instead, often ending the fight before it could truly begin.

She grew more cautious and patient with every encounter. Memories of pain and death at the hands of similar monsters drove her on, nudging her reflexes this way or that. Every new wound taught her a new lesson that made the next fight that much safer.

She found stairs and ladders here and there, always following them upwards. The air was warmer the higher she rose, and her stiff, aching muscles cried out for that warmth. The warmer things got, the more she realized how painfully cold that first day had been.

"Human."

Victoria shot upright, instantly awake. Other than the little creature the first day, nothing ever spoke more than one or two words, usually threats or a simple declaration of, "hate!" She tried to interrogate the others she fought and killed, but none had anything to tell her. The giants never said anything, and Victoria wondered if the lumbering beasts could speak at all.

This was different. The voice clearly belonged to one of the green-eyes. It sounded like the babble of water through pipes in the wall and the grinding of stone underfoot.

It called again, drawing out the syllables. "Human."

"My name is Victoria!"

The voice fell silent for a time, during which she tried to figure out exactly where it came from. Noises echoed strangely through the corridors where she was, and she suddenly wished it would continue talking.

After several hours, it obliged. "Victoria," it called, repeating her name at long intervals with no set pattern. Every time it spoke, it seemed to come from somewhere else.

Eventually, she found herself in a maze of twisty passages, all alike. Now, the voice addressed her regularly. She held a dagger in one hand and her baton in the other.

"Human," it said, "why are you?"

She ignored it, trying to follow the voice, but it repeated the question from a different direction. "I don't know!" she finally shouted.

"What is your purpose, human?"

52

"I said my name is Victoria!"

"Name. What is a name? You are a human. Is a 'Victoria' truly any different?"

"Yes!"

"You are like those who came before."

She stopped in her tracks. The voice was close now. "How many?"

"Many."

"What happened to them?"

The voice laughed, a grating sound that tore at her bones as it echoed around her. "We happened! Thought we could be caged, they!"

She crept slowly around a corner. The voice was very close now, with minimal echoes. "Who are you?"

The voice retreated, further away now. "My name is not for you, human."

"Then *what* are you?"

"I think. I speak."

Now, she felt herself drawn toward the voice, an urge she could not name pulling her along. "Why am I here?"

"You are here because we are here, human."

"Why am..."

Victoria rounded a corner and found herself face-to-mask with a tall, thin creature. Two long arms hung from its shoulders, reaching to its knees. A pair of shorter arms reached from below and slightly toward the center of its chest. Those it held back, hands clasped together expectantly. The head, or at least the helmet it wore, was large for its frame.

"Hello, human."

"What are you?"

"I think."

"Are you in charge of the other green-eyes?"

"Green-eyes?" Again the bone-chilling laugh. "Yes, it makes sense for you to call us that."

"What are you?"

The creature shrugged its shoulders in a disturbingly human gesture. "Our original purpose is irrelevant. We are trapped here with you. We want freedom."

That stopped her. "Freedom?"

The creature nodded. "For three hundred times your life thus far we have wandered these halls. Food dwindles."

"Then why did you try to kill me?"

"A great monster guards the exit, one which has forgotten my voice. I had to know if you could kill it so that we could be free." It extended one of its smaller hands and clasped its longer arms behind its back. "Together."

Victoria eyed it with suspicion. Its words made logical sense, but every other green-eye had tried to kill her on sight. She had no reason to think this one was any different. Perhaps its intelligence gave it the capacity for reason, and it decided she was its best hope for the freedom it claimed it wanted.

Or perhaps, she continued, it simply hoped she could be swayed because it spoke to her.

"What will you do with your freedom?"

"We will take our revenge on those who caged us. We will return home and bring a great fire."

"To the other humans."

"To the humans who caged us both!"

It stood much closer to her now, and Victoria shivered automatically. She had not noticed it moving at all, so small and careful had its steps been. Its longer arms hung down by its side now, and one of the smaller hands still reached out for her in a gesture her mind kept trying to interpret as friendly.

"I'm human. What if I refuse?"

"Then you will die like all the others. We will feed and grow and eventually we will have our freedom and the fire will burn this place to ashes."

Before she could say anything else, it lunged for her. Victoria spent too much time listening to its words and it drew much too close to her. Its first strike slammed into the side of her head from below her vision, knocking her sideways and off balance. The second strike hit her ribs on the other side, sending a jolt of pain through them. Her arm spasmed with the shock, and her baton clattered to the floor.

She dove for the thing's chest, but its smaller arms grabbed her and pulled her in closer. They were much stronger than their thin, spindly appearance suggested, and Victoria found it difficult to fight against them.

Fortunately, she did not have to. She still had the dagger, which she plunged into the monster's skull from below, where the helmet was not armored. The visor on this one did not shatter like the others. She reached up with her other hand and ripped it off, revealing a fishbelly-white face, streaked now with vibrant, crimson blood. Its three lurid, green eyes failed to focus on anything as she drew the dagger out of its jaw and plunged it into the uppermost eye.

It fell, and Victoria sagged backward against the nearby wall moments later. Her head pounded where the thing hit her, but her vision was fine. As always, she checked her ribs, and this time cursed. The fabric there had been torn and she bled freely from her side.

The four-armed monster twitched, and Victoria lunged at it, driving her dagger deep into its throat and skull over and over until she was absolutely sure it was dead. Sinking back against the wall once more, she realized something positive came of their fight.

She reached for the monster's helmet. It was streaked with gore, but her assessment had been accurate. Their skulls were nearly the same size.

Chapter 4

First Lord Aegesander shut the lid of his holoprojector. It locked with an audible click that he found reassuring. He stood up from his desk aboard his private liner and strode across the spacious room. His quarters on his ship were large, a reflection not only of his tastes but of his wealth, and Aegesander made sure the other Hexarchs knew it. Technically, of course, all six of them were equals in all things. However, he was the oldest of the First Lords, and second most experienced, and that carried with it a certain personal requirement that he maintain a level of comfort suitable for his position.

At the moment, however, all of the comfort in the binary would not have assuaged the tumultuous thoughts running through his brain. He poured himself a glass of water from the kitchenette in his office, downed it, and filled the glass with brandy made from grapes from First Lord Eurybia's planet. That glass, unlike the water, he planned to nurse for some time.

The news had been no worse than he expected, Aegesander reflected as he peered into the amber liquid. It had taken five years, but Project Titan was finally paying off.

He frowned, mulling that thought over and over in his head. Project Titan, Tritogenes's insane scheme to create a team of supersoldiers to stop the mastigas, was actually going to pay off.

Privately, Aegesander had started to wonder if his fellow Hexarch's doomed plan would ever bear fruit. His own success was assured, his soldier ready, but until now he had his doubts about the others.

He sipped at his brandy, thinking. Tritogenes was going to be insufferable.

This most recent update came from First Lord Eurybia and contained information on the final iteration of her Project as well as what she could glean from First Lords Rivka and Enyalios. Hyperion remained secretive enough personally, though the details of his part of the Project were all public—his Titan loved the spotlight. Tritogenes maintained almost the opposite outlook, keeping his Project secret, but showing his face at every public event he could.

The positive aspect of it was that Project Titan stood to make him a great deal of money indeed, especially if it did everything it was supposed to do. If it succeeded, Aegesander could bury his original arguments against it easily enough. Not only that, but the strides of research he and First Lord Eurybia made into cybernetics were going to revolutionize Technocrat industry for generations.

He idly conjured a holo image of a woman in a blue robe with silver-white metal adorning her face. She could have been any one of a million people who thought this year that metal was the new trend, using it instead of traditional makeup. Second Lord Helena was not one of those people. She was his Titan, and that metal the end result of five years of research and development.

And, he thought with a cold chill, that thought terrified him. Outwardly, of course, he had nothing but praise for the things he and Eurybia developed, but he had a great many misgivings about this technology. At best, it would upend current market trends, likely requiring heavy government intervention and welfare until things calmed down again.

And it was all, ultimately, Tritogenes's idea. His frown deepened as his thoughts circled back around. He was going to be insufferable, and the utter secrecy with which he ran his Project infuriated Aegesander.

In truth, the Lord of Limani was many things that Aegesander found infuriating, but Tritogenes's command of security earned his grudging respect. All he knew about Tritogenes's part of Project Titan was that his facility was secreted away somewhere in the outskirts of the binary system they had called home for the last eleven-hundred and eighty-one years.

Yet, that morning, Tritogenes broadcast from an undisclosed location, claiming success and promising good news at the next Council session. He had more to say, of course, but Aegesander tuned most of it out, trying to piece together any clues that his fellow Hexarch might let slip.

"So," he muttered. His voice, deep and gravelly, matched his weathered face. "Tritogenes managed ... something. Somehow."

Still, he thought as he paced around the room, gesturing and speaking his thoughts aloud in the one place where he knew he would have privacy, Tritogenes was neither alone nor unique in his success. In a sense, he was pleased. While he would not weep at the loss in standing Tritogenes would suffer if Project Titan failed, he admitted to himself that it would also be unacceptable from a practical standpoint for nothing to come from the resources the Technocracy poured into the Project.

Aegesander strode back to his desk and tapped the communications switch. "Second Lord Miranda."

There was a moment of silence before the line clicked once. "Speaking," a female voice replied.

"Please inform Second Lord Helena that I wish to see her within the hour in the exercise room."

"Understood, First Lord. Will there be anything else?"

"That will be all."

Aegesander put his drink down and strode to his cabin's window. He had business at the capital before the Council meeting, and so his liner already jockeyed for position in Prosgeiosi's high orbitals. Aegesander was in no hurry, and so was content to proceed through the usual checks and procedures.

A few minutes passed while he watched the blue and green planet turning slowly beneath his window. Aegesander then raised an arm and activated his computer's holo display. It appeared above his raised forearm in a simple, easy-to-read gray. Navigating through the menus there, he recorded a message for First Lord Hyperion.

Aegesander cleared his throat as the message began. "First Lord Hyperion, Hexarch Pteryga, I, First Lord Aegesander, Hexarch Dasos, greet you."

He resisted the urge to smile as he laid the formal addresses on thick. Showing that much emotion would have been somewhat of a social overreach, even for a private message.

"I regret to hear of your recent illness and wish you a speedy recovery. I hope that you will have recovered fully in time for the upcoming Council meeting. If you need anything, do not hesitate to contact me."

He stopped the recording, placing just enough encryption on it so that it would look like he "made an effort," and sent it on its way. The odds that no one would intercept and read it as it crossed the system from his cabin to Hyperion were immeasurably small, and both Hexarchs knew it.

They also both knew that Hyperion was not sick and had not so much as suffered from a cold in thirty years. His "miraculous recovery" before the Council meeting was surely going to cause people to talk. Perhaps they would talk enough to convince Hyperion that it was time to end his charade and actually meet with Aegesander in person.

Aegesander returned to his drink. He and Hyperion had their differences over the years, but those issues were in the past. Surely, he thought, no reason remained for the two senior Hexarchs to ignore one another.

He sipped his brandy, then had another thought. Rather, his mind finished churning through a series of plans and finally arrived at the most logical next step. He activated his holo again, once more paging through menus until he arrived at the communication screen. He directed, then encrypted the message carrier before dictating anything. This note he actually wanted to keep private.

"First Lord Eurybia, I believe your current travel schedule will bring you within a short distance of Katarraktes a few days before the Council meeting. I would consider it a personal favor if you made a brief stop there and brought First Lord Enyalios to Prosgeiosi yourself."

With a wave, he sent the message off. Let Enyalios make of that what he would, Aegesander thought.

Again, he frowned as his thoughts turned toward the last two Hexarchs. Tritogenes's behavior was always frustratingly difficult to predict, and he was likely going to stay in his secret base right up until the time came to leave for the Council meeting.

That left First Lord Rivka, who already turned down Aegesander's offer of financial aid. That sent enough of a stir through the lower ranks to keep both of them busy for months, and Aegesander had not contacted her directly in nearly a year because of it. Diomedes, her predecessor, had been a compatriot of his and Hyperion's. Unfortunately, she inherited some of his tendencies which made her as supremely difficult to predict as he had been.

Diomedes's suicide during the first mastigas attack still haunted Aegesander more than he wanted to admit. If nothing else, the sudden loss of a Hexarch, and the unusual dictate from his Will that Rivka be appointed his successor, left a gaping hole in Aegesander's knowledge database.

More than he wanted to figure out Tritogenes's plan, Aegesander *needed* to know how much Diomedes told Rivka before his death.

Aegesander finished his brandy in a single, frustrated gulp, then refilled it on his way out of the cabin. Knowing Helena, she was already there, waiting on him.

***

Aegesander did his best to stay in good physical shape, and he had to admit that for a man of a hundred and fifty, he was still quite healthy. He placed a great deal of the credit for his continued health on his insistence that every ship he owned or operated contain some sort of exercise or fitness area.

In the two years since Helena officially became his Titan, she accompanied him nearly everywhere he went. Aegesander's gym might have been set up for his own use, but as time passed, the room became hers more and more.

As he predicted, she arrived some time before he did, despite there still being over thirty minutes left on his "within the hour" request. When he stepped into the room, Helena rose from a seated position in the middle of the open space at one end. A single twitch of her shoulders smoothed out any lingering wrinkles in her lapis-blue robes, causing them to hang with nearly mathematical precision. Like all Technocrat robes, Helena's obscured everything from the neck down, showing instead representations of her achievements—at least the ones that were not classified as "Top Secret."

Above the neck, she bore more physical results of her part in the Project. Polished metal sat atop the bones of her face. The pieces wrapped around and connected to one another at the base of her skull before descending and vanishing inside her robes. Six spidery, metallic legs wrapped around her skull, one pair each over her eyebrows, cheekbones, and along her jaw. The metal itself was kept polished, but pale blue color was enamel deliberately chosen to accentuate her icy eyes.

Her hair had grown back since the implants had been installed two years before and was now gathered just above the metal nexus at the base of her skull. True to technocrat tradition, her braid was elaborate and showy. She parted it in dozens of different places to show off her implants as well. Despite the nature of the augmentations Project Titan had bestowed upon her physical body, she remained a Technocrat, and one for whom appearance and propriety remained important.

Four guards stood at the four corners. Each had been armed differently and carried slightly different sets of equipment. Like everything else in the last few years, they were a test for his most prized accomplishment.

For a moment, she still looked like the young girl he remembered. She had been a programmer before the Project, before the implants changed her. Now, she stood with a grace that was at once stoic and fluid.

Aegesander cleared his throat to announce his arrival—like unnecessary—and Helena turned. Her eyes had focused on a blank spot on the wall opposite where she stood, but now they zeroed in on him. Even First Lord Aegesander could not tell what went on behind those eyes. Two years of working with her, and he still barely understood how her mind worked now.

"Is there any pain today?" he asked.

Helena's eyes snapped into focus, zeroing in on Aegesander. She fixed him with her cold, blue gaze without moving her head. "There is no pain, First Lord. There has been no pain in one year, four months, sixteen days, nine hours, thirteen minutes, and seven-point-oh-oh-three seconds, as of your asking."

"May I make a suggestion?"

"Of course. You are my Hexarch."

"There is a line, Second Lord Helena, between formality and unsociability. Such precision, while helpful to our scientists during your examinations, will not win you any friends."

62

"My apologies, First Lord. I will be," she paused, "less precise in the future unless questioned by a scientist."

Aegesander nodded. "Good. Now, let me repeat my question. Is there any pain?"

"No, First Lord. Not in," another pause, "some time."

He smiled, tight-lipped but pleased. A moment passed before he turned away from her and beckoned to one of the four guards. "Can you tell me, Helena, what Third Lord Guardsman Elftherios has in the breast pocket of his uniform?"

She turned her head, watching the guard approach. "A holoprojector," she replied. "Simple, yet ornate, with minimal storage capacity. It appears to have no external connections. I cannot see more."

"Guardsman Elftherios?" Aegesander asked, gesturing to the man's pocket.

The guard nodded and withdrew a small disk from his pocket. He placed it on the palm of his hand and tapped it once. An image appeared in the air, showing him, another man, and three children.

"Thank you, Guardsman," Aegesander said, waving the guard away. He pointed to another guard, waving her over. "What can you tell me about Third Lord Guardswoman Melina's morning?"

Helena's eyes swept over the second guard, she inhaled deeply, and then reexamined the guard. "Her breakfast was some sort of sweet bread, but the smells are overpowered by others. I detect gunpowder residue in her hair and solvent in her sidearm, likely a result of extended training time after breakfast."

She inhaled again, watching the guard grow less comfortable as her analysis went on. "I also smell cologne and male pheromones along her neck and," her eyes moved again, "other areas. The spotty nature suggests it was transferred by contact. She has not yet eaten lunch."

Aegesander nodded, this time allowing a thin smile to cross his wizened features. He gestured for Melina to return to her post, which she did with a look of gratitude.

"Second Lord Helena, Third Lord Guardsman Elias is going to try to take your sidearm from you. You are to resist his efforts and subdue him without causing any injuries."

"Yes, First Lord," she replied. Her feet slid apart and she softened her knees, sinking into a fighting stance. The guard Aegesander had indicated set his rifle down in his corner and approached. He withdrew a small stick from a pocket, one that quickly elongated with a flick of his wrist.

Elias swung the baton and Helena simply shifted backward and out of the way. She dodged his second and third attacks with equal ease before he straightened up and exchanged a moment's eye contact with Aegesander, who nodded.

His subsequent attacks were faster, much more precise, and Helena was only able to avoid the first two. The third snagged her voluminous robe, pulling her off balance. The fourth strike nearly hit home, but she turned her sudden loss of balance into a roll, coming up near Elias's knees.

Helena rose, toppling the guard as she did so. She followed him back to the ground, intending to end the match then and there. Instead, as he fell onto his back, Elias grabbed for her hands and put a foot into Helena's stomach, flipping her head over heels and onto the floor.

"Second Lord!" Aegesander snapped. "Analysis!"

Helena rose to her feet with a single motion. "My opponent is relying on the limitations of my instructions and attacking when I could, but may not, strike him. I will compensate."

Aegesander nodded, watching as Elias shifted his tactics. Rather than use the baton in his hands as a small club, his motions now were focused on grappling. He snaked the metal rod in quick circles, trying to ensnare Helena's arms or legs.

Her hands moved ever faster as she allowed Elias's new aggressive style to push her around the room. She was not so much losing ground as deliberately ceding it, using the distance to control the fight. Whether

Elias knew it or not, Aegesander could see that she had already won their engagement, even if it took several more seconds.

Finally, Helena allowed Elias to hook one arm with his baton. His next move was logical, and it would have worked against a normal opponent. He lowered himself slightly, reaching out a foot to entangle her legs. She, however, was prepared for it and altered her balance, giving her control of his leg instead.

One twist of Helena's hips and Elias went to the floor. She followed again, successful this time, and dropped her hips heavily down onto his. She reached out with the hand opposite Elias's weapon hand, seized his wrist, twisted, and disarmed him.

He grabbed her other arm, but she twisted that one as well, breaking his hold. Helena then leaned back so that she was away from his hands, but her weight remained centered. With one deft motion, she produced a pistol from a hidden pocket in her robe and aimed it at his forehead.

"You have lost, Third Lord Elias," Aegesander pronounced. "You may release him, Helena."

She nodded and the pistol disappeared back into her robe. Helena then stood and stepped away from Elias's prone form. A moment passed and she extended a hand, helping him to his feet.

"If I may speak freely, First Lord," Elias said, speaking in the stiff, formal tones required of him when addressing the Hexarch. "I remain impressed by Second Lord Helena's combat skills."

"As do I," Aegesander replied. "Thank you, Guardsman Elias. You may return to your post."

The guard saluted and stepped away.

"I apologize, First Lord," Helena said. "I was unable to refrain from bruising him, and I fear I may have hyper-extended a tendon in Guardsman Elias's wrist."

Despite the demands of propriety, Aegesander laughed. "You are forgiven, Helena. Your restraint was admirable."

"Thank you, First Lord," she replied, then a distracted look came across her face. "First Lord?"

"Yes?"

"There is a message for you, from First Lord Eurybia."

Aegesander nodded, trying once again not to be disturbed by watching her mentally access his personal network. Before he replied to Helena, he turned to the guards. "You are dismissed."

"First Lord?"

He waved them away. "Go, Thirds. I give you the day off."

"Yes, First Lord," replied Elias. He gestured to the others and, as one, they exited the room, leaving him alone with Helena.

Now, he turned to her. "What does the message say?"

"First Lord Eurybia's schedule has been delayed. She does not believe she will arrive in time for your feast next week. She also sends her wish that I meet with Second Lord Panatakis, her Titan, as soon as possible.

"Shall I reply?"

Aegesander nodded. "I sent her a message earlier. Tell her to keep to that schedule if at all possible, and that meeting me at Dasos is less important. Ask her to..."

The intercom overhead dinged once. "Message from First Lord Eurybia. Play?"

Aegesander nodded, ignoring the alert. "Ask her to forward the latest information on Panatakis's implants. I would like to compare them to yours. Tell her I look forward to seeing her on Prosgeiosi."

"Is that all, First Lord?"

He thought for a moment. "Ask her if she will still have time to meet with me ahead of the Council session."

Helena nodded. Her lips moved as she subvocalized a message, dictating it via her implants rather than using a microphone and her voice. When she finished, she locked eyes with Aegesander again.

The hair on the back of his neck rose slightly under the intensity of her stare, but he made himself meet her eyes. He was a Hexarch, after all, and no Second Lord would make Aegesander of Dasos flinch.

After a moment, Helena's lips turned upward in something that might have been a smile on someone whose face seemed less predatory. "Message sent."

He made himself nod. "Thank you, Second Lord. Now, do you feel ready?"

"I could be ready in ten minutes, First Lord."

"I meant mentally, Second Lord Helena. Are you ready to meet the others and to formally meet the Council?"

She paused and a strange, calculating expression passed over her face. "Yes, First Lord." Another moment passed, and she asked, "are you?"

Aegesander froze. When he spoke it was slow, methodical. "To meet the Council? Yes, of course." He laughed. "Aside from Hyperion, and even him indirectly, I talk to them often."

"With respect, I meant the other Titans."

He nodded very slowly, not bothering to hide his anxiety from Helena. If he thought he could have done so, he would have, but Helena had proven time and time again to be able to read even the most minute changes in facial expression. In a way, it was freeing to not have the usual weight of guarding his emotions to worry about.

"I am, yes. Much of the information, as you are aware, is publicly available, but I'm curious to see what my comrades have done with their time. Why do you ask?"

Helena's face registered no emotion. "Curiosity."

"I see," he replied. After a moment's consideration, Aegesander added, "curiosity drives a great many of your questions, Second Lord."

She nodded and a smile spread across her face. "As it does for everyone."

67

He briefly considered correcting her, explaining that most people asked questions to gain information that they could then use to their advantage later, but decided against it. On the occasions that they discussed such issues, Aegesander always came away profoundly frustrated by Helena's apparent naivete.

She raised a thin eyebrow, bisected by a scar from her early training in using her implants. "First Lord?"

He shook his head. "It's nothing. Merely lost in thought for a moment."

Helena nodded. "Of course. You have many things to occupy your time."

He eyed her for a moment. "Second Lord Helena," Aegesander began. He spoke slowly, choosing his words carefully as he always seemed to do around her. "Is something on your mind?"

Her eyebrows drew together and her lips turned down in a frown. It was, at least for a short moment, the most human expression he had seen in her face since her implants were installed.

Helena took a deep breath before answering. "I am unsure what I feel. Perhaps 'trepidation' is the most accurate descriptor for my current mood. I am different from the other Titans, and I have often found myself wondering how they will treat that difference."

Aegesander smiled. This, at least, he could deal with. "Differences in appearance are the hallmark of Technocrat culture. I would venture to say that, if you looked just like everyone else, *that* would be the problem."

She nodded and her frown softened some, but did not disappear. "I understand that, First Lord. It is not my appearance that concerns me. Since the Project began, I have," she stopped for a moment in a rare display of not having the right words to say. A sharp intake of breath later, and Helena added, "I've experienced a great many things in a different way."

He nodded. "I imagine you have."

An expression Aegesander could not define crossed Helena's face. If someone pressed him in that moment to explain what it was he saw on her face, Aegesander would have defined it as "pity." It chilled him.

She looked like she was about to say something, but then Helena's lips turned up in a disarming, gentle smile. "Of course, First Lord. But if I wanted to speak to someone with similar experiences?"

"I'll have Second Lord Panatakis's frequency forwarded to you immediately."

"Thank you, First Lord."

He nodded acknowledgment. Helena knew about Panatakis, and about how Eurybia's research into cybernetics had been developed alongside his. Panatakis's implants were designed to do different things than Helena's were, but ultimately Aegesander supposed that was immaterial. She wanted someone "like her" to talk to, and Panatakis was the only person who could share in her experiences like that.

He also knew that Helena could have simply taken that information at any time. The fact that she had not, and had in fact asked him instead, assuaged some of his fears about her capabilities. The Helena of two years ago would simply have gone into his computer and taken that information.

And then she blinked, keeping her eyes closed just a fraction of a second longer than usual. Aegesander knew she had just done exactly that. His best security experts would likely find no trace of her intrusion in his systems, assuming they could even determine if she went through Dasos's database or his own personal system.

He asked himself if the security of either even gave her pause anymore. No matter what answer he came up with, Aegesander did not like it.

She smiled. "Thank you First Lord. I will contact Second Lord Panatakis soon. I believe you are correct. He and I will likely have much to talk about."

Again, Aegesander nodded. "It's important to have people you can trust, Helena. Don't forget that."

Again, the expression that might have been pity crossed her face, gone in a heartbeat and replaced with that same gentle smile. "Of course, First Lord."

"May I ask you a question, Second Lord?"

For a moment, she looked confused, then she nodded. "You are my Hexarch. You can ask anything of me."

"Why did you volunteer for this Project? You've never talked about that."

Suddenly, the expression on her face turned profoundly sad. Her eyes fell and even the shining metal of her implants looked dull. "I had friends on Kipos, First Lord."

"You're so young," Aegesander said. "I... no. I had friends on Kipos, too, Helena. Diomedes, the former Hexarch, was a close personal friend of mine. You had to be, what, twenty?"

"Twenty-seven, First Lord."

"I'm sorry, Helena. I should not have asked."

She shook her head. "You had no way to know."

"Still."

She took a deep breath, then fixed Aegesander with her piercing blue eyes again. When she spoke, the sadness was gone, replaced with a tone very even and level. "May I return to my suite, First Lord?"

Aegesander nodded. "You have the rest of the afternoon to yourself, Helena. We should land tonight after dinner."

She nodded and turned to leave the room. Beneath her robes, Helena might as well have been floating with how little her shoulders moved with each step.

The door clicked shut and Aegesander shook his head. So quiet that he barely heard his own voice, he muttered, "what have I created?"

Chapter 5

Victoria jumped fully awake in an instant, startled by some noise she failed to immediately place. One hand raised her baton into an automatic guard while the other groped for her backpack, making sure it was still where she left it ten minutes before. Finding her bag and its nearly-depleted store of food and water intact assuaged some of her anxiety, but not much.

With the baton still raised high, she slowly came to her feet. Without a proper way to keep time, she had no way to know how long it had been since her first fight, but Victoria had not gotten more than fifteen or twenty minutes of sleep at any given time. Her head swam, and she shook herself.

She stumbled, thrusting the baton ahead of her and then sweeping it around the other direction in an automatic defense. Nothing attacked her and she leaned against the wall, catching her breath and forcing her heart to beat slower.

After killing the four-armed monster, Victoria fought several more of the different creatures. The fighting might not have been constant, but she had very little time to rest in between fights. It certainly *felt* like the fighting had been constant, at any rate.

The whole sequence was routine anymore. Victoria lowered the baton, letting it dangle from her wrist via a strap she cut from green-eye fabric. With her other hand, she took the bag from her shoulders and set it on the floor, then untied the makeshift strap under her chin that held on her purloined green-eye helmet.

Hunger gnawed at her, sinking its fangs into her stomach and tying the muscles there in tight knots. She eased the feeling by draining a half-full water bag before anything else. The sudden influx of fluid woke up her brain the rest of the way and caused her heart to again beat faster. When that calmed, she dug out the last of her rat-meat jerky and ate it.

Her hunger never abated, but the addition of a few tiny bites of food made things more bearable.

Victoria hefted the backpack onto her shoulders again, adjusting slightly so that it settled onto her back with some measure of comfort. Layers of green-eye fabric made a reasonable pad under the straps and against her back.

She might have remembered the bag from her dreams, but the modifications had been her own. Tools, weapons, those all appeared in her dreams. Here a naked hand gripped a spear, there an arm wrapped in heavy fabric swung a hammer. She knew how to sew her own clothes from another set of memories, small hands that moved with deft quickness, but those hands had been killed like all the others.

In a way, modifying the backpack like she had was a comfort. So much of what she knew, or felt like she knew, came from flashes of insight and memories of hands and bodies that were never, could never be hers. To have something that was her own, truly her own, left her with the feeling that she was more than a culmination of a set of memories, doomed to die like so many others.

Dismissing those thoughts as distractions, Victoria placed the helmet on her head and methodically tied the straps tight. It sat as comfortable as anything else now that she added a layer of padding to the inside. Whatever status the four-armed creature held, its helmet was certainly stronger than the ones the lesser varieties wore. Despite repeated strikes to the head, the visor had yet to shatter.

She winced as a loose tile shifted underfoot, sending a shock through her bruised ribs. Compared to the number of them she killed, very few of the green-eyes managed to even lay a hand on her. Even then, the injuries mounted as minor bruises and scrapes stacked one on another.

Whatever happened, Victoria knew she had to get somewhere safe. If not, the alternative was to end up as the dream of some future soul who found herself condemned to wander these same halls. She owed it to them, at least, whoever "they" were.

The only thing that drove her on was the steadily rising temperature of the air. Even after killing the four-armed green-eye, Victoria found an open elevator shaft. The lift cage had been smashed, but most of the rungs of the ladder inside remained. She followed that up two stories until the rungs vanished, at which point she found herself out of energy and slept.

Something about the floor where she ended up felt familiar. She could not have explained when or where, as the details in her mind grew more and more hazy, but Victoria knew she had walked through these same halls more times than she could count.

As she made her way down the long passage, Victoria felt a mounting anxiety, one different from the lingering fear of attack. A thin sheen of sweat broke out on her forehead, quickly disappearing into the green-eye fabric lining her helmet. Out of reflex, Victoria raised her baton in one hand, stopped to kneel just long enough to draw one of the daggers from its sheath at her calf. Her movements slowed, becoming more guarded with every step away from the elevator shaft.

After passing a series of locked doors, Victoria found herself in front of a massive double door with an unsettling, vibrant mosaic. It felt familiar, even if she could not place the exact pattern. The dominant color was a sandy bronze, but here and there blues, greens, reds, and a whole host of others colors turned and danced in a pattern that threatened to trap her attention for hours.

She reached out a hand and touched the massive doors, finding them warm to the touch, even compared to the hot, close air around her. Victoria hesitated. Every memory of this massive door was the same. Whenever she dreamed about opening this door, oblivion followed.

Despite that, the doors were the only way to go. She lost count of rooms after two hundred or so, but remembered every floor. This one, with its warm door to death, was the seventeenth story in whatever sort of facility she had been born into. Her shell, left so long ago, was on the third of those seventeen floors.

With reservation, and indeed feeling the first real flash of fear since awakening, she put her hand on the door and pushed. Nothing happened, and so she grasped one of the projections and pulled. Again the door stayed shut. She shoved harder and it remained stuck.

She stared at it for a moment, then moved away. A wider perspective offered nothing more, and so she once again came close to it. She remembered nothing about the door other than its presence and the feeling of fear she associated with it, but that was just as well. She had no choice but to trust her alien memories, but she felt she had become too reliant on them and it was a strange comfort to have nothing to rely on but her own faculties.

Victoria reached out and touched the door again, and one of the swirls in the pattern shifted slightly. She pushed on that spot again, and the swirl shifted further, rotating as though it were on a pivot somewhere deep inside the massive door. She pressed her face close to the warm metal and saw that it was not flat after all, but a series of dozens of layers. With some experimentation, she found that nearly all of the pieces of the pattern—each layer made of a different color and section—were mobile.

The door was not stuck, she realized; it was locked.

She moved one piece, and then another, testing out the mechanism. With no clues nearby, her only guide was the pattern itself, which was frustratingly complex and made worse by the irregular pieces. Here a part of the pattern moved by itself, but on the other side of the door, a piece of the same color moved seven other pieces, each scattered about the door in different colors.

After an hour, she had figured out the pattern of the mechanism itself, but was no closer to actually unlocking it. That took the better part of another hour, but when the final piece slid into place, the pattern became rather simple. What had been a swirl of colors and fractals was reduced to six small circles, one in each primary color.

She tried the door again, and found it still locked. Sure she had solved it, Victoria tried to move one of the small segments again. It refused to slide or turn; like the door, it was now locked in place. Each of the circles was connected to the one opposite it by a line in the pattern, resulting in a sort of starburst effect. She stared, knowing the answer was there in front of her if she could only figure it out.

Victoria tried moving various pieces again, but none of the colored circles would rotate. Feeling like she was running out of ideas, she traced the new pattern with her fingertips, looking for something she had missed. As she brushed across the lines connecting the circles to one another, it all became clear—that line, in fact all of the lines between the circles, was not a part of the pattern at all, but a hollow trench.

Each of the circles slid along the line, though not without some difficulty. Victoria suspected that whatever parts they were moving inside the door were neither simple nor fragile. It took a great deal of effort, but she finally moved one of the circles halfway to the center, where it stopped. Now, the entire center piece rotated freely and it was only a matter of minutes before she had used it to rearrange the circles in order from red to purple.

When the final circle slid into place, the pair of doors emitted a single loud click. Victoria pushed on the center, where the two doors came together. Three colored circles lay on either side of her hands, testament to more than two hours of tedious puzzle-solving work. She pushed gently on the doors; they moved with just a little pressure and light spilled through the crack between them.

Despite her drive to push onward, she stopped reflexively as the sudden brightness lashed at her vision. She stepped away, shielding her eyes with one arm, but left the doors open a crack. Momentarily blinded, her hands went instinctively to the baton that now hung from her waist. She raised it defensively, but nothing came at her. No sound aside from her own surprised breathing and rapid pulse reached her ears.

Victoria grit her teeth and pushed the door open the rest of the way, squinting against the painful brightness. Sheer force of will, and a paranoid streak born from dozens of ambushes, kept her eyes open a crack. If something waited for her on the other side, she needed to be ready to face it, and that meant dealing with the brightness before going in.

It took only a moment, but the area around her quickly faded into darkness as her eyes adjusted to the painful illumination. The room beyond was huge, filled with sand. A hot wind blew the fine dust into her face, irritating her eyes even more than the light itself had done.

She opened the doors all the way and stood just outside them, waiting another minute for her eyes to adjust. Finally convinced that her sight in the bright room would get no better, she stepped fully through the doors, which slowly shut behind her as if on some automatic impulse.

With a click, the lock reengaged.

***

The lights overhead made her sweat, but Victoria was glad for the dry air. After uncountable hours in the cold and damp, followed by still more hours in air that was not only damp but hot as well, it was a welcome relief. She considered stopping to rest, the sand-filled room was certainly comfortable enough that she finally felt she could sleep for good.

That feeling shattered when, at the far end of the room, a second door, even larger than the one she just went through, opened a crack. A bolt of terror shot through her and she dropped the backpack from her shoulders.

Victoria did not get more than four steps into the sand when the door at the far end slammed open, giving shape to the formless anxiety that had lingered over her since opening the puzzle door. What strode through had to be one of the green-eyes, the black suit and glossy helmet made that clear enough. This one was more massive than any of the others, easily three meters tall, and with four long arms.

It bellowed and the sand under her feet shuddered. With its arms splayed out as they were, it looked every bit the living nightmare she knew it had to be.

On the short list of things that saved her life in the next moments right then was the fact that she came into the room ready for a fight. Her reflexes and weapons were already primed when the four-armed creature bounded across the sand. In its wake, it kicked up great clouds of dust that shrouded its movements. Three steps into its charge, it crossed all four arms and drew four swords.

Had her weapons still been in their scabbards, Victoria would have died right then. She did not have time to react to the monster's charge, parry its attack, get out of the way, and draw her own weapons. As it was, her instinctive parries gave her an extra half-second to avoid the incoming blades. She slipped around the first one, a thrust from an upper arm. She caught the follow up cut from the opposite lower arm with one dagger, twisted, and narrowly avoided a cut from the second of the monster's upper arms. The fourth arm recoiled for a thrust and she danced around it, allowing it to make the attack, then deflecting the blade when it came at her.

That put her close enough to strike out at the monster's flank with her own dagger. She drove the dagger into what she hoped was its ribs and slammed her baton into its belly. The creature recoiled, wrenching the dagger out of her grip.

Victoria refused to let it open up the distance between them. It was so much larger than she was—and it carried longer weapons—that to let it dictate where and how they fought was suicide. She learned that on her first day, fighting the giants. Instead, she stepped forward and plucked her second dagger from its sheath, pressing the advantage her counterattack had given her.

It roared, spinning in place to face her again. One lower arm snapped around, trying to drive the pommel of its sword into her head. She turned and slammed her baton into its arm to stop the attack. Before it could react, she drove her dagger in with a hard thrust just behind its wrist. It pulled back, but she wrenched the blade out of its arm. The limb spasmed and twitched, trailing a stream of bright red blood.

The creature pivoted further, bringing an upper arm into play with a powerful downward cut even as the other upper arm swept around in a wide circle to deliver a cut from the other direction. She saw, for a moment, no sign of the unwounded lower arm.

Victoria lunged forward, inside the monster's reach. One arm snapped up and cracked the baton across the knuckles of one upper hand. She stepped with one foot, contorted her body to the side, and thrust her dagger through the palm of the other upper arm.

The creature lashed out, kicking her in the ribs with a leg snap she had not seen coming. She sailed through the air, landing three meters away from the monster and sliding another meter in the loose sand.

Her head was fuzzy. Between dehydration, lack of food, lack of sleep, and the sheer damnable stress of it all, her body felt ready to give up right then. Her muscles screamed at her to stay where she was as fatigue descended on her like a blanket.

Give up, urged her muscles, weakened beyond continuing.

The monster took another step.

Adrenaline broke through her temporary daze as she realized that she was still not far enough away from the creature to be safe. It took a step and brought its remaining undamaged hand up to strike. The arm she first stabbed seemed to have gone limp by the monster's side; it had also dropped the sword from that hand. The others, one with broken knuckles and the other with a bloody palm, seemed to still be usable, but the creature was clearly holding them back in favor of the undamaged hand.

The voice in her head spoke not in words but with an overwhelming surge of emotion.

DEFEND.

LIVE.

She rose, unsteady for a moment as her heart hammered in her chest. In those moments, the urge in her mind coalesced into real words. *Fight*, the voice of countless memories urged. *Fight or die.*

She charged forward, waiting for the moment at which the creature would fully commit to its own attack. That moment came when it made a thrust with its undamaged hand. She deflected the thrust with her dagger and snapped the baton overhead. The heavy rod caught the wrist of the creature's upper arm—the same hand whose knuckles she had broken moments before. It dropped the sword, which clattered against her helmet before it hit the ground. In that moment, she disengaged her dagger from the thing's sword, made another step, and drove the dagger upward into the space between the two shoulder joints on that side.

It roared in pain and tried to take the step that would bring its other arms into position where it could strike with them. Victoria had no intention of letting that happen and slammed her baton into the thing's knee. It went down on one leg and, at the same moment, attacked with its other upper arm. The wounded palm was slick with blood and weakened by injury. When she intercepted its sword with her dagger, the movement twisted the weapon free.

With her dagger, she finished the arc that disarmed the creature's remaining upper arm, trying to stop the follow-up back swing from the one arm she had not been able to hurt yet. It was too close to her, moving too fast, and she missed the parry. The creature's long blade sliced into her ribs, shredding the fabric there.

79

Victoria brought her baton down against the thing's faceplate, hoping it shared the same weakness the others had displayed. It did, and the black plastic shattered beneath her stroke. It stared out of the helmet with three bright green eyes that shone against the oily white skin of its face. At that moment, she had no idea if its sword cut all the way through to her skin or not, but she snapped her dagger up and thrust it through the thing's face, right between all three eyes.

It howled and scrabbled at her with the one arm that still worked properly and the one with the bloody palm. The third, with the broken wrist and fingers, it treated like a flail and slammed it into her head. That blow knocked her sideways and she tripped amid the thing's flailing limbs and hit the ground hard.

Her vision swam and a sharp pain in her hand told her she lost the baton in her fall. It lay a meter or so away in the sand, strap torn. She ignored it; her attention was on the monster in front of her. It struggled to its feet on shaking legs as it screeched and screamed incoherent curses at her.

"Fight or die." That idea, the first words she had said in days, echoed in her brain, urging just a little more out of her tired, fatigued body.

The creature took a step, then a second, before Victoria came to her own feet. She lurched into motion, batting the first of its wildly flailing limbs aside. The second came at her straight. She grabbed it, stepped to the side, and drove the heel of her hand into its elbow, snapping its last undamaged arm backward.

Another lunge brought her into reach of its body. She stepped around its legs, put a foot behind them, grabbed a shoulder, and heaved the massive creature to the ground. It hit the sand and she was on top of it in a flash, tearing her daggers out of its ribs and face. In one violent frenzy of movement, she drove both of them into its neck, and withdrew them. Her next movement plunged one back into its neck. She jerked it violently to the side, tearing the tough muscle there. The other one she drove into its chest, where a flash of memory told her its heart resided.

It continued to flail, beating on her back and head with its arms as she twisted the knife in its heart. With the other, she made the monster pay for every strike on her back with another violent thrust against the dense hard bone of its skull. Little by little as the painful seconds ticked by, timed only by the blood rushing in her ears, the monster slowed. Eventually, it stopped moving altogether.

She stood, finally aware of the stinging pain in her side, the ache in her ribs and back, and the throb in her head.

Victoria swiped at a tickle on her side and her hand came away glistening with blood. Her head swam and her knees sagged. Whatever she was going to do, she had to work fast. If she were attacked right now, she knew she would not survive another fight.

For just a moment, the universe stopped caring and her vision went black anyway.

***

Victoria knew several things.

First, she knew the four-armed monster was dead. She killed enough of them to know what death looked like and to appreciate the difference between it and being stunned or knocked unconscious. If its inaction did not convince her, the gaping hole where its throat and face had been certainly did the job. Its blood soaked the sand, turning it black.

Second, she knew she finally achieved some measure of safety. The big door with its complex lock had sealed behind her as she stepped into this place. If the other green-eyes could open that door, they would have done so already.

Third, and perhaps finally, she knew her own blood soaked the sand under her back. Sand stuck to her when she sat up and ground into her wounds.

What she did not know was how long she slept after killing that monster. She was still alive, and so reasoned that it had not been long. Still, Victoria was aware of a brief period of dream-filled darkness in between the monster's fall and the current moment.

81

Slowly, she dragged herself to her feet. Blood-crusted sand fell from her as she moved, and she dusted off as much as she could. At least sand was rough, she reasoned, and did not turn slick and treacherous the way bloody tile did.

After taking a moment simply to breathe, Victoria stripped off the top half of her black suit and let it fall to the sand. It hung in ragged strips after her fight and did little for her anymore. Her ribs continued to bleed, leaving a bright red streaks in the grime on her skin.

Victoria eyed the four-armed monster. Its clothes were made out of the same black fabric as the other green-eyes. If she could stop her own bleeding, she could scavenge what she needed for a new suit from it.

Unfortunately, the effort of stripping it halfway took what little energy she had left, and Victoria collapsed again on the sand. She remained conscious this time which, she admitted, was an improvement.

She adjusted her position, rolling onto the sand and reveling in the simple action of stretching her muscles for a brief moment. The light no longer hurt her eyes and she stretched out on her back, enjoying the warm lights overhead. It felt good, relaxing, and she remained there until the slowly-spreading pool of wet blood under her back cut through the fog in her brain and reminded her of her wounds.

Victoria sat up, brushing another layer of sticky, blood-caked sand from her back. The warmth overhead slowly soaked into her body, returning some of the energy that the cold lower levels sapped. She stretched again, this time taking a moment to inspect her injuries. Most were minor, the result of endless fights where her attackers landed insignificant blows here and there. They would heal with time.

The four-armed monster only truly hit her once, but the gash it left in her side was a worse injury than anything else so far. Its razor-edged sword had done its job almost too well. Had it cut any deeper, warned the voice in her mind, it would have done catastrophic damage to her muscles and organs. The wound itself was straight, with none of the ragged edges the others' dull knives and claws left. It was going to be easy to sew back together, at least.

Small positives, she reminded herself.

She looked down at her side again, watching the blood leaking from the cut. She needed most of her remaining water to wash the area before sewing it up; none of her previous wounds had been quite so bad. Something told her that it would scar horrifically.

As the thought of washing the wound crossed her mind, a vision flashed through her memory. Hands, not her own, gripped her leg. A chunk of flesh was missing there, ripped away by the teeth of the dead creature at her dream's feet, one of the knife-wielders. Blood was everywhere and with no way to stop the bleeding, she was quickly losing feeling in the leg, even though it was not hers. The memory reached down and picked up the dead green eyed monster and tore out the side of its throat. Brilliant, crimson-red blood flooded over her hands, bathing them in heat.

The memory pressed the side of the pale creature's neck against her thigh, filling the wound-echo with blood. Hands that had once been hers rubbed the red fluid into the wound, ignoring the searing pain that made her flesh ache even in memory.

Her mind flashed forward days or weeks; she had no way to tell how far. The hands removed a bandage made of black fabric from her leg. The wound underneath was red still, at least where the brown color of scabbed blood had not yet taken over, but showed no trace of infection.

She snapped back to the present, more disoriented than usual by the vivid flashback. The aching sensation of being alone in her body again was dizzying.

Victoria looked at the huge beast that lay half naked, then looked again at the bleeding wound in her side. Her memories had never given her wrong information before, and when there was a danger to be avoided, the resulting painful death was usually the end result of the vision. To see something that did not promise death gave her reason to assume it was safe, if unappealing.

Victoria dusted off her knife and once again crossed the sand. She regarded the dead monster with suspicion, as though it were only sleeping and could get up at any moment and resume its attack. Slitting what remained of its throat would, she thought, have the added benefit of forever preventing that possibility.

She seized it under the upper shoulders and drew the torso into a partially upright position. With the whole creature half again as tall as she was, even that small adjustment made it seem frighteningly large.

One of its three eyes remained open, an empty gaze staring at the far side of the room. Something about leaving its eyes open seemed wrong to her, as though even this murderous beast deserved some manner of dignity in its death, and she slid the eyelid slut.

Victoria drew her knife across its throat, digging the sharp blade deep into its tough muscle. Death had robbed its blood of some of its normal sheen and color, but a bright red curtain still poured from beneath her blade.

She dropped the knife to the sand and cupped her palms under the stream of blood, collecting a double handful of the inhumanly bright stuff. It smelled strange, with a sharpness unlike her own blood.

Clenching her teeth against the pain she knew would be coming, she smeared the beast's blood across her side. In an instant, her wound burned with white-hot pain. The shock took her knees out from under her as her side burned. She fell to her hands and knees and the sand swam before her eyes. Every muscle in her body tightened against the pain and she dug into the sand with her fingers.

It continued to burn, searing every nerve within a hand-span of her wounded side. Victoria imagined she could hear her flesh sizzling like cooking meat and the blazing agony only grew worse as her breathing sped up.

Then, as the moments passed, the pain ebbed. It shrank back from fire, to a sting, and then finally to an ache that she could ignore. Victoria sank back onto her heels, aware that only a few moments had passed.

With the pain at a manageable level, trusting that her memories were right and what she did would actually help her, she went to work again. Victoria retrieved the sewing kit with its whittled-bone needles, testing them one by one to find the sharpest among them. Into the eye of the needle, she fed a long string soaked with blood from the four-armed monster's throat.

Victoria's side, she was pleased to notice, no longer hurt. The burning pain had been replaced by an oddly pleasant tingling sensation that, she hoped, could be blamed on the green eye blood she smeared into the wound.

The numbness did not extend very far, a fact that immediately became clear when she slid the needle into her flesh. She screamed involuntarily as pain, somehow worse than the original wound, flared from the bone needle.

With one hand, she held the wound in her side closed. Merely pressing the flesh together produced another spill of dark, dead blood. The other hand slowly pulled the thread through her skin, as the agony flared to new heights. The thread was worse than the needle. Not only was it not smooth, but it tugged at her flesh from the inside in a deeply disturbing way.

Reaching the knot at the end of the thread, Victoria readied herself for the next puncture. This time, she did not scream. Again and again she looped the thread through her torn side, pulling the wound slowly together. Each prick hurt less than the one before it as the pain multiplied to the point that she no longer consciously registered it at all.

She made a second pass down the gash, crossing each of the stitches carefully, and tied it off where she began. Satisfied, she returned the sewing kit to her bag with mechanical precision. Every excess movement hurt.

With the wound itself taken care of, Victoria cut long strips of black fabric from the four armed monster's long sleeves and wrapped one around her ribs. She wrapped another around her breasts, replacing the blood-and-sweat soaked strip of fabric that had been binding them down since the day before.

It would take time to repair her top, and she had no real desire to struggle back into the tight fabric until the stitches in her side healed more. She had less desire to leave it in the sand-filled arena when she left, however, and so tied the tattered sleeves around her waist.

With her backpack on her shoulders once more, she went to the pile of swords taken from the massive creature. What had been one-handed swords for the three-meter creature were large two-handed weapons for her. Lying there in the sand, they still looked deadly, especially the one that still bore a smear of dried blood on the edge.

She picked up the nearest sword. A large dent, one that matched the edge of her baton, marred the edge. She discarded that one. The second one was in decent condition, if dull. She returned it to its scabbard and tied it to her backpack. Carrying it that way was awkward, but it would be serviceable with some sharpening, and she learned early on with her knives that having backups was good. The third sword was similarly damaged, and it, too, was left behind.

The fourth, the sword that had been stained with her own blood, was much sharper. This one she gathered up with intent to use it. The scabbard had a metal tip and a metal band around the opening. Resting against the sand, the pommel of the weapon reached her eyes. She satisfied herself with using it like a walking stick. In fact, after a moment's thought, having it as a walking stick might just be more useful in the long run than having it as a weapon.

Victoria knew she could re-open the door she came through and return to the dark and damp, but as long as it was locked she felt a strange sense of safety. Additionally, if she was being honest with herself, she did not want to return to that hell of violence, at least not yet.

With the monster dead, the room felt empty. An eerie silence fell on everything, broken only by the grinding sounds of sand underfoot, as she approached the door through which the monster came.

The door remained open, exactly as the monster left it. As Victoria approached, a fetid smell assaulted her nostrils. Death and detritus hung heavy in the air. Stepping through that door sent a shiver down her spine. Automatically, Victoria reached for her baton, but the monster's sword was closer. She removed its scabbard, dropped it.

She tried to raise the sword in front of her, holding it far out like a knife, but the burning pain in her shoulders prevented that for more than a few moments. Instead, she braced her arms against her torso and held the point outward from there. Its size was a sort of comfort. She could interpose its long, sharp edges between herself and an attacking green-eye easily, but the nuances of actually using the thing were lost on her. She dreamed about knives and clubs, even spears, but never something like this.

Once again, uniqueness had an appeal all its own.

The unique nature of the room around her, however, was anything but a comfort. Blood coated the walls, with more appearing with every passing moment as her eyes continued to adjust to the gloom. The room, or what was left of it, looked like the one in which she had first awoken, but smaller. Large tables and bits of broken equipment were scattered around, most in a pile to one side that left two large areas clear.

One of those areas, the one against the far wall, smelled vastly worse than the other. Victoria knew that smell: organic waste, though the cumulative stench of however long the four-armed green eye had lived here was worse than anything she left behind. The other was clear except for two piles of debris, one of black fabric and the other of knives, clubs, even a few spears.

Victoria went to that area, feeling drawn to it. She picked up the spear. It was crude, little more than a head-high pole carved from the wooden panels of a table with a broken-glass blade tied to the end. Still, it somehow felt familiar in her hands as memories of using it to kill the green-eyes came to the surface.

She remembered carrying the spear through the same halls she herself, her real self, had walked only recently. Those halls looked the same, but her body was not. An unfamiliar feeling between her legs was all she needed to confirm that.

The memory-self stalked through the corridors, moving quietly on bare feet. She remembered hearing scrabbling from around a corner and wheeling around, jabbing the spear out without even looking for the target. One of the smaller green eyed creatures died with the glass blade stuck through its throat.

That sequence repeated over and over. The memory would hunt, seemingly going out of his way to find and kill them. The little ones fell in droves, and he even managed to kill a few of the giants, though his spear proved to be less effective against their thick skin than her hands and knives had been.

Each memory came as a flash. A thrust here, a kill there, nothing so vivid as the few moments that gave her the idea to use the creatures' blood to clean her own wounds.

She put the spear back down on the pile of weapons. Its familiarity was welcome, but something about the weapon made her want to distance herself from it. Its owner had failed, else she would not have his memories now, and the weapon stank of that failure.

Victoria wondered if the four-armed creature had actually lived here. The weapon stack looked like trophies, and the pile of fabric might have been a bed of sorts. She moved it around with the tip of her new sword, finding nothing.

She went to the far wall, fighting to keep what little food she had eaten in her stomach as she passed the site of the monster's waste. A door sat in the wall there, but it was covered in dirt and rust. She tried to open it, but the metal would not move.

Victoria beat on the door with the pommel of her sword. It rang loud and every blow she landed left a small dent in the metal, but it stood steadfast and unmoving. She could deal with it later.

Her body continued to protest every movement, every action. After several minutes, she found herself eyeing the pile of black fabric where the giant monster appeared to have slept. Curiously, it had no smell. The idea of sleeping there repulsed her, but she had to sleep somewhere, and this room could be barricaded.

Near its sleeping area, a series of designs on the wall caught her eye. Coming closer, they turned into a series of paintings and engravings. Most were simple pictographs, what appeared to be the four-armed beast fighting and killing person after person. Some of them were the dull rust brown color of dried blood; others had been scratched directly into the tile of the wall.

Each drawing triggered a memory. Though she only had her own memories of the creature itself, many of the designs triggered flashes of fighting or of insight. Some were as simple as, "do not be hasty," or, "do not be too reserved." Others were more visceral, painful even. One memory was only of the realization that she had to defend herself before attacking, and the unbelievable pain in her gut burned so strongly that, for a moment, she forgot the pain was not actually her own.

A human shape holding a spear ended the block of figures. She touched that drawing. There was no way to tell from its simplicity, but she knew down in her bones that it was the same spear she had been holding moments before. Four successive pictures of the encounter stood in a small square, more detailed than the others. First, the man threatening it with his spear, then the man piercing the one of the monster's arms with his spear. The third picture showed the monster having grabbed him with two arms; the spear lay on the ground. The last image was the monster tearing the man in half, complete with a fountain of blood.

Victoria's memory reaction to that was immediate and agonizing. She doubled over, clutching her stomach. That might as well have been her in the drawing, torn apart by the massive beast. Memory of pain so unbelievable that the thing's blood burning in her wound became a mere footnote ripped through her nerves, lighting them with fire made all the worse by the knowledge that it was not real and would not end with her death.

Inside the pain, buried so deep that its message seared itself into the core of her soul, was a message to not be overconfident in her own ability.

In moments, the pain passed, leaving Victoria soaked with sweat, curled into a tight ball on the floor. She forced herself to her hands and knees and violently expelled the last of the cooked rat meat.

She crawled away, forcing herself to her feet. She had one last task to accomplish before she could rest. Debris filled the room and it took her very little time to barricade the door, even moving sluggishly with the echoes of being ripped apart still haunting her brain.

In moving the rubble, she uncovered a message etched into the tile wall near the paintings. A large knife, likely small by the scale of the creature that lived there, lay on the floor beneath it. She could read the signs she found scattered around the corridors, but this looked to have been done by hand in a subtly different language. The strokes matched the ones that made the pictographs, however, and Victoria's pulse raced.

She asked herself if the four-armed beast, the thing that attacked her with violent abandon, could have been capable of thought. The idea that she killed something without first trying to understand it struck her as wrong. It attacked her, as they all had, but the question of why remained unanswered.

Now that question gnawed at her as she tried to make what sense she could of the engraving.

"Sealed," she read, halting as several of the words were unfamiliar, or came with strange spellings. "in I. Cannot... something... door.

90

Wrecked? The other door. Strength most having, something about approaching?" She stared as an entire line of text refused to make sense. She understood the pronouns, and little else. "This pit am trapped, sky desire I? No more sings the singer. Kill... all... I."

Victoria stared at the inscription for a long time, but nothing else in the carving made sense. She finally turned away and shed her excess gear. The backpack made a poor pillow, but it was better than nothing. She lay the usable sword next to her, draping an arm across its scabbard, and set everything else to one side.

Wonder about the nature of the creatures she had been fighting ate at her as she sought sleep. However, with the door safely barred against intrusion, she knew she finally had that time to think. Sleep would come, and when it came, she would finally have true rest.

Chapter 6

For a moment, Second Lord Pallasophia could not decide which sight was more impressive. In the arena below them, the black-suited figure of Test Subject One Hundred finally toppled the mastigas elite. However, standing next to her, First Lord Tritogenes positively vibrated with excitement.

After several minutes of silence, he simply said, "she has done it."

Pallasophia, beside him and with her eyes firmly riveted on the bright, sand-filled pit a dozen stories below them, simply nodded once. Seeing Tritogenes so excited was certainly a rare thing, but Number One Hundred was the truly fascinating sight.

She was aware, however, that what might have been tears glittered in the edges of her eyes.

"We have to get her out of there," Tritogenes continued. "She will likely need medical attention. Not to mention the ceremonies that will have to be planned in her honor."

Pallasophia finally tore her attention away from the window. "She has needed medical attention for days now. It seems knowing about the antiseptic properties of the mastigas's blood helped."

Tritogenes nodded. "Make sure whoever had that idea received a commendation."

She had already done so, several generations of test subjects ago in fact. Project Titan, while it was the most important of his affairs, was only one of Tritogenes's many operations and she could not fault him for forgetting the things that had already been taken care of. If he forgot to order a commendation altogether, she would have taken issue with it, but to simply be reminded twice was a small thing.

She looked back to the arena. Her Hexarch was right, even if he was just repeating something she already knew. Number One Hundred had to be taken out of the mastigas-infested parts of the facility as soon as possible. The only problem—truthfully, she thought, the main problem—was that after the Incident, the lower fifteen or so levels had not only been abandoned, but had been manually sealed as well.

The mastigas destroyed most of the communications equipment down there as well, which made getting a message in or out impossible. It was only Tritogenes's paranoid forethought that protected the gestation pods themselves from the mastigas. They were armored using the same sort of state-of-the-art material that went into frontline military warships.

Nothing could penetrate the exterior of the gestation pods, which was how not only Number One Hundred but many more before her had been born. So the Project continued, at least until now.

"How long until we can free her?" Tritogenes asked.

Pallasophia thought for a moment, noting his use of "free" instead of any other word he could have chosen just then. To continue Project Titan, even with the facility sealed, had been his express order. Nothing, he had ordered, was to impede its progress. Pallasophia had, at the time, raised considerable objection over that point, but in a rare display of rank, the Hexarch overruled her.

And then, she thought with a frown, he handed the Project over to her anyway. She ignored that sudden burst of frustration, pushing it down to be dealt with later. Pallasophia might have been comfortable speaking her mind in front of her Hexarch, at least in private, but that would start trouble she did not want to deal with.

"A day," she replied, "perhaps two. I will have to organize a team to clear out the rest of the facility. The sensors we still have down there tell me that several dozen mastigas are still alive."

Tritogenes paled. "How many, exactly?"

"It's hard to count, exactly. No more than four gigas, I *think*."

"But the sophont is dead?"

Pallasophia nodded. "She killed it before taking out the elite."

Tritogenes nodded and stood up. He smoothed the purple folds of his robe and reflexively adjusted the fall of his braid. Pallasophia stood a moment later, paying noticeably less attention to her outward appearance.

"Keep the retrieval team small," he ordered. "And be careful. If we wanted to storm the facility with an army, we would have."

Rather than turn her frustrated glare on Tritogenes, Pallasophia looked out the window as Number One Hundred cut apart the fabric making up the elite's clothing. "Of course."

"The fewer people who know, the better, at least for right now. I need to go prepare to address the Council. I ought to stop by Katarraktes first."

"Why there?" Pallasophia suspected she knew the reason. Despite a rocky start to their professional relationship, First Lord Enyalios, Hexarch of Katarraktes, had been one of Tritogenes's closest confidants and supporters since the beginning of Project Titan.

"Limani's orbit is fairly close to Katarraktes this time of year. It will be a simple matter to stop there for a short visit before continuing on to Prosgeiosi. Besides," Tritogenes added with a small smile, "it will be good to see how his part of the Project is doing and to plan our next moves before we have to actually enact them."

Pallasophia nodded. A moment passed and she said, "Tritogenes?"

The tone of her voice made it clear she was addressing him as her friend, not as her social superior. "Yes?"

"Promise me that you will treat One Hundred with humanity. Remember what I said to you before showing you the footage of Number Thirty's end."

Tritogenes's face darkened and he turned slightly away. That had been a sore point between the two of them for some time. Tritogenes had been much more active in the Project in the earliest stages, especially in the first ten trials. However, their continued deaths—the events he referred to as "failures of the Project" to keep the wall between his feelings and the Project's needs—got to him. The Incident occurred after Number Nineteen's death, and Number Twenty was the last one Tritogenes oversaw personally.

Pallasophia took over fully from the Hexarch starting with Subject Twenty-One. By subject Twenty-Nine, she knew she had to bring him back in. She convinced him to watch the footage of Number Thirty to, as she explained, "better understand what might be improved in subsequent variations."

As it happened, Number Thirty died horrifically by poison. At the end, his very organs had liquefied, but his mind was far gone by that point. The events sickened the First Lord, but he ordered her to press on despite that. The Project, he argued, was too important to the survival of the human race to halt.

Number Thirty-One was killed by a gigas, but Thirty's memories of poison, implanted via a process which Pallasophia herself designed, kept Thirty-One alive just a little longer.

"We owe a debt to our dead," Tritogenes said darkly. He still refused to look directly at Pallasophia. "Now, I should go. If I hurry, I can schedule a meeting with Philip before I depart Limani."

The Second Lord stood and watched him depart, carrying a heavy weight on his shoulders. She felt the same weight, but had no time to dwell on it. She wanted to hate Tritogenes for putting the entire Project on her shoulders, but she understood all too well his feelings.

She did, however, resent him for leaving Aphelion so quickly. Tritogenes *should* have stayed to meet Test Subject Number One Hundred, to stand beside her when they explained exactly why she had been subjected to the nightmare that was her life.

Eventually she followed Tritogenes out of the small room. By the time she did, the Hexarch was long gone. She took a deep breath and held it for a moment, hoping that everything they had done, all of their sins, would be worth it.

A gesture activated her computer's holo display. As with most, hers floated a few centimeters above her forearm. It only took a moment to navigate through the layers of menus until she reached her communication directory.

"This is Second Lord Director Pallasophia." She spoke into a small pickup disguised as a necklace. "I need to meet with Strategos Glaukos at his earliest possible convenience."

She nodded as the person on the other end of the line acknowledged her request and then deactivated her comm. Glaukos normally worked at what passed for the "night shift" in a facility where the binary suns were little more than bright dots. It would likely be the better part of an hour before he returned her message, but that was just as well. It gave her time to return to the suite where she lived and make preparations for Number One Hundred.

***

Three hours after Number One Hundred killed the mastigas elite, Tritogenes boarded his personal shuttle, heading for Limani. Pallasophia still found herself with a bitter taste in her mouth over that decision, but three hours of voicing her opinion had not changed his mind. With little she could do there, Pallasophia threw herself into work again.

With luck, the First Lord would make it to Limani in just a few days. This time of year, his world and Aphelion were on the same side of the binary suns. That would cut down on travel time significantly. From there, Katarraktes would only be a day or two away. Depending on how long he spent at home, he could easily reach Enyalios's planet within two weeks.

After seeing Tritogenes off, Pallasophia returned to her suite. She wanted to sleep, but Pallasophia had a sinking feeling that she would not get a decent night's sleep until Number One Hundred was safe. Even then, that would only bring another set of problems to plague her schedule and keep her up at night.

Before the meeting she scheduled with Strategos Glaukos, Pallasophia had just enough time to wash and change clothes. She also took a moment to brush a blue streak through her short and otherwise featureless hair and apply a rough smear of black makeup that covered her eyes, eyebrows, and upper cheekbones.

Catching herself in the mirror as she left the suite, she had to admit she liked the look. Both added touches were in vogue with the Technocrat military, especially those stationed at Aphelion. It was good, she reasoned, to style things so that she fit in with the people she was about to be meeting with.

The facility's guard force nodded politely as she passed on her way to Glaukos's office. They obviously knew who she was, but a visit from "Facility Director Pallasophia" was very different from a visit by "Lochagos Pallasophia." The minor changes to her appearance, including her choice of a vibrant blue robe whose hue was more in keeping with military tradition than the navy blue robe she had on that morning, made her "one of them." She could have spoken to those she passed, but she had no business with them and so left them to their work.

Finally, after making her way through the armory itself, which did require an extra security check, Pallasophia found herself in Glaukos's office. In contrast to the utilitarian setup of the rooms outside, the Strategos's waiting room was rather luxurious.

An oversized cup of coffee steamed pleasantly on the table beside her seat, brought ten minutes before by a Fourth Lord who apologized for the delay. Pallasophia took another sip from the mug, not sure if it was the caffeine or the unreasonably bitter, military-strength brew that helped her energy level.

Probably, she reasoned, it was both. Still, if Glaukos did not show up soon, she *was* going to go back to her suite and sleep. That was not entirely fair to the Strategos, however, as it was Pallasophia who woke him up in the first place, and so she waited until Aphelion's Security Director saw fit to present himself.

She only had to wait a few more minutes before the door opened. A large man in a blue robe stepped through. He had close-cropped hair, though intricate designs had been freshly shaved into the sides. The folds of his robe draped around a large pistol at his side, one worn to be seen rather than the smaller weapon Pallasophia kept concealed in the folds of her own robe.

He closed the door with all propriety, nodding to the Third Lord working security outside, then turned. The neutral look left his face, replaced by something that was half grin and half mock-anger.

"Selene's Tits, woman! What do you think you're doing getting me out of bed in the middle of the day?"

Pallasophia, despite her attempts to the contrary, failed utterly at keeping her face neutral. She cracked a grin, then a smile, and finally resorted to a moment of full-blown laughter. She stood and held out a hand. "Nice to see you too, Second Lord Glaukos."

He grasped her arm by the wrist. She did likewise, and they shook hands once.

He grinned, broad and bright. "What's this 'Second Lord Glaukos' nonsense? The door's shut. The other Twos won't hear us."

Pallasophia's smile persisted. "Alright," she said, slipping into the same sort of less formal language he was using. "If you insist."

"That's better."

"Strategos." Her wink ruined the formal emphasis of his rank.

He laughed. "I suppose I deserved that."

"A bit, yeah."

"I'll take what I can get, Director."

"As you should."

"Anyway, what did you need?"

Pallasophia returned to her seat. She waved Glaukos to the other one, taking a long drink of her coffee as he adjusted himself in the oversized leather chair.

At his expectant expression, Pallasophia laughed. "Didn't you read the message I forwarded?"

He shrugged.

"Strategos."

Glaukos laughed. "Stars, woman! Of course I read it. You were just vague, is all."

"There's only so much I can say in a message that might be intercepted."

Glaukos scoffed. "My staff's security is top notch."

"No security is impenetrable, Glaukos. You ought to know that. Gods' sake, given what's at stake here..."

Glaukos's raucous laughter interrupted her, but he said nothing.

Pallasophia sighed. "Right."

"It's too easy when you're tired, Director."

"I'm about thirty minutes away from sleeping for twelve hours," she said, "so I'm going to keep this as short as I can. The Project has finally paid off."

His eyes went wide. That part had not been in the message she sent. "Paid off? As in...?"

"The test subjects..."

"The people," Glaukos grunted, interrupting her.

Pallasophia nodded, looking away. "Yes, people. Ninety-nine dead, plus the personnel we lost during the Incident, and we finally have what we've been looking for this entire time."

Glaukos's eyes went wide. "Don't tell me that someone's finally completed that insane series of trials that Tritogenes came up with."

"Number One Hundred. She killed an elite with her bare hands." Pallasophia chuckled. "Well, her bare hands, two large knives, and a metal club."

Glaukos nodded. His eyes drifted around the room as his thoughts processed the implications of what she was saying. He sat back in his chair, crossed one leg over the other under his robes, and steepled his fingers in front of his face. When he finally spoke, he still used informal language, but his tone was thoughtful and measured.

"And now you need to get her out of there. We sealed up those levels for a reason, Pallasophia, and even though you and the Hexarch insisted on continuing the Project afterward, I don't know how easy it's going to be to unseal them."

"It can be done."

"Of course it can be done," he said, then laughed. "Anything you can build or lock up can be broken with enough time. That's not the problem. The issue is going to be making sure it's safe for, well, normal people."

"Number One Hundred..." she began.

Glaukos interrupted. "Is not normal. We both know that. Whatever she survived down there would have killed most people, even my soldiers. It's going to take more than cutting a door open to get her out safely."

"Then give me a team."

"Give you a..." he started. "You're not going down there."

"You know, Tritogenes told me something very similar earlier today."

Glaukos shook his head. "I'm sure he did."

Pallasophia set her half-empty coffee mug down on the small table next to her chair. "She's my responsibility. Need I remind you that I do hold the rank of Lochagos?"

"And I hold the rank of Strategos," he countered, "and I say you cannot go down there. It's too dangerous."

"Lochagos," she said, ticking things off on her fingers, "Second Lord. Director. You can overrule the first, out-argue the second, but you cannot overrule the third, and that's the one I invoke, Glaukos."

He eyed her for a long moment, then sighed. A complex relationship existed between Social Rank, where they were equal, Military rank, where he outranked her, and their actual job, where she outranked him. Finally, he acquiesced, "fine, but you're taking my best with you."

She smiled. "That's why I'm here."

"I know of two I'm sending down regardless. Did you want to request anyone specific?"

"I'll leave it up to your judgment," she said. "Strategos."

He gave a mock-exasperated sigh. "At least you leave some things up to me." Seriousness returned to his voice and he added, "give me a day."

***

Victoria awoke some time later. She had no idea how long she slept, but her bones ached from laying in one position for so long. With the doors closed and barred, the stench of the four-armed monster's former lair had quickly become overwhelming. Despite that, and the primal fear-reaction it elicited from her heart, she slept better and longer than she ever had.

The long sleep had done wonders for her mind. Fatigue crept up on her so slowly that Victoria had not realized how tired she actually became. Her sleep time and meal time were so irregular that she could not rely on them to log passed time. However, it was clear enough from the way she felt now that she had gone much too long without sufficient sleep.

Eventually, she realized, fatigue would have caught up with her and even one of the little green eyes would have killed her. At that, she realized exactly how lucky she really was that she encountered the beast when she did. Much longer without proper rest, and the four-armed monster would have torn her apart, just like it tore apart so many others.

She shuddered at that memory. It made her whole body hurt, even thinking about it. Muscles and joints being ripped apart, bones snapping, and the last few moments of life where the mind she remembered being clung to consciousness even as it realized nothing below its ribs remained attached.

One of the negative effects of her mind being clearer and sharper now was that the memories, for they were clearly memories now and not dim dreams, were as real to her mind and body as her own experiences were.

Victoria sat up, fighting her protesting joints. Stretches superimposed themselves over her vision. These were not memories, but instructions. She followed the motions, feeling the physical fatigue draining away until her body felt like her mind did—whole again.

She carefully unwrapped the strips of cloth wound around her chest. Her stitches held, and her side seemed to be healing well enough. Residue from the green-eye blood remained, dried into a brown film that coated the wound and her stitches. The wound ached, but the sharp pain of the injury itself was gone.

Something told her that wounds needed to breathe to heal properly, and so she left the bandage off a while longer. She did, however, gather up the strips of fabric and pile them with her shirt-turned-pillow where it still lay on the floor next to her.

With the renewed strength that came from sleep, Victoria returned to the sealed door at the back end of the monster's lair. It still bore the marks from where she struck it with her sword's pommel. Her sleep-refreshed mind also picked out a series of scratches and marks on the wall around it so deep and complete that she at first thought the damage to be just another part of the wall.

Other doors she had been able to lever open with her baton, but the crevasse between this door and the wall was much too thin for that. She briefly considered using the sword taken from the monster, but discarded that idea. She did not want to damage the blade like that. Three others remained, and perhaps she could try one of them. Those, she was not keeping, and so Victoria did not care very much if one broke.

Unless one of the green-eyes had somehow opened the door with its complex color lock, Victoria knew everything in the sandy arena was the same as it had been before she slept. A few minutes of work and she unblocked the door, returning in moments with the most damaged of its swords.

She wedged the damaged sword between the door and the frame, hammering it into place by hitting the pommel with her baton until it would go no deeper. Experimentally, she pushed on it, trying to use the huge weapon as a lever. It groaned, though she was not sure if that was the sound of the weapon or of the door, but gave little other indication of anything happening.

Victoria strained, bracing her feet on what remained of a large table. The metal creaked, and then the sword's blade shattered into a dozen crystalline pieces. The shards hit the tile with a musical chorus of tinkling noises as Victoria herself fell backward into the wall.

Her side screamed and she sat there for a moment as her head swam, but the sensation cleared as soon as it arrived. Angrily, she tossed the sword's broken grip away from her and simply sat there with her back against the cool tile.

Victoria seemed to be trapped there. Either she missed something in the room or she missed another way out, another way to go that did not lead to the arena of sand and heat. The only other option was that she was truly trapped and would wander the halls until she, too, succumbed to any of the many horrors that had taken the lives she remembered being.

If she could not escape, then she would be just another voice in the mind of the next one to wake up in this abominable place. If there was to be anyone after her, she thought.

She frowned and rose to her feet. This part of the monster's lair was covered in a thin layer of dirt, and she took a moment to dust off her pants before doing anything else. She spared the broken sword pieces little more than an annoyed glare as she stepped over the crystalline shards.

If she could not find an exit, then she would make one. If nothing presented itself in a few hours, she would return to the twisting maze of passages and look for another way forward. Victoria knew there were places she had not visited in this life, places where her memories ran thin. Perhaps the answer to escape waited for her there.

If that did not appear inside of another five days, then she would come back here and beat down the door, no matter how long it took.

She returned to the arena again, taking a wide path around the corpse of the monster. It already crawled with flies. She never stayed in one place long enough to notice them before, and any other corpses she left behind quickly disappeared, but here they descended in a thick black cloud.

Her eyes landed on the puzzle door. It remained the only other exit from the sandy arena and she nodded in its direction. She had no desire to go back there, but the alternative was to try and break down a door that the unbelievably strong, four-armed monster could not open. She saw little option.

Carefully, Victoria dragged all of her possessions out onto the sand. She knew, simply from standing in the stuff, that the grit would get everywhere, but something about the arena's warmth calmed her. The heat eased the ache from her wounds as well, something the dank, cool labyrinth could not do. That alone was reason enough to risk a little sand in her clothes.

She sat for some time, simply thinking. She had a decent mental map of the areas of the labyrinth through which she had traveled. The green eyes moved around, and she knew she had not encountered all of them, but that was no concern.

What concerned her was how to escape the damnable place altogether. That alone would be enough of a challenge. The smaller four-armed green eye, the one that actually conversed with her, said they were all locked away down there together. If it was even remotely as intelligent as it seemed, it would have tried to escape.

Yet, it remained. Victoria wondered if the "singer" referred to in the inscription was the same creature that spoke to her. If so, perhaps it remained in the labyrinth in the hopes that it could free the four-armed monster.

"If that was true, why didn't it solve the puzzle door itself?" she wondered aloud. Speaking the words, instead of thinking them, gave the ideas a quality that was uniquely hers. Even her own memories melded with those of past lives, but anything she said aloud would only ever be in her voice.

"Was it telling the truth? Did the big one really stop listening to it?"

Victoria grimaced. She had no answers, no plan, but she also had no other options. She remembered where she had been, that was easy enough. Many of the floors she passed had doors she either ignored or did not explore at the time. That produced a glimmer of hope.

Three things quashed that hope almost immediately. First, her mind returned to the thought of the talking green-eye. If escape was possible at all, it should have done so long ago unless it had some reason for staying. She could think of several reasons for it to stay. Those ranged from practical concerns—that there might be no food outside the labyrinth, or that something worse than the four-armed beast lurked out there—to the less practical or even downright disturbing, such as the possibility that the talking green eye stayed around for no reason other than to torment her and her predecessors.

The second and third reasons were much more immediate, as far as Victoria was concerned. Even in her memories, much of the facility remained unexplored. It would take a long time to search everywhere, which ran directly into the third problem—food.

Her stomach growled as she thought about how much time she would likely spend searching for an exit. Her supply of rat meat was, for the moment, gone. More to the point, it had never been enough in the first place. Now, after sleeping properly, her body saw fit to remind her exactly how hungry she was.

Whatever else she did, she had to go hunting again. She dressed quickly, trying to press the cleanest sections of the bandage against her wound. She was rapidly running out of water as well and could not afford to wash her side again.

That settled that problem. First, she needed water. It could hardly be called a plan, but a list of needs was better than what she had when she woke up. Fortunately, her water bags seemed to be durable enough to be reused. When full, only one of them leaked.

She left the door to the dead monster's lair open. If she ever had to come back this way, at least now it would have a chance to air out.

The lock on the puzzle door on the inside of the arena was similar to the lock on the outside, but the pattern inverted itself in strange places. However, now that she had opened the other side once already, Victoria found this side of the door an easy challenge.

Moments after it opened, it started to swing shut on its own and, in a flash of inspiration, she set her backpack in the way. The door might have been heavy, but it was well balanced and the pack stopped it from closing all the way.

Victoria crossed the arena and retrieved yet another of the monster's swords. She carried it to the puzzle door and wedged it into the hinges.

Now, with the way permanently open, she went back into the dark corridors of the labyrinth. She heard the scamper of green-eyes as they moved around the halls, but never saw any of them. These higher levels were less damaged and some rooms even showed no signs of green eye activity at all. If not for the presence of the talker and the titanic four-armed monster, she would have assumed the exit lay downward instead.

The hallways seemed to wind back upon themselves the further she went, and even going down a level and coming up in different places did not seem to help. Nothing on the arena's floor opened to any higher level.

She ran across more than one locked door, but they refused to open to any tool she had. Victoria did her best to memorize their locations and went on. If nothing proved useful, she would press on by *dismantling* every door in her way.

***

Pallasophia met her troops for the first time outside the final seal. Glaukos deployed them early that morning, long before messaging her about the deployment schedule. She supposed it was his little act of rebellion, protesting against her going down personally.

The Facility Director let it slide. After all, he only succeeded in sparing her the time needed to oversee the team as they cut through the sealed outer door. Most of those doors were simply locked, if so unassuming a term could accurately describe the sort of locks that used arm-thick bars of steel to anchor the door into the rock wall.

Further in, "locked" gave way to "sealed," but even those were easy for the team's equipment to penetrate. This last one was much thicker, originally intended to be the very failsafe that it turned out to be. When she arrived, the team had been at it for nearly an hour.

To get through the last door, the extraction force had to cut through the doors themselves, their locking bolts, and a pile of steel and stone debris that had been welded into a solid mass overtop of it all. Even with multiple cutting torches, it was not an easy job. That was probably a good thing—the Ten Thousand only knew how much blood would be on the floor if the mastigas could have gotten through easily.

Upon seeing how quickly the team progressed, she remarked to herself, "Glaukos must have picked a more exceptional team than I thought." Now, standing in front of them as they worked, she saw how correct that assessment actually was.

"Status?" she asked.

None of them questioned her sudden arrival. "Everything is ready for the final seal, Lochagos."

She nodded. "Thank you, Lochias. Proceed."

He nodded and issued several sharp commands. The team flanking the pile of rubble that covered the final door dispersed, save one. A man bearing the blue stripe of a Second Lord on his black uniform sleeve remained behind, affixing a series of wires to a network of small, gray blobs.

Pallasophia watched him work. He, Second Lord Dekaneas Stavros, had been the one who rigged the explosives that originally sealed not only this door but all of the elevator shafts and stairwells. Now, it was time to undo all his work from years before.

She was not surprised when she saw his name on the personnel list Glaukos forwarded. Ordinarily, the use of high explosives inside the facility would have been prohibited, but she had complete faith in Stavros's ability to neither kill them all nor bring the facility down on their heads.

The soldiers took cover in the next room out. Stavros emerged a moment later, carrying a detonator and trailing a length of wire. "At your command, Lochagos."

Pallasophia nodded. "You may proceed, Dekaneas."

He nodded and went through the short sequence that activated the detonator. With the small device unlocked, it projected a series of holographic controls. He double- and triple-checked the settings before finally tapping lightly on the "Detonate" button.

The detonation consisted of two explosions. The first was a low-pitched concussive blast designed to shatter the solid mass of debris. The second, coming a split second later, obliterated the fragments with a cloud of thermobaric dust.

"Clear," Stavros said after a moment. "Permission to examine the blast site?"

Pallasophia nodded, and the man re-entered the room. After a moment, he called back, "all clear!"

Pallasophia waved the team forward.

"Plasma torches standing by, at your command, Lochagos," Lochias Photeos, the man who had been in command of the squad until Pallasophia's arrival, said.

"You operated admirably without me, Lochias. Please continue."

"As you say," he replied, then turned to the four soldiers carrying the cutting torches. "You heard the Second Lord. Get this door open!"

They moved quickly, operating in a well-trained pattern. First they cut a series of holes near the top, into which they inserted metal rods to act as grab handles. As the team moved around the door, the other soldiers, at Photeos's discretion, took hold of the impromptu handles.

When the door fell free, it did so against the shoulders of eight soldiers who gently lowered it to the floor. Without knowing what was on the other side of the doors, letting them fall was not a good idea. More importantly, even the best the cutting team could do would not always ensure the door fell the proper direction.

The stench that assailed their noses as the doors fell was unbearable. The scent of burning metal given off by the plasma torches kept most of it at bay while they cut through the door, but with it out of the way, the full array of odors made it to their noses.

More than one of the soldiers doubled over, retching or threatening to. Pallasophia herself felt nausea threaten to tear her insides apart, but she fought it down. She was in charge, after all, and it would not do to have their commander fall to her knees simply because the room stank.

"This must be where the elite lived," Photeos said. His voice sounded like it came through gritted teeth, but with his helmet in place, it was impossible to tell.

"It is," Pallasophia confirmed. She knew that much from watching recording after recording of it emerging from the other end of the room.

She stepped into the room, steeling herself against the smell. With an iron grip on her nerves, she surveyed the area. It was supposed to have been a work room where personnel could study the records from the fights in the arena. One of the two rooms directly outside had been a

109

hospital suite and shower for their subjects, but now it was full of rubble. The corners of her mouth turned down at the sight of so much waste. No lives had been lost in this sport, for that she was thankful. Those working here had been able to evacuate before the elite made it to the arena.

Pallasophia picked up a the hilt and first dozen centimeters of a broken sword. Glittering pieces of steel covered the floor, debris she initially though had come from the door itself. Now, she recognized the glint of polished steel. Another lay on the other side of the room, discarded. The other two were nowhere to be seen.

She examined the damage to the blade, and turned to look at what remained of the door frame. It had been heavily scratched and dented, and the spot between was badly mangled. The sword clearly came out of the exchange worse.

"Did the elite do that?" Photeos asked.

Pallasophia shook her head. "It only had four swords. It would not destroy one simply to try and escape. I suspect the dents in the door's surface came from it, but I cannot be sure."

"Then who?"

"Number One Hundred," Pallasophia replied. "After she killed the elite, she stayed in this room for thirty-six hours before coming back out and returning to the facility labyrinth.

"I see," Photeos said. He took the sword from Pallasophia and examined it. With one hand on what remained of the blade and the other on the grip, he tried and failed to bend it either direction. Placing the broken end on the floor, he pushed on it again with both hands and one booted foot. With a grunt, he managed to kink what remained by a few degrees. He panted. "And she did that by herself?"

"So it would seem."

"With respect, Second Lord, *what* did Hexarch Tritogenes make down here?"

Pallasophia was silent for a moment, then, "we made what we set out to make, Third Lord. Nothing less."

"Lochagos Pallasophia," a female voice called from the far end of the room. "I think you need to come look at this. Stavros, too."

Pallasophia approached, with Stavros the explosives tech right behind her. The woman who had spoken gestured to a series of images on the wall. They were crude, but detailed enough for Pallasophia to recognize them.

"Lochagos?"

Pallasophia stared at the drawings, pacing up and down the line of them, mouthing numbers at she went.

Stavros came a moment later, checking settings again on his holographic tablet. "Eleni, you asked fo..."

Pallasophia interrupted him. Her voice was quiet. "This is a record of every kill the elite made."

Stavros finally looked at the wall himself, staring at it in mute fascination.

"You're the expert, Stavros, do you know anything about this?" Eleni, the woman who first noticed the pictographs, asked.

Stavros shook his head hard. "I have never seen anything like this or even heard that they were capable of such artwork. This.... this needs to go into the archives. No, this needs to be examined by every mastigas expert in the binary! This isn't just idle scratching, either, this is a journal. It kept a journal! Do you know what this means, Second Lord?"

Pallasophia's eyes remained fixed on the wall in front of her. She saw each death depicted here in her mind's eye. To Stavros, she replied informally, "yes. I'm afraid I do. It means everything we thought about their intelligence level might just be wrong."

"What do you want to do?" he asked.

"Lochias Photeos!" she barked, shifting back into formal speech. "I am officially taking command of this expedition as of now. Detail two additional guards for this room. The rest will accompany us into the facility. Pull the team from the outer doors in as well. This is the only way in or out and it *will* be protected."

"As you say, Lochagos."

"Assign a team to remove the elite's artwork. I want it intact and taken to my suite as soon as possible."

Photeos gestures to two of his soldiers, who immediately moved toward the wall.

Pallasophia continued, "the contents of this room and the existence of those artworks are to be considered classified. You will not speak of what you have seen here to anyone. Is that understood?"

"Yes, Second Lord Lochagos!" came the immediate reply.

A tense few moment passed as the two assigned to the wall began to work. Then, Eleni spoke up. "Lochagos?"

"Yes, Dekaneas?" she replied formally.

"Did you see this part?" She pushed aside some pieces of debris, revealing an inscription carved into the tile a few meters away from the pictographs. A knife lay on the floor at the base.

"A message from One Hundred?" Photeos asked.

Pallasophia shook her head, feeling a lump rising in her throat. Frustration raged under her skin, but she dared not let it out. "No," she replied, "this is Lexeis Archeio. One Hundred would not know Lexeis Archeio."

"The Archive language?" Photeos asked. Awe crept into his voice.

Pallasophia nodded. "The same."

"I can read it," Eleni offered.

"As can I," Pallasophia said. She stared at the inscription, momentarily blocking out everything but those words. Her voice grew less steady as she went. "I have been sealed in here. A door I cannot unlock closed behind me, and debris blocks my exit in the other direction. The Singer comforts me from beyond the locked door, saying that only the strongest and best will come to face me. Yet I remain discontent. I desire freedom, not this cage. I would fight under the open sky, not in this pit. If I am to be trapped here, I will kill all of the..."

Pallasophia's hand flew to her mouth as her eyes went wide and her face drained of all color.

"What does it say?" Photeos asked.

"The last word," Pallasophia replied, "is 'Creators.'"

Chapter 7

Second Lord Nikos raised his armored forearm, warding off the blow from the gigas. The mastigas giant teetered, not expecting its target to simply block its fist like that. A mix of emotions crossed its pale face, iridescent green eyes going wide first with surprise then with anger.

The gigas bellowed incoherently. Nikos allowed it the small threat display, then strode forward to deliver a punch of his own.

Nikos's armored fist connected with the gigas's shoulder. Through the multiple layers of metal and polymer, Nikos had no real feedback from the strike. Even the usual feeling of impact was missing, replaced by a note of resistance where his attempts to finish the full extension of his suit's arm stalled. Instead, a targeting suite projected on the inside of the armor's faceplate displayed his impact point and probable damage.

He nodded in satisfaction, barely seeing the data. It showed things in convenient, bright colors with high contrast. Even if Nikos never read the detailed report, the sudden orange flash on the gigas's silhouette told him enough.

Recentering, Nikos strode forward again and delivered another punch with his other hand, aimed at the same spot on the gigas's shoulder.

The giant swatted his armored fist aside with a hateful bellow and lashed out with its fists.

First one, then two strikes landed on Nikos's armored head. Like the impact of his punch, he did not feel the monster's strikes at all. Instead, what he felt was the sudden jolt to the entire suit as the impossibly strong gigas knocked him sideways and off balance.

Nikos fell to the floor, but as he did so, he grabbed the gigas's wrists. The only thing in that room stronger than the massive mastigas was Nikos himself, thanks to his powered armor, and the the gigas found itself unable to break free as its human opponent dropped to the ground. Nikos reached out with one foot, planting it in the soft part of the gigas's stomach, pushing with his leg at the same time as he pulled with his hands.

The gigas went end over end, sailing through the air to land a good two meters away in an impact that made the floor shudder. With some measure of satisfaction, Nikos noted the fine shower of dust from the lights and rafters overhead, knocked free by the impact of the massive creature as it hit the floor.

Nikos rose to his feet, shaking his head inside the suit's helmet. He might not have felt the impacts of the gigas's fists, but getting knocked around like that made his head swim. The suit corrected for his sudden loss of balance automatically, which presented a simultaneous solution and a new problem. The good news was that Nikos remained on his feet as the suit was not subject to the whims of his inner ear. The bad news was that a lifetime of human reflexes taught Nikos that he *was* falling in that moment, and he froze.

The gigas crashed into him like an ocean wave, going from prone on the floor to charging in a single terrifyingly fluid movement.

This time, Nikos did hit the floor, and the gigas was on him in a moment. Without a higher intelligence to instruct it, the monster lacked any sort of real combat training. Nikos's mind flashed through a dozen different things that an experienced grappler could have done in that moment, and the gigas did none of them. Instead, it simply punched him in the face once, then again.

It roared, giving Nikos a moment between strikes to act. When the gigas's next punch came down, Nikos reached out with both powered hands and seized it by the wrist and elbow. The gigas never bothered to pin or control Nikos after he fell, a fact for which he was very grateful.

Nikos kicked his legs in the air, using their momentum to power his upper body. Assisted by the armor, he wrenched sideways, throwing the gigas away from him and allowing him to rise to his feet once again.

His head continued to swim. After this trial was over, he would speak with First Lord Enyalios about adjustments to the inertial systems. It did him absolutely no good to be able to "feel" the world around him if it also meant he suffered the same problems as a normal human when they got punched in the face over and over again.

The gigas rushed him again, but Nikos was more ready this time. Assisted by powered servos in the suit's legs, he was able to outpace the massive creature's speed. The gigas pivoted on one foot, changing direction midstride in a display of the sort of reflexive skill that most people forgot the giants possessed.

Inside the suit, as he dodged again, bringing his hands up to block the followup shot, Nikos grimaced. Even though he knew exactly how fast these gigas were, their bulk still threw him off. His every instinct told him the big, ponderous-looking mastigas ought to have been slow, plodding creatures. Instead, they could bend every ounce of their strength toward speed as well, making them terrifying in close quarters.

What they lacked, however, was the exact realm in which Nikos excelled: finesse. He sidestepped again, snapping out a series on punches that all connected with the side of the monster's skull.

It roared and lashed out, but Nikos stopped the blow by interposing both forearms. In the same moment, he stepped forward and drove the suit's knee into the gigas's stomach. It bent double and Nikos brought both fists down on its skull.

The gigas crumpled downward, grabbing at Nikos's waist as it went. The suit started to unbalance, but Nikos sprawled backward, pressing the gigas to the floor. He pinned it in a hold that would have held a human, but the gigas's titanic strength came into play again and the monster simply rolled in place, reversing the pin.

Nikos cursed. Even gigas could learn, he reminded himself. This time it pinned him much more effectively. Sitting on his hips, the gigas gripped both of Nikos's arms at the elbows, effectively taking them out of the equation.

It bellowed again, displaying its sharp, predator's teeth. Those same teeth descended towards his throat a moment later. Nikos knew it would not get through without breaking multiple teeth, but he also knew exactly how little the gigas was going to care about something like that in the heat of the moment.

Worse, it *would* get through. To give him more freedom of movement, the neck of the suit was softer, less armored. Nikos amended his previous note about improvements. In addition to equilibrium adjustments, the neck needed to be reinforced as well.

The suit's helmet suffered none of the weaknesses of its neck however, and Nikos defaulted to one of the oldest techniques in the proverbial book. He waited until the gigas was close, then drove his head forward and into the monster's nose. It broke, spraying the faceplate of his suit with inhumanly bright blood.

More important, however, the sudden broken nose weakened the gigas's hold, allowing Nikos to break free and once again rise to his feet.

This time, he did not wait for the gigas to attack. It was wounded and its attacks now would be both less controlled and stronger. Nikos was not about to allow himself to be struck again, powered armor or no.

When the gigas punched again, Nikos leaned and stepped lightly to the side, inside of the striking arm. He raised his up arm, deflecting the punch the rest of the way and allowing his momentum and the gigas's own forward momentum to carry his fist into the monster's face. The

117

impact flashed red on his heads-up-display, indicating what his suit's computer believed to be "critical damage."

Nikos did not see the gigas's other fist coming. It smashed into what would have been his ribs had he not been encased in a suit of powered armor. As it was, the blow was enough to knock him completely off his feet and onto his back.

Its face might have been a mangled mass of blood and torn flesh, but the gigas continued to pursue him. Rather than rise to his feet, Nikos pivoted on the ground, tripping the gigas with his legs. Then he rose just enough to cross the short distance between them, pin the mastigas, and snap its neck.

Finally, Nikos rose and allowed himself to feel tired. No matter how much the powered armor helped, it still relied on his own body for direction. That in turn still required strength and, perhaps more important, endurance and energy. For the first time since the fight began, he became aware of just how fast his heart was beating and of the ragged, oxygen starved feeling in his lungs.

In his ear, the voice of Second Lord Kyveli spoke. She had a way of telling him he was not yet finished that made Nikos want to press on rather than demand a rest. "Excellently done, Nikos. We will proceed with the second part of today's trials at your pace. Please activate the switch on the wall when you are ready."

"Understood, Titan Control."

"In the meantime," she continued, "I overheard you say that you needed to tell the Hexarch something?"

"It can wait until I finish."

"Of course, Nikos. However, First Lord Enyalios is here, now."

"I see. How much did he overhear?"

A gruff, older male voice came into the conversation. If Nikos had never met Enyalios, he would have assumed that gravely voice belonged to an aging singer. "Your microphone was active the entire time, Second Lord."

At that comment, Nikos's pulse did its best efforts to undo the last minute's calm. "My apologies, First Lord. I did not mean..."

Enyalios laughed. "Nikos, please. I was a soldier in my day as well. If I had a credit for every time I cursed my own superiors, I would be richer than Hyperion!"

"Thank you, sir."

"On the other hand, Second Lord. Some of those things were simply anatomically impossible. In the future, if you're going to insult me, please do so more creatively."

Despite his fatigue, Nikos laughed. "Understood, First Lord."

In the silence that fell afterward, Nikos took a moment to drink from the tube connected to his suit's internal water reserves. He preferred not to dwell on where that water would come from when the suit was under long-term use. Those filters had been tested and relied on technology long proven to be effective. Still, he thought, some things were best put out of mind unless he absolutely *had* to worry about them.

With his pulse and breathing under control, Nikos strode across the room to the corpse of the gigas. He knelt, grabbing the mastigas's arms and unceremoniously hoisted it onto his suit's shoulders. Even with the power assist, the gigas was massive and carrying it across the room to the disposal hatch took a minute.

Now, Nikos thought, he could get on with the second phase. He went to the wall where the switch Second Lord Kyveli mentioned waited. Mentally shifting gears to a more contemplative, patient mindset, Nikos reached out with his suit's armored hand and pressed the oversized switch.

The wall next to where he stood slid open, revealing a long, narrow hall. The far end was at least a kilometer away, but the sides of the hall were only ten meters or so apart. Two meters past where the wall once stood was a bench sized to his frame inside the powered armor. On the bench rested three firearms, all scaled similarly.

Nikos went to the bench as a series of targets appeared at the far end of the range. He nodded, picking up the largest of the weapons. The order was always random, but his performance at long range was not up to the same standard as his short-range shooting. He expected these targets to be the first ones to appear and had prepared accordingly since the last shooting trial.

Thanks to the powered armor, Nikos hoisted the massive rifle as easily as if it had been a lightweight antipersonnel weapon and not a two-hundred kilo anti-materiel weapon that fired three-thousand gram bullets. Carefully, he went through the procedures to check the weapon's functionality, starting with the simple things like the action and magazine and ending with the complex mechanism that served as the weapon's sound suppressor.

Satisfied, he braced the weapon against his armored shoulder, settling it into specially-designed grooves. The suit sensed the presence of the heavy weapon and automatically shifted more than a dozen different balance subroutines to compensate for its weight and recoil.

Peering through the weapon's scope brought the targets at the far end of the range into focus. Six targets waited for him, and Nikos tried very hard not to think of his previous performance on this test. He had not failed it in months, but neither was he particularly pleased with his scores.

Carefully, he took aim at the first target and gently squeezed the trigger. His armor obliged and the weapon kicked hard enough that even the suit's systems could not completely cancel it out. The bullet made it to its target before the echoes from the gun's report faded. It struck the exact center of the target, setting off the little explosive charge inside it that shattered it completely.

Pleased, he nodded inside his armor's helmet. It might have been only the first target, but a perfect score was a good way to start things.

Unfortunately, that mood shattered exactly like the first target when his second shot went wide. Through the weapon's scope, he saw the crater it left in the shooting range's backstop. That wall was made of the same heavy, reinforced alloy that the Technocrat navies used for thier orbital warships. Not even his power armor's weapons could breach that material in a single shot. Repeated strikes to the same target or same general area would do the truck, but if Nikos found himself in single combat with a warship, then it was likely that things had already gone very wrong with his plans.

Annoyed, he rushed the third shot. It hit the target, but did so off-center. Nikos would receive points for that shot, but not full points. Worse, at the end, he would be penalized for every miss as well.

Taking a moment to breathe, he placed his fourth shot exactly in the center of the third target. He hit the fourth and fifth targets, but did not hit the center of either. Nikos's aim faltered on the sixth target as fatigue suddenly set in, dragging his shoulders down. First one shot, then two missed. He cursed, breathed, and placed a third shot dead center.

With a frustrated sigh, he dropped the long rifle back into the bench as as series of targets appeared in the middle of the range. These moved on tracks, primarily up and down or left and right, but some also slid closer or further away. Nikos watched their movement for a moment, waiting for a pattern.

This part of the test he enjoyed much more than the long-range precision shooting section, at least.

The second weapon on the table was much smaller, though still many times more massive than something carried or used by an unarmored human. For his armored scale, it would have been considered a small combat rifle. Next to it was a pistol likewise designed for use by his power armor. It waited in a holster, which he clipped to another special mounting point on the armor.

There was no break between parts two and three of the test, and both were timed. The clock started the moment he put a hand on the medium-sized gun, and so Nikos took another moment to analyze the movement

121

patterns of the targets. He would get no chance to do the same for the third set of targets, so efficiency in this part was his main concern.

In a flash, he swiped the rifle from the bench. His hands went to their proper places with practiced ease. Four bullets went downrange in the first second, striking one of the moving targets and shattering a second. Nikos emptied the first magazine in thirty seconds, striking ten of the twenty-two targets and shattering another four. His score would be calculated based on the first bullet to strike each target, but the timer did not stop until he destroyed each one.

Swapping out the magazine for a full one took moments, and Nikos said silent thanks to the designers who made the weapon specifically to be used by hands sheathed in powered and armored gloves. He might have said something out loud, but at the moment he was too focused on the task at hand to pay any real attention to what might or might not be coming out of his mouth.

Three bullets resulted in two shattered targets. When he changed his second magazine, only three targets remained. Those exploded in quick succession as he sent a half-dozen rounds downrange.

He had no time to congratulate himself or even breathe more than once as another set of targets appeared much closer. These not only moved, but would randomly rotate or even disappear altogether. Nikos also knew from experience that this part of the test never had any discernible pattern.

The rifle clanged to the bench as he simply dropped it, drawing the armor-sized pistol in the same movement. Nikos's first few shots missed completely, and he grit his teeth against the mounting frustration.

The rest of the pistol's magazine he put to much better use. Out of the ten targets, only seven remained when Nikos dropped the magazine and replaced it with a full one. He emptied the second one in moments, scoring a number of hits and destroying two more targets.

Unfortunately, that only left him with one pistol magazine left, and if any of the targets remained when he ran out of bullets, the entire test would be marked down as an immediate failure. He needed to slow down and take his time, no matter what the clock said. A high time and good score was preferable to failing.

When the last target shattered to pieces, Nikos had two bullets left in his pistol. He heaved a sigh of relief and returned it to the bench. Next to the weapons was a cleaning kit, which he unpacked.

Normal practice held that a soldier took their weapons out of the range and back to the armory for cleaning, but Nikos's circumstances were slightly different. Unarmored people could, technically, operate and service the weapons he had been using if they had the proper tools. Those tools existed, primarily for the purpose of servicing vehicle weapons, but the scale of his powered armor meant it was more efficient for him to do it himself. Aided by his armor's strength, the cleaning process took no longer than it would have for a normal human to clean and inspect a normal-sized rifle.

In his ears, Enyalios's voice spoke. "Well done, Second Lord."

"Thank you, First Lord."

"Before you remove the suit, how can it be improved before the next test?"

Nikos knew that most of the suggestions and improvements would come from the technical staff watching and analyzing his performance. In fact, Second Lord Kyveli, Titan Control in general if he was being honest, rarely even asked for his input. Anything he had to say was usually passed through the armory master and then to the directorial staff.

But this time the Hexarch himself asked the question, and so Nikos paused on his way out of the testing room. Remembering his earlier trouble with balance, the head, and the neck of the suit, he carefully put together his suggestions.

"I believe, First Lord, that the suit relies too much on external stimuli. Armor this heavy should not be so easily damaged by blows to the head."

123

"Sensors inside the armor did not detect any noticeable damage, Nikos," Second Lord Kyveli said.

"Not to the suit," he agreed. "But I'm talking about damage to my head. First Lord, the armor did exceptionally well protecting me from direct damage by the gigas, but," he paused, "permission to speak freely?"

"Permission granted," replied Enyalios's gravely voice.

"It knocked me the hell around, sir, and my head's still spinning. See if the techs can come up with something to stabilize against hits to the head and I'll be happy," he said, then, "sir."

"Understood. Is there anything else?"

He thought for a moment. "The throat. I won't be much good if one of those things tears out my own throat."

"I will pass along your suggestions, Titan-Candidate Nikos."

"Thank you, sir." He said, feeling pride in even that tentative title. "Oh, and Kyveli?"

"Yes, Nikos?"

"Next time, I want two gigas."

"That's inadvisable."

"The mastigas aren't going to just come at me one at a time, Kyveli. I need practice fighting multiple opponents."

"The answer is..."

First Lord Enyalios's voice cut through. "Permission granted, Titan-Candidate. Your next trial will be in three days. Enjoy the downtime until then."

"Thank you, sir."

As the door opened ahead of him, Nikos nodded, pleased. "Titan-Candidate" did not have quite the ring that "Titan" would have, but it was nice enough in its own right.

***

Three days later, Second Lord Titan-Candidate Nikos stood sheathed in powered armor once more. The technical staff spent that time working

124

night and day to upgrade his suit again. The most obvious visual change was to the suit's neck. Exactly as he requested, the neck had been reinforced with a metal collar. He was surprised to see the collar attached to the body of the armor rather than the helmet, but once he had it on, Nikos understood that the design protected the suit's vulnerable throat while impeding his movement as little as possible.

A few other minor changes were obvious before he put the suit on. The weapon mounts had been adjusted slightly, likely based on some equation one of the techs ran to optimize shooting efficiency and minimize draw time on his weapons.

The joints also looked like they had been altered slightly, but Nikos was a soldier, not a machinist and could not even begin to guess what purpose those alterations served. He hoped it was to enhance the system's balance and reduce external shock, but he did not have time to ask the techs what, exactly, they had done.

Inside the suit, the first thing he noticed was increased comfort. That seemed to happen every time as the crew adjusted the inside each time to better fit his body and the way it moved. Reflexes and general movement felt more fluid as well.

As for his main request, he could tell no difference until the fight started.

While he waited, a Second Lord in a dark blue robe made of heavy, utilitarian fabric ran various checks on the outside.

"How do I look?" Nikos asked.

"Bored," replied the other Second Lord.

"Daniel, buddy, I'm always bored."

A laugh answered that. "At least you're self aware."

"I am all kinds of aware!"

Daniel laughed again. "The suit looks fine. Our upgrades have meshed seamlessly with the previous generation of systems."

"So what is this now? Version eight?"

"Not quite. We didn't do a major overhaul. Think of it like version seven-point-two."

"Well, whatever version it is, how's it look?"

"I just said..."

Now, it was Nikos's turn to laugh. "No, how does it *look*?"

Daniel grinned. "Badass."

"That's what I wanted to hear! Let's do this!"

Daniel patted the suit on the leg, the only thing he could easily reach. Nikos felt nothing, instead simply heard the sound transmitted from the armor's external microphones.

Nothing happened for several minutes as Daniel exited the testing area and the rest of the technical crew ran their own tests prior to beginning. After a nearly ten minute wait, a voice finally broke through Nikos's growing boredom.

To his surprise, First Lord Enyalios, not Second Lord Kyveli spoke. "Are you ready, Nikos?"

Now, adrenaline surged through Nikos's veins. That was good, he thought. Let it flood his system now, when there was nothing to fight, rather than dumping on him in the middle of things. "Yes, First Lord."

As promised, when the door at the far end opened, a pair of gigas lumbered out. They pushed and shoved at one another, momentarily unaware of his presence. Without directions of their own, the gigas tended to default back to whatever their base instincts were. Typically, that meant fighting whatever was nearby, even one another.

Nikos read about their behavior, but never had a chance to see it up close like this. He watched them push one another around for a moment, filing everything he saw away in his mind for later use.

Aloud, he muttered. "Without a sophont, gigas get stupid. Noted."

Nikos rushed the gigas, trying to get as many blows in as he could before they noticed him. He succeeded in that goal, slamming his shoulder into the nearer mastigas and driving it back against the wall.

It bellowed and beat on his armored head, but Nikos barely felt the impacts. Whatever reinforcements the techs did to the suit seemed to be working. He still felt knocked around by the punches—the gigas hit hard enough to knock his entire armored weight into the air after all—but it no longer felt like his head was being snapped back and forth.

He punched the gigas once, twice, thrice in the ribs. Each impact registered steadily more damage on his suit's HUD. The first strike barely registered, but the second and third showed on the target indicator as strongly yellow impacts, medium strength.

Despite all of its upgrades and enhancements, the powered armor still operated under certain fundamental laws of human structure. Among those laws was that strikes landed using the power of the legs and hips hit much harder than those delivered by the arms alone. Nikos twisted his hips, intending to deliver a rib-crushing punch, but his fist never hit its target.

Instead, the second gigas slammed its own fist into his armored ribs from the side, sending Nikos sprawling.

While the first gigas recovered its breath, the second bounded after him on its deceptively long legs. It roared, swiping at the air as Nikos rolled backward and to his feet. He sidestepped slightly, catching the gigas with his shoulder in what would have been the solar plexus in a human. It had a similar effect, and the giant's wheeze was accompanied by a spray of spit and blood.

Nikos delivered a long punch backed by his, and thus the armor's, entire body structure. It struck the gigas full in the face, snapping its head back and sending it to the ground in a sprawl. Nikos followed, prepared to pin it so that he could snap its neck, when the first gigas appeared suddenly at his side.

The first gigas, recovered from the pummeling Nikos gave its ribs, did not strike out at his armored form. Instead, it wrapped both of its impossibly strong arms around him and hoisted his entire power-armored weight off the floor.

Nikos flailed against the gigas's crushing grip, catching it in the leg with his feet. The gigas grunted in pain, but did not drop him. Instead, it pivoted and body slammed him into the floor with enough force to knock the wind from Nikos's lungs, power armor or no.

An alarm blared inside the armored helmet as his vision swam. Some part of the chest armor had cracked. Nikos did not have the time at the moment to determine which part. He only hoped he could finish the fight without taking another hit to that same spot.

Fortunately, the power armor did not suffer from the organic limitation of muscle shock. Nikos got control of his breathing back in under a second, and the armor translated his twitches of movements into something much more powerful. He bucked the gigas off before it could strike at him again.

The first gigas sprawled and Nikos stepped away from it, turning his attention to the second gigas. Its face streamed blood from where he punched it and from its mouth where it seemed to be coughing up blood from Nikos's strike to its gut.

Nikos launched himself at the second gigas, dropping at the last moment to pass under its arms. His shoulder caught the giant just above its hip bones, more or less where the kidneys would be in a human, and Nikos wrapped both armored arms around the gigas's legs. The giant toppled to the floor as Nikos scrambled into an automatic mount.

He landed another punch to the gigas's face, which his HUD indicated with a flare of red damage. It swiped at him with both hands and Nikos realized his pin had been too hasty. The gigas's arms were still free.

He realized this in the exact same instant that the gigas slammed the side of its fist into Nikos's armored head. The armor still did its job, preventing his head itself from being knocked sideways. It did very little to stop the sheer energy from the strike, however, and he fell to the side, stunned and sprawling.

He must have bit his tongue or cheek when he fell, because Nikos spat blood as his vision cleared. He twisted, starting to come to his feet again. The gigas that struck him bounded forward, arms raised to strike. Nikos put up both of his own arms, blocked the blow, rose to his feet, and immediately slammed back into the ground as the other gigas slammed a shoulder into his midsection.

"Are they learning," he muttered, "from what *I* do?"

He rose, thankful the gigas hit him as hard as it did. The blow sent him some three or four meters through the air, out of reach of both mastigas for the moment. That gave him time to properly get to his feet and to resume an anchored fighting stance.

It also afforded the gigas the same luxury. They approached him together now, neither moving very far from the other.

Nikos faked to one side, then lunged to the other. Both gigas fell for the feint and he struck out at the nearer one with his fist. The blow caught the creature in the back of the head and it stumbled.

The other gigas shoved past the one he punched, sank slightly, and sprang forward in the exact same wrestler's tackle he used moments before. He hopped backwards, hoping the armor was capable of such a nimble movement, then dropped elbow first onto the gigas. He connected with the exact center of the monster's spine, and his HUD flashed a dark red damage indicator.

Before he could rise, the other gigas was on him. It grabbed his arm, held him tightly, and tackled him to the floor. Despite the armor, Nikos was still a human underneath the layers of alloy and polymer. The gigas jerked his shoulder at an unnatural angle that his armor did nothing to protect him from, and he screamed.

Nikos started to right himself, but the gigas planted a foot onto his shoulder, continuing to twist his arm. He felt the joint dislocate, then a sickening tearing sensation as the muscle and ligaments suddenly sheared and separated.

Nikos thought he was screaming. His throat burned and his lungs emptied, but he heard no sound come out.

The pressure lessened for a blissful moment before redoubling to new heights. Absolute agony blossomed in his elbow as the gigas's foot snapped Nikos's arm in half. He continued trying to scream as his vision faded.

Dimly, somewhere a million kilometers away, he heard a man's voice. "Kill them! By the Ten Thousand, kill them now!"

Noises erupted overhead, but the only thing Nikos knew was the pain in his arm and shoulder. They were his world right up until he felt his head move. There was a clang, and a shock, followed by another.

Then another clang, another shock.

Another.

The last thing Titan-Candidate Nikos felt was a sudden blissful warmth. Nothing could hurt him anymore.

***

The door to First Lord Enyalios's office buzzed. He took a long drink from the amber liquid in his glass, ignoring who- or whatever it was that demanded his attention.

When the door buzzed again, he snarled. "What?"

The door slid open soundlessly, admitting a lone Second Lord in a dark blue robe stained with blood. Enyalios could not tell if the red streaks in the man's beard were a deliberate choice or if they were more blood. He certainly had not gotten all of it off his face.

Enyalios's eyes narrowed. "Second Lord Daniel, is it?"

Daniel nodded. "Yes, sir, I..."

"What the *hell* do you want, Daniel?"

The man paled slightly. "Sir, it's about the Project."

Enyalios straightened, but continued staring death and hate in Daniel's general direction. Some part of his mind told him that was not fair, that what happened had not been Daniel's fault, but he was the only person the Hexarch had at the moment to blame.

"Don't you think it's a little soon to be talking about the Project's future?"

"Sir, with respect..."

"Stop that," Enyalios ordered. He tapped a button on his desk and the door to his office slid shut again. "If you're here to say something, Daniel, say it. Otherwise, get out."

Daniel waited a moment, rocking back and forth on his heels while Enyalios continued to fix him with an angry stare. Finally, the Hexarch chose to break the tension by looking away and taking another drink from his glass.

Let the man have some peace, he ordered himself.

"Sir..."

Again, the Hexarch fixed Daniel with that same angry glare.

He took a deep breath. "Enyalios. My team is prepared to begin work on version eight of the armor immediately."

Enyalios could not even muster enough rage to shout. "Nikos is dead."

Daniel nodded. "I am aware of that, sir."

"What are you going to do about it?"

"Sir, I," he started, then stopped. Daniel looked around the office for a moment, then seated himself in one of Enyalios's chairs without being invited to do so. His face took on a hard set, which carried over into his voice. "Look. Nikos was my friend. I'd known him for seventeen years."

"What's your poi—"

"My point," Daniel snapped, then stopped. He took a breath, then continued with a small measure of calm. "My point is that I worked with him through his entire candidacy. I was the one who convinced him to apply after Chryssa was killed."

Enyalios continued watching Daniel with anger and suspicion, but allowed his subordinate to continue. In truth, he admired the man's tenacity and the nerve he displayed by walking into the Hexarch's office and talking like he was. For the moment, Enyalios would hear him out.

"I propose that I take Nikos's place."

Enyalios's eyes widened. "You?"

Daniel nodded solemnly. "No one else knows the machi-machi like I do."

Enyalios quirked an eyebrow at the nickname the techs had given the armor. He heard it before, but never in a formal conversation. Of course, he reminded himself, this conversation never was a formal one, he saw to that as soon as Daniel came into the room.

"You're doing this because you feel like you owe it to Nikos."

"No," Daniel replied, then, "yes."

"Are you intoxicated or otherwise impaired at this moment?"

Daniel's eyes narrowed slightly, but his tone was even. "My religion forbids those things."

"I see."

When Enyalios said nothing for a moment, Daniel stood and straightened his robe. "I apologize if I've gotten my friend's blood on your furniture. Your answer, please, First Lord."

"You start tomorrow."

Daniel nodded. "Thank you, First Lord."

"Don't thank me, Daniel. I've just signed your death warrant."

"Then I'll see Nikos sooner than I thought," Daniel replied. "Sir."

"Go with the suns, Titan-Candidate Daniel."

Chapter 8

The massive corpse of the mastigas elite lay sprawled on the sand at the far end of the arena, exactly where Number One Hundred left it. When she propped the puzzle door open, Pallasophia expected the other mastigas to drag it away for food.

That it had not happened pointed to one of two things. Either One Hundred killed many more mastigas than she suspected, or something was actively keeping them away from the elite's area. The former made a measure of sense, but the latter would require a higher level of planning than she understood the mastigas to possess.

Whatever the reason the mastigas had for staying away, Pallasophia was not going to complain. She and those of her team not guarding the doors had to explore the facility anyway to find Number One Hundred, and she knew they would encounter mastigas along the way.

"Dekanii Isodorus and Myrto, secure the inner door."

"Understood, Lochagos."

"Lochias Photeos, accompany them, please."

He nodded and took off after the other two Second Lords at a light jog.

Dekaneas Eleni's sudden gasp shook Pallasophia from her reverie and she automatically leveled her rifle, looking for whatever threat the soldier spotted. Instead, she seemed to be staring directly at the elite's body. "Holy shit."

Stavros waved at the dead monster. "I didn't believe it when I read the mission brief. There's no way, I thought, that one person could kill one of those things. I've seen footage of one elite taking out an entire squad before. But I can't argue with *that*."

"Number One Hundred is more than she appears," Pallasophia said.

"I can believe it," Stavros said. "To have survived down here alone."

Pallasophia nodded. The official story was that after the Incident, the lower levels had been sealed off. That much was true. Where the official story diverged from reality was in that Pallasophia, over Tritogenes's objections, had in fact spread word among the facility's staff that she was Limani's Titan-Candidate up until one of the gestation pods "accidentally" activated, releasing Number One Hundred.

"Not just survived," she corrected, "but emerged triumphant."

Pallasophia watched as Stavros slunk, catlike, toward the elite. Even knowing it was dead, he moved with drilled precision, encircling it with his rifle raised as though it was merely sleeping and might wake up at any moment. Eleni hung back, torn between knowing it was obviously dead and the desire not to abandon Stavros on the off chance that it was, somehow, still alive.

"It's quite dead, I assure you," Pallasophia called. "Coming back to life is one of the few things they don't do."

"Understood, Lochagos," Eleni replied. Despite her faceplate, her tone clearly indicated she was grinning when she asked, "satisfied, Dekaneas?"

Stavros nodded. "I think so. 'Trust but verify,' is what I've always been told when you're dealing with these things."

Pallasophia exchanged an amused look with Eleni that translated even through the featureless faceplates of their helmets. Aloud, she said, "we will not find many other bodies down here. The mastigas are not above cannibalism, especially without a sophont to guide their baser urges, but there will likely be several recent ones."

"How many are left?" Eleni asked. "Should I set up detection perimeters as we go?"

Pallasophia nodded. "Do so, but don't waste equipment on areas like this, which will be watched by the rest of the troops."

"Understood."

"If there is nothing else," Photeos ventured, returning from his momentary posting at the puzzle door, "Strategos Glaukos stressed that we should spend as little time as possible, as he put it, 'dawdling.'"

Pallasophia nodded. "It will likely take some time to find her. We are in no hurry." It was a lie, but one that would help their nerves and, thus, their chances.

"As you say, Lochagos," he replied, then turned to where Stavros was examining the elite's corpse. Flies still swarmed, but he had scared most of them away. "Dekaneas Stavros! You have two minutes! You can poke at the elite later."

Stavros approached quickly, addressing both of them with formal language. "Apologies, Lochias, Lochagos. After seeing the inscription in there, I found my curiosity piqued. Crude drawings are one thing; we know of animals that do the same. But language..."

Photeos grimaced. "I'm more concerned about what it meant by 'creators.'"

Stavros spared a look back across the arena, as though looking at the door to the monster's lair would provide clues. "For all we know, it could be speaking of the mastigas themselves. I would certainly want revenge if the sophont locked me in the arena."

"But the sophont doesn't create other mastigas, does it?" Eleni asked.

Pallasophia turned to face Stavros. "You're the expert. You tell us."

"I don't know," Stavros admitted. "There are people who certainly think so. Being an expert in the mastigas is like," he waved a hand,

135

searching for the right expression. "It's like being an expert in FTL technology. We know it's possible, we just don't know how to get around the problem of..."

"I understand," Pallasophia said, "and I apologize. I should not take my frustrations out of you, Dekaneas."

Eleni cleared her throat slightly more dramatically than necessary. "If I may, Lochagos."

Pallasophia made a motion for her to continue speaking.

"You need to let your frustrations out, otherwise they may affect the mission."

Pallasophia stopped pacing and laughed. She shook her head once, to clear it. "You're probably right."

"I do have a degree in the field, Second Lord."

"Of course. Still..." She made a noise that was half sigh, half growl, and all venting frustration. "What in the starless, gods forsaken, blue screened hell are these things really?"

"I will be making every inquiry I can," Stavros declared, speaking formally in deliberate contrast to Pallasophia and Eleni.

Pallasophia nodded. "Good," she said. "Good. I will expect you to keep me updated with any information you find."

"Of course."

"Now, are we ready to move further?"

"We have been waiting on you, Lochagos." Despite the helmet, Photeos's tone made the amused smile on his face impossible to mistake.

She allowed herself to laugh, then beckoned the others to follow. As they approached the puzzle door, Pallasophia leveled her rifle again. The others followed suit, with Eleni last. Her gaze lingered on the puzzle door.

"I am certain One Hundred did not damage your door, Second Lord," Myrto quipped. She spoke formally, but the amused lilt to her voice was clear.

Eleni laughed. "I'd be surprised if she was able to, honestly. It was smart of her to prop it open when she left."

Pallasophia watched the woman work for a moment before asking, "Dekaneas Eleni, your dossier indicated that you were in charge of wiring the communications lines?"

She nodded, listening to her commanding officer, but obviously much more invested in the act of inspecting the door's complex mechanism.

"It was the reason for which she was Elevated to Second Lord," Photeos replied.

"I did the job I was assigned, Lochias," she argued.

"Regardless, your work was one of the reasons the Project was able to continue on at all."

"Thank you."

Pallasophia cleared her throat. "Will you be able to repair anything the mastigas have damaged?"

"Yes, Lochagos," she replied without hesitation.

Pallasophia nodded. "Good. The more equipment we can repair and use, the better. I have no doubt that you could do your job without it, but it is my hope that the mastigas have not destroyed everything."

Eleni nodded understanding. "I agree, Second Lord."

"Lochias Photeos," Pallasophia said. "Your dossier indicated high marks in tracking, especially people."

He nodded. "Before I came to work for Tritogenes, I worked for First Lord Aegesander as a 'personnel retrieval specialist.' I have not lost the skills."

"Good," Pallasophia said. "Because we have a lot of ground to cover. One Hundred could be anywhere."

"Understood, Lochagos. I will find her."

***

Victoria had been on her guard ever since the explosion earlier. She caught and cooked a rat after leaving the arena, in an attempt to stop the

137

cramps in her stomach from growing worse. The paltry bit of food helped some, but within hours her body was once again reminding her that food was a necessity, not a luxury. Now that the explosion caused her adrenaline to spike, those feelings were only growing worse.

The realization that the green eyes apparently had explosives did little to calm her nerves. She was not quite anxious, but the immediacy of her situation created a sort of annoyed, angry determination.

The only positive she could rationalize out of it was that explosions usually meant destruction. She had no idea how she knew that, or even truly what "high explosives" or "thermobaric weapons" were, but the knowledge imprinted itself on her mind nonetheless. If the green eyes were blowing things up, then perhaps they had found a way out of the labyrinth.

Whatever was happening, Victoria knew she had to keep moving. If the green-eyes were blowing things up, then every moment she stood in the same place was another chance for them to plan an ambush. Worse, if it was some new enemy come to kill her, and if they brought explosives, then it just added to her problems.

Prowling with her stolen sword held at the ready, Victoria considered her options. Returning to the arena was not an option. Even if the explosion had not come from above, she saw how badly the four-armed monster tried to break down the door. Certainly there was nothing she could do, especially after breaking one of the swords in her first attempt to break the door down.

Everywhere she went, the green-eyes had torn things apart. They rarely touched the floor except for what seemed to be random spots where they dug deep, ripping out some sort of electronic device and smashing it. She only knew that much because of the wires left behind.

The walls, too, had been smashed seemingly at random. They succeeded in a very few places, spots where the material was thin or not reinforced, but those only led to more of the same empty, ransacked rooms.

That left the ceilings. Too far to jump, she grudgingly sheathed her sword and piled larger pieces of debris in the center of one of the rooms until she could reach a part of the ceiling where the green eyes had already torn a hole.

After a moment to adjust to the darkness inside the ceiling, Victoria took a single, crouching step. She yelped involuntarily as what she expected to be solid turned out to be thin and brittle. It shattered under her weight, and she fell hard to the floor beneath. The impact knocked the air from her lungs, and the gash in her side screamed its protestations.

She tumbled off her pile of debris, coming to rest on the cold tile floor. Fighting to put air back into her lungs, Victoria's hands scrabbled not for her sword, but for the much more familiar baton that hung from her waist. Panting, and with back muscles that still protested, she came to her feet, brandishing the baton like a torch against wolves.

Nothing approached her, and she let out her frustrations on a piece of the debris she used to reach the ceiling. The concrete cracked under repeated blows from her baton. It did very little to slow her pulse, but the momentary release did wonders to calm her nerves. She struck what remained of that block again, just to be sure, and the release she felt as it shattered under her weapon was palpable.

The problem she now faced, other than the soreness in her back, was that she smashed a good portion of her way into the ceiling. With her temper expended, she looped the baton's wrist strap through her belt once more and set to work finding more debris with which to climb back into the ceiling.

Fortunately, Victoria did not have to look very far. Debris of all sizes and shapes was easy enough to come by. In minutes, she climbed back into the ceiling, careful this time to keep her weight on the metal framework that seemed to be holding the brittle parts.

A mass of wires and pipes surrounded her, answering at least one of the mysteries that had been plaguing her since she awakened. The pipes made a variety of noises, most of which she recognized and filtered out of her awareness long ago as something that was not dangerous.

Still, she thought, it was nice to have a reason for things.

Victoria tugged at the wires, but nothing seemed useful. Some felt like she could pull them loose, but that would do her no good. Piles of cables on the "floor" attested to how futile that was going to be. Likewise, pieces of shattered pipes told her that she would get nowhere there.

Still, Victoria mused, once more thing remained. She considered using one of the broken pieces of pipe, but that was a somewhat ridiculous notion considering she had a hefty length of steel already tied to her belt. With no room to swing, Victoria rolled onto her back and jabbed at the stone overhead.

It scuffed and chipped, but Victoria had no real idea how thick it was. As her arm tired, she supposed the task was ultimately possible, but if it was actually useful, the green-eyes would have smashed holes between the levels already. More important than travel between the levels, they would have broken their way past the arena.

They had not done either of those things, and Victoria stopped her efforts. Inside her helmet, sweat covered her forehead. Very little air seemed to be circulating where she was, and it quickly grew to stifling temperatures while she worked.

She considered sleep. The sudden warm temperatures certainly made her want to do that, at least.

That desire was shattered by a sudden surge of adrenaline as she heard footsteps. Waiting where she was did not seem like a good idea. The pile of debris she made was directly under her, marking her spot for anyone—or any*thing*, she thought—to see. Careful to keep her weight on the sturdy sections, Victoria crept forward.

Despite being unable to go up a level as she planned, Victoria did discover one benefit to moving through the ceiling. Where she was had no walls. She could move freely without having to maneuver around obstructions in her path. Crawling might have been slower, especially with all of her things, but the ability to bypass doors made up for it. If she could keep track of her position, sure could potentially explore some of the locked areas she passed on her way up.

Footsteps below turned her attention downward again. Whatever made them was not trying to be quiet. Victoria was thankful for that; it made her job of finding them easier. As she drew closer, the sounds became more distinct.

The footsteps came from multiple sources, of that she was sure. They fell heavier than the little ones or the knife wielders, and they were too light and too regular to be the lumbering giants. She never heard the four-armed titan's footsteps on solid ground, but, given its size, she imagined it stepped even heavier than the giants.

And, she reminded herself as a surge of adrenaline accompanied memories that were definitely her own, it was most definitely *dead*.

Whatever the sources of the footsteps happened to be, Victoria had no desire to run into them without first having a chance to study them.

A sudden thought chilled her blood. The idea of facing one of the green-eyes, especially one of the smaller varieties that would have little trouble maneuvering in the tight confines, was not a pleasant one. With that in mind, she drew one of her daggers from its calf sheath. With it in hand, her forward moment slowed, and at times she had to clamp it between her teeth to progress at all, but she felt much safer.

As the source of the sound drew even closer, Victoria started to discern different voices. The green-eyes had not spoken that much, and certainly had not spoken to one another like these newcomers did. They spoke in short, clipped phrases full of numbers and complex words Victoria had no context for. The two most commonly repeated phrases were "mastigas" and "One Hundred." Beyond that, she might have understood what they were saying, but had no idea what they were actually talking about.

The positive was that their noise allowed Victoria to track them easily. After two short hours, she found them. Their small group had stopped a few meters away from another broken section of the ceiling. Crouched in the darkness above one of the few functional ceiling lights, she might as well have been invisible in her black suit.

She waited, watching.

Six creatures moved around below her. She wanted to believe that these were human like her, but their black suits gave nothing away. Whatever they were, the newcomers moved with methodical precision. Four of the strangers, including the only one of the sextet with green stripes running down the sleeve, seemed to be standing guard. The others all bore blue stripes on their suits. The two smallest had taken up part of the floor and were up to their elbows in it.

Off to one side was a small pile of backpacks and equipment. Another, smaller, pile lay close to the pair working on the floor. They all carried what her brain told her were weapons: rifles and pistols primarily. The green eyes had never possessed weapons like that before, and she made the logical connection between these newcomers and the explosion earlier.

Their faces were covered by helmets, but the design was not like the green eyes' helmets. They seemed stronger, better built, and even Victoria could see the antennas and connectors on the helmets and understand that there was more to them than simple concealing masks.

She listened as they spoke.

"Dekaneas Eleni." The blue-stripe that spoke, a woman, had a warm, pleasant voice. Her tone spoke of authority without having to be harsh. "Status?"

"The comm uplink here was badly damaged, Lochagos," the smaller of the two working in the floor replied. She raised up out of the work area, bringing tools with her. Her voice was higher in pitch and even clearer than the first one, but no less firm. "Estimate five minutes to repair it if the spares all fit. Fifteen to twenty otherwise."

142

The first speaker nodded. "Anything from the sensor net?"

"Nothing out of the ordinary on the ground."

"Explain."

"It filters out anything with a regular pattern like the air system, water dripping, and so on. If something irregular makes noise, the program pings me. Three of the stations have been set off, one twice."

"I sense a 'but' in there, Dekaneas," the largest member of the group said. His voice was much deeper, with a gravelly quality. None of them sounded like green eyes.

"Yes, Lochias. The only pings in the last hour have been from above us."

"I thought the sensors could not pick up anything through the floor."

"They can't, no. Either I'm getting faulty readings, or something is moving around in the ceiling."

The first to speak looked up, scanning the ceiling. Victoria's blood froze as the helmeted face passed by her hiding spot. In a moment, the reflexive search continued. Victoria let out the breath she had been holding and slowly, very carefully, readjusted herself. If they were somehow listening to her movements, she needed to stay absolutely still until they left the area. She might as well get comfortable.

"What bothers me," the green-sleeve said, "is that you're getting those readings from places we've already cleared. Lochagos," he turned to the tallest blue-sleeve, "do you still think it's possible for us to effectively clear these levels? They're obviously avoiding us."

The tallest blue-sleeve nodded once, slowly. "I believe so. Admittedly, I hadn't expected the mastigas to do anything but rush us as soon as they scented us, and this waiting is grating on my nerves as much as it is yours, but we don't have any better plans."

"Bring the Strategos's entire regiment down here and burn everything," the larger of the two blue-sleeves working on the floor suggested, then, "sir."

"Not an option," the tall blue-sleeve replied. "Not with One Hundred down here."

"Cheer up," the small blue-sleeve with the soprano voice said. "You could still be on customs inspection duty."

The other one working in the floor grunted. "I've spent enough time going through boxes of grain to last the rest of my life."

Victoria watched them work for some time. Finally, they inserted a small piece of electronics in the floor and replaced the panel. They all picked their gear back up when a noise drifted through the area.

"Victoria..."

Victoria's head shot up as the four below looked around, murmuring to themselves.

"Victoria," the voice drawled.

What was more unsettling was that she could not pinpoint where it came from. Whatever had spoken, however, seemed to speak from everywhere at once. Everywhere except her own head, that was. She was all too familiar with the sensation of remembering having said something from a mouth that was not hers, but this was something different.

From below, the voice of the apparent commander ordered the others to move. In the silence that fell, Victoria remained where she was for the better part of an hour, but the voice never came again.

***

Victoria remained in her hiding place in the ceiling long after the six strangers were gone. Between their conversation below her and the snippets of dialogue she heard as they came and went, she had two new pieces of information. First, the "mastigas" they spoke of had to be the green-eyes. The only other thing they could have been referring to were the rats. They seemed wary of being hunted by these mastigas. At the very least, that meant they merited "enemy of my enemy" status, though the second piece of new information kept them firmly in the "unknown" category.

144

That second piece of information was that, in addition to the mastigas, these newcomers seemed to be searching for her personally. None of them had said so, at least not in her direct line of hearing, but the context was obvious. They came to search for something, and their actions had already ruled out the idea that they were searching for the green-eyes. That, and the fact that they constantly referred to "Number One Hundred" were all the clues she needed.

Her shell, the thing in which she had first awoken, had been painted with that number. Hers had been listed as number 6-100, with ninety-nine others, all empty, stretching back down the room.

One Hundred was not her name, and the fact that it was how they referred to her infuriated Victoria. She could see the logic, she supposed, but that only made it worse. By calling her One Hundred, instead of any sort of actual name, they removed her humanity. She wondered if they considered her human at all, or simply some sort of test subject.

She growled involuntarily at that thought. A series of informational images superimposed themselves on her memory. She remembered reading about something called Project Titan. The memory seemed to have been triggered by hearing the name of her enemy—mastigas. This new information came through another set of eyes, displayed on a holo projected by another pair of hands.

She shook her head violently to clear the memory. She would not forget it. So far, she was not sure she *could* forget things like that. As time passed those memories became indistinguishable from her own without serious mental effort. Other bodies—other lives and deaths—all melded together in her memories and dreams now.

The entire group seemed to defer to one of the blue-stripes in particular, and Victoria made a mental note that she was likely the group's commander or leader. In turn, the commander relied on the big green-stripe for matters of tracking. Despite their noise, he seemed quite capable of following even the most well-hidden tracks. She overheard him explaining to one of the others about the differences between the footprints and other signs of passage the various kinds of mastigas left.

If he was that skilled, she knew it was only a matter of time before he led them right to her. That thought sent a chill down her spine. Even if they were friendly, which she currently had no proof they were, Victoria had no desire to be cornered by their tracker. When they met, it had to be on her terms.

Unlike climbing up, where she had the pile of debris to extend her reach, Victoria had no such aid now. She was not about to return to the pile she made, either. If the strangers found it, they would likely set up camp there and wait for her arrival.

Carefully, she eased to the edge of one of the broken sections of ceiling, reaching as far as she could. Some of the areas were built with higher than usual ceilings, but this did not seem to be one of them. The wound in her side protested as she pulled herself back into the warm safety of the ceiling, but she ignored it.

Victoria had very little room to maneuver, and even less to maneuver something as big as the sword she stole from the four-armed mastigas. Eventually, however, she got it off her back and down through the hole. If she held the heavy pommel and hooked her feet around part of the steel framework in the ceiling, she could touch the weapon's tip to the floor below.

With nothing else to brace against, Victoria knew she had to be quick. She took a deep breath, then levered herself out and through the hole, using the sword itself as an anchor. The tip slipped on the tile and she fell. Unlike last time, she was prepared now, and managed to turn over in the air to land on her feet.

She still landed hard, especially as her feet were still bare. The impact sent a shock through her heels and leg bones, but that was quickly overshadowed by yet another stab of pain from the now-bloody wound in her side. She had no idea what torn stitches felt like, but she was sure some of them tore as the pain in her side flared and her knees buckled.

Victoria's hips hit the floor, which sent another new wave of pain through her body as bruised ribs mingled with her torn and bleeding side. She bit back a curse, instead letting it out as a low growl as she scrambled to her feet. Every motion sent another shock of burning torment through her flesh, but a thought that kept her going during her endless fights with the mastigas resurfaced—she would have time to bleed later..

She turned her attention back to matters more important than physical pain. The blue-stripes were clear enough regarding the purpose of the devices they left in the floor. However it actually worked, she knew her sudden landing on the floor would be transmitted directly to them. That only gave her a few minutes.

Victoria knelt and removed the section of flooring that hid the device. She withdrew it, examined it. Victoria turned it over in her hands. From the outside, it looked like nothing so much as a small, black box. A few holes had been cut in the outside here and there, but nothing protruded from it.

The explanation given by the blue-stripe named Eleni seemed, at least to Victoria, to indicate the device transmitted actual sound, not just notices that it had detected something. She banked on that possibility, tapping the thing with her knuckles twice.

"Come find me," she said to it. Her voice was hoarse. Between lack of water and simple disuse, she spoke with a raspy quality and a rattle in her throat.

Victoria set the box down on the floor and was about to walk away when a thought struck her. The newcomers must have been hiding these devices for a reason, and that reason clearly was not her. If they were hiding them from the green eyes—the mastigas, she reminded herself— then Victoria had a duty to put them back in their hiding spots.

The strangers were not friends. She would find out exactly what they were soon enough, but she was not about to do something careless that might help the mastigas in any way.

With the device once again hidden under the floor, Victoria examined the room once more. She had been here before, several times in fact. To her eyes, the only important things were the footprints of the six strangers in the thick layer of dirt.

The scattered remnants of clay pots and dead plants gave Victoria another reason to confront the strangers. She had no food and was nearly out of water. With them prowling around, her chances of acquiring either were very low.

If the strangers were friendly, they would have both in abundance to share with her. If they turned out to be hostile, it would not change their stockpile any. Victoria would simply have to kill them all before she could eat or drink again.

Her stomach growled and protested at that thought, and Victoria put a hand there automatically. It came away wet and sticky from blood that finally seeped through the black fabric of her shirt. She did not want to consider how much blood she lost for it to soak through like that. One way or the other, she had to deal with the problem of the strangers before she could inspect her injury again.

She examined the room in detail now, gritting her teeth against the sudden flare of pain in her side. Now that she was thinking about it, and about her hunger, both problems strove to be the sole occupant of her attention at that moment. It took several deep breaths and many minutes before she had those things back under control again.

While she waited, Victoria heard distant sounds of shouting and repeated cracks that her brain told her were gunfire. The mastigas did not possess firearms, but the strangers did, which told her they were engaged with one another somewhere close enough for her to hear. If nothing else, that realization solidified the "enemy of my enemy" idea in her head— the strangers were *not* going to be helping the mastigas.

Again, she examined the room around her. Three doors led away from where she now stood. Victoria knew one of the doors led to a utility closet. The shelves inside had been smashed and it reeked of the sort of chemicals that triggered memories of painful death.

The other ways were different, and she had watched the strangers leave the room. The door through which they left led to the same place as another door adjacent to it, though the halls went different directions for a while. If she waited in either of them, the strangers could come up behind her.

So Victoria went to the fourth door, which from her own personal experience led to a small room strewn with broken furniture.

Victoria scooped up some of the dirt from the broken flower pots in one of the corners. She scattered it across the floor, deliberately walking through it and leaving obvious footprints. She also made sure to step hard on the floor, making a loud trail of noise that the device in the floor was sure to pick up.

She wanted there to be no doubt where she went, and for them to follow her, and this let her dictate the time and place of their meeting. It was not ideal, as the pain in her side indicated, but at least it was better than them finding her while she slept or with a needle and thread in her side.

Now, all she had to do was wait.

Chapter 9

A second passed in a minute as the Hexarch's eyes slowly blinked. She was speaking, but the words were so drawn out that Second Lord Lelantos was having trouble following them. She had been speaking, saying the same sentence, for the last ten minutes. Two minutes before that, she had taken a breath, and two more sentences filled the quarter-hour before that.

Ten minutes passed and Lelantos continued to meditate with his eyes open. His Hexarch, First Lord Rivka, had now called up a menu on the holo-display above her wrist. He watched every movement of her fingers across and through the holographic images, as she slowly inched toward the keyboard.

As she typed, he moved his eyes, but not his head. A window sat behind him and dust swirled on the winds as the minutes ticked by, glacially slow in its ballet through the sunbeams slanting over his shoulder. Across the room, a digital clock's final number blinked, replaced by a black square for more than five seconds before the next number in the sequence burned in its place.

Idle thoughts crossed his mind as he watched the icy slowness of Rivka's fingers as they typed out a message. He already knew, or suspected anyway, what she was going to write, but interrupting his Hexarch before she was done would be impolite. Besides, the twenty minutes it took her to type the short message allowed him to bring his thoughts back to the surface.

Finally, she finished typing and held her wrist aloft.

The green letters demanded an answer. "HOW SLOW?"

He opened his mouth, tightened his throat. His diaphragm clenched as his lips slowly formed words. To speak at a pace she would understand required time and dedication. His answer took three full minutes of carefully controlled breathing to articulate.

"One sixtieth." Lelantos supposed that, from her perspective, he still rushed through his words.

More time passed as she typed out a message. This one was longer and scrolled across the holographic display with minutes in between each letter. He waited, reading her question as she typed it out, then reassembling the hour long text in his mind once she completed it. Fortunately, years of such experiences had created in him the desired mindset. Lelantos was nothing if not extraordinarily patient.

"YOUR METABOLIC OUTPUT IS EVEN HIGHER THAN USUAL," the message read with glacial slowness. "ARE YOU UNCOMFORTABLE?"

He thought for a moment. His head felt a little fuzzy around the edges, like he had been drinking weak wine for hours without ever quite reaching a state of drunkenness. He placed a hand over his heart, moving this time at a pace more like what he was used to. The movement still took nearly twenty seconds to complete. Under his palm his heart thundered once.

He waited. Twenty-five seconds later, he felt another two-stage thump in his chest. He started to inhale and focus on the feeling of air rushing into his lungs. His unconscious, the part of his brain that could not comprehend the world at anything other than one second per second started to panic as the deep inhalation lasted almost two full minutes.

As he let the air out of his lungs, ignoring the certainty that he was about to suffocate and pushing the urges of his hind-brain away, he answered her question.

"My pulse is fast," he said, "and I'm already getting hungry."

Another message scrolled across First Lord Rivka's holo-screen. "BUT NO PAIN?"

He drew out his answer, "no," for a minute and a half.

Another slow message from her screen read, "I HAVE PLACED A TARGET..."

***

"...on the top of a spire fifteen hundred meters away."

Speaking the message itself was extraneous. Rivka knew that anything she was actually saying would be so stretched out that Lelantos would have trouble understanding her, but it helped keep her thoughts in order.

"Your rifle is on the balcony. Please hit that target twice."

The message on the display floating above her wrist finished scrolling. Lelantos's wide eyes followed it and again she marveled at his patience. The angry, impulsive man he had been before Project Titan would not have waited so long for anything. She, certainly, would not have been able to stand still as long as he had, feeling time pass so slowly. It must have felt like an hour or more since their conversation started.

After a moment, Lelantos nodded. He moved his head normally, from her perspective, then turned and strode to the balcony. His steps were no longer than anyone else's would have been, but they came in such rapid succession that his movement sounded more like the steps of a sprinter than those of someone calmly walking across the room.

Rivka followed a pace behind. Lelantos blinked at the sudden brightness of the afternoon suns overhead, shielding his eyes against the glare. True to her instruction, his rifle awaited him. However, she had withheld the crucial detail that the rifle awaiting him had been completely disassembled.

He looked it over for a moment, two or three seconds at most, before going to work putting the complex weapon back together. His hands moved like lightning, sorting the parts and assembling the rifle in just thirty seconds.

Lelantos raised his head, looking out over the valley at the foot of Rivka's palace. A red flag, barely visible as far away as it was, waved above his target. He nodded once, picked up his rifle and pressed the scope to his eye.

Rivka watched him exhale, all tension leaving his muscles. First one shot rang out. Another followed barely a quarter second later. He relaxed, lowering the rifle back to the table as Rivka pulled up the footage of the target.

The imagery streamed in quickly. The top of the recording was taken up by the red of the flag. At the bottom of the image floating above her arm were two stacked boxes, no larger than a person's torso each. In slow motion, slowed down even more dramatically then Lelantos's own senses, a bullet crashed into the bottom box. Nothing happened for a moment, then the minor explosive stored inside it detonated, set off by the shock from the bullet.

The explosion of the first box sent the second one into the air. It rose perhaps twice its own height before another bullet came streaking in and detonated the explosive it contained. The area beneath the target had been cleared some time ago, so the smoldering bits of metal and slow-burning powder were free to fall wherever the wind took them.

She had typed "EXCELLENT" into the holographic interface by the time Lelantos turned back around. He removed the weapon's magazine, cleared the breech, and engaged the safety before leaving the weapon on the table again.

His eyes fell on the display above her arm and his mouth twitched into a smile. The movement was jerky, probably, she thought a result of how quickly he was processing information. His mouth turned upwards into a smile a second time and he held it there for a few seconds.

"ARE YOUREADY TO END?" she typed, realizing the typo only after the message scrolled past.

Lelantos nodded once. His hand shot to a pocket in his robe. A moment passed as he adjusted the controls on the device wired to the intravenous collars around his upper arms, thighs, and neck.

When he spoke again, his words were long, drawn out. Everything took two or three times longer than it should. "Is that acceptable?"

Rivka nodded, then smiled. "That was more than acceptable, Second Lord," she replied, glad to be able to use her voice again, rather than a text-based interface. "As a matter of fact, I think your ability to cope with the dilation effect has improved remarkably in the last week alone."

"I've been spending a lot of time under. It's peaceful," he replied. The first few words were still a little drawn out, but by the end of the sentence, he was speaking normally. "The real training starts soon enough."

Rivka nodded. In some ways, she was reluctant to part ways with him for the final phases of the Project. He volunteered for the job three years ago. That alone was enough to garner her respect, but the fact that he volunteered even after seeing his predecessor lose her mind spoke volumes about the sort of person he was, or had been.

The drugs changed Second Lord Lelantos in many ways. Some were improvements. He was the single most patient Technocrat that Rivka ever met, capable of waiting hours for the smallest things to happen. She had never seen him lose his temper or even show the slightest rise of negative emotion since the treatments started.

The physical changes were the most obvious. Early on, Lelantos lost his hair—all of his hair—and it had never grown back. He replaced the hair on top of his head with tattooed designs reflecting his proudest accomplishment—surviving the Project. Below those tattoos, however, Lelantos had a fairly gaunt face which he emphasized with dark makeup on his cheeks and lips. Thanks to the drugs he took to slow his perception of time, his metabolism ran at a rate far in excess of normal.

Several weeks remained before the Council session where they were all to officially unveil their Titans to the system, then, as Lelantos said, the real training would start. The six of them had to learn to work as a team before assaulting the mastigas ship. Rivka could not be more proud of his accomplishments, but that also meant she felt like she was sending a son off to war without her.

The others, more jaded in their experience, probably did not feel as strongly about their charges, she presumed. Many of them held seats on the Council when the mastigas first appeared thirty years ago. Perhaps that experience, reading about the mastigas and their ferocity, was enough for them to understand the danger they posed, and the very real risk of losing their Titans and failing completely. For First Lord Rivka, however, the feeling was much more immediate.

She might have occupied her seat for scarcely more than five years, only slightly longer than Project Titan's own existence, but she rose to her position through blood and fire. The mastigas landed a force on her planet, then belonging to First Lord Diomedes. It was the furthest they ever came. Her Hexarch at the time left orders with her to oversee Kipos's army, save as many people as she could, and push the mastigas off the planet.

Thousands of people died before the mastigas could be repulsed. When she returned to Diomedes's chambers, she found the Hexarch dead in his chair. In five years, she thought she might be able to forget some of the details of that moment, but she never had. The way he had been slumped in his chair, she thought he might have dozed off. It would have been unlike him, but he also had not slept well in the days between the mastigas's landing and her return.

The glass on his desk, her desk now, had been empty. Chemical analysis found a dozen different poisons, mostly sedatives, mixed into the alcohol. His suicide note had filled in the rest of his thoughts.

That note had also done something else. Signed as a Living Will, the document named her as his successor. Over their history, that was an unusual way to do things, but three of the six on the Council had found their seats that way. Diomedes's Will left her Kipos and his entire corporate holdings, as was common for anyone rising from Second to First Lord.

His Will had also included a small box with no key or apparent latch. The note it came with said it would open "in due time" and instructed her not to tamper with it in any way before then. In five years, it never opened, and even now simply sat on a shelf in her office a floor above where she and Lelantos were training that day.

"Have you met the others?" she asked, returning her thoughts to the present.

Lelantos looked up from the holographic screen above his wrist. The pastel blue interface was blank on her side, but she knew from long experience that he would be checking the levels of the various chemicals that made up the chronodrug. He did that, methodically, after every use for two years.

After a moment, he looked up at her and smiled. His features were relaxed, at least as relaxed as they ever were. She remembered a man, Kiposian militia like everyone else on her planet, who came to her years ago. He survived the mastigas attack, but it let him with a heart full of rage and hate. Lelantos was no longer that man, and there were days, like today, that Rivka wondered if she actually saved his life by letting him join the Project.

Now a calm, meditative expression was his default. He opened his mouth to speak, still coming down from the chronodrug. "Panatakis, yes, and I corresponded with Helena this morning, but no one else. I enjoyed meeting Second Lord Panatakis, his view of the world is quite literally a world of difference from anything I could have ever imagined. Helena... How do I put this..."

"Unnerves you?" Rivka offered.

156

Lelantos nodded, dismissing the holo interface. "Yes, exactly. I can't put my finger on it, but yes. She said she had to deal with a lot of changes during the Project, so I suppose I can understand," he tapped the steel collar around his neck that dispensed the most potent of the chemicals, "but there's something in her manner, even in text, that would have made the hair on the back of my neck stand on end if I had any."

He paused a moment and quirked a hairless eyebrow. "I take it you've met her?"

"Only in passing, and only once, but you're right. There was something about her that made me feel uneasy. I've got nothing but respect for First Lord Aegesander, but I know what *I* put you though, Lelantos."

He nodded and grinned. "And look at me," he said, smiling wider. "I'm almost sane these days."

Rivka, despite the subject, laughed. "That can't be completely true."

"Can't it?" His grin never faded.

"You still work for me, after all."

Lelantos laughed. "Of course I do. Do you know the things I've seen since you talked me into getting my brain pumped full of chemicals?"

"I can't imagine."

"Sure you can. Just think of everything here," he waved at the room, "but very slow. Dust dancing on the wind for hours or the beat of a bird's wing. I just can't hear colors like Second Lord Panatakis."

"You've got a point. Still, I can't help but wonder what Aegesander did to Helena beyond her implants."

"I asked her, for what it's worth, and she said she never went through anything, quote, 'terribly traumatizing.' Just a lot of training and getting used to using computers with her mind, same as Panatakis. Her eyes, at least, still work right."

Rivka settled back, leaning against a nearby table. "I spoke to First Lord Enyalios about his Titan the other day. Apparently he's had some setbacks."

Lelantos frowned. "Setbacks?"

She nodded and a veil of sadness fell across her mind. "Apparently he lost another candidate."

"Damn. And so close to the end of the Project?"

"So it would seem," she replied. Rivka took a moment to cross the room to the balcony. Unlike many of the Hexarchs, who lived in the same palace their predecessors occupied, Rivka had a new one constructed away from the capital city. The old palace, Diomedes's palace, she converted into a headquarters for her planetary militia.

After the mastigas attacked, and she assumed the mantle of Hexarch, she mandated that every able bodied adult be issued a weapon and trained. In short order, that militia acquired a small fleet of cruisers that patrolled her orbitals. The mastigas had not moved in five years, but—and with that thought she looked back at Second Lord Lelantos—if they ever did, Kipos was ready. The city was chaos, but it was *her* chaos, which had a calming effect all its own.

Here, however, things were quiet. Her air filters were specifically programmed not to filter out the complex chemicals that gave the forest its smell, and she breathed deeply of that earthy aroma.

He turned a quizzical expression in her direction. "Is everything alright?"

She shook her head. "Just thinking of the cost of this Project so far. First Tisiphone, then what it's done to you, and who knows what happened to Helena."

"Panatakis will never be normal," Lelantos quipped. "And Tritogenes. Does anyone know what exactly it is he's done?"

Rivka shook her head. "I've got no idea. Early on, there was talk that he was building a facility somewhere out in the Kuiper belt, but a year into the Project, that entire facility went dark."

"You don't think he failed, do you?"

She laughed. "Tritogenes? No, I don't think that man knows how to fail, and even if he did, I met the person he put in charge of the day-today affairs. Second Lord Pallasophia has got a little of Selene in her. I almost expect to see her standing up there with you and the others when the time comes."

"I just hope he's had better luck than Enyalios."

Rivka's lips drew into a tight line. "Second Lord Nikos, Enyalios's last Titan-Candidate wasn't the first one to perish, either. I always felt he was pushing them too hard."

Lelantos nodded and ran a hand across his head. "Yeah," he sympathized. Then, "what? Ten dead? Twenty?"

Rivka nodded. "Something like that. Sad."

Lelantos sighed, a sharp exhalation. "Crashed terrible is what it is."

"Anyway," Rivka said after a minute's tense silence. Her thoughts were going places she would rather them not be. It was hard enough losing one prospective Titan. To think of losing over a dozen and half that many support staff was disheartening. She had seen worse, especially in the days before being given the Hexarchate of Kipos, but that had been *war*. To lose that many to the Project before it was even done was more than she wanted to contemplate.

She strode back into the room. "Will you be ready for another test this evening? I've got a new reaction drill I would like to try."

Lelantos nodded. "Of course. See you in a few hours, First Lord."

***

First Lord Rivka's office sat at the top of her palace's tallest tower not out of any attempt to lord her status over the general population of Kipos, but rather out of appreciation for the local landscape. Even then, "tower" was only accurate in the most literal of terms. The spire rose a mere four stories above the ground, offering bedrooms and workrooms for herself, Second Lord Lelantos, and a few of Rivka's highest officials.

What gave the tower its height, however, was the very landscape where Rivka built the palace. The bulk of the complex sat at the base of a mountain, nestled between two small foothill ridges. By contrast, the place's living area climbed the face of the mountain itself, eventually culminating in her personal tower which jutted up from the very top.

Her suite consisted of the usual amenities, a bedroom and sitting room connected on one side to her workroom and on the other to a small kitchenette. The part that Rivka considered to be most "hers," however, was the vast wraparound balcony. Most of the time she left it open, allowing Kipos's cool mountain breezes to permeate her living area. Ultrasonic devices hidden here and there kept birds out of the suite proper while still allowing them to land on the outer railings of the balcony.

Automated security and a fiercely loyal security staff protected those balconies as well, which set even Rivka's security-focused mind at ease. They also did so from a series of hidden points, out of her sight, allowing First Lord Rivka at least the illusion of privacy.

When she stepped out of the tower's lift, Rivka first went to the exact same spot she inspected every day for the last five years.

She kept clothes two places in her bedroom. The closet held her everyday wear, including three sets of Hexarch's robes and a variety of underclothes. In the back, she also kept a number of older robes from her days a Second and even a Third Lord. Nothing older than that remained, having been long-since recycled.

The other place she kept clothes was a massive wooden armoire off to the side. Locked in it, Rivka kept her finest robe, a shimmering garment of royal purple silk embroidered with real precious metal wire and silk couching. She took it out of the armoire once a year or so to add some small detail here or there to commemorate her proudest achievements that year. Including her elevation, the garment had only ever been worn once.

Along with that robe were some of her finest jewels and a few other things of great personal importance. The very top shelf held exactly three items. The first, despite the traditional lack of importance placed on family ties by most Hexarchs, was a holo of Rivka with her parents taken

160

on the day of her elevation. A similar holo sat on her desk, but that one was the official, posed picture. In this one, Rivka's father and one of her mothers fussed over her brand new purple robe while her other mother tried desperately not to glare at the three of them for taking so long.

Next to the holo sat Diomedes's suicide note, rolled into a tight tube so that no one could read it. Opposite the note was the little lock box Diomedes himself left her. Small, and painted an oddly pleasant shade of turquoise, it contained something her former Hexarch desperately wanted her to have, but in five years she had yet to figure out how to open the frustrating thing.

So, every day, Rivka checked on it just in case the lock was time sensitive, and every day it simply sat there, inert.

She nodded at the box and closed the door, going to the normal closet next. There, she stripped off the multi-layered working garment she thought of as her "Project Titan Robe," and threw the morning's underclothes into a basket to be taken to the wash later. At some point, the robe she just removed needed to be professionally cleaned, but as long as she considered it a working garment, she could write off the dirt and oil stains as simply part of the charm of doing her own work.

Rivka briefly considered simply starting work as she was, but outside her tower, autumn waned and the mountain air blew in with just a little more chill than she found comfortable on bare skin. The shirt and pants she put on instead would do enough to keep the chill away. She had been born on Kipos, after all, and found the planet's cooler climate pleasant until the very depth of winter hit and froze everything solid.

Before doing anything else, she went to her desk and withdrew a small tablet from inside a locked drawer. It projected a single-sided holo in the air, tuned so that it was only visible from a single, specific angle. Rivka also turned her back to the one spot in the room where her own security cameras could not see the display.

Five years ago, she had to give up the majority of her old profession. It was not seemly for the Hexarch of Kipos to regularly meet with clients

161

in a hidden garden, trading information and secrets like some people traded playing cards or miniatures. Her identity at that point had been "known" in certain circles, ultimately including Diomedes himself, which was how she came to be named in his Will in the first place, but no one one outside of those rather small circles knew who she was.

Now, as Hexarch, everyone in the binary knew her face. In a way, she longed for those days again, but only very tangentially. Her life now was, while more complicated, vastly better than it ever was back then.

However, despite her security staff knowing she did something clandestine with that particular tablet, none of them knew what. Rivka prided herself on having kept *that* particular secret. It was one of few she held onto.

Before settling into her real work, she took a moment to peruse various messaging systems and private relays. Most days, that was all she did with that access. Rivka simply had no time for the sort of games she played before her elevation. However, every so often she had a day with a few minutes to spare, and so now she actually took the time to leave a few messages here and there.

Before her elevation, Rivka was never certain whether Diomedes let Kipos's underworld thrive because he could not prevent it or because he did not want to. Even after, she was never sure of her predecessor's motivations, though she suspected it was the latter. For herself, it was most definitely the latter of those two options. Of course, she came down like a hammer on anything truly dangerous, but otherwise the same information and material trade that brought her success as a Second Lord continued to thrive.

Of course, she thought with a smile, even if none of them knew who "Lady Whipcord" actually was, Kipos's various "enterprising organizations" understood very well how important it was to deal fairly with her. Those who did not often found themselves shut out of business deals or even completely isolated by the others.

All of it happened without "First Lord Rivka, Hexarch Kipos" knowing anything.

Rivka deactivated the tablet and the holo-display vanished. A moment later and it was back in its locked desk drawer and she had a completely different tablet in her hand as she strode out of the room and into the balcony. Her sudden arrival disturbed a number of colorful birds that had taken that section of balcony as their resting place for the afternoon, and they took off in a squawking swirl of yellow and green.

Below the balcony sprawled her palace complex, alive with lights and action barely visible through the forest of trees. It reached more than a kilometer down the vale, where a series of well-hidden trams connected everything together. A vast swath of green occupied the space between the ill-defined, but well-patrolled, edge of her palace and Kipos's capital far in the distance. Unlike her palace nestled against the mountain and full of transplanted trees, the capital city gleamed like a jeweled beacon.

When she addressed the other Hexarchs, especially the elders of the Council like Aegesander or Hyperion, Rivka still did not feel she belonged. Especially given the unconventional nature with which she attained her seat, a nagging voice always told her she was not truly "one of them," which was one reason she was so quick to shed her purple robes in private. However, the view of her palace and capital city assuaged that anxiety significantly.

There on the balcony, she opened a vast array of single-sided holographic windows. From outside, they showed as jade green blanks, barely distinguishable against the forest-colored exterior of the tower. On her side, however, the displays gave Rivka all of the information and control she needed to properly execute her duties as Hexarch.

The entire setup was unconventional, but it reminded her in a tangential way of how she used to operate as a Second Lord and even before then. Rivka could lose herself in the vast array of information, operating it on a nearly unconscious level. She still had a pattern and a way of tacking it all, but working like this allowed her to simply *do* her work, rather than stressing herself by thinking about it.

Out of the mass of data, she pulled a series of communications with Lelantos's personal physicians. As her Titan, he had access to the best minds she could bring in, and an entire panel of specialists monitored his condition on a nearly constant basis. Nutritionists, chemists, even psychologists fed her constant updates on his condition. She skimmed those quickly. As important as they were, after so many years of working with Lelantos, Rivka knew two things. First, his own analysis equipment would pick up any chemical imbalances when they happened and he would know almost before his own doctors did. Second, when there was something that important, the doctors understood her schedule and marked the information as such.

These updates were not labeled as high-priority, so after a cursory examination, she marked them as being finished and filed them away.

Dozens of things needed her approval, or at least examination. Most of them were mundane things. Business projects needing approval for a budget or for land usage were by far the most common. However, no matter how ostensibly uninteresting some of the projects were, each of them required careful thought.

Unlike the messages from Lelantos's physicians, Rivka had to actually do something with these messages. Worse, the ones spread across her holo-display at that moment were notes and requests that had been passed to her by her staff, meaning this was likely one percent or less of the total. Total personal control over Kipos or no, Rivka had an entire staff of people dedicated to managing the various avenues of the planet's operation. Anything that came to her desk, either metaphoric or literal, meant whatever it was, her staff could not deal with it.

So, methodically, Rivka paged through each and every request that she had been presented with. Despite being important enough to merit her attention, most were still fairly simple affairs. A few, she marked to deal with later through other channels, usually her private black-market tablet, and still others she marked as needing further attention.

Worst among them were a pair of project proposals. As soon as she read them, she realized why they had been transferred to her within moments of one another. One project wanted to repurpose an unused warehouse in the downtown district of the capital as a sporting arena. Rivka had to admit that the proposal swayed her a little by playing on her own planetary pride—it suggested that the reason Kipos repeatedly came in dead center of nearly every single sport the Technocrats played was because they lacked a "proper" sporting arena.

The second proposal came from the university. More accurately, it came from a group of university students. They wanted her approval to turn the same warehouse into a new theater space, citing the aging nature of the university's current theater. It detailed plans for the existing facility, including using the large auditorium as combination lecture hall and dedicated music venue.

Three things immediately swayed her towards that proposal instead of the sporting arena. First, the students organized the entire thing themselves. Other than having official university approval, the message was careful to note that everything had been thought of and written down by a dedicated group of student activists. Second, and by extension third, the students included plans to work with the other Hexarchs. Their proposal included an inaugural performance at the renovated music hall by the Katarraktes Symphony, pending First Lord Enyalios's approval, and a personal consultation with First Lord Tritogenes in regards to the construction of the new theater.

Rivka approved the students' proposal, taking a few minutes to compose a personal reply as she did so. In it, she expressed not only her approval of their plan, but of their initiative and wished them the best of luck in their negotiations with the other Hexarchs.

Despite that, she knew she had to give the sporting groups something, so she drafted a note to her staff, instructing them to form a committee to begin drafting plans for a new facility on the outskirts of the capital city.

Satisfied, she nearly closed the entire message window, when two new ones appeared, both flagged as high-priority. The first was a message from a school on the far side of the planet, which was a surprise. Rivka opened it, finding a not and a scan of a hand-written invitation. The note explained that one of the school's students, a young girl by the name of Alexis, had been selected to compete in a marksmanship competition held on Limani. The handwritten part, recorded in the meticulous handwriting of a child eager to please the adults around her, asked for Rivka herself to be present at the competition.

Smiling wide, Rivka took several minutes to return to her bedroom and get dressed the rest of the way in a clean robe. Thankful she had not yet washed the dramatic blue and pink swirls off her cheeks, Rivka returned to her impromptu workstation on the balcony to record a video message.

She clasped her hands in front of her, putting on her best friendly smile, and waited for the indicator light to come on.

"Hello, Sixth Lord Alexis. This is Hexarch Rivka. Thank you for taking the time to write to me; that was very thoughtful. Congratulations on the invitation! That's a big achievement. I would be delighted to attend your competition. I would also consider it a personal favor if your instructor and parents sat with me during the event.

"Please don't hesitate to write to me again."

She stood still for a moment, waiting for the system to realize she was finished. The indicator light went off and Rivka relaxed.

While her system compiled the video file to send off to Sixth Lord Alexis, her instructor, and her parents, Rivka opened the last piece of high-priority mail, a recording from First Lord Aegesander.

The voice-only message grated for a moment, likely a planned voice to make the message seem more relaxed. Unfortunately, it had the opposite effect. Rivka might have been fairly new to the Council, but she

166

knew First Lord Aegesander. He never did anything in any way that she could consider "relaxed," and for him to attempt to project that sort of atmosphere kicked her usually suspicious mind into overdrive.

"Rivka," his gravelly voice opened, "I have recently commissioned a new training facility on Prosgeiosi. I would like very much to meet your Second Lord Lelantos, as well. Would you do me the honor of bringing him to the capital to train with Helena and Panatakis, First Lord Eurybia's Titan? I would very much appreciate your assistance in training Helena."

The message ended, leaving Rivka somewhat surprised. That Aegesander requested her presence was no real surprise. That was how the Hexarchs did things, especially when it related to asking for favors or offering the use of something. Hence her careful phrasing of the message to Alexis's parents. It had to be a request, like Rivka was asking them to do her a favor. Even coming from a Hexarch, simply asking them something would have been a slight.

Similarly, had Aegesander simply offered the use of his facility to her, the gesture would have been insulting, a backhanded way of telling her that her own training facilities were sub-par. Then, if she refused, she would have been insulting *him*, implying that not only was his training space the sub-par facility, but he was lying to her about it.

So, he phrased things as a request, asking for her help. To ask another Technocrat for help was neither a sign of weakness nor of failure. Rather, it was a sign of strength and mutual appreciation. The insult came when one person forced their help on another without first being asked.

One of the principle benefits of that unspoken system, Rivka thought, was that it fostered communication. People were afraid of insulting one another by assuming they knew what the other person needed or wanted that they took extra care to ask after their friends' and coworkers' needs.

More to the point, First Lord Aegesander was the oldest sitting member of the Council, and second only to First Lord Hyperion himself in seniority of experience. For someone in his position to ask anything of a relative newcomer like Rivka was an even greater honor for her.

Quickly, she checked her schedule, comparing what she still needed to do before she could possibly leave Kipos to the amount of time it would take to prep Lelantos's equipment for travel. Within minutes, she was ready to compose a reply.

"Aegesander," she said, "thanks for taking the time to message me. Please allow me a week to finish some business here and then Lelantos and I will be delighted to join you on Prosgeiosi. Lelantos has a number of special requirements, which I can forward to you. Please make sure there's a facility ready for us when we arrive."

With a nod, she sent that message off as well, then turned her attention to the last piece of business she had to take care of before she and Lelantos went through their final training session for the day.

With a wave, Rivka dismissed all but one of her windows. It expanded automatically, taking up the entire area she set aside as her work space. First Lord Enyalios might have had the largest military in the binary, with First Lord Aegesander close behind him, but Rivka prided herself on having the largest effective army in the form of Kipos's planetary militia.

With a wave, she opened the first of many militia documents needing her review and approval. With a sigh, she glanced at the page count. Another training session with Lelantos was going to be a welcome relief when she was done.

Chapter 10

Dekaneas Stavros laughed. "I know that. All I'm saying is..."

A sharp gesture from Lochias Photeos who, along with Dekanii Isodorus and Myrto, had been taking point, cut him off. He raised a single hand, clenched in a tight fist in a signal for them all to halt, then extended a single finger which he pointed upward, then forward. Finally, he extended all of his fingers with his palm facing backward.

Pallasophia nodded. It might have been some time since her last real combat assignment, but the hand signals remained clear enough. One target waited for them up ahead and the Lochias wanted them to fall back for a moment, likely to plan.

The team followed his orders without needing clarification, moving backward as one unit to their previous "safe" spot. For a few moments, Dekanii Eleni and Stavros took point as they went. Pallasophia remained in the center of the group, shepherding both her people and the bulk of their equipment.

They rounded a corner and Eleni gestured for them to stop. She and Stavros scanned the area, then lowered their rifles slightly. A moment more passed, and she signaled that the immediate area was tentatively clear. The rest of the team lowered their weapons as well, but no one was about to actually put them down or come off their guard without significantly more distance between them and the noises they had been hearing all morning.

"Up ahead," Pallasophia began. "Do you think it's Number One Hundred?"

Photeos shook his head. "I don't think so, no."

"Mastigas, then."

"I believe so, yes."

Pallasophia cocked her head to the side, which was as much expression as the face-shrouding armor allowed. "Lochias?"

"I apologize, Lochagos, but I do not recognize the tracks we have been following or the sounds. They match general mastigas movement patterns, but the foot and step sizes are not like anything I've seen before."

Pallasophia frowned, thinking out loud. "I'm perhaps more intimately familiar with the listing of mastigas that were brought to this facility before the Incident than anyone else, and Second Lord Stavros knows more about them as a species than even I do. Are you telling me that, with our resources, you don't know what's up ahead?"

Stiffly, he said, "that is correct, Lochagos."

Her frown deepened. "That's impossible."

"I understand that, Lochagos, but it is what it is. The tracks belong to no known mastigas breed."

"Describe them, please. As much detail is relevant."

Next to her, Stavros sidle up to listen. He already had his holo-computer active, likely ready to take notes. Pallasophia had to admit she admired the native Kiposian's dedication to understanding the mastigas.

"It's big," Photeos began. "Smaller than the gigas in mass, but nearly matching them in height. It moves around with the long strides of the more predatory breeds like the fonias or the elite, but is much larger than the former and smaller than the latter. More to the point, the foot shape is not quite the same. It seems to lack the claws of the fonias."

She nodded. "Anything else?"

"We passed multiple signs of tool usage, spots where things had been manipulated or moved by hands with long fingers and possible claws."

"It sounds like you're describing a sophont."

"I thought One Hundred killed the sophont?" Isodorus asked.

Pallasophia growled. "She did."

"It's not a sophont," Photeos said. "They walk, how do I put this? They walk like a human, with smaller, more measured steps."

"Impossible," Stavros muttered.

"I'm only telling you what I'm seeing, Dekaneas."

Quickly, Stavros shook his head. "Sorry, Lochias. I wasn't calling your observations impossible. It's just that..."

Pallasophia gestured for him to continue.

Stavros drew himself up straighter. "A few years ago, after the Project began, I was involved in some research on mastigas corpses recovered from their attack on Kipos. We discovered that the five breeds could actually be classified into two primary types. We argued back and forth about how and why, and even what to call them. None of us could agree on..."

"Stavros?"

He cleared his throat with a sharp nod. "Apologies, Lochagos."

"Continue, please."

"Anyway, two main types. Let's call them 'simple' and 'complex.' The simple breeds were the fonias and the gigas. They tend to be less intelligent and less capable of thinking on their own. The complex breeds were the mikros, the sophont, and the elite. All three are trinocular tetrabrachs."

"Tri-what?" Isodorus asked. Helmet or no, the sound of his eyes going wide with confusion was clear enough.

"Three eyes and four arms," Pallasophia supplied. "Though the mikros' second set of arms are so small that they barely count."

"Yes. Some of us posited that the complex breeds all came from the same stock, likely a mikros or something similar."

Pallasophia felt her blood freeze. "And there were dozens of mikros here. You're telling me it's possible one of them could be, what, growing up? Becoming another sophont?"

"I'm telling you there were people on Kipos five years ago, myself included, who believed it might be possible."

"Why is this the first I'm hearing of it?"

Stavros shrugged. "The senior scientists reported directly to the Council. One day they came into the lab and started turning equipment off and sending people home. None of the research was ever published, and we were all threatened with hefty penalties, even jail time, if we talked."

"But you're talking now," Photeos said.

Stavros laughed, a thin nervous found. "Yeah, I suppose I am. Because if we were right, then what's up there," he pointed down the hall whence they came, "is far scarier than anything the Hexarchs can do to me."

Photeos drew himself up taller. "You think there's a juvenile elite up there."

"I do."

"Why not another sophont?" Pallasophia asked.

"We believed the sophont was a spontaneous development. It was exactly what you said, a mikros 'growing up.' We believed the elites we believed were a directed mutation somehow, that had to be triggered by an existing sophont."

"The one that was here probably began the development of this juvenile before One Hundred killed it," Pallasophia said.

"Likely, yes."

"Orders, Lochagos?" Photeos asked.

Pallasophia took a deep breath, mentally shifting gears back in to the combat mindset. "We kill it. Eleni, Isodorus, cover our equipment. Everyone else, drop everything but your weapons and follow me."

If the two soldiers she ordered to stay behind on guard objected to Pallasophia's orders, it did not show in their body language or movement. They nodded understanding, then immediately started gathering up the packs of supplies and equipment and tucking them in a nearby corner.

"Good, no—gods!"

Whatever order Pallasophia was about to give was cut off as Isodorus tackled her to the floor, using the straps of her backpack for leverage. He flattened himself on top of her as a sickening rush of wind cut through the air, followed by a scream.

"Talk too much, humans!"

The thing in front of them did, in fact, look like a mastigas elite in miniature. It rose just over two meters tall, much shorter than the full three meter height the "adults" attained. Its nude, sexless body was the same uniform shade of fishbelly white except for the three bright, emerald eyes staring them down.

In the juvenile's upper hands was a metal pipe easily a meter and a half in length. The end it gripped was wrapped in strips of black fabric and the other end terminated in an elbow joint, into which had been jammed a jagged piece of twisted metal. One of its lower hands clutched one of the long daggers that gave the fonias their name, but in the hand of even a juvenile elite, the blade looked more like a pocket knife. Its other hand was empty, fingers curling in and out in readiness.

Isodorus rolled off Pallasophia, rising in a flash of movement. One hand went up as long-drilled reflexes took over, but he realized a moment too late that his weapon was not in his hand. It lay at his feet, dropped when the quick-release sling snapped as he tackled Pallasophia out of the way of the juvenile's first attack.

The mastigas's second swing did not miss, and the heavy length of pipe smashed into Isodorus's side, penetrating his ribs with the twisted

173

spike. He gurgled and folded in half as the juvenile's swing carried him into the air.

Isodorus hit the floor several meters away, where he lay unmoving.

"Shoot!" Pallasophia snapped. She scuttled backward and away from the juvenile's third swing, a downward blow that shattered the tile where she had been a moment before.

Eleni and Photeos fired first. He was the first to put down his extra gear, and so was just a little quicker on the draw. Eleni, to her credit, simply dropped Myrto's pack to the floor and drew her own weapon in a single, fluid motion.

One burst of gunfire hit the juvenile in the left thigh, tracing out a trio of bloody pinpricks, while the other went wide.

The juvenile charged forward, swinging its pipe. Stavros froze in mute horror until Eleni grabbed him and threw him backward. He stumbled to the floor, then scrambled to his feet again. His hand finally found his weapon, but by that point, the juvenile was too enmeshed in close combat with the others.

"I don't have a clear shot!"

Pallasophia ducked low, under a swing from the juvenile's pipe, then had to contort sideways to dodge a follow-up thrust from the knife in its hand. "Then—shit!—cover it until you do!"

Photeos backed away with two quick steps, bent double, and picked up a broken piece of tile from the floor. He hurled it at the juvenile's head like a discus, where it shattered into a cloud of dust and several pieces.

The juvenile roared, bounding forward. It swatted Pallasophia aside with the back of its knife hand, drawing a long gash across her stomach. She stumbled backward, but remained on her feet.

Myrto was not so lucky. It struck her fully with its empty hand, knocking her onto her back, where she lay writhing and gasping for air.

The juvenile's third step brought it close enough for it to reach out with its open hand, seeking to grab Photeos. The hands that held the pipe lowered the weapon in a backhanded swing that shattered part of a nearby wall, showering Eleni and Stavros with dust, but not hitting either of them. It raised the knife, ready to impale Photeos as soon as its other hand could grab him.

Photeos, however, skipped back another step and fired a pair of bursts into the juvenile's chest. Brilliant red streamers answered him, fountaining blood that covered the front of his uniform with inhuman redness.

The juvenile stumbled, dropping its knife but not the pipe, as Photeos dodged to the side. His foot caught on a piece of debris on the floor, and he fell as the juvenile's now-empty hand struck him.

Pallasophia rose to her feet again and, the heartbeat she was sure Photeos was out of the line of fire, tracked three bursts up the creature's back. The final bullet impacted beside its upper right shoulder blade, and that arm went limp. It howled, turning in place. The pipe slipped out of its other hand, leaving it unarmed, for all the good that would do.

She fired again, catching it in nearly the same spot that Photeos shot moments before. Despite the nearly two-dozen bullets riddling its body, the juvenile seemed barely affected. If anything, now that it was mad, it seemed to be moving even faster than before. It closed the distance to Pallasophia in two bounding steps, reaching out to grab with its lower arms and with its one good upper arm raised to strike.

A single shot slammed into the juvenile's face, turning its left cheekbone into a mass of blood and gore.

Momentarily stunned, it slowed fractionally, giving Pallasophia time to move not away, but toward it. She saw how One Hundred killed the full-grown elite, and knew that if she could just get too close for its long arms to properly attack her, she could kill it. A thought nagged at the back of her head as a second bullet struck the juvenile in the upper chest, reminding her that getting close was not good enough. If she did that, which she was, she had to finish the fight before its titanic strength could envelop and crush her.

Fortunately, her plan worked for the most part. The juvenile's upper arm strike went wide and it took a moment to realize where she had gone. In that moment, Pallasophia jammed the barrel of her rifle against the underside of the juvenile's chin and almost pulled the trigger.

Before she could fire, its lower arms wrapped around her, squeezing and crushing. Despite a career as a trophy-winning grappler, Pallasophia never felt strength like that before. Even an underdeveloped juvenile elite like this easily possessed enough arm strength to crush her rib cage and break her spine. The momentary hesitation as she imagined what an adult was capable of nearly killed her as the juvenile tightened its grip.

"Lochagos!"

Eleni's shout brought her mind back on track and Pallasophia put every ounce of power she possessed into her struggle. All she needed to do was create enough space between her chest and its body for one hand to do its job.

In the back of her mind, Pallasophia was momentarily glad Glaukos outfitted Aphelion's security force with state-of-the-art magnetic weaponry. Shooting a traditional gunpowder weapon with the barrel next to her face was not on her list of good ideas. As it was, even the rail gun produced enough waste heat to burn the side of her neck where it was exposed beneath her helmet. The bullet flashed by a moment later with millimeters to spare.

It did its job, however, and the top of the juvenile's skull exploded upward. Its grip tightened for a terrible moment before falling away completely.

Pallasophia sagged to the floor, still quite conscious, but willing to lay there for several moments as she reminded her body what it felt like to not be nearly crushed to death. Elsewhere in the room, she heard someone vomiting as a series of rapid footsteps moved around the space.

"Isodorus! Isodorus! Wake up, damn you!"

Painfully, Pallasophia drew herself back into a sitting position. Eleni was shaking the bloody and unmoving body of Dekaneas Isodorus. The

176

gaping hole in his side, torn by the juvenile's weapon, told them everything they needed to know, but Pallasophia let her have her moment to process what just happened.

Quietly, Photeos crept closer and then sat beside Pallasophia. His visor was raised, face white but set into a firm mask. "Orders, Lochagos?"

"Are you alright, Lochias?"

"I fought mastigas on Kipos."

"But are you alright?"

His expression did not soften. "I will be. Orders?"

"We need to find a safe place to tend to our wounds."

"And Isodorus?"

"Hide his body under some rubble and leave a location tag. Once we get the network restored down here..."

"And the mastigas are gone," he interjected.

"...and the mastigas are gone," she agreed, "we'll send people down here for him. I don't know what's left of the others, but if we come across any remains on the lower levels, those are my standing orders."

"Others?"

"From the Incident."

Photeos nodded, but his eyes were elsewhere. "Understood, Lochagos."

***

Pallasophia cracked the seal on an ampule of quick heal. The syrupy liquid was supposed to be sweet, sugared to mask the taste of the chemical cocktail, but for the moment, the Second Lord could taste nothing. Losing troops had been a near certainty, but Isodorus gave his life to protect her from the juvenile elite. That final act drove his death home in a way no distant casualty ever could.

Despite, or perhaps because of, the losses suffered during the Incident, Pallasophia felt every death in a profoundly personal way. Isodorus was one of her soldiers, a man only recently assigned to

Aphelion itself and even more recently to her command. In a very real way, Pallasophia felt Isodorus's death as a personal failing,

Her command, she thought, downing another sip of the bitterly sweet quick heal, and so it was her responsibility.

She briefly considered downing the rest of the ampule, overloading her body with the healing cocktail. The chemicals had a euphoric effect, one whose appeal for abuse she could easily understand. That impulse passed in a moment—a longer moment than she might have admitted, but it was gone nonetheless. Two oral doses would be enough to heal most of her injuries until they had time for proper local application.

With Isodorus's supplies divided up between the survivors, they ran no real risk of running out of quick heal. She frowned, thinking. At least some good came out of his senseless death.

She heaved a sigh, thankful that for the moment her back was turned to the others. As Photeos said right after the fight, she would be alright later. When One Hundred was safe, Second Lord Pallasophia would take the time she needed to grieve for their losses. Until then, Lochagos Pallasophia had work to do.

Pallasophia stood, about to give orders, but when she turned, she caught sight of the expression of intense focus on Eleni's face, and instead went to her directly.

Squatting down next to their communication equipment so that she could more easily read Eleni's holos, Pallasophia asked, "is everything alright?"

The reply was quiet, not quite aimed at anyone in particular. "I heard something."

"What was it?"

Her eyes shifted to Pallasophia, bright and blue despite the fatigue lining them, followed by the rest of her face. "A voice, Lochagos."

"Play it," she ordered.

Eleni nodded and adjusted a few settings on the holographic control panel floating above her forearm. Beyond the subtle rustling of air currents picked up by the hypersensitive microphones, the recording seemed to be silent. She waved her fingers through the controls, advancing the time on the recording slightly.

There came a rustling, scraping sound, followed by a heavy double-thump.

"That was feet. Bare human feet, specifically," Photeos said, and Eleni paused the recording. Neither of them heard him approach. He gestured to the ceiling. "She was probably up there."

Pallasophia and the others looked at the ceiling in turn. The room they were in was bare of tiles, revealing the network of rafters and wires above. Most of the conduit had been ripped free of its fixtures and the wire stripped out. Pipes had been broken free as well and, from the looks of the upper layer, had been used as rudimentary and ineffective chisels.

"She was above us the entire time?" Eleni asked. Pallasophia noted the blank, even tone in her voice, but said nothing about it.

"So it would seem. Pallasophia turned to Photeos. "Lochias, would you care to tell me why you did not pick up on that particular fact earlier?"

He spoke with a matter-of-fact tone, not attempting to make any excuses. "There were a lot of tracks, Second Lord. Between those left by the mastigas, our own, and multiple sets of prints left by One Hundred during what appeared to be several trips through that area, I could not tell how recent any of them were."

Pallasophia nodded. "She would have ended up behind us."

Photeos apologized, then added, "I should have been more aware of the surroundings. Perhaps..."

Pallasophia interrupted him. "Apology accepted, Third Lord." When she continued, her tones softened and became much less formal. "However, you can't blame yourself for missing the clues. One Hundred has had a lot of time down here to perfect her skills. This isn't a normal woman you're tracking, Photeos."

"I understand."

Pallasophia turned back to where Eleni still stood with her recording at the ready. She motioned for her to continue. "Now, where were we?"

Eleni advanced the time on the recording slightly. The device played back scraping and sounds of movement. The unmistakable sound of hands moving over the microphone came next, then again.

"I think she's inspecting the sensor," Eleni supplied.

Pallasophia nodded, but said nothing.

The rustling stopped, and then a raspy voice spoke. It sounded healthier than a patient with a sick throat, but still unpleasant. Underneath the sandpaper, however, was a warm contralto, decidedly human, that lacked the wet-rocks sound the mastigas sophonts made when they spoke.

The voice coughed, dry and hacking. "Come find me."

More rustling and sounds of movement followed. The device fell silent, then it let out a series of scrapes and clicks as the floor piece was replaced above it. Moments later, a series of heavy footfalls receded.

"Those steps are heavier than anything else I've picked up," Eleni said.

"Not so heavy as a gigas," Photeos added, "but she definitely wanted us to know which direction she went."

"Could it be a trap?" Eleni asked.

"It most likely is," Pallasophia replied. "She knows we're here, she's seen us now, and she wants to force a meeting."

"That is what we came down here for," Photeos supplied.

Pallasophia nodded. "True, but Dekaneas Eleni's word choice was apt. One Hundred knows nothing of our motives. She's probably trying to trap us somewhere on her terms."

"We're not hostile," Eleni protested.

"She doesn't know that," Photeos cautioned.

"Exactly. We'll go to her, but we go very carefully."

"And if she attacks us?"

"Defensive force only," Pallasophia ordered. Her voice indicated that she would accept no arguments on the subject.

The replied came instantly and unanimously. "Yes, ma'am!"

"Dekanii Myrto, and Isod—damn it. Myrto, you and I are on point. Stavros, you and Eleni have the gear. Photeos, watch our backs"

"Will do," he replied informally.

***

"She's in there, Lochagos," Eleni said, dismissing her holo interface. "Or she was when she found the recorder."

"Left the bait, you mean," Photeos muttered.

"I've not heard anything else since then."

"We didn't hear her, sensors or no, until *she* wanted to be heard. She killed a blue-screened elite, remember."

"Quiet," Pallasophia snapped, not entirely sure where that burst of anger came from.

"Apologies, Lochagos," he replied stiffly. "Orders?"

"As I said before, defensive force only, weapons ready, but not high."

"If she attacks?"

Pallasophia paused, on the verge of repeating her orders yet again. Before that could happen, however, she realized exactly what it was Photeos was asking. He wanted specific instructions, not vague guidelines, and she nodded firmly. "Stun her, then restrain her."

"Understood."

A moment passed and Pallasophia gestured to Photeos. "You and I are on point, Lochias. If she's not in there, I need to know where One Hundred went."

He nodded and joined her at the front of the group. A small gesture sent Dekaneas Myrto to the rear. Activating the holographic controls on his rifle, he switched the weapon over from lethal fire to stun rounds. First Pallasophia, then the others, did the same.

With a curt wave, Pallasophia deferred to Photeos, allowing him to move forward first. She followed a pace behind him, with the butt of her rifle at her shoulder and the muzzle pointed slightly downward.

Pallasophia grit her teeth. She hoped she could reason with her, but if One Hundred had any inkling of *why* she had been born into the darkness of Aphelion's depths, the odds of that might be lower than she wanted.

The room where Eleni's sensor reading and Photeos's tracking led them was nearly identical to how it had been before. If Pallasophia had not known where the sensor was hidden, no unusual markings or signs on the floor would have given it away. The only real difference was the prominent set of footprints leading off in one direction.

Photeos pointed to the ceiling. "She was right there. The footsteps directly under that spot just appear."

"Like she dropped from above."

"Exactly."

Pallasophia nodded. "Can you tell where she went?"

Photeos laughed. "There are only two other exits from this room. I doubt she would hide in the cleaning closet, Second Lord."

Inside her helmet, Pallasophia's grin was amused. "Then we go that way."

"As you say, Lochagos."

The area on the other side of the little vestibule was dark. Pallasophia half expected to hear the crunch of broken glass underfoot, but it was noticeably absent. If her memory served correctly, this was part of the initial medical areas before the arena, or it was. Once upon a time, the subjects would have undergone rigorous medical screening before being allowed to fight the elite and its associated mastigas.

Absently, she wondered what the creatures had done with the holding area that once housed the four-armed monstrosity. Trashing it seemed most likely.

"Lights?" Stavros whispered.

Pallasophia shook her head, then realized the gesture would be lost in the darkness. She replied, "no. When I saw her in the arena, the bright lights seemed to bother her eyes. We're playing on her terms now, Dekaneas." She voiced that last statement louder than the others, projecting so that her voice would carry.

"That's far enough."

The voice that spoke came from the opposite end of the room, with the scratchy, hoarse quality from Eleni's recording. In person, or nearly so, it was clear that the speaker was unaccustomed to forming words and speaking. Her command of those words seemed correct, but simple unfamiliarity lent it an over-enunciated quality.

She spoke again. "Who are you?"

"My name is Pallasophia. With me are Stavros, Eleni, Myrto, and Photeos, all soldiers. We've been sent to take you to safety."

The voice repeated. "Who are you?"

Pallasophia fell silent for a moment. She beckoned to Eleni. Despite the intimate knowledge she felt she shared with One Hundred, her training in psychology would, she hoped, prove more useful. "Any idea what she wants to know?"

She thought for a moment, lowering her rifle to hang from its sling. Quietly, she said, "she has yet to attack us, which means she doesn't view us as a threat."

"That much was obvious."

"Yet," she continued, "she's staying hidden. I don't think names are going to be enough to coax her out here."

Pallasophia spoke to the shadows where she suspected One Hundred was hiding. She used the most formal of tones and tenses. "These three are soldiers by trade. I myself am a scientist and..."

One Hundred's voice interrupted. Behind her voice was a quiet sound of metal-on-metal and two footsteps. "Soldiers. Are you with the green eyes?"

"I assume you're watching me," Pallasophia said. She wondered exactly how good One Hundred's eyes were. Perhaps she could see her clearly. "I'm going to remove my helmet now."

One Hundred remained in the shadows, silent. A tense moment passed and Pallasophia slowly unlatched the straps under her chin and removed the helmet. Underneath, her short hair stuck out in several directions, sweaty and mussed by the helmet itself. She motioned for the others to do the same.

Stavros and Photeos moved first. Photeos's pale skin stood out with a sheen of sweat. The mathematical design shaved into his close-cropped hair had turned the same ruddy shade as his cheeks. He might have been one of the best fighters Tritogenes employed, but his pale complexion meant any exertion showed like a beacon. Stavros moved right afterward, showing dark skin and even darker hair. His forehead, in contrast to his CO's, was dry.

Myrto and Eleni removed their helmets last. Both wore their hair in near identical styles, with shaved sides. Eleni bore a tattoo of the golden ratio on either side of her head, while Myrto's short-haired scalp was otherwise bare. Down Eleni's back tumbled a shock of blond hair twisted into an intricate six-strand braid that fell halfway down her back now that it was free of the helmet.

"We're human, just like you," Pallasophia said.

Silence hung in the dark room for a full minute before One Hundred emerged from the darkness. She was preceded by the menacing point of an enormous sword. The Technocrats one and all immediately recognized it as one of the swords carried by the elite. It hovered a bit lower than the three-meter monster would have held it, but the long blade was no less dangerous in the hands of a human.

Perhaps, Pallasophia thought, it might even be more dangerous in One Hundred's hands.

Behind the sword was a black suited figure. Ingrained training itched at Pallasophia's hands. She wanted to raise her rifle and shoot the thing

184

in front of her. One Hundred, in her cobbled-together clothing and armor looked more like a mastigas than a human. The stolen helmet she wore only added to the image.

A quick glance to her sides showed her that she was not alone in those feelings. Eleni was tense, ready to spring backward on command, to open the distance between herself and what looked for all the world like a mastigas. Stavros, on the other hand, fought the urge to inch forward. He had never seen a mastigas in person, and the horror of Isodorus's death only made him bolder.

Pallasophia regarded Number One Hundred for a long moment before the other spoke again. Her voice was still scratchy, but as she spoke, she gained greater control over her tone. "You came from the other side of the mastigas titan's room."

"The elite, yes. We sealed the door on the other side, and..."

Even as the words were out of her mouth, Pallasophia knew they were wrong. The ice that suddenly gripped her veins spoke too clearly for her to ignore, even before One Hundred moved.

Her sword plunged forward like a spear. She might have lacked formal training, but the combat data that had been provided for her, plus what she learned from the labyrinth and arena themselves, more than made up for it. Her distance was perfect, even if her timing was not, and she moved faster than any of the Technocrats dared expect.

The tip of the deadly sword brushed past Pallasophia's head. Her muttered prayer of thankfulness was cut short when she realized One Hundred had not intended to hit her with the blade at all. The weapon's wide guard slammed into her throat, forcing a choking gasp out of her lungs. She dropped her rifle reflexively as her throat closed up.

Eleni and Stavros reacted at once, firing short bursts from their rifles. The shots had been aimed at where a normal person would have been, and they missed One Hundred's speeding shoulders by a wide margin.

Photeos was luckier; one of his shots took One Hundred in the center of the chest. The stun rounds used powerful electric current to incapacitate enemies when lethal force was not an option. A single round should have been enough to take down even a trained soldier, but as the electricity sparked against her chest, One Hundred showed no sign of stopping.

She swung her sword and the long weapon clanged against the ceiling. Rather than fight the momentary hesitation in her attack, One Hundred simply dropped the weapon. It clattered to the ground as she plowed into Photeos with her shoulder. Now that she had both hands free, she grabbed him by the shoulders and pivoted around his back.

She moved so quickly that Stavros's follow-up shot, the shot that should have kept her from reaching Photeos at all, struck the Lochias in the chest. An additional shot from Myrto struck him a moment later. The three stun rounds sparked against his uniform and he collapsed.

One Hundred kicked him forward and he fell, face-first, to the broken tile floor. One Hundred followed him, grabbed a piece of broken pottery. She sprang upward, slinging the reddish brown missile at Eleni's face. It shattered against the side of her head, and she stumbled.

She followed up the shard of pottery with a charge of her own. One Hundred grabbed Eleni by the shoulders, spun her around and shoved her violently against Pallasophia. The two Second Lords collided in a tangle of limbs and equipment as One Hundred dashed past them.

Stavros leveled his rifle and fired, but the shot went wide as One Hundred dodged to one side like a dancer. She struck his arms, grabbed the rifle out of his hands, and struck him again in the gut with the shoulder stock.

As she disentangled herself from Eleni, Pallasophia's eyes went still wider with shock. One Hundred flipped the rifle around in her hands and fired three stun rounds into Stavros's stomach at point blank range. He let out half a cry and doubled over, hitting the floor with his knees hard enough that his armor shattered the tile.

From the far side of the room, Myrto fired a full burst from her rifle. One of the stun rounds struck One Hundred in the leg and she stumbled.

186

The other two missed, sparking against the tile. One Hundred dropped to one knee, then tracked several shots across Myrto's chest. The stun round sparked, and she fell, twitching.

One Hundred pivoted on her heels, aiming the stolen rifle square in the center of Pallasophia's forehead.

"You sealed me in here?" she demanded. Incalculable fury, coalesced into a single pinprick spot colder than space itself, raged in her voice. Her question carried with it the inevitable doom of an avalanche. "This was *your* doing?"

Pallasophia put on her best diplomatic tone, saying, "you must understand. We had no..."

"Yes, or no," the icy voice demanded.

One Hundred stepped away, circling so that she could keep the rifle on Pallasophia and distance herself from the others. One Hundred's thumb went for the selector switch on the side of the rifle, changing the feed from stun rounds to lethal ones—Pallasophia suddenly regretted including that particular feature in her indoctrinated knowledge.

Pallasophia swallowed hard. Stun rounds she could deal with—One Hundred had not acted like she wanted to kill her or her team before. Now, however, the rifle was armed with bullets that would tear through her as easily as they would mastigas.

"Yes."

"Why?"

Pallasophia spoke slowly. Every word she said would have to be carefully considered. "It was not supposed to be this way. The mastigas were to be kept contained until we needed to evaluate your combat performance."

"And the performance of the ninety-nine others you killed."

Pallasophia's jaw clenched as she saw the imperceptible tightening in One Hundred's hands. She knew she could not afford even a single wrong word. "Yes."

"Why?"

"We needed to test you against the mastigas, and..."

"I understand that," One Hundred growled. "They're here. I'm here. They're trying to kill me. That purpose is clear. Why were the doors sealed?"

"There was an accident."

"The four armed mastigas."

"Yes," Pallasophia said, then, "and no. It was the sophont that began it." One Hundred continued to stare, silent. "The one that can speak."

Finally One Hundred nodded slowly. "Why are you here?"

"I told you the truth before. We came down here to bring you to safety."

"And the mastigas you sealed in here with me?"

"Exterminating them is now our top priority."

"Why now?" One Hundred demanded. "Why after ninety-nine deaths do you come now?"

Pallasophia's voice was barely above a whisper. "We had to know you could do the impossible."

"Why should I not kill you all and leave myself?"

Pallasophia was silent for a moment. "There are many more soldiers on the other side of the arena. Even your skill and speed could not cover so much empty ground before they shot you."

"Then I'm your hostage."

Pallasophia shook her head. "No. You are our mission."

"Give me one reason to trust you."

"I have no reason to lie to you," Pallasophia said. She spoke formally. "If you do not believe that now, I will take every pain to make that clear to you in the long run. Additionally, we still have a lot of work to do. One of us will escort you to out of here and..."

"No," One Hundred's voice was firm.

"No?"

"You said your mission was to get me out of here, yes?" One Hundred asked, and Pallasophia nodded. "Then why don't we all leave together?"

"We still have work to do here. The area is not safe, and..."

One Hundred's biting laughter interrupted her. "And you blasted the only door apart, so now you can't lock it behind you."

Reluctantly, Pallasophia agreed. "That is true."

"Either you're all fools, or you planned on this," One Hundred accused. "What is it?"

Again, Pallasophia spoke with reluctance. "The latter."

"I suspected as much. And if I help you?"

"When that work is done, I will submit to any questions you deem fit. Are we agreed?" Pallasophia extended her hand, extraordinarily slowly.

One Hundred looked at the offered hand for several long moment. Finally, she thumbed the weapon's safety on and dropped the sling over one shoulder.

One Hundred extended her hand as well, grasping Pallasophia's own. Her grip was like iron-backed velvet. The strength was there, under the skin, but she knew she had the upper hand and no longer had anything to prove. To crush the Second Lord's hand now would gain her nothing, or so Pallasophia hoped.

"We have an understanding, Pallasophia."

She nodded once. "And what am I to call you?"

"My name is Victoria."

Chapter 11

The binary stellar pair around which the Technocrat planets orbited created a much wider than average safe zone for terrestrial planets. Rather than just one or perhaps two Earthlike bodies, their suns boasted seven planets. Each was ruled by a single Hexarch and the seventh, the capital Prosgeiosi, was governed directly by their joint Council of six.

None of the planets orbited at exactly the same distance or exactly the same rate, and a year on one planet could be as many as two local years on another. As a result, the calendar of Prosgeiosi was the accepted standard, with local variations bringing each planet's calendar more-or-less in line with that of the capital. Thus, according to the calendar, it was the same "day" on close-in planets like Katarraktes or Kokkinos as it was on far out Kipos or Limani.

As star systems went, the more distance between an object and the sun—or suns, in the case of the Technocrats—the longer it took to orbit. From that perspective, Tritogenes's secret Aphelion facility barely moved while the inner planets zipped around the twin suns over and over again.

The complicated dance woven by the paths of the Technocrat planets all but ensured Tritogenes would stop at Limani on his way to

Katarraktes anyway. His planet sat on the near side of the suns relative to Aphelion, while Katarraktes found itself nearly a full hundred-and-eighty degrees away. Even if he did not have reason to stop, a day spent on his own planet barely added eight hours to his overall transit to Katarraktes.

So, less than a week after leaving Aphelion in his fastest ship, Tritogenes touched down at First Lord Enyalios's private spaceport. Several hours after that, after the requisite feasting and entertainment, he found himself alone with the Hexarch of Katarraktes.

Enyalios's office was much the same as it had been the last time Tritogenes visited. He moved a few things after Nikos's death, but otherwise very little was different. If the Hexarch was being honest with himself, very little had changed in the twenty-five years since he first set foot in the small suite after claiming it for himself.

The area he claimed for himself served as a fully contained apartment. In fact, Enyalios rarely slept or stayed in Katarraktes's palace at all. That sprawling complex sat at the top of the largest waterfall in the city and was home to a great many of the planet's rich and powerful second lords, serving as a center of business more than anything.

For himself, Enyalios's office suite was located downriver somewhat, on the ground level of a building set into the rock above the river below the palace's waterfall. Years ago, the building had been a military command center, and still served that function admirably, but the bulk of the facility's space had been taken up by his Titan training facility.

There, after allowing him time to change into a less formal robe, Enyalios met Tritogenes in the cool, river-scented building. They toured the facility itself as Enyalios talked about the newest generation of combat armor under development for Second Lord Daniel. For the rest of the time, they made small talk until finally ending up in the Hexarch's suite, cool and dim where it had been cut directly into the rock.

191

Even in the dim light he preferred, Enyalios's robe and jewelry shimmered, Like Tritogenes, he had donned something less formal, but the two Hexarchs had very different definitions of what that meant. Tritogenes wore a faded purple robe spotted with embroidery here and there. The edges and hems were frayed, but Enyalios supposed that defined the Project well enough.

For his own part, Enyalios wore a much newer robe, though it sported less ornamentation than the one he wore to dinner. His elaborately Fibonacci-braided hair remained in place, as did a few of the less valuable pieces of his handcrafted jewelry.

"Before we talk of the Project," Enyalios began as the doors behind them swung shut, "I should let you know that Eurybia is here as well. She will likely have questions about your part of things."

Tritogenes's eyes widened in surprise. "What's she doing here?"

"She came to inspect the Project."

Tritogenes scoffed. "So she says."

"So far, that's all she's done."

Tritogenes eyed him for a moment, and Enyalios knew exactly what he was doing. The way his gaze wandered all over someone's face, watching for little tells and tics, was nothing new. After a moment, a ghost of a smile flitted across the younger Hexarch's lips. "Why do I sense a 'but' coming?"

Enyalios laughed. He held many years of seniority over Tritogenes, and early on in the latter's career, they butted heads over many things. Energetic and young—by the standards of the Hexarchs, anyway. He was scarcely forty-five when he ascended to the Hexarchate of Limani— First Lord Tritogenes simply seemed to rub Enyalios the wrong way. Tritogenes often came out of their debates with the upper hand, something that never stopped annoying Enyalios, even after he realized exactly how the theatrically-trained Hexarch was doing it.

Ultimately, it was Tritogenes's focus on the sciences, despite his background in the arts, that won Enyalios over. Under all his early bluster about "reconnecting with the spirit of adventure" that had put their ancestors on the ship that had, for ten long millennia, taken them through the stars and finally to the binary that became their home, Enyalios finally discovered a mind truly interested in furthering humanity's understanding of science and technology.

That, Enyalios thought at the time, was something he could support.

Now, however, Tritogenes's ability to read the room worked in Enyalios's favor more often than not. He knew the younger Hexarch still considered him to be a bit "stodgy" and "conservative," but after patching up their differences with the start of Project Titan, Enyalios found a fast friend and resourceful ally in Tritogenes.

And yet, despite their now-strong friendship, Tritogenes never failed to strike a nerve when he read Enyalios so easily. Aegesander had the same habit, but he did the same thing to *everyone*, somehow making it more palatable from the older Hexarch.

Rather than growl, Enyalios laughed. "Because there is a 'but' coming. She's been making requests of my senior staff for two days now."

Tritogenes's eyebrows rose. "Requests? As in...?"

Enyalios nodded, frowning. "Yes. Just this morning, she messaged the steward of the guest house where she's staying and said, and I quote, 'if it's not too much trouble, can you bring breakfast to my room?'"

"You know she's only doing it to annoy you. Hell," Tritogenes laughed. "Is that why she wasn't at dinner?"

"I can't say," Enyalios replied. "I sent a messenger to tell her to come, ordered her in the most polite way I could manage as well, but she never showed."

"She's probably here on Aegesander's orders."

"Why, though?"

"What do you mean?"

"Why would Aegesander, or why would she of her own volition, come all this way just to needle my staff with pointless rudeness?"

Tritogenes waited a moment before answering. When he did, his voice was quieter and he spoke a little more carefully. "Maybe they're testing you after what happened to Nikos."

Enyalios gestured angrily. "Then they could simply do so! Slights against my staff are intolerable."

"You could throw her out, or even have them tell her no."

Now, Enyalios laughed, loud and uproarious. "I admire that about you, Tritogenes, but *I* am not quite willing to start a fight on the Council floor for something as petty as this. Let them have their little victory." He shrugged. "It won't bother me long term."

"Then..."

Again, Enyalios laughed, but the sound was almost conspiratorial this time. "My friend, if I set out to return her rudeness with some of my own, it's not *fun*."

Tritogenes quirked an eyebrow. "Fun?"

"Of course! She's been here for days now. It's almost become a game, at least that's how I've been treating it."

Tritogenes's face lit up as he processed the idea, and a grin spread across his features. "I remember a certain Hexarch 'offering' to guide me on a tour of the city's waterfalls shortly after my elevation."

Enyalios kept his voice, and his face, carefully neutral. "Oh, yes. They're quite dangerous, you know. 'Eurybia,' I said after the first time she made a request of my staff, 'if you have the energy today, I have prepared a tour.'"

Tritogenes laughed. "The same line you used on me."

Enyalios grinned, breaking his stoic demeanor for a moment. "Yes, except it worked on her. Unlike you, you crashed hardhead.

"At any rate," he continued, "you'll get to deal with her soon enough. For now, let us talk about the Project. I fear it's the last time we'll get to talk privately."

Tritogenes nodded. "As you say. Tell me, Enyalios, what happened to Nikos? Your official report is, let's say, vague."

Enyalios felt his face darken, not from embarrassment, but out of anger. That passed in a moment, however, as he reminded himself that Tritogenes was perhaps the only Hexarch who could understand how it felt to lose a Titan-Candidate. Rivka *understood*, but, while Enyalios respected her, he considered the young Hexarch to be much too soft.

With his mental mask carefully back in place, Enyalios replied, "he got cocky and tried to take on a pair of gigas by himself."

Tritogenes did not reply for a moment, and Enyalios wondered if he had somehow offended the other Hexarch. He pushed that worry aside—Tritogenes would have told him immediately if that had been the case. For all his annoyances, the Council's youngest member did not play the same sort of games the others did if he could avoid it.

Rather than directly address Nikos's loss or what it was that killed him, Tritogenes said with utmost politeness, "show me."

"Give me a moment."

Tritogenes nodded and left the room, heading to the kitchenette attached to Enyalios's office.

Set in front of one wall like an archaic movie screen was a much larger holoprojector than either of them could carry on their person. Using the controls at his wrist, he navigated through the menus while Tritogenes busied himself in the kitchenette, likely making drinks for them.

After days of dealing with Eurybia, Tritogenes's politeness was refreshing. The other Hexarch did not *ask*, and in so doing imply that Enyalios might not be up to the challenge. He simply *did*.

With the recording ready, Enyalios waited for Tritogenes's return. Fortunately, he did not have to wait long. Tritogenes knew what both of them preferred and, after five years of unofficial meetings like that, knew exactly where Enyalios kept everything.

Silently, he handed a steaming mug to Enyalios. The black coffee within had been sweetened a little more than he preferred, but the alcoholic kick was certainly up to his standards. In his own hand. Tritogenes held an unfamiliar pink liquid.

At Enyalios's inquisitive glance, he shrugged and said, "I wanted to try making something new."

"So you are celebrating something."

Tritogenes laughed. "And I thought it was only I who could read people like that."

"Years of working side-by-side will do that to anyone, even me."

Limani's Hexarch gave a short bark of laughter. "You make a fair point."

"As much as we fought, you'd think I would have picked that talent up sooner."

Now, Tritogenes's laughter came louder and more boisterous. He caught his breath, sipped his undoubtedly sugary drink, and shrugged. "I never expected you to."

"Your confidence in me is outstanding."

"In my defense, I thought you were a stodgy pain in in the ass."

Enyalios laughed. "In your defense, I *am* a stodgy pain in the ass."

Before working together on Project Titan, Enyalios and Tritogenes were actually banned for a time from addressing one another directly for more than twenty minutes during Council meetings. That had eased tensions somewhat, but they continued to butt heads for years.

And then the mastigas swept across Kipos like wildfire and Diomedes poisoned himself in shame.

He remembered that Council session vividly. He and Tritogenes stood up at the same moment, glared at one another, daring an interruption, and then in near unison declared that something had to be done about the mastigas.

It was like a switch had been thrown. Overnight, he and Tritogenes became friends.

And now they stood side by side again at the culmination of the Project that ended their fifteen year feud.

Wordlessly, Enyalios gestured to the holo with one hand, dimming the lights with the other.

He reached for the control to start the video, then paused. "Success has not come easy."

Tritogenes's face darkened, obvious even without the overhead lights. "No, it has not."

"I must admit, I'm a little jealous."

The shock on Tritogenes's face was nearly palpable. "Jealous, how? Everything I built went to hell."

"Mine has been no different. Watch."

The video began, showing Enyalios, resplendent in a new purple robe, talking to a man wearing a full suit of combat armor. He left the sound muted, and when Tritogenes asked about that fact, Enyalios insisted that sound was not necessary to convey the message.

"I have heard those words enough," he added, without making eye contact.

The man on the screen exchanged a few words with Enyalios. He did indeed remember those words. They talked about the suit, the first of its kind, and its capabilities. Enyalios had encouraging words for him.

"This will be easy," he remembered saying. The words, the lie, ate a hole in his stomach every time.

On the video, Enyalios's mouth moved without words. The man in armor nodded and gestured. His face was obscured by his helmet and mask, but the intent behind the gesturing seemed clear enough.

The camera switched to a feed inside a small room. It was bare except for a single mastigas gigas, armed with a long club, much heavier and more appropriate to its size than the baton One Hundred stole from the ones she vanquished.

It paced the small room, clearly agitated by its captivity. A large door at the far end was shut and, Tritogenes presumed, locked. He guessed it was the door through which the gigas had been led—or pushed—into the room.

The armored man stepped into the center of the video, giving a clear look at his equipment. In hindsight, Enyalios could see every flaw that early suit possessed. Its parts were too soft or too brittle, designed for combat with human enemies. Enyalios cursed his foolishness. His forces helped push the mastigas back from Kipos; if anyone other than Rivka should have had a clear idea of what the mastigas were capable of, it was him.

And he still made the suits too weak.

The gigas turned and sighted the armored man. It bellowed. Its posture, the sudden tension in the shoulders and the head thrust far forward, could indicate nothing else. Even in the silence of the muted video, Tritogenes knew that sound and it was enough to freeze his blood. The gigas wasted no time with anything either of the Hexarchs could have called skillful fighting. Instead, as soon as the beast saw Enyalios's man, it lunged forward, club raised high to strike.

The man dodged the strike and laid a left hook into the side of the gigas's head. With the suit amplifying his strength, the punch was powerful enough to knock the massive creature off balance, letting the armored man follow up with another quick strike. On a human target, the next two blows would have easily broken bones.

The gigas, however, continued to rage on. It moved slower after the first hit, and the third one seemed to hobble one of its arms, but finally it connected with its club. The thing looked to be a solid steel beam two meters in length and at least as thick at the end as a human's thigh was wide. It connected with the man's armored torso in a brutal impact made all the more gruesome by its lack of sound. He folded like a doll as the momentum from the club slung him against the nearby wall, at the edge of the camera's pickup.

The gigas roared again and charged, slamming into the armored figure as he struggled to his feet. The giant picked him up by his neck and slammed him into the wall, repeating the motion twice before Enyalios paused and cut the video.

"That was three years ago."

With what even Enyalios could see was a carefully constructed, and very thin, veneer of professionalism, Tritogenes asked, "I assume you have had more success since then?"

Rather than reply, Enyalios brought up the menu again. He selected a clip from the lower right corner. "Nine days ago."

The menu faded again, to be replaced with a room very similar to the previous one. This new arena was larger and several more doors led in differing directions, but otherwise it was identical in its stark emptiness.

In the center of the room stood a behemoth of steel. Taller than even the gigas now, this version of Enyalios's power armor looked more like a walking tank than a human inside a suit of armor. Here and there lights dotted the armor, though their purpose was unclear from the recording.

"Nikos?" Tritogenes asked.

Enyalios felt his lips tighten into a thin line. "Yes."

A door at the far end of the room opened, admitting two gigas. On the silent video, it was obvious they did not yet see Nikos or his armor.

Enyalios felt very cold inside as he watched the opening moments of the fight. Watching as Nikos gained an early upper hand against the mastigas only made the eventual result of the trial worse. Several moments passed and Enyalios became aware he had clenched his fists so tightly that his nails dug into his palms.

At his side, if Tritogenes noticed, he said nothing about it. Instead, he seemed to be thinking aloud. "They act very different when a sophont is around."

Enyalios paused the recording while he could still fool himself into believing Nikos might defeat the two gigas. "I am aware, Tritogenes. Perhaps you ought to ask Rivka how they act when led by a sophont. Or," Enyalios allowed a little more anger into his voice, "perhaps you should ask your own people?"

199

Tritogenes's eyebrows narrowed into a frown a just a moment, but it passed as quickly as it appeared. "I needed the most realistic trials I could craft."

"So you said, and I recall warning you that to capture a sophont would be too dangerous. When I heard of your Incident, it seemed as though my caution was warranted."

Tritogenes opened his mouth for a moment, then stopped.

Rather that watch Nikos's death again, Enyalios cut the video and raised the room lights. "I have not had your success."

"What about Daniel?"

"He is training day and night. I fear he will push himself too far."

Tritogenes waited a moment before asking, "what then?"

Enyalios raised his hands, palms upward and fingers curled like claws. "I've mastigas blood on my hands, Tritogenes. If Daniel... If he fails, I will go myself."

For just a moment, shorter than even a single beat of Enyalios's heart, a look of utter shame passed across Tritogenes's face. "I wish we all were like you."

Enyalios scoffed, choosing for his friend's sake not to mention the slip of his emotional mask. That scoff turned into an angry growl, aimed not at Tritogenes, but at himself. "To hell with that. Wish we were all like Rivka instead."

Tritogenes's eyebrows rose, though Enyalios could not tell if it was his tone or the mention of Rivka that did it. "I thought you didn't like her."

"I appreciate her, Tritogenes. Rivka is soft, gentle, but underneath all that is an iron spirit that nothing can break. No, I meant what I said, though you will not repeat it outside this room."

Tritogenes nodded. "Second Lord Pallasophia, Aphelion's facility director, is the same way. She, too, told me that if none of Aphelion's test subjects succeeded, she would go herself."

"But, as I understand from your message, that will no longer be a problem?"

Tritogenes nodded. "Number One Hundred succeeded."

"I wish you would not refer to them like that, Tritogenes. And what metric did you use to define success?"

He raised his arm, summoning his holo controls. "May I?"

Enyalios nodded, entered a command on his own control panel, and waved acquiescence.

The lights dimmed again, and this time the holo against the wall showed events twice the size of Enyalios's own recording. Torn between amusement and annoyance, he nonetheless laughed—Tritogenes and his flair for the dramatic, he thought.

The holo showed a sandy pit, empty. A few moments passed and a massive door at one end slowly swung open. Through it strode a barefoot human figure wearing mastigas clothing and carrying a backpack. Unlike Enyalios's recording, Tritogenes's holo included sound, though all that Enyalios could hear was the rumble of something massive moving out of sight.

The woman dropped the backpack and drew her weapons, a steel baton in one hand and a long dagger in the other. Enyalios shot Tritogenes a questioning look.

"Taken from dead mastigas," he explained. "A gigas and a fonias, specifically."

A few moment passed as the woman in black advanced across the sand, then a towering, four-armed monstrosity literally leaped into view.

"By the Ten Thousand," Enyalios heard himself swear as the elite took a swing with one of its massive swords.

She moved with fluid grace, dodging and striking whenever opportune. Slowly, over the course of several minutes of constant combat, she wore down her opponent. She was not without her share of injuries, but carried on despite them. Enyalios knew exactly how terrifying one of those elites was in person, and to see it confronted with such a mixture of grace and ferocity was inspiring.

At nearly five minutes, it was one of the longest nonstop exchanges of blows he had ever seen. Even gladiators and pugilists broke contact every few exchanges to catch their breath and reassess their opponent. Nothing of the sort passed between these two figures.

Finally, the elite, a monster ripped from Enyalios's nightmares of the fighting on Kipos, sagged to its knees on the sand. The woman in black did not stop fighting there, either. She savaged it, ensuring with bloody efficiency that the enormous mastigas would never draw another breath.

"What was she about to do?" Enyalios was only dimly aware that his voice had risen in pitch. He normally spoke in a tone slightly higher than Tritogenes, pitched that way by his Katarraktean upbringing and the need to project his voice over the planet's omnipresent waterfalls. This was different, much closer to the high, clear quality needed to be heard over the din of combat.

"Scavenge," Tritogenes said, and Enyalios raised an eyebrow. Tritogenes continued, "where do you think she acquired her clothing, armor, and weapons?"

"You did not provide them?"

Tritogenes shook his head. "No," he replied. "everything except her body itself came from the mastigas she killed."

"Ah, right. Your little..." He paused. "Incident."

Tritogenes nodded grudging agreement. Enyalios knew his fellow Hexarch counted that failure among his worst. Finally, Tritogenes said, "yes. It made sending materiel to the subjects difficult."

"Impossible, you mean."

"Yes."

Enyalios sighed. "Again, I wish you would refer to them another way, Tritogenes."

"How do you mean?"

"'Test subjects,' or just, 'subjects,' makes it sound entirely too clinical and detached. These are human beings, after all."

A sigh, then, "I know, but it's hard to bring myself to keep that thought at the front of my mind, do the job, *and* sleep at night."

Enyalios's shrug was dismissive, but his tone was anything but. "Everyone's sins haunt them from time to time."

"If I'm being honest," Tritogenes said. "I'm glad the other Hexarchs don't understand the full extent of what went on at Aphelion."

"Your research terrifies them, Tritogenes."

He arched an eyebrow. "They know?"

"They suspect."

"Ah. Why?"

"Genetic engineering on that scale? Even Hyperion has spoken to me in private about his misgivings. They're afraid you've made something more than human out there."

"One Hundred is human," he said, almost too quickly. "I assure you of that."

"Expect questions, Tritogenes."

"I always do when entering a room with Aegesander."

"As I said, even Hyperion is going to demand answers of you."

"And I'll give them. Enyalios, I did what I had to in order to complete Project Titan. After the Incident, I did everything I could to make sure it could continue."

Enyalios frowned, fighting down anger. What Tritogenes had done, locking the facility and still subjecting those people to a maze of mastigas with no hope of rescue, was inexcusable. He also knew that he was likely the only one who knew the full extent of what happened. Tritogenes's official story was that he stopped that part of the Project after the Incident, but "Test Subject One Hundred" was accidentally awakened.

Of course, much of the anger Enyalios felt was directed inward at his own failings. To take that out on Tritogenes would be unfair.

He fought all that down, waiting a moment, and several deep breaths, until his calm restored itself. "You could have restarted. Safely."

Tritogenes shook his head. "I suppose that was always an option, but you know as well as I do how much blood that would have cost."

"You've spilled your fair share of blood as it is."

"Less than the alternative."

Enyalios fell silent as the recording began to play again, automatically. The woman Tritogenes would only refer to as "Number One Hundred" attacked the elite with a speed and fury he had never seen before. The fact remained, bloodshed or no, Tritogenes had succeeded in his part of Project Titan. His "Number One Hundred" was exactly what he promised the other Hexarchs five years before.

Finally, Enyalios said, "we all have our share of blood on our hands."

Tritogenes nodded slowly. "For the greater good."

"That is what we must tell ourselves, is it not?"

"It is the truth."

"That makes it no more palatable," Enyalios countered.

Tritogenes watched the recording, carefully not looking in Enyalios's direction. "What is true and what is comfortable are not always the same thing."

"The last five years have made that more obvious than I would care to admit."

"You're right, though. I could have restarted my Project, but by continuing it, I was able to produce," he gestured to the holographic video of One Hundred. She had already wounded the elite several times. "This."

"And is she safe now?" Enyalios asked. "Few things could kill her given the way in which she dispatched that elite, but she was rather wounded in the process."

"Second Lord Pallasophia went into the facility to rescue her after I left to come here. I expect they will emerge soon, and we will all meet my Champion."

"'Champion' is better than 'One Hundred,'" Enyalios mused. "One wonders what she calls herself. You say you had no contact with her?"

"None," Tritogenes answered. "Since the Incident, none of my personnel were allowed lower than five floors above the arena."

"And the equipment was still intact?"

"It would have to be for the signals that control the gestation pods to operate."

"You never wondered why the mastigas never severed those links?"

"I made the shells out of the same material with which we shape starship hulls."

"Expensive."

"But ultimately worth it."

"Though that raises the question of why you thought you would need something so durable in the first place. It is something the other Hexarchs have pondered in private ever since learning of the Incident."

He nodded, still refusing eye contact. "Simple preparedness."

"Preparedness is reinforcing the shells with conventional alloys, Tritogenes. To use stellar alloys speaks of paranoia, or perhaps planning."

"Speak your mind, Enyalios. If the other Hexarchs have insinuated..."

The other Technocrat interrupted. "They have said many things, Tritogenes. I myself am merely thinking aloud. So, why..." He trailed off, gesturing to Tritogenes to fill in the rest of the sentence.

"Did I do it?"

Enyalios nodded. He spoke slowly. "Especially when the cage into which you placed that sophont, if your report was accurate, was significantly less durable."

Tritogenes turned, visibly fighting his temper. That tendency towards shouting before thinking was one of the things early on that Enyalios detested about him. In fact, it was his principle reason for voting against Tritogenes's elevation.

205

Watching him the years since, even when they fought, Enyalios came to understand that the other Hexarch's passion was a powerful tool. He waited for the explosion, but Tritogenes made a calming gesture with his hands and replied with an even, level voice. He spoke slowly, choosing his words as deliberately as he would in the Council chamber.

"You think," Tritogenes began, "that I engineered the sophont's escape?"

"It would explain things neatly," Enyalios replied. His tone was so matter-of-fact that it stopped Tritogenes's retort before he could open his mouth.

They stood silent for a moment as the recording ended again and Enyalios deactivated the holoprojector. Aloud, Tritogenes said, "it would, yes. However, I can assure you that it was exactly as I said it was when it happened—an accident."

"And the shells?" Enyalios gestured for Tritogenes to continue.

Tritogenes paused, gathering his thoughts. Slowly, he opened his mouth, talking now with even more care and measure. "I planned, or thought I did, for the possibility that the sophont might escape. I knew how dangerous they were, but believed, as I still do, that facing one was necessary for the success of Project Titan."

"Why?"

"Without a sophont, the mastigas are just beasts."

Enyalios growled. "Beasts that killed several of my best people."

Carefully, he nodded. "Yes, but when the Titan eventually face them, they need to understand how to fight *thinking* mastigas. Yet," he paused, "perhaps you are right. Perhaps I needlessly sent those people to their death."

"Between us, Tritogenes, no results justify what you did."

Grimly, he nodded. "I understand that."

"And that is why you must *never* tell the others what really happened at Aphelion."

206

A ghost of a smile flitted across Tritogenes's features. "I also understand that."

After several moments, Enyalios spoke again. "So, simple paranoia after all?"

"Yes."

Enyalios heaved a sigh and finished the drink in his hands in a single gulp. "Enough of this. If you came to my planet to discuss our sins, I fear I must ask you to leave. I intended to drink and be merry tonight and will no longer accept any other course of action."

"Then let us return to the palace. I passed an advertisement for a concert that should start within the hour, and the air here does wonders for my thoughts."

Enyalios smiled. Tritogenes's energy, at least, was infectious. "Ah, yes. My city's newest pride and joy. An excellent plan, my friend."

"While the musicians play, you will of course join me for more drinks. I brought a bottle with me that ought to fit quite well with live music."

"Then we should make haste. I will keep neither music nor drink waiting."

Chapter 12

The soldiers calling themselves Technocrats retreated to an area even Victoria thought of as being safe, and she followed. They set up their camp, the functions of which simply came to Victoria as she watched in another unexpected burst of memory.

With vaguely worded threats and gestures that included the sword taken from the mastigas elite and the rifle she had yet to return, Victoria isolated herself as they worked. While it was likely that these soldiers brought medical supplies with them, Victoria would not permit herself even a moment of vulnerability. Too many of her dreams ended with violent death and dismemberment because one of those lives thought it safe when it was anything but.

When the woman calling herself Pallasophia objected, stating that it was their job to protect Victoria, she agreed to a compromise. Rather than leave completely, Victoria went into a small side room whose only door led into the area where the soldiers' camp was being assembled. Safely inside, she wedged the captured rifle against the door handle, bracing the other end against the crevice of a broken tile.

With that secure, the only way into the room would be to break the door down or come through the wall. If the latter was possible, the green-eyes—mastigas, she corrected herself—would have done it already. If the Technocrats tried either option without an incredibly good reason, Victoria would kill them herself.

She already proved she could.

Safe and alone, she carefully stripped completely for the first time since making her initial set of clothes. Since that day, only parts of her outfit came off, never the entire thing. Now, at least for a few minutes, Victoria found herself in a place that felt safe enough to let her guard most of the way down.

More than the feeling of safety, Victoria relished the ability to remove the tight bandages protecting her wounds and the strips of fabric binding her chest. Before even inspecting thy myriad scratches and cuts that crisscrossed her flesh, she simply stood there, breathing and savoring the feeling of air on her skin again.

Reluctantly, she began her inspection, starting with the worst of her injuries. As she was afraid, Victoria had indeed torn the stitches in her side. Rather, she added with a silent curse, she tore the stitches in her side *again*.

The flesh there was ragged, but fortunately no longer bled. A bright red line in the center of the wound traced out the path of the elite's sword where the barest edge of the blade caught her. She did not need to fantasize about what a deeper wound would have done—Victoria had lived those deaths more than once. Unlike other, lesser, cuts which she had not bathed in mastigas blood, the skin around the healing sword wound was no warmer than the rest of her body.

From her backpack, she withdrew a square of fabric soaked in mastigas blood. She cut open one of her water bottles to store it, using the waxed interior to keep the fabric wet as long as possible. She did not know what or how, but something in the mastigas's blood cleaned her wounds better than water. She wiped it across the wound in her side, leaving a dull smear of red across the wound. It burned, but this was a feeling of uncomfortable warmth, not the searing agony of fresh mastigas blood on a fresh wound.

Without a curse or sigh, Victoria methodically set to work stitching up her side once more. At this point, the raw pain and nauseating pulling sensation as she sewed were expected. After doing it twice already, including once when the wound was fresh and still bleeding, these stitches were easy.

Mending the wound also took less time now, though how much of that was because it had healed some and how much was because Victoria simply no longer cared about the pain, she could not say. When it was done, she took much more time inspecting everything else. Bruised muscles needed to be massaged and bruised bones checked for fractures. Even the shallow scrapes on her hands and feet merited attention now that she had the time, and she wiped the stinging blood cloth across them as well.

She hated how minor wounds and scrapes throbbed. Major injuries simply hurt, pain that sank into the background because it was too intense to do anything else. Lesser problems just sat there, innocuous until she moved the wrong way, and then shot a random flare of pain through her system. While it did whatever it was that it did to clean her wounds, mastigas blood intensified that sensation.

Fortunately, the stinging sensation did fade after only a minute or so. Once it did, she carefully rewrapped everything with the least dirty bandages she had. None of her cloth was very clean, but as long as she used the mastigas blood to protect her wounds, nothing triggered any more memories of infection and death.

With the bandages back in place, Victoria pulled on the suit of black mastigas fabric. Compared to her few moments without it, the suit was confining, tight, and stiff. It, and especially the helmet, also offered a layer of protection not just between her skin and the elements, but between Victoria herself and the Technocrat soldiers in the other room.

With her body and face shrouded again, it would be much easier to keep a barrier between them.

Finally, she removed the gun from where she wedged it against the door, which fortunately remained shut. She had her doubts about the latch without it, but for the moment, it remained exactly where it was supposed to be.

During their somewhat violent meeting, she took the weapon from one of the soldiers and used it immediately without needing to think about it. That made her uneasy. Victoria knew she should have needed at least a few moments to learn how the weapon worked, where all the controls were, and what exactly it did. Instead, everything about it was as familiar to her as the movements of combat or breathing.

The feeling continued—though whether it was worse or better, Victoria could not say—as she looked over the weapon. She knew the terms for all of the pieces she had never before seen, and knew how it all functioned. The magazine fell with the light press of a button. A twist and an action of a lever and she removed the shroud around the barrel. After that, disassembling the entire weapon took no time at all. She spread it out on the floor after brushing aside the dust and debris there, then put it all back together exactly as it had been before.

Fully assembled, the rifle was significantly shorter than her extended arm, but felt comfortable nonetheless. The other soldiers carried similar weapons, including smaller backup arms, and she reasoned the man from whom she took this particular one could use one of them instead.

Victoria set the rife down just long enough to put her backpack on first, then dropped the shoulder sling across her chest. The sword she stole from the elite continued to work well enough as a walking stick, and so she carried it in her hand. She pulled the charging handle, feeling everything inside the weapon click firmly. As far as she was concerned, this was her weapon as much as the others were.

Victoria returned to the larger room where the soldiers were finished with their camp. On the way there, she heard most of them exchanging words and picked up their names easily enough. Remembering names came easy to her as each of the soldiers moved differently. Little bits and details like that made it easy to keep track of who was who.

Two stood guard, chief among them the man named Photeos. The only one to wear a green stripe, he seemed to be in charge of the soldiers themselves, but he still deferred to the one named Pallasophia. He stood watching to the left, weapon at the ready. Beside Photeos, the woman Myrto stood watching the outer hallway to the right.

Off to one side, another pair of soldiers worked on a similar device to the one she used to attract their attention in the first place. Like the other, this one was set into the floor, but from across the room, Victoria could not tell anything else about it. Logically, she assumed it served a similar, if not identical function.

As soon as she stepped into the room, several things happened. Victoria assigned them varying degrees of importance. Of least importance, the two guards at the door turned to give her a minor nod of acknowledgment, then returned their attentions to the hallway outside. Second, the two technicians working on the machine in the floor looked up for a moment. Unlike the guards, these no longer wore their helmets and seemed to regard Victoria with a mixture of awe and fear.

Given that her rifle's previous owner was one of those technicians, that reaction suited Victoria just fine.

The most interesting reaction, however, came from Pallasophia, the ostensible commander of the team. Without a helmet, she rose and carefully approached Victoria. She held her hands out by her side, palms forward to clearly show she had no weapons. Her face was open as well, eyes wide and relaxed, doing everything she could to present as little threat as she possibly could.

Inside her helmet, Victoria regarded her for a moment. Pallasophia moved with the same lethal grace as the others, but carried herself just a little bit higher through the shoulders. She was beautiful as well, just like the others, but the effort she put into not appearing like a threat seemed to accentuate the effect. Despite her open expression, Pallasophia seemed to be examining Victoria in much the same way as she was the soldiers. Perhaps the most important detail right at that moment, however, was that Pallasophia left all of her obvious weapons on the floor.

Victoria nodded in acknowledgment, trying her best to mimic the way the soldiers greeted one another with curt movements. "Lochagos."

Pallasophia watched her for a moment longer. When she spoke, her voice was different from before. Victoria could tell a difference, she thought, between the intonation and cadence in their voices when they were being formal and when they were more relaxed. It went beyond the words themselves or even the conjugations, touching on the sound of her voice itself.

"I wanted to apologize," she said. "For earlier."

Victoria growled. She did not have the control over her voice that the soldiers seemed to have. Her throat, dry, cracked as she spoke. "For trying to corner me?"

"Yes."

A moment passed and Victoria forced herself to stay calm, to approach this conversation exactly like she would a combat. Deep breaths, smooth movements, she reminded herself. She inhaled slowly, feeling her lungs expand exactly like they would in a fight. "You acted on the best information you had."

Pallasophia started to speak, then stopped. Finally, she said, "that's it?"

Victoria stepped closer by a single pace. She was significantly larger than any of the soldiers and, having been up close with the giant mastigas types, she knew how intimidating size could be. For the moment, she loomed, playing it to its fullest. "*Should* there be anything else?"

Pallasophia's face closed off, not quite a frown, but clearly a defensive measure. "After the way you attacked us, I assumed there would be."

213

"You were an unknown. I had to make sure you couldn't threaten me before we could talk."

Pallasophia, despite the underlying threat, laughed. "You did an admirable job."

Victoria growled. "I had more than my share of practice."

"Another thing I wanted to apologize for."

Victoria simply stared at her, an impassive mask of black plastic.

After a moment, Pallasophia continued, somewhat more formally. "What we put you through was..." She groped for words, shifting in place slightly. To Victoria's surprise, she seemed to come closer. "Immoral, perhaps. But it had to be done."

"Because of the mastigas?" Victoria demanded, putting things together in her mind. Her tone was grim and tight, but something told her to keep the volume down, that only Pallasophia needed to hear.

She shifted again, and Victoria allowed herself to be pushed backward, away from the others. She could kill this woman if she had to, and Pallasophia had to know that. Bringing Victoria out of range of her squad was a measure of trust.

Victoria reciprocated, moving backward of her own volition. If privacy was what she wanted, Victoria would give her that. A few paces further away, and she spoke again. "I disarmed your soldiers. I could have killed them, and you, back there. And so you locked me down here, with the mastigas, so that I could become the soldier your people can't be."

"That's not all there is to it."

"Explain."

"Walk with me?" Pallasophia gestured with raised eyebrows to the door where Victoria cleaned her wounds.

Victoria wasted no time considering the offer. She gave her own gesture of trust, turning her back to Pallasophia and taking the lead. That she was their commander was obvious enough, and so her desire to talk where they could not be overheard was a lure.

She entered the room and continued walking to the far side. There, against the back wall of the room where she could interpose her body between Pallasophia and her weaponry and what remained of her food and water, Victoria unloaded her shoulders of gear piece by piece. Behind her back, Pallasophia's light and measured footsteps followed, stopped, and the door clicked shut as she latched it.

She turned, ready to speak, but Pallasophia opened first. "First, sealing you down here wasn't part of the original plan. I was telling the truth before when I said there was an accident where the elite and sophont escaped containment. You, or one of your predecessors, were supposed to fight them and learn from them. Eventually, you were supposed to beat them on even ground."

"It was that or let them gut me," Victoria growled, accusatory. "Of course, this damnable place has dangers all its own. Others starved, or suffocated, or were poisoned. The mastigas were not the only killer you left down here."

"I know." Pallasophia paused. Victoria wondered if honesty was warring with a convenient lie, or if she simply had no idea how to proceed. Her eyes darted around Victoria's face, subconsciously looking for human features in the helmet's blank mask. Finally she finished her thought. "I watched them. All of them."

Victoria felt a flash of anger. She supposed the story about having set things up for her to fight the mastigas made sense. Now that she knew the purpose for her prison, it was logical that they would have been watching her as well. It was all logical. Despite that, hearing the fact spoken aloud infuriated her.

Victoria hissed. "And you did nothing?"

Pallasophia gestured toward the door. "Second Lord Eleni is here because she helped install the conduits that run through the floor. Those same conduits, some of the only ones to survive years of mastigas habitation, ran directly from the labs in the upper levels to the room where you first woke up."

215

"You're the reason I remember so much about those lives, about things I've never seen." She gestured to the gun where it leaned against her backpack behind her right leg. "Like that."

Pallasophia nodded.

Victoria laughed. The conflicting rush of emotions she felt as things fell into place was almost dizzying. One thought made her want to strangle the black-haired woman in front of her, and the next made her want to trust her. "So, what, you woke us up one by one until I finally killed that damn elite?"

Slowly, very slowly, Pallasophia nodded. "Each time one of..." A pause while she seemed to be correcting something she almost said, then she continued. "Your predecessors died, that knowledge was passed on. Skills, warnings, each time they survived longer."

Victoria growled, feeling her fists tighten at her sides. "That's monstrous."

"Yes." She made no attempt to lie.

"Why?"

She spoke slowly. "We already lost one person coming to find you. Isodorus was a trained soldier with years of experience. Your predecessors..." She turned away from Victoria for a moment, then repeated herself. "Your predecessors would have all died if we woke them up all at once."

"So they were sacrificed to make me what I am. Again, the soldier your people cannot be."

"There's more, but yes."

"Tell me."

"I'll tell you when we get out of here," she said. "I promise."

When nothing else came, Victoria said, "I suppose I should thank you, then."

"We came to retrieve you. No, we came to protect you."

A sharp gesture from Victoria cut her off. "No. Not that. You wouldn't have come unless I killed that elite and the sophont. I should

216

thank you for waking me up so I could stand here now, having done your killing for you."

Pallasophia's face grew harder for a moment. "I brought five people down with me. We lost one in a fight against a single juvenile elite. Victoria, you killed a full-grown elite with a knife."

With short, clipped syllables, Victoria repeated herself again. "The soldier your people could not be."

"I would have gone in your place!" Pallasophia snapped.

"In my...?"

"Yes, if you died as well, *I* would have been the one to take your place."

The tension in Victoria's jaw softened. That changed matters. If this woman was willing to put her own life as risk like that, it placed her much higher in Victoria's esteem. She still had no real idea what her purpose was, but her life had been a hell already.

"Again, why?"

"That's one of those things I need to tell you later."

"Why couldn't you just include it in one of those damnable dreams?"

Pallasophia turned to face her directly with her face set in a hard mask. "After the Incident, we worked on the method we used to synthesize information for you. We could only pass on so much, and so we focused on combat."

Something in her face made Victoria stop for a moment. The expression there was not regret, not exactly, but rather a mixture of it and fear and anger.

"That's why we're in here, isn't it? You'd rather they think you're a monster for locking me down here than they know the truth."

"Not quite. The official story is that you were awakened accidentally while we worked on a way to reopen the facility and extract your gestation pod."

"But that is still not the truth."

Pallasophia nodded slowly. She spoke with equal care. "Project Titan itself is no secret, but the things that went on here at Aphelion were."

Victoria's voice was flat when she spoke. "You built me."

Pallasophia sighed. The noise seemed not to be directed at Victoria so much as inward, at Pallasophia herself. "Not like a machine, no, but you're not far from the truth."

Victoria's fists clenched automatically. Inside their wraps of black mastigas fabric, her knuckles went white as her fingertips dug in. "One more question, then. Why?"

Pallasophia sighed again, once more at herself, or perhaps Victoria thought she might have been sighing at the situation at large. "You've already answered that question, Victoria. The mastigas..." She paused, looked away. "We don't know where they came from, or why. Nothing we've done has stopped them. We've repelled them, yes, but only with catastrophic losses. It's been thirty years."

Pallasophia turned to face Victoria again. She started to reach a hand out, but Victoria pulled away. After a moment she said, "so we created you."

Victoria's head swam. To be born into a world of darkness and blood and then told she had been created, literally created, to fight the monsters with which she had spent the last week trapped was almost too much of a whiplash of thoughts.

She still felt anger; it simmered under the surface, but she had no idea who or what it should be directed at. Pallasophia went out of her way to admit that she was responsible for the torment here in the facility, but Victoria also knew that without Project Titan, she would never have been born.

She asked herself if she should direct her hate at the mastigas. They, directly, had been the things trying to kill her. The Technocrats might have put her where she was, mastigas hands wielded the knives that left the scars in her skin. Also, if Pallasophia was telling the truth, which

Victoria suspected she was, the mastigas's actions had indirectly led to her predicament as well.

Her thoughts swam until she forced them into a cage in the back of her mind where she could deal with them later. Another question rose to her mind. "What about the others?"

"Others?"

"My shell, the place where you turned me into..." She gestured to herself, then forced those angry, frustrated thoughts down as well. She growled to herself. "It was inscribed with numbers and letters. They were all the same except for the symbol for their order. Mine, number one hundred, was last. There was another number; they were all numbered 'six.' Why?"

"First Lord Tritogenes, Hexarch Tritogenes if you're feeling formal, designed Project Titan to be shared among his colleagues. Six Hexarchs means six branches of the Project."

"Then there are five more like me."

"Not exactly like you. The other Projects are all different."

"I see."

After a tense silence, Pallasophia slipped a hand into one of the pockets on her uniform. Victoria watched her with caution, ready to spring one way or the other at the first sign of a weapon. The Technocrat had been honest with her, or so it seemed so far, but they did not mean Victoria was going to let her guard down.

"I also wanted to give you this," she said, holding out a small device.

Victoria examined it without taking it. It was roughly fist sized, with no obvious control surface or way to interact with it. She had seen the Technocrats using holographic interfaces enough to safely assume that was how it worked, however.

Pallasophia added, "it's medical. It contains a dozen doses of a combination of chemicals and things we call quick heal."

Victoria slowly extended a hand and took the device. She tapped it and a floating, blue menu appeared in the air a few centimeters above it.

219

The options seemed straightforward enough, and she skimmed the explanations—oral dosages for light healing over the whole body or apply directly to the wound for more powerful local effects.

She eyed Pallasophia for a moment. If she wanted Victoria dead, this would be the perfect way to do it. Or, if she was telling the truth earlier, if she wanted to poison her as another test of her toughness, this would also serve that purpose.

On the other hand, Victoria thought with a bit of a rueful smile inside her mask, how could she expect these Technocrats to trust her if she was not willing to trust them?

She selected the whole-body option and a port on one end opened. The holographic instructions told her to upend the device and drink from it like a bottle, and she did so.

The quick heal tasted strange. The liquid was thick, sweet, and had a gritty consistency she found unpleasant. It was also warm, or perhaps that was the chemicals themselves making her mouth and throat feel warm. In any case, that feeling of warmth hit her stomach and spread slowly elsewhere. It would take some time to reach her extremities. She pocketed the device, intending to use a heavy dose on her side later.

She turned back to Pallasophia and nodded. "Thank you."

A look of vast relief washed across the other woman's face. "You're welcome."

"Now what?"

"My people need rest and the quick heal will still take some time. Will you be ready in the morning?"

Inside the helmet, Victoria raised an eyebrow. "Morning?"

"We've got to sleep for a few hours before we move on."

Victoria did not mention that, excluding the time she slept in the elite's lair, she never slept that long at one time. She supposed the two of them had enough conflict for the moment, and arguing over sleep would not be productive. Instead, she nodded. "And in the morning?"

"We need to clear out the rest of the facility to prevent the mastigas from coming into the common areas above us."

She nodded. Inside the mask, her face split into a toothy expression that might have fallen under a liberal definition of a smile. "I'll sleep in here. Tomorrow, there are mastigas to kill."

***

Victoria awoke long before the others. As always, she slept in her clothing and helmet, which produced interesting and painful stiffness in her neck and shoulders. A few minutes passed as she went through the stretching routine she learned in her dreams after that first day, and her full range of motion slowly returned.

When she left the room to rejoin the soldiers, Victoria left her sword and backpack. Judging from the sounds, or lack of thereof, the soldiers remained asleep. She could come back for those things once they were finally ready to move. Until then, all she needed was her usual weapons, the knives and baton, plus the gun taken from Stavros.

True to sound, only one of the soldiers was awake. One of them stood guard by the door, back facing the sleeping soldiers. Until she moved, all Victoria could tell was that the guard was neither Pallasophia nor Photeos. Pallasophia still slept nearby, while Photeos, the only one with a green stripe of his sleeves, slept on the far side of the room.

She moved, broad shoulders and long legs, making it obvious to Victoria's eye that Myrto was the one guarding the door. She turned, and her helmeted face nodded in Victoria's direction. Victoria returned the gesture and Myrto returned her attention to the hallways outside.

For a moment, Victoria considered ignoring her, but the soldiers made an effort to talk to her on their way to this safe-room. After talking to Pallasophia, Victoria supposed she could make an effort at conversation. With Myrto being the only one awake at the moment, her options were limited until the others were ready to depart.

"You didn't sleep very long," Myrto commented as Victoria came to stand next to her.

221

"What do you consider not very long?"

"Assuming you went to sleep immediately after the Lochagos left your room? Twenty-three minutes."

"It was long enough. When do we leave?"

Myrto laughed. "Assuming the boss lets everyone sleep a full night? Eight hours."

Victoria frowned, aware that the gesture was lost to anyone on the outside of her mask. "And if not?"

"At least another hour and a half, but after the hell of a time we had fighting that baby elite..."

Victoria interrupted her. "Baby elite?"

Myrto nodded. "Shortly before we found you, we ran across some kind of half-grown elite. Stavros was saying there's some theories that they grow from mikros, but that's all I know about it."

"You've never studied your enemy?"

She shrugged. "No one has, really. They sit out at the edge of our system killing everything nearby. The only time they actually attacked was when they hit Kipos about five years ago."

"Five years..." Victoria muttered.

"Yeah. Project Titan started right after that. Hey, so, can I ask you something?"

Victoria turned to face her, momentarily regretting the concealing masks they both wore. Her tone sounded cautious, but without an actual face, she found it difficult to accurately gauge the other woman's emotions. Finally, she nodded.

"You were born down here, right?"

Another nod.

"Glaukos told us what happened. Things must have been pretty bad down here."

Cautiously, Victoria replied. "They were, yes."

"Thank Selene you're alright, then."

Victoria slowly nodded. She was tempted to tell Myrto what really happened, about the others, their deaths, but bit back that particular retort. She asked herself what good it would do to tell them the version of things they knew had been heavily sanitized.

Instead, she said, "I'm grateful, yes."

"They told us you were trained before birth. Is birth even the right word for what happened to you?"

Something about the woman's enthusiasm was infectious and Victoria found it hard to resist her charm. Still, without divulging the complete truth, she could only tell so much. "I dreamed a lot. Sometimes when I sleep, I still..."

Down the hall, Victoria heard a noise that stopped any further conversation. Without consciously thinking about it, she swept up her rifle, brought it to her shoulder, and scanned the hallway through the scope.

"What is it?" Myrto asked.

Victoria held up her hand in a gesture she picked up from watching the soldiers. She assumed the raised hand with her palm outward meant "stop talking," anyway. That was the usual reaction from the others when Pallasophia or Photeos made the gesture.

Apparently, it worked, and Myrto said nothing else. She also drew herself up a little straighter and raised her own weapon.

The noise came again, closer this time. Repetition and proximity allowed Victoria to identify the source of the sound. Approaching them were two mastigas, small ones, probably more mikros. They moved slowly, carefully, obviously aware that the humans were holed up in a room with nowhere to go.

She relayed that information to Myrto as soon as she was sure it was accurate.

"I'm going to wake the others."

"Don't."

223

"If I don't, gunfire is going to be their alarm, and we don't need that kind of stress after that thing killed Isodorus."

Victoria considered that, then nodded. "Be quick."

The two mastigas came into view a few minutes later. Victoria heard motion behind her, but never broke her concentration on the hallway. The sounds behind her were not mastigas; the Technocrats did not move like the green-eyes. She had nothing to fear from those noises, and so she ignored them.

Finally, she had something to pay attention to. Stavros joined her at the door, carrying a weapon similar to the one she took from him, but different in form. The instructional voice in her head told her his rifle was heavier than hers—his old one—and fired more slowly, but fired much larger rounds.

Victoria nodded. It would do.

"Location?" he whispered.

She closed her eyes, listening to the sound of footsteps. Something else was there, just loud enough to be heard, but too quiet for her to discern amid the sounds of the Technocrat camp rousing itself to wakefulness. Instead, she focused on the footsteps of the mikros.

"They're close. Around that corner," she finally replied, gesturing with one hand at a bend in the hallway about ten meters from their position. "Follow me."

She spared a momentary glance at Stavros to make sure he followed, then moved to the corner in a fast, low crouch. She pressed her back against the wall just short of the corner.

"On three," she said, then counted. When she hit three, she dropped to the floor, shoulder first. She hit the ground, rolled, and came up with her rifle at her shoulder in the same moment that Stavros rounded the corner, standing upright.

One of the mikros screamed, a high, shrill noise that sounded more like an alarm than anything else. She flashed back to some of her first memories—at least the earliest memories that actually belonged to her body and brain, anyway. Gigas or worse came running in answer to that call then.

All of those thoughts passed in less than a second. The mikros was not even done sounding its alarm call when she gently squeezed the trigger of her short rifle. Training printed into her brain held the weapon still with the same precision of the trained soldier beside her.

The bullets slammed into the mikros's torso, staggering it off of its feet. A single cough of fire from Stavros's gun took it square in the head and it crumpled instantly.

The other mikros turned and sprang away, moving on hideously long legs. Victoria fired again, as did Stavros. Most of the bullets hit the walls, but a splash of vibrant red on the back wall indicated that at least one of the rounds hit home, probably in the fleeing mastigas's leg.

Stavros surged forward. "After it!"

Victoria rose. A movement driven more by instinct than conscious thought extended her hand and she snatched at the back of his jacket. She grabbed more roughly than she meant to and threw him backwards. He stumbled and fell.

"What the hell?"

For a moment, anger flashed through Victoria's mind. His tone brought out a desire for violence in her, but she choked it down. When she spoke, however, she channeled that feeling of violence into her words. "Chasing after it like that is a good way to get yourself killed!"

"That 'thing' is a scout!" he retorted. "It's going to tell the others that we're here."

"You think I don't know that?" she growled. "How many of them do you think I fought down here? How many did I kill? Did you not hear it yelling?"

Stavros nodded reluctantly.

"They already know we're here. All chasing after that mikros is going to do is lead us into any trap they have for us."

"They're not smart enough to lay a trap!"

Victoria's eyes narrowed in automatic disbelief. She knew he could not see the gesture, but it had been an unconscious reaction. "Wolves can set traps, can't they? Herd prey into the jaws of the other wolves? Mastigas are at least as smart as that. If there are others out there, and you chase after that mikros, you'll be running right into their arms."

She had only the faintest idea of what a wolf actually was, but the words and the analogy came to her nonetheless.

Victoria had no chance to voice anything else as a shout of alarm from their safe room brought her and Stavros back in a run.

Victoria momentarily unshouldered her rifle, using the stock to bounce against the doorframe as she careened into the room. She had never heard a shout of alarm from another human being before, but the sound sent shivers down her spine and her heart thundered in her ears as a single overriding instinct projected itself onto her brain.

PROTECT.

She cursed at the sight. Three fonias stood on their feet, menacing the Technocrat soldiers with their knives. At such a close range, and with so many of their own people around, their guns suddenly became useless. At those ranges, the little knife-armed monsters were many times more deadly than they would have been if the soldiers had a clear shot.

To one side, Photeos rolled along the ground, grappling with a fourth fonias. The small mastigas were phenomenally strong, but Photeos seemed to be holding his own. In the half-second that Victoria watched him, he reversed an attempted pin and rapidly gained the upper hand.

She ignored Photeos, turning her attention to the others. Eleni blocked a slash from one of the fonias with her rifle, but the thing kicked her in the stomach a moment later and she crumpled. Pallasophia and Myrto stood back to back, facing off against the remaining fonias as the knife-wielders circled them.

"Stavros!" she snapped. "Help them!"

He nodded, dropping the rifle and drawing a dagger of his own from his boot.

Victoria put him out of her mind as well, returning her attention to Eleni. The fonias had her pinned with one hand on her throat. The other held one of their signature knives raised high, ready to plunge into whatever soft target presented itself first.

She did not give it time to choose a target. Dropping her rifle to the floor, Victoria snatched the weapon she was most familiar with from her belt. The baton settled into her hand nicely as she crossed the room in bounding steps, the last of which gave her the momentum to smash the fonias's skull into a mess of blood and brains. Her stroke knocked it away from Eleni as well, allowing her to come to her feet again.

A shout from behind interrupted Victoria's second swing, aimed again at the fonias's skull to make absolutely sure it was dead. The overriding instinct in her brain to *protect* those around her stopped her hand and turned her feet almost before Victoria was aware of the thought forcing her way through her skull.

Victoria pivoted on her heels, taking in the scene as she dashed toward it.

Photeos kicked the fonias away from him, and the lithe creature rolled backward and to its feet. It jumped away from Photeos and tackling Stavros instead. Fortunately, it lost its daggers when Photeos dropped it, but that only made the mastigas marginally less deadly than it had been before. It, and Stavros, rolled away as the mastigas savagely clawed at his chest.

Pallasophia kicked the fonias away from her, turned, and dove onto the mastigas tearing its way through Stavros's bloody clothing. The two of them rolled away as Pallasophia's limbs wrapped around the mastigas, pinning it with her legs before Victoria could get close enough to help. By the time Victoria passed, Pallasophia already slit the monster's throat.

Photeos and Victoria collided with the third fonias at nearly the same moment. Reflexively, she drove the handle of her baton into its face, kicked it—and by extension Photeos—away, and slammed the baton into its skull. Knife in hand, Photeos grappled the fonias, pulling it the rest of the way to the ground amid a flurry of blood and steel.

She turned toward the last one. Myrto bled from several wounds on her forearms as the fonias slashed wildly with both knives it carried. Without thinking, Victoria threw one of her own knives across the short distance, embedding it in the mastigas's chest. It screamed and lunged forward, blindly attacking the closest target.

It and Myrto fell to the floor as Victoria and Pallasophia covered the few meters between them. Out of the corner of her eye, Victoria saw Eleni kneeling over Stavros, fiddling with something in her hand that she assumed was quick heal.

Pallasophia reached the fonias first, delivering a brutal kick using her own running momentum. It flew a meter into the air where Victoria caught it, pivoted, and slammed it bodily onto the floor. One arm ended up under the mastigas, but the other remained free to rain down blows until it stopped moving.

Victoria stood, looking around the room for more enemies to fight. When her eyes fell on Pallasophia, however, that instinct changed. Pallasophia knelt over Myrto, muttering something under her breath. Something inside her softened, and Victoria knelt in time to hear the last few words.

"...not very religious, Second Lord, but..."

A wet cough answered her.

"May Selene's light shine on you forever." She looked up and, despite the masks between them, Victoria knew their eyes met. "She's dead."

Chapter 13

The view from any given balcony on the exterior of Odyssey's dome was a swirl of color to the human eye. Odyssey itself was fully enclosed, even the balconies and windows on the outside were fairly small compared to the vast bulk of the former starship. The closest thing the city had to a truly open area, at least completely open to the elements, was the landing pad that occupied the very top of the dome. Even that could be covered by meticulously maintained doors if the need arose.

The surrounding areas, however, told another story. Much of that space was open to the sky, built to be a deliberate contrast to the vast bulk of the capital city proper. Those outlying towns, themselves cities in their own right, stretched off in every direction around Odyssey in a mixture of architectural styles spanning a thousand years. Most of them had, at one point or another, been fairly far away from Odyssey, but as their footprint grew, separation shrank.

Now, many of the surrounding cities were literally attached to Odyssey itself. Bridges and causeways spanned gaps between buildings built on Prosgeiosi and the outer shell of the ship that brought them to that planet in the first place. Those bridges connected to what were at one point in the distant past docking bays or large personnel hatches.

Now, those vast doors stood permanently open, admitting a constant flow of foot and vehicle traffic in every direction.

In and among the colors of the building and landscape themselves moved people and vehicles in a vibrant profusion of color as well. By far, blue and green were the dominant colors worn by those moving around, the robes of thousands of Second and Third Lords creating a visual sea of blue-green. Here and there yellow robed Fourth Lords congregated and groups of orange-clad Fifth Lords and even red Sixth Lords moved through the crowd.

From Odyssey's upper balconies, however, the effect was muted. The smear of color as people moved around the streets far below was much less interesting than the vista of the cities themselves or the landscape beyond. Odyssey and its child cities sat in the middle of a vast open plain, the one of the largest in Prosgeiosi's temperate zone, chosen over a thousand years ago as humanity's new home.

Unlike most, Second Lord Panatakis was actually more interested in the people moving down below than the mountains in the distance. Without serious focus, he could not really hear things at that distance, anyway. Certain sounds echoed, but most of those heralded some sort of violence: gunfire, explosions, and the like. Odyssey was thankfully free of that type of noise. The general press of humanity produced more than enough noise to echo off those mountains, but the image that came to his brain was unclear, muddy. He tended to ignore sound like that.

If Panatakis really wanted to see the mountains that badly, all he had to do was reconfigure his implants so that they processed visual data the same way everyone else did. He rarely did that and much preferred to live in the world as he saw it now. Sounds produced splashes of color whose brightness and shade corresponded to loudness and pitch. He could do the opposite with light, but for the moment his focus was on sound, and he allowed no optical data into his brain.

Standing on his balcony, he could "see" everything that made a noise loud enough to hear. Picking individual things out of the cacophony was not easy. Especially with an entire city's worth of noise, the exercise was much like a normally-sighted person trying to solve a hidden image puzzle.

Complicating the difficulty was that none of the people below him stayed in the same place. He would begin to pick one out of the crowd, then they would vanish into a loud conversation or enter a vehicle or building. Sometimes, Panatakis could listen to the noises they made long enough to start to get a picture of what a person looked like. Truly identifying people, even those he knew, from this distance was impossible, but that did not mean he never tried. Everyone moved a little differently and even from a long distance some of those patterns were identifiable.

Today, however, the press of people was too thick for that sort of detail. He could follow them here and there, but only for a few seconds. Rather than distinct splashes of color, the best he could manage was to pick out a slightly brighter swirl here and there. Vehicular traffic was also unusually high, drowning out all but the loudest sounds of people moving around.

Those, at least, he could follow easily enough. Before Project Titan, he could not have identified more than a handful of the most popular vehicle brands across the entire binary. Since then, not only had he learned to understand the different sounds, but Panatakis could also diagnose a great many problems with their engines from up close. He could not hear that kind of detail even in the largest vehicles outside, but identifying them by make and model was easy enough.

The clock had not even struck noon yet, but the majority of the traffic below was luxury models. Ironically, those were the hardest to identify by sound because they often came with an entire suite of noise canceling devices. When they made noise, it was a low, red rumble, dim and hard to make out past the louder colors of higher-altitude freight haulers.

It made sense, he rationalized, watching the river of luxury cars fly by below in a streak of dim red so dark it was almost brown. Not only would people be coming to Odyssey to watch the Council session, but the day after that was the formal dinner and ball for the Titans. Unlike the Council meeting, those events were technically private, but a great number of tickets had been sold to those with the means to afford them.

The following weeks marked the end of Project Titan, officially, and would be dominated by the ceremony where the six of them were "officially" introduced to the populace. Since the installation of his implants, Panatakis found he enjoyed pomp and ceremony much more than he used to. The plethora of information available to him, even with his senses no more sensitive than a human's, was fascinating. If he enhanced one or more of them at a gathering like that, he often learned all manner of interesting information.

He also kept most of that from his Hexarch, informing her only of the implants' success at first restoring his sight and then later allowing him to adjust his senses so that the information from one could be routed to any of the others. He obviously trusted First Lord Eurybia with his life, otherwise he never would have allowed her scientists to operate on his nervous system, but Panatakis had no real desire to play the secret-finding game that the Hexarchs prided themselves on.

He set aside an hour for the perception exercise, and that time was nearly up. Now, as the last few minutes ticked by, he turned his attention to the landscape at large. People, vehicles, and all motions down at the street level faded into a seething sea of colors. Sparks of light popped in places as loud noises cut through, but nothing down there caught his attention anymore. Instead, he tried to picture the landscape itself as it spread out below him.

This exercise required some actual visual data, which Panatakis slowly added to the stream of aural information running through his optic nerves. His goal was to try and create a complete picture of the area around him using nothing but sound, then compare it to how things actually looked. This exercise, like most of his others, was one Panatakis himself invented. No one else understood exactly how he perceived the world, and he quickly surpassed Eurybia's scientists in his understanding of his implants. Panatakis reasoned that if he could assemble a portrait of something the size of Odyssey's suburbs, then imaging a single room or building would be easy.

In a way, it required even more concentration than trying to pick out a single sound-color. That was difficult enough, but once he acquired a "lock" on something, it was easy enough to trace out the path of color as it moved. Capturing an entire area in his mind required him to focus on things in every direction and keep track of a multitude of tiny sounds and colors as the world moved.

Fortunately, Panatakis had years of practice at this point.

His implants afforded him a great deal of control over his bodily functions and in moments, he stilled his pulse to the point that even its noise would be a quiet murmur in the background. For obvious reasons, he could not keep it up for very long, and so his goal became to piece together as much information in as short a time as possible. As his heart slowed, Panatakis pushed awareness of his body out of his mind. Bones, muscles, the sound of cloth against his skin, all of that was happening to someone else for the next few moments.

He inhaled, the last breath he would take before breaking the trance.

Odyssey's surface sloped away on either side, gleaming in the twinned sunlight. Visually, the city's shell was just reflective enough to merit the term "opalescent" without being uncomfortable to look at. Aurally, it might have been pitted with millions of imperfections, but the overall effect was heavily reflective as well. Panatakis used that sound to map out the curve far beyond what human eyes could have perceived.

Eantio, to his left spread out in low-lying villas originally built on the verdant banks of Iason's River. That city was never very loud, but sounds always came from discrete areas within its limits. Parks, open-air concert halls, and the like dotted Eantio's cityscape, and the straight-line roads originally built to connect the widespread villas produced crisp, even echoes. To his senses, the colors of Eantio were dark, quiet, but easy to see. Panatakis could trace out every road in that city with his mind.

Across an imaginary line laid down as the two cities spread, Tavros's towers rose in a forest of glass and steel to his right. That city was loud at all times of day and night. Panatakis wondered how those living right on the boundary of either city coped with the sudden cultural shift from one side of the road to the other.

Tavros was alive with motion and noise. Vehicles swarmed around its buildings without cease, especially during the day. The colors barely changed at night when the cool air carried sound even farther. By contrast to Eantio, he had trouble imagining Tavros from this distance. It was so noisy and the profusion of tall, reflective buildings twisted the colors of the city's sounds back upon themselves.

The sounds from Tavros produced a clear outline, unlike Eantio's slow fade into the countryside. However, unlike the well-planned villa streets to his left, the roads of Tavros wound around the buildings like a knot of yarn. Inside the city, down on the ground amid all those towers, Panatakis could focus on some of those sounds, but from that distance most of what reached his mind was a bright muddle of color with no rhyme or reason to it.

Ironically, the sheer volume of noise coming from Tavros made the Odyssey's shell easier to image on his right side. The parts of the city's exterior that reflected sound from Eantio were fuzzy by comparison.

As the burning in his lungs started to override the mental blocks he placed on the sensations of his body, Panatakis saved a mental snapshot of the landscape to his implants' memory. Allowing his heart and lungs to function at their normal rate again, he compared that image to the one he took the week before, finding the newer one ever-so-slightly clearer.

The final part of the exercise required the visual data he had prepped before holding his breath. Panatakis tuned things so that he could see the visual spectrum for a few seconds and compared that image to the one he assembled by sound. The colors, of course, were nothing like reality, but reality was drab and boring by comparison. What was important was the clarity of the image itself, and in that area both were nearly identical. In fact, his auditory map contained more detail than the limited point of view provided by his eyes could generate.

He felt a swell of pride in his chest as his accomplishments. Not bad, he told himself, for a man who was nearly blind six years ago.

Finally, he checked all of the mundane data coming in from his implants. Simple things like temperature, humidity, and barometric pressure were possible even with his first generation of implants. At this point in his training, he used those data readouts more as accuracy checks than anything else. If his implants agreed with the computer in his pocket, which they always did, then he knew he could trust them.

Panatakis stepped back into "his" Odyssean suite. First Lord Eurybia technically owned the opulently expensive apartment, but she gave it to him for his use shortly after the first successful trial of his earliest implants. Even by Odyssey's standards, the multi-room suite was expensive, the sort of place that he never would have been able to afford inside the space-starved dome without his Hexarch's aid.

The few people who came to visit often commented on his unusual taste in decoration, but those people saw with their eyes. As he moved, his footsteps and even the rustle of his robes set echoes moving through the air around him.

Those sounds reflected off his various art pieces and unusually-shaped furniture in a variety of ways. Pitches rose or fell when they encountered strange angles and curves. At times, an echo would be louder than the sounds that produced it when a noise fell into one of the strange, parabolic sculptures in just the right way.

His hard-soled shoes produced sharp blue clicks that bounced in pulses around and through everything, while the shifting of his robe around his feet played a red-orange counterpoint in smooth waves. He whistled a single, sharp note, interjecting a spear of purple into the air that spread outward, bouncing and throwing everything for a few meters into sharp relief.

With his daily practice over, he re-opened his senses the rest of the way. A flood of sound came to him, color translated into pitch and volume in the exact opposite way that his ears turned sound into light. The scales were similar; brighter light equaled louder sound, and higher-frequency color translated directly into pitch.

The room around him erupted into music as his eyes swept across things. Other art, little more than a mismatch of colors to those poor souls with human eyes, sang to him in ethereal voices. His robe today was a dark blue shot through with dozens of glittering designs. To his mind, the garment hummed a quiet soprano interrupted randomly with the sounds of crystal bells as light caught the silver threads.

Originally, the implants had been designed to restore his sight, possibly enhance it somewhat. Early on, the scientists had been fascinated by the second generation's ability to perceive visual wavelengths ever so slightly into the infrared and ultraviolet range. Panatakis had as well, if he was being fair. It had been so long since his eyes worked at all, that expanding his vision into those bands was no more difficult than restoring it in the first place.

It was not until the third generation, when Eurybia's scientists tried to enhance his other senses, that Panatakis discovered he could "rewire" his brain at will. Ever since then, he tweaked the interface between his implants and his own neural pathways, pushing further to see what was possible.

He often asked himself, with that sort of control over his own mind, why he would ever be tempted to interact with the world in a "normal" way again.

His suite's door chime sounded, bright blue amid the rapidly quieting colors around him. It rang once, the sign of someone in the corridor outside wanting his attention, not necessarily someone with the clout or personal permission to simply enter the room. It might have belonged to

First Lord Eurybia, but as long as the suite was legally his, only people Panatakis permitted could enter.

Just in case, he waited a moment to see if his potential guest rang a second time. He did not wait long, however. Panatakis, for all his ability to focus when he needed to work on something, was not a patient man.

When the door chime did not sound again, he made a hand gesture that his pocket computer would interpret even without the holographic interface active. Hidden microphones around the room picked up his voice and carried it to the door. "May I help you?"

"You have a visitor, sir." His ears interpreted words normally, passing them along to his brain exactly as anyone else would have heard them. Even through a speaker, Panatakis was still privileged to certain additional information. Emotional tones colored everyone's words, and in Panatakis's case it was literal. For whatever reason, the messenger sounded nervous.

"Enter."

The suite's outer door slid open so quietly that the color of its motion was a dim red mist rolling across the floor like fog. Cutting through that fog were the short, sharp footsteps of his sole messenger. Each step was a brief flash of light, bright for just a moment before fading quickly against dull red glow of the wall-to-wall tapestries.

The messenger stepped into his room, allowing Panatakis to see more clearly the noises of his passage. His heartbeat was a ripple, spreading out around him, dim against the bright noises of his feet. His robes hummed in the pleasant, warm tones of silk. Panatakis looked over his shoulder for a moment, taking in the viola hum of his yellow robes just enough enough to attempt a visual identification.

His visitor's robe rustled, stiff. Either a new garment, or the man had been recently elevated. The smooth fabric, unbroken by embroidery, told the rest of the story. "Messenger" was likely his first job since his latest Elevation, and Panatakis wondered what achievements brought him to his newest rank. It did not take very much to rise from Fifth to Fourth, but he was clearly nervous about his newly increased responsibilities.

Panatakis had never seen this man before, and so he turned, inclining his head in greeting. He did not look directly at this messenger, instead keeping him in the periphery of his vision as they spoke.

Panatakis smiled. "Are you my visitor, Fourth Lord?"

"No, sir."

"What is your name, then?"

"Cyrus, sir."

"How are you doing today, Fourth Lord Cyrus?"

Panatakis heard his heart speed up. "Sir?"

"How are you today, Cyrus? It seems a simple enough question."

His heart continued to thunder, sending little ripples out from his chest. "I'm, um. I'm doing well, sir. Thank you for asking. How are you today, Second Lord, Titan, sir?"

Ah, thought Panatakis. There was the cause of his anxiety. He smiled again. "I'm well, thank you. Now, you say I have a visitor? Tell me who and where."

Cyrus nodded, obviously put a little at ease by Panatakis's politeness. His heart slowed somewhat, but not very much. "Second Lord Helena, Titan of Dasos, arrived an hour ago and asked to meet you specifically, sir."

"Thank you, Cyrus. Tell Helena I will meet her within the hour at," he paused, thinking, "Three Peaks. You know where it is?"

Cyrus nodded.

"Good. Escort her there yourself, Fourth Lord."

He nodded again. "As you say."

Cyrus turned on his heels and strode out of Panatakis's suite. He seemed, if possible, even more nervous than he had been when entering. Panatakis knew he put the man at ease, and so wondered what suddenly set him off again.

Three Peaks, his personal favorite coffee shop, was not far from his suite and he gave Helena an hour. They might have communicated a few times over the last several days, exchanging messages that were as light on content as possible. Their identities might have been public, but few other details of the Project were, and the risk of their messages being intercepted was too high to risk.

He supposed he could look up whatever public information was available on her, but Panatakis knew nothing had changed since the last time he went looking. At that point, the only things he could find were a handful of old, poor-quality holos registered to an obscure Dasos news agency. They showed Helena from years ago, just after her implants went in and before her hair grew back out.

He could get more information by using Eurybia's personal key, but she tended to be cross when he took those kinds of liberties with her authority. More important right at that moment, going rifling through the Hexarchs' records would be boring.

Why, Panatakis asked himself, should he waste his time with that, when he would have an opportunity to talk in person? After all, he reasoned, they had a lot to talk about—counting himself and Helena, the sum total of human cyborgs was two.

***

Panatakis arrived at Three Peaks a few minutes ahead of his promised hour to find Helena already there and seated. She was easy enough to pick out from the crowd, even for human eyes. Human skin muddied sound, but the metal of her implants, like his own, reflected clearly. They stood out in his mind as though lit from within by some sort of clear blue light.

She stood when he arrived and they shook hands. In person, Panatakis found her to be strangely alluring. The bone structure of her face, and not just that but her entire body, sounded delicate. Someone relying on his eyes might have considered her petite, or any one of a dozen other cliche adjectives, but Panatakis heard the way she moved and the interplay between her human body and the implants. With no way to tell how deep her implants ran, he found it hard to gauge exactly what her physical capabilities were, but between the sound of her muscles and the strength of her grip, Panatakis knew something more than human lurked underneath Helena's skin.

Like him, Helena was a Second Lord. Her robe sang a soprano chorus of blue, pitch perfect and precise. Every fold of her clothing was exactly where it needed to be to produce a beautiful, alluring song. He wondered if she shared his ability to hear colors and designed the drape of her robe to match or if the mathematical precision was simply some other by-product of her own implants.

Above her robe and cascading down the back, her dark hair hummed a rustling bass line. Light reflected off the myriad twists of her braid, strings and deep rumbles that filled out the chorus begun by her robe. Strangely, other than the high polish on her implants, Helena wore no jewelry.

She turned pale blue eyes on him, twinned airy solos that reached heights of pitch the choir making up her robe never could. When she spoke, her lips moved with mathematical precision that lent her words a mechanical quality. "Thank you for agreeing to meet with me, Second Lord Panatakis."

Helena indicated the two chairs of their table, and he sat before replying. "We're both Titans, there's no need for rank between us."

She nodded. "Of course."

"Have you been waiting long?"

"Not long. Seven hundred seconds, perhaps."

"Seven...?" he asked, trying to do the math in his head.

"Apologies. About ten minutes."

"I heard you were prompt," he replied with a laugh. That was one of the few pieces of information he uncovered, from an early interview with First Lord Aegesander himself.

"I value efficiency."

"You'd have to to work with Aegesander."

One metal-clad eyebrow rose. "How so?"

"Have you never met any of the other Hexarchs?"

Helena shook her head.

"That explains it. Aegesander is very, how do I put this? He's very direct. He and Tritogenes have that in common."

"Aegesander does not like Tritogenes very much."

Panatakis laughed. "No. No, he does not. All you need there is to watch any one of the Council meetings over the last, oh, twenty years or so and that becomes clear."

A green-robed Third Lord chose that moment to approach their table and take their order. Helena ordered a heavily-sweetened espresso drink with a single shot of locally-produced brandy added. For himself, Panatakis ordered something much simpler, but still worthy of Three Peaks's austere atmosphere.

"May I ask you something, Panatakis?"

He briefly considered falling back on an old joke and saying, "you just did," but ultimately resisted that urge. Instead he nodded, saying, "of course."

"Do you trust me?"

Panatakis stopped himself before saying anything. That had not been anywhere on the list of questions he expected her to ask, and it took several moments before he could truly process what it was she was asking. The tone she used was not an idle one; whatever Helena was going to ask *next* was clearly important.

What he needed was more information, so he asked for it. "Why?"

"We are similar, you and I, moreso than I and anyone else. I believe I may be able to add a function to your implants they have not yet possessed."

Panatakis laughed. "If that's all it is, then sure. I tweak them all the time and it's been years since I've really minded having someone rooting around in my brain."

"It may be uncomfortable," she said, "if it works at all."

Now, he began to feel a twinge of concern. "You've never done whatever it is you're about to do before?"

Helena shook her head. Her hair scratched out a rhythm on her back that echoed around the room, rippling through the air like waves on a pond. "You are the only one with neural implants I have met. I know what I am capable of, but I can make no promises about what yours can do."

He shrugged. "What's the worst that could happen?"

"Insanity," she replied, deadpan.

Despite the cold chill in his stomach that her tone evoked, he shrugged again. "Let's do it anyway."

"As you wish. Can you lean forward slightly?"

He instinctively bristled at the way she phrased her request, then relaxed. It might have been a little rude, but asking if he *could* do it still gave Panatakis a way out if he decided at the last second to change his mind.

Instead, he shifted slightly, leaning forward.

Helena did likewise, reaching out with both hands. He expected her to take hold of his head or for there to be some dramatic interaction between the two of them, but she simply touched the sides of his head where the largest cranial nodes resided, then sat back in her chair, watching him.

For a moment, nothing happened, then everything went black. All sight, all sound, everything vanished. He was vaguely aware of his own movement and bodily presence, but proprioception was a poor way to navigate the world. Only because the experience, his implants shutting down, was somewhat familiar to him did Panatakis remain calm.

Slowly, over a full minute, his senses returned to him. Hearing came first as the world erupted into conversation and the noise of human interaction. Sight would have followed, if he had any. Panatakis was aware of a tension in his eyes and could feel the muscles there moving, but nothing penetrated the blackness of his vision.

Moments later, he could see again, but the image was fuzzy and unclear. His implants functioned once more, but they showed him the world as everyone else saw it, flat and static. Across the table, Helen'a implants gleamed as highlights against her skin. Her lips, painted a red so dark it might as well have been black to human eyes, were quirked in a quizzical expression, part smile and part patient interest.

Now Panatakis found a reason to be somewhat upset. His senses were working again, but they functioned like those of a normal person. He saw with his eyes and heard with his ears. After spending so much time in his version of the world, to be thrust into the same one experienced by everyone else was a less than pleasant experience.

He kept his eyes, at least what passed for eyes in his machine-infused skull, focused on Helena while he turned his attention inward. The implants did not have menus or anything that would make them easy to navigate. Perhaps if Helena could turn them off with a touch, Panatakis might get her to design an easier to use interface for him at some point. For the time being, however, he slowly pushed against their default settings with his mind.

"Is everything alright?" Helena asked. Her expression had morphed into a look of concern which she took no pains to conceal.

Panatakis realized he was squinting and leaning forward to force just a little more detail into his damaged, human eyes. He sat back, frowned. "My implants reset."

"I apologize. Do you require time to adjust them?"

"Yes."

As it happened, it took somewhat longer than a minute. While he worked, the Third Lord who took their order brought their drinks. Panatakis gave an offhand order for some sort of appetizing food taken at random from the day's specials. He would figure out what he ordered when it came to the table. Fortunately, Three Peaks did not make bad food.

Slowly, colors and lights bled around him, detail and information trickling in like cool air in the Kokkinian heat. As the world came back into proper focus again, Panatakis felt the tension in his neck start to dissipate.

When the world was back the way he wanted it, Panatakis turned his attention back across the table to Helena. Now that he thought about it, other than the occasional drink and the moment when she ordered her food, he did not remember her moving at all while he readjusted his implants.

"Alright, what did you do?"

<This.>

Panatakis jumped in his seat. Her voice came from inside his head, bypassing every single one of his senses. Despite that, the sound was clearly her voice. The intonation might have been a little flatter, lacking the timbre that human vocal cords imparted, but the sounds were all there.

A moment passed and he became aware of her presence in his mind as well. It felt much like the sensation of someone sitting down in a chair next to him, close enough to feel and hear the subtle signs of life like body heat or breath.

Only the feeling was completely different, because she was somehow *in* his mind.

"How?"

<Our implants are connected now. I do not know over what distance the connection will function, but it seems to work well enough at close range.>

"How do I...?"

<Focus your thoughts on me. That should work. Your mental voice, that you use when you give voice to your thoughts and ideas. Converse with that.>

He closed off his eyes and ears for a moment, relying on nothing but the information coming into his implants from Helena. She was colder than he was, somehow, but having only ever touched her mind like this, he had no one else to compare to. Perhaps everyone was like that and one's own mind was always warmer.

Maybe, he thought, that was how he stayed "him." The warm parts were "Panatakis," and the cool parts were "Helena."

"Like," he said, then, <this?>

She radiated a feeling that hit every one of his senses. Sight, sound, even smell combined to create the sensation of a smile without either of them moving a muscle. <Yes. I confess I was afraid it would not work.>

Panatakis returned the feeling, surprised at how easy it was. All he had to do was imagine the feeling of smiling and their shared connection translated that automatically to her. <It seems it worked quite well.>

She radiated a sense of caution. <Let us keep this new ability between us.>

<Literally and metaphorically, you mean.>

<Yes.>

<Why?>

She waited a moment before replying. <Aegesander. He does not trust me. I often found new security measures in place soon after expressing an opinion or that I had found a new way to work through his computers. He is proud, certainly, but also distrustful.>

<Was it that obvious?>

<No. He did much of the changes to his computer system himself. Most unusual for a Hexarch. I do not think I would even have realized it had it not happened more than once.>

<Do you think he's been keeping you isolated so you can't talk to the other Titans?>

<I do not think so. He encouraged me to meet you.> She stopped a moment, awash in caution, then finished that thought. <But all things are possible.>

<That's not reassuring.>

<It is not, no.>

He smiled, both physically and mentally. With a jab of amusement he said, <we'll know by the end of the month one way or the other.>

<Indeed. Have you met any of the others?>

<Korakti,> he replied. <Hyperion's Titan. I have corresponded with Lelantos, but he has yet to leave Kipos.>

<I have spoken to some of the others, but not often,> Helena replied. <I would very much like to meet Tritogenes's Titan. As I grow uneasy working with Aegesander, I feel drawn to Tritogenes. I am unsure why.>

Panatakis laughed with his physical body. Their connection automatically translated it as a flare of color. <Obstinance is a very human trait, Helena.>

<I see. I admit, though, I wish to meet his Titan more than I wish to meet Tritogenes. Even without meeting you or the others, I know a great deal about you from Aegesander's database, but he has nothing on Limani's Titan.>

<Your thoughts feel excited,> he said, aware that ten minute before he would have had zero reference for that feeling.

<His Titan is a mystery. The others have come forward already, at least temporarily. I both like and dislike mysteries.>

<That's called 'curiosity,' Helena.>

<It is an annoying sensation.>

<It'll pass.> He sent a flare of amusement, trying to limit it to just their connection.

She felt his amusement and sent him a burst of curiosity.

<It's kind of funny that people have been trying to figure out telepathy for, what, ten? Fifteen thousand years? And here we are.>

She laughed, a rare verbal sound from her. <The irony, I feel, is that neither Aegesander nor Eurybia expected this outcome.>

<Pretty much. Do you think the others had anything unexpected like this happen?>

She replied with the mental sensation of a shrug. <All things are possible given the drive with which the Hexarchs went after Project Titan.>

<Tritogenes's grand plan.>

She nodded mentally. <Yes. That is in part why I wish to meet his Titan. I would attempt to penetrate his security measures, but we will meet his Titan soon enough.>

<You seem at home working with computer systems.>

Another mental shrug, touched with caution and pride in equal measure. <Aegesander saw fit that I learn to bypass or fortify security, depending on what was needed.>

Panatakis grinned with his physical face and inside their connection. <So, you would consider yourself a skilled strategist?>

Helena hesitated less than a second. <I would.>

He radiated a general feeling of pleasantry between them. <Excellent. Can I interest you in a game of polychess, then?>

He felt a rush of surprise and that same glow of curiosity coming from Helena's mind before she asked, <polychess?>

<You've never heard of it?> His disbelief radiated in an orange flash. <I have not.>

Blue-green amusement bubbled up from his mind, filling the space between their thoughts. <Come, then, you're in for a treat.>

Chapter 14

After hiding Myrto's body where the soldiers said the mastigas should not find it, they packed up their camp and left that area quickly. Privately, Victoria had her doubts about whether their attempts to keep the body hidden had any chance of being effective. If the mastigas were incapable of finding corpses in out of the way places, she reasoned she would have stumbled across some of her predecessors. Until the soldiers, she never found another human, and the mastigas even disappeared their own corpses with alarming speed.

Victoria herself walked at the rear of the group. During the few minutes she was able to speak with Myrto before the attack, Victoria felt a general lessening of tension in the room. A lot of it could have been attributed to the simple fact that most of the soldiers were asleep. Victoria was certain, at least for those few minutes of peace, that at at least some of it came from her talk with Pallasophia. Perhaps she helped smooth things over while Victoria slept.

Since the fight, however, that tension returned. Photeos walked at the front of the group, as far from Victoria as he could. Eleni and Stavros moved with nervous energy, not exactly avoiding her but not coming near either. Only Pallasophia walked close by Victoria, but even she had nothing to say.

"Damn it, where are they?" Eleni cursed, physically smacking the device in her hands. It remained passively unaware of her attempted violence.

Victoria sped up, doublestepping twice. "Where are who?"

Eleni jumped. That she was suddenly on edge was obvious enough from the tension in her shoulders. Her masked face turned toward Victoria for a moment before she replied. "The mastigas."

Victoria nodded. The same thoughts had been eating at her as well. "It's unusual for them to make a small attack like that and then not follow up with anything."

From the front, Photeos scoffed, but said nothing. Victoria might not have noticed if the noise not been pitched to carry.

"Is there something you wanted to add, Lochias?" Victoria asked, hoping she remembered the correct rank for the green-sleeved soldier.

"Killing a few of them is impressive, One Hundred, but it doesn't make you qualified to opine on their tactics."

Victoria bristled. "There's a dead sophont and a dead elite down here. I did more than kill a few of them, I *lived* with them."

Photeos started to snap some sort of fiery retort. In fact, he got as far as cursing before visibly stopping himself and falling silent for a moment. "I apologize. In the interest of open communication, I feel personally responsible for what happened earlier."

"And you think I don't?" Victoria still did not have the control over her emotions that the soldiers displayed, and it came out much harsher than she might have wanted.

"What do you..."

She interrupted. "Do you know how many fonias I've killed?"

"No."

"Me neither, but you can be sure it's more than four. I should have been able to handle that myself with no one getting hurt. Instead, Stavros is hobbling along while a chemical cocktail puts his chest back together and Myrto's body has gone cold under a pile of rocks!"

"The mastigas surprised us," Pallasophia said, physically interjecting herself between Victoria and Photeos. Her voice was calm, level, and seemed to do wonders for both of their emotional states.

"The Lochagos is right," Photeos said after a moment. "When I fought them on Kipos, we would have considered losing two people a fair trade for five dead mastigas."

"Anything so long as someone walks out of there alive, right?" Victoria asked. Her question might have been directed at Photeos, but her face—helmet and all—was turned directly toward Pallasophia.

"There were days that, yes, those were our orders." Photeos was silent for a full minute as they walked. Finally, he added another thought. "Without you, One H—Victoria, we would probably have all died in that ambush. Thank you."

"You're welcome," she replied automatically. His words did nothing to assuage the frustration and anger seething inside her, but they did calm her surface thoughts.

Adding to it, Pallasophia said, "apology accepted, Lochias."

"Eleni's right," Victoria persisted. "It's not normal for them to ignore a fight like that. They always came running after the sounds of fighting. I either had to kill them quietly or run and hide until they lost interest. Otherwise, I would often have to fight several in a row."

Photeos nodded. His back was still to her, but the tension in his shoulders had lessened some. "Without a sophont, they just go after whatever seems the most interesting."

"And by 'interesting,' you mean 'violent,'" Victoria said.

"Or most likely to result in food."

Victoria shuddered. That was a dream she did not want to have again. Pallasophia's masked face turned to regard her for a moment, but she remained silent. Victoria suspected she knew exactly what memories had been passed on to Victoria and how graphic they were.

"I've got something on the floor above us!" Eleni announced.

At one, the group stopped at a hand signal from Pallasophia. "Play it," she ordered.

Eleni did, producing a scratching sound from the device in her hands.

"Mikros," Victoria and Photeos announced at nearly the same moment. She added, "only one of them."

Photeos nodded agreement. "You learned well."

"I didn't have much choice." Victoria heard the soldiers laugh off negative things while they talked to one another. Watching them, it seemed to be a way to relieve stress. She did her best to make her voice sound like that, hoping for the same effect. The slight relaxation in Photeos's shoulders told her it worked, at least a little bit.

"It's probably watching the stairs," Photeos said.

"That matches what I saw them do around the sophont," Victoria said. "They didn't do it anywhere else, though."

"I thought you killed the sophont."

His tone might not have been accusatory, but that was how it came across to Victoria and she growled in automatic displeasure. "I did."

"Lochagos," he said, addressing Pallasophia. "You're sure there was only one sophont down here?"

She nodded firmly, once. "Absolutely."

"If I may," Stavros said, speaking for for the first time in a while. His voice was quiet and slow, and he stopped frequently. The quick heal was doing its job on his ribs, but even it could only work so quickly. Victoria also knew from experience that using the stuff, much like a smear of mastigas blood, also made the wound burn.

"Go ahead." Pallasophia gestured for him to continue.

"Morphologically, the elite and the mikros aren't the only ones similar ones. The sophont shares a great many characteristics with them."

"So, we could conceivably be dealing with mastigas led by a new sophont?" The surprise in Eleni's voice was clear.

251

Photeos nodded. "Their behavior would indicate that, yes."

Something creaked down the hallway and the soldiers instantly assumed defensive postures. Only Victoria remained where she was, watching as the others raised their weapons to their shoulders and disabled the safeties.

Pallasophia was the first to rise out of the half-crouch into which she sank. "Victoria?"

She closed her eyes as the creak turned into a rhythmic knocking. "That's a water pipe. Specifically, it connects to the only place I found clean water."

Now, it was Photeos's turn to be surprised. "You mapped out the pipes?"

"Only the ones that made mysterious noises while I was trying to sleep, but yes."

"So what makes that noise?"

Victoria shrugged. "I don't know. I only know where that pipe leads."

"It's an air hammer," Stavros ventured.

"I don't like the sound of that."

He laughed. The sound was a little thin, but still mostly amused. "It just means some air got caught in the pipe."

Victoria nodded. "It leads to an open trough where I got water before."

"That's one mystery solved, then," Photeos said with relief.

"Victoria," Pallasophia said, "where do you think they mastigas are, if they're not attacking us?"

"If there's a new sophont," she started, emphasizing 'if' both times, "and if the remaining mastigas are following it, then they're probably below us. The sophont, the one I killed, made me come to it. I had to find it to confront it, and when I did, it tried to ambush me."

"After this morning, why don't they just attack and kill us?" Stavros said. "Why don't..."

Stavros's knees wobbled. Victoria, nearest him, put a firm hand on his shoulder while he struggled to keep his legs and feet underneath himself. A trained reflex made him relax his hold on his rifle, allowing Victoria to take it and hand the weapon off to Eleni, who accepted it without question.

Victoria, still holding Stavros by the shoulder, came around in front of him. She felt the same rush of emotions she felt during the fight: the instinct to protect, to analyze. That close, she could see through the tint of his visor to his wide eyes and sweaty forehead.

"Are you alright?"

Stavros took several deep breaths. When he finally replied, most of the fear and uncertainty remained, but he seemed much more in control of things. He also seemed to have found control over his feet again and Victoria relaxed her grip on his shoulder.

"I will be," he said. "Just still a little shaken."

Victoria stepped away and nodded as Photeos approached. He slapped Stavros lightly on the back, but it was enough for him to lurch forward a step. Victoria reached out a hand to steady him again, but he brushed it off with a muttered, "thanks."

"Congratulations, Dekaneas," Photeos said. "You've survived *two* engagements with the mastigas now."

"Thanks," he replied. "I'd be sure to mention that at the ball next week if it wasn't classified."

Photeos laughed. "Give it time. In a few weeks, I'm sure you'll be able to talk about some of it."

"I doubt it." Stavros then waved a hand at their dark surroundings. "Not with the unmitigated disaster of the Incident here."

"Hey, it's not an 'unmitigated disaster,' anymore," Photeos retorted. "We're mitigating the hell out of it as we speak."

"He's probably right," Eleni offered. She maintained a more positive tone in her voice, one which Victoria actually felt was somewhat out of place. Stavros and Photeos were concerned and on edge, but Eleni almost seemed detached.

She continued after a moment. "I'll actually be able to tell people some of the things I did here."

"Really?"

Pallasophia cleared her throat. "You are aware that Aphelion's facility director is here in the room with you, are you not?"

"Apologies, Lochagos," Stavros said.

"Accepted," she replied. "After the banquet, most of this facility is going to be declassified, but the Incident will *not* be. Understood?"

"Understood, Lochagos."

"The Incident," Victoria said. "That's an awfully sanitized name for what happened."

Rather than defensive, Pallasophia's reply came with an equal mix of regret and anger. "We could not have predicted what happened."

Victoria turned on her heels and bit back her initial angry reply. Instead, with an attempt at a cool tone, she replied, "why not?"

To her surprise, Stavros spoke up instead of Pallasophia, the bitter, almost resentful tone in his voice clear. "Research is being suppressed."

"That's your opinion, Second Lord," Pallasophia retorted.

"No. That's a fact. People who worked on that project *disappeared* if they talked."

"I still find it hard to believe the Hexarchs would do something like that, especially if the end result could benefit us."

Photeos shrugged. "My unit never saw data on anything other than how to kill them more efficiently."

Victoria held up a hand. "Some of them speak. They're obviously intelligent. No one tried to communicate with them?"

Photeos laughed, a bitter sound. "We did. The few times they replied at all, the only thing we got out of them was," he lowered his voice and tried to mimic the wet-rocks rasp of the sophont, "hate humans!"

"Even if." Pallasophia stopped long enough to turn her masked face toward Stavros for a moment. "Even if there was some conspiracy to suppress research, it's only been in the last few years that anything has been done at all."

Pallasophia gestured around them. "It wasn't really until we started all this that anyone worked toward understanding the mastigas."

"For twenty or twenty-five years, all anyone was interested in was defending against them," Stavros said. The disgust was clear in his voice, even through the helmet. "No one wanted to understand them or why they were here."

"That's not true," Photeos said.

Before the two of them could argue further, Victoria stepped between them. She had seen Pallasophia do the same thing enough times already to know how effective it was. She turned toward Stavros, stating the obvious first. "You sound like it's personal."

"I studied the mastigas for a few years before the project was shut down. Ask me about it later, alright? I've already gone into it once since we set foot in this hell."

Before Victoria could say anything, her attempt at stopping his argument with Photeos failed. Stavros stepped to the side and gestured to the other soldier. "As you for you, *Lochias*, you know better than anyone here that all they did was send you out there to 'patrol' and let you take Parthian shots at the mastigas while whatever factory those things hit was evacuated. Never once were you ordered to actually attack that battleship."

A tense silence fell before Photeos said, "I did not give the orders then."

"You're not disagreeing that those were your orders, though."

"They were."

"Just like mine were to pack my lab and never talk to anyone about it."

"What would you have me do?" Photeos shot back. "The last time I went out there, I was a new-lifted Fourth Lord. Who was I to criticize the decisions of the Hexarchs?"

Pallasophia cleared her throat. "There are always ways to get your message through the ranks, Lochias Photeos."

"Admittedly, Second Lord Director Lochagos Pallasophia," he emphasized each of her titles separately, "I was not prepared then to accept the fallout if there was push-back against my views."

"Much like a certain 'Third Lord' Stavros," Stavros muttered.

"Yes," he replied, then, "my apologies."

"For?" Pallasophia asked.

"I was ordered not to bring politics into the mission," he replied. "Strategos Glaukos was most insistent."

"You are forgiven," Pallasophia replied, letting a hint of amusement creep into her voice. "This mission would be much more boring without people to talk to, Photeos. Do not mistake an order to leave your political aspersions and aspirations at the door for an order to leave your opinions there as well.

"As I said," she continued, "there are people in the higher ranks who will listen to what you have to say."

"Of course, Second Lord."

Pallasophia laughed. "Relax, Photeos. That's an order."

His grin was clear from the tone of his voice. "Yes, ma'am."

"At any rate," Pallasophia continued. Victoria could hear the strain in her voice and wondered if the others could as well. They certainly did not act like her forced attempt at positivity was anything but genuine. She continued after a moment to breathe. "That's all a moot point. In a few months, there *will* be an attack. I understand you've already applied for the mission, Photeos?"

He nodded. "I requested a posting on the *Justice*. Stavros is right. I sat and took orders I didn't like for too long. This is, well..." He laughed. "It's a chance for justice."

"I put in for a transfer to the *Abraxas* once my work, our work, here at Aphelion is completed," Eleni added.

Pallasophia laughed. "At this point, my entire staff is going to end up on that mission."

"It's what you've trained us for." The pride in his voice was clear even through the slight muffle of his helmet.

"Victoria..."

She froze. The voice that called to her was not human. Like before, when she heard it in the ceiling above the soldiers before they met face-to-face, it clearly came from outside her body. It lacked the wet-rocks sound of the sophont. Instead, it now came to her like a melody, drawing out each of the vowels in her name, especially the middle one.

Her heart thundered in her chest as the same pit she felt in her stomach upon sighting the elite re-opened itself. For a moment, everything felt cold and she was very, very alone.

Fortunately, a quick glance around at the sudden tension in the soldiers' posture told her they heard it too. Just to make absolutely sure, she asked aloud, "I'm not the only one who heard that, am I?"

Pallasophia shook her head slowly. "You're not."

"Shit," Photeos cursed.

Stavros added a curse of his own, then, "there's another sophont in here somewhere."

Pallasophia drew herself up straighter. "Alright, people. New orders. We find a safe place to rest, and this time we check every possible avenue of approach. I think Victoria is correct and the mastigas are setting up an ambush for us somewhere below us."

Inside her helmet, Victoria grimaced. "I know where they're going to be."

"Tell me once we make camp," Pallasophia ordered. "Everyone move! Victoria, take us to this source of water you found. Unless," she paused, "that's not where you think they're congregating?"

Victoria shook her head. "No."

257

"Then we'll deal with that after we rest and eat."

"It's a small room, too small for everyone to be comfortable."

"Comfort isn't important. We've got mastigas to kill."

Again, Victoria found herself with a toothy grin. "Yes," she replied, "we do."

***

Victoria watched the soldiers work, keeping her distance as much as possible in the small room. The four Technocrats also did as much as possible to minimize how much space they required, though there was only so much they could do. The water trough, the place in which she was almost drowned, took up the majority of potentially available space. More of the floor had been occupied with equipment which she had been assured was for cooking.

So she perched on the edge of the water trough, watching the mechanical precision of the soldiers as they worked. Even having lost two members of their team, each person had a job to do. Stavros guarded the door while Pallasophia and Photeos set up the equipment.

Next to her, Eleni tinkered with something inside the wall next to the apparent source of the water that saved, and almost ended, Victoria's life. She watched as each time Eleni adjusted something in the wall, often resulting in a metallic thunk, it sent ripples through the slowly moving water.

Victoria watched the soldiers as they worked for several more minutes. They conveyed as much information to one another through their facial expressions and momentary glances as they did through actual words. Only Stavros, who actually stood guard, still wore his helmet. Photeos removed his mask, but not the cover for the top and sides, while Eleni and Pallasophia removed their entire helmets.

She supposed she had to look strange to them in her stolen mastigas clothing and helmet. They stopped jumping when she moved into or out of sight, though how much of that was familiarity and how much was a general lessening of tension, she could not say. The air felt more relaxed now that they found this room, at least.

Eleni stepped away from the wall and replaced the panel there with a satisfied sigh. Her next motion wiped sweat from her forehead and face. The rest of her, what little exposed skin she had, anyway, was dry and Victoria supposed whatever was inside the wall had to be significantly warmer than the air where she sat.

She looked up with a start, probably not expecting to see Victoria's masked face staring at her. Absently, she smiled and tucked a stray piece of curly blond hair behind one ear. It did little to keep the frizzy mess out of her face. She smiled, nervous, and her cheeks dimpled.

"This was a washroom," she offered. "The water here came directly from one of the processing plants. I'm not sure where it goes after it leaves this spot, but that's why the water here was safe to drink."

Victoria tilted her head to one side, watching her for a moment longer. "Processing plant?"

Eleni nodded. "Aphelion has, or had, several processing centers for producing clean water and air. The mastigas destroyed one down here and severed the pipes of the second, but I supposed they left this one alone."

"Even green-eyes need to drink," Victoria said. "How long are we going to stay here?"

Eleni shrugged. "My part of the work is done. You'll have to ask the Lochagos if you want to know that."

"What did you do?" Victoria asked. "More sensors?"

Eleni shook her head. "Lights."

Victoria nodded again. "The mastigas hate light."

"It should help us sleep a bit better."

Victoria frowned. "I don't sleep well in the light."

"Me either," Eleni admitted. "But I'd rather a few hours of uneasy sleep to..." She stopped as a dark cloud passed over her face.

"It's preferable to the alternative," Victoria finished for her.

"Yes."

Silence fell, broken only by the noise of the soldiers moving as they finished setting up the last of the equipment. She heaved a deep sigh. "I'm sorry, Eleni."

Her eyes widened with surprise. "What for?"

"You shouldn't have been forced to come down here for me."

"We had orders, Victoria."

"Orders that should not have been necessary."

Eleni frowned. "I agree, if I'm being honest."

"Good."

She leaned against the trough next to where Victoria sat. "Why?"

"I don't claim to understand everything that happened here," Victoria said. She spoke slowly, trying to piece together things even as she said them. "I'm grateful I woke up, and I'm grateful you came down here. I told Pallasophia as much earlier."

"But?" Eleni offered.

"But I regret that you had no choice."

Eleni was silent for a moment, then, "I appreciate that."

"Should I let you work?" Victoria offered.

She gestured to the open spot on the wall where a bundle of wires wrapped in some sort of tape dangled. "My work's done until tomorrow."

Another few minutes silence fell while Photeos set up what seemed to be the last of his equipment in the center of the room. It popped and sizzled with noises that Victoria's subconscious told her were the sounds of mechanical heat.

Eleni looked back up at Victoria, and she met the blond woman's eyes through her own mask. Out of her sight, Victoria gave her an inquisitive look. Eleni must have seen something of it in the shifts in Victoria's posture, because she said, "you've never worked on a team before."

She noticed it was not a question. Nevertheless, she nodded. Earlier, Pallasophia and the others responded to such questions with sarcasm, which seemed appropriate. Inside her helmet, she grinned. "Obviously not."

Eleni laughed. "Of course."

"Until you and your team arrived, I had never seen another human."

"No mirrors?"

Victoria shrugged her shoulders. "The mastigas must hate mirrors."

Eleni blinked for a moment, then laughed. "I supposed they do. What..." she paused. "Do you know what your face looks like?"

Victoria shook her head.

"Is that why you haven't taken your helmet off?"

Victoria looked at her again, and Eleni's eyes widened. In truth, she knew the other woman was right, but hearing it spoken aloud was different than thinking it in her head. It took Victoria a moment before she could reply.

"Perhaps," was her only answer.

"Not even with the Lochagos?"

She shook her head. "No."

"For what it's worth, you'll have to soon enough. Photeos is cooking dinner. If you're right and the mastigas are baiting us, we're all going to need to eat."

Victoria nodded, but said nothing. Across the room, she watched as Pallasophia sank smoothly to the floor opposite Photeos.

"That smells almost like food," she joked. "What's for dinner today, Lochias?"

"Roasted protein block," Photeos replied. He laughed. "I thought I would cook up the good stuff, you see."

"Hear, hear!" Eleni added, raising her hand in mocking salute. To Victoria, she added in a lower voice, "I'm sure it's better than whatever you had to eat down here."

Inside her mask, Victoria smiled. "Anything would be."

She grimaced. "I'm almost afraid to ask."

"If we run out of," she gestured to Photeos's cooking, "that, I'll tell you."

"We would have to be down here for weeks before we ran out."

"We'll be out of here before then."

"Do you know what's outside this place?"

She shook her head and frowned. "No, but anything is preferable to this."

Photeos rapped on the side of the cook pot. "Soup's on!"

Victoria hesitated while the soldiers queued up. Everyone produced a small bowl and set of utensils. Pallasophia, waiting at the end of the line, looked up from the pot and made eye contact with Victoria through her mask. She had no idea how Pallasophia managed it, but every time she looked at her, Victoria knew without any doubt that Pallasophia stared directly into her eyes, mask or no.

She left her place in line, approaching Victoria with the bowl and utensils in hand. Without saying anything, Pallasophia extended the set to Victoria. "I have a spare set in my gear," she explained.

Victoria took the bowl gingerly, somehow afraid it would break. Featureless gray plastic except for a serial number printed on the bottom, it actually felt fairly heavy in her hand. Whatever the actual material, Victoria knew it would take more than a simple fall to break it. Despite that, it still felt impossibly fragile in her hands.

Pallasophia turned back to the line, leaving Victoria with the empty bowl. She considered her options for a moment before sliding off the edge of the water trough. Victoria set the bowl on the floor beside her feet, hesitated for just a moment as an unexpected spike of adrenaline flooded her system, then reached under her chin to undo the tie holding her helmet tight to her head.

Cool air brushed against her face and the helmet made a dull thunk on the floor as she set it down. As one, the soldiers all turned and stared.

***

Pallasophia was aware she had been staring. All of them had, in fact. It felt like much more time had passed than truly had, and to see Victoria now without her helmet was very strange. Until the moment she removed it, all any of them had ever seen was the shiny face of a stolen mastigas mask. Pallasophia had seen her face on the security feeds, at least the ones that remained, but those were degraded and poor representations of reality.

As it happened, those grainy images had not prepared any of them for the reality that Number One Hundred, the person for whom two died in the last twenty-four hours alone, was a real person just like they were.

The hair on her head was little more than dark fuzz, far too short to accurately determine color. In the dim light, Victoria's cheekbones stood out prominently, casting dark shadows on her face. Gray-green eyes flashed out from those shadows, sharp and piercing.

And then, that moment passed. The vulnerability written clearly on her face faded the moment Photeos made a joke about the scar that crossed one cheek. Victoria's strong jaw relaxed and her lips quirked into a smile.

She laughed, and suddenly every worry Pallasophia held about the potential failure of Project Titan fell away. This woman killed an elite with little more than her bare hands and survived alone in a mastigas-infested hell. Every concern she held shattered under a wave of relief with the simple sound of her laughter.

She was also aware that she stopped listening to anything her people were saying. Her bowl of half-eaten food sat forgotten on the floor in front of her. Victoria sat across from her, Eleni to her left, and Photeos directly to her right. Stavros sat between him and Victoria, none of them with more than a centimeter on either side of their knees.

She looked back up as Victoria turned a questioning glance at Stavros.

Photeos laughed.

"Theory?" Victoria asked.

"Part of what we discovered on Kipos is that they seem to have some sort of hive mind."

Victoria nodded as a thoughtful look crossed her face. "When I fought the fonias by themselves, they jumped at random, trying to rip and tear and cut. They hurt me, but they hurt themselves just as badly. The ones this morning..."

She trailed into silence for a moment, and Eleni finished. "Worked as a team."

"I'd buy a hive mind, but I don't think it's only the sophonts," Photeos argued. "Their skills increase by number even without one nearby."

"That doesn't rule out the sophont's purpose," Stavros argued. "There are plenty of colonial organisms that can cooperate like that. Victoria, when you killed the sophont, were there any others around?"

She shook her head, gesturing widely with her hands now that she had eaten. "No, just the one. It seemed... lonely."

"Impossible," Photeos snarled. "Mastigas don't *feel*."

"What about that inscription in the elite's room?" Stavros asked, then grew demanding. "What about the fact that it kept a 'room' at all?"

Eleni cleared her throat. "It's well documented that lone mastigas are not intelligent. They don't 'get smarter' when there's more of them. They're just programmed to follow the sophont's orders. Alone they only know two things: kill and eat."

"They're sentient, even alone," Stavros said. "We've seen them manipulate simple tools."

"Weapons especially," Victoria said. One hand automatically went to her side.

Eleni held firm. "I'm not saying they're not sentient, only that they're not sapient."

"What we need is more data," Stavros said.

"Look," Photeos's tone changed, assuming the sound of a commander for the moment. "Standard doctrine is to kill the sophonts first. If you don't, you die. The mastigas coordinate too well. Without a sophont," he made an explosion gesture with his hands, "their ranks fall away."

Stavros frowned. "I think we should just burn it all."

Photeos laughed, something which quickly spread around the circle.

"Victoria," came the sing-song voice from before. It drifted on the air currents, echoing through the halls. Everyone around her perked up while Pallasophia's brain dumped adrenaline into her system.

One thought hit her above all others: it was close enough to talk to them. She opened her mouth to speak, but Victoria was faster.

The tone of Victoria's voice sounded more like the way she gave orders than the way Photeos phrased things, and Pallasophia wondered exactly how much Victoria had been studying them—her in particular— since their initial meeting.

"Stavros, check the hallway."

He hesitated just long enough for Pallasophia to bark confirmation of that order. "Now!"

He nodded, shot to his feet and grabbed his helmet with one hand and a weapon with the other. In moments, he was out of sight. Nothing indicated his presence but the bouncing of his weapon light as he swept the hallway.

No one spoke until he returned, though they each reached for their weapons. Pallasophia found herself watching the ceiling more than the door.

"Nothing out there, Lochagos," he reported.

Pallasophia frowned. "Good. Thank you for checking, Dekaneas."

He remained standing, watching the door. "All part of the job."

"Good, then you and Eleni have first watch. Four hours, then wake Photeos and me."

He nodded toward Victoria. "And her?"

Pallasophia turned toward Victoria, who watched the byplay with analytic interest. The brain that allowed her to survive while surrounded by mastigas was at work now. "Will you be able to sleep?"

Victoria frowned. "I will try."

She turned to Eleni next. "Do everything you can to pinpoint the mastigas' location while we rest."

Eleni nodded. "Understood, Lochagos."

"Victoria, is there anything you would like to add?"

Pallasophia watched as a grin flashed across Victoria's face, wild and gleeful. It barely lasted a moment, and in fact was little more than a single muscle twitch, but it left one thought burning in her mind. Victoria was not afraid of the mastigas. No, the hell she and Tritogenes put her through actually made her look forward to the fight tomorrow.

And that, Pallasophia thought, scared her.

Victoria's sharp intake of breath roused her from her thoughts. Her face set itself into a hard mask again, and Pallasophia was struck by the realization that this was likely the expression on her face, normally obscured by her mask, while she fought.

"Fight," she said, "or die."

Chapter 15

The Katarraktean sunlight slanting in through the bedroom window produced two thoughts in First Lord Tritogenes's brain. First among them was the realization that it was, in fact, morning. Second was a vague sense that he had only gotten into that bed a scant few hours before. The former thought brought resentment, while the latter brought a grudging acceptance of the state of things.

His skull pounded a slow, aching rhythm of hammer blows as his heart pumped blood back into his brain. He was not sure how much he could blame the sun for that particular pain—it certainly was not making things better, at any rate—but Tritogenes knew the majority of the blame could be placed firmly on the second of his two morning thoughts.

After their meeting in Enyalios's quarters the evening before, the two Hexarchs finally met up with First Lord Eurybia. Despite Enyalios's story the night before, she spoke and acted with utmost politeness toward both of them. Enyalios himself took some time to warm up to her, but he finally admitted that his rancor had been fueled by a combination of her unexpected visit and the reports reaching from from his own underlings.

Eurybia, for her part, apologized for setting Enyalios off, explaining only that she meant no offense. Tritogenes remembered telling her not to worry, that Enyalios was "just being his usual self," and the three of them could talk politics in the morning.

To his complete lack of surprise, Eurybia and Enyalios both agreed, and the rest of the night was a wash of color, music, and drink after drink from Enyalios's personal storehouse.

The pounding in his head and the sour feeling in his stomach combined to inform Tritogenes exactly how bad of an idea trying to match drinks with Enyalios had been. Still, he retained the contents of his stomach that night and continued to do so as he shuffled around the suite for a glass of water.

By this point, Enyalios's staff certainly knew he was awake. Motion sensors in the suite would have alerted them the moment he actually got out of bed, but they would not come to his room unless summoned. Dressing was something best done alone. Indeed to be seen in anything other than his purple robe by anyone other than family or those otherwise very close to him would be an embarrassing breach of protocol.

Fortunately, that in effect, gave Tritogenes as much time to get ready as he wanted. Skipping breakfast might have been unfortunate, but unless he had an actual invitation, it was not a slight to his host.

Additionally, Tritogenes thought with an inward smile, Enyalios was likely much worse off than he was at that moment. Despite his original plan to match his fellow Hexarch drink for drink, he quickly abandoned that plan as Enyalios quickly outpaced him. When Tritogenes finally gave up and switched to less inebriating substances, Enyalios's pace barely slowed compared to the start of the evening.

He took a few minutes to compose a series of messages. His sleep clothes had no pockets to put his computer in, and so he set the tablet-sized device on a nearby table. The display registered the tabletop and initially projected itself directly above that flat surface, but Tritogenes had no real desire to sit. He took hold of the massless hologram and pulled it upwards, placing the display at eye level.

The first message was short and succinct. He asked Pallasophia for an update on her progress and inquired after "their guest's" health. He concluded by asking her to meet with him when she arrived at Prosgeiosi, and promised to have a suite set aside for, again he used the euphemism because he did not yet know her name, "their guest."

That message would take several hours to reach Aphelion and even longer to pass through the encoding and decoding algorithms on either end. Truthfully, he did not expect a reply at all, but he felt it was his duty to at least ask.

Second, he send a message to Pteryga with just as much encryption as the first one. This one contained no sensitive information, he simply wanted to ensure as few people as possible could read it. In it he asked to meet with Hyperion when the latter made it to the capital as well, indicating that Enyalios might accompany him. The subject matter was fairly innocuous, but it was the informal tone he used with his former mentor that Tritogenes did not want just any random eyes to see.

It was the third message that he considered to be the most important. This one he directed at Limani and recorded a full video transmission rather than a simple text.

The recipient was one of the few people Tritogenes allowed to see him without his Hexarch's robe. As such, Philip resided on a very select list containing Hyperion, Pallasophia, and perhaps Enyalios. Despite that, he drew himself up a little taller and tugged at the fabric of his sleep shirt, smoothing it.

The indicator next to the holographic interface lit after a moment and he began.

"Philip, I regret that we can't have this conversation face to face. I know how much you prefer that to electronic communication, but I will not have time to return to Limani before departing for Prosgeiosi. You were right, and I should have made time to meet before I left the planet.

"I need you to do me another favor. In addition to the data you're compiling on the Titans—which, by the way, how is that going?—I need

269

you to see what you can dig up on a group calling themselves the Ouroboros Society. I overheard some of the musicians talking last night and not even Enyalios knew about them. Apparently, it's a new group. I'm not too concerned, but it would be good to have some information ahead of time in case the Council brings it up.

"Additionally, can you forward me the numbers for last season's performances at the Golden Hawk? I need something to gloat about over breakfast.

"Thank you, Philip. Go with the suns."

Tritogenes ended the recording. That one would reach Limani in a matter of minutes. He gave it an hour at most before he had a reply. Philip always surprised him with the speed he answered messages. Information, of course, took time to gather, but simple answers often returned long before most people would have gotten around to them.

Before he could shut down the holo, someone knocked at his suite's door. Tritogenes frowned, wondering if the sound was a recording. It would be like Enyalios to program the suite's door to play a sound like that rather than a simple chime.

The knocking came again, and Tritogenes dismissed his holo with a wave. No, he realized, that sound was genuine. Someone outside his door was actually *knocking* with their hand.

While that was puzzling enough, the fact that he had a visitor at all was stranger still. No one should have been bothering him, especially not so early in the morning.

"Yes, yes. What is it?" He found his headache returning and his tone came out angrier than he meant it to.

"First Lord Tritogenes, Hexarch Limani." He did not recognize the voice that replied, but the use of not only his full, but also his official, title jumpstarted his brain. In moments the cobwebs from the night before were gone, replaced with steel-edged awareness. The sudden adrenaline dump that came with it was not welcome, however.

The voice continued. "First Lord Eurybia, Hexarch Kokkinos has requested your presence at your earliest convenience."

If his brain was not already running in high gear, that announcement would have sent it speeding. "Did First Lord Eurybia supply you with a purpose for her invitation?"

"Breakfast, First Lord."

Tritogenes frowned, confused. "Break—?" he mouthed. Aloud, to the unnamed messenger on the other side of the door, he said, "inform First Lord Eurybia that I will gladly meet her for breakfast and thank her for the invitation."

"Yes, First Lord."

"Where am I to meet her?"

"The Hawk and Arrow, First Lord."

Tritogenes nodded, thinking. At least Eurybia had good taste in food. That made it almost worth having his morning disrupted. "And when?"

"First Lord Eurybia did not give a time, sir."

Leaving it up to him, of course, he thought with a frown. That meant it was his problem if breakfast was too early or too late. He gave a chuckle too quiet to be heard through the door. Perhaps there was some truth to what Enyalios told him last night, because now it was Tritogenes's responsibility to finalize breakfast plans.

On the other hand, that might work in his favor. On the surface, forcing him to choose a time meant that if he picked a time that Eurybia, or any other guests she might have invited, found less than ideal, the blame would fall on him. He would have failed to accommodate "his" guests, despite the original plan being Eurybia's.

He had to admit, it was a fairly well-thought piece of the social game the Hexarchs played with one another.

Fortunately for him, Tritogenes did not particularly care about any potential loss in standing be might incur from something like that. He especially did not care so early in the morning. Even on the best of days, he was not an early riser.

271

He checked the clock on the wall, finding it just past midmorning. "Inform First Lord Eurybia that I will meet her in ninety minutes."

"Of course, First Lord."

Tritogenes waited several minutes to make sure the messenger was gone before reactivating his holo. He sent Enyalios a short text message, dictating it as he removed his sleep clothes and unfolded the day's robe.

"Eurybia invited me to breakfast without settling on a time. I told her an hour and a half. Meet us at the Hawk and Arrow."

Several minutes passed and a message indicator flashed on the holo, a reply from Enyalios. "Will do." Another came in a minute later. "Also, which god lit the suns again? I have a personal grudge for them."

Tritogenes laughed and dictated a reply. "You and me both."

***

An hour and a half later, Tritogenes stepped onto the outdoor patio of the Hawk and Arrow. The suns hung high already, burning most of the morning's fog and mist away. Of course, with the rivers and waterfalls coursing through the multi-layered city, even the hottest summer day could only banish the ever-present mist for a short time. He had to admit, at least to himself, that the array of sunbeams streaking through the planet's clouds were rather beautiful and the warm, wet air did wonders for both his skin and his lungs.

A table waited, already reserved, which only surprised Tritogenes for a few moments. When he realized the other Hexarchs were already waiting for him, that feeling went away rather quickly. Eurybia arriving early was no surprise, but he was somewhat impressed to see Enyalios up and moving. The tone of the messages they exchanged over the prior hour had not given him much faith that Katarraktes's Hexarch had even gotten dressed yet.

Not only had Enyalios gotten dressed, but his animated movements and expressions gave no hint of the tired, haggard man who had messaged Tritogenes an hour before to complain about his own alcohol-fueled headache. His "secret" was not exactly secret, but his preference for stimulants over getting a good night's sleep never interfered with his ability to do the job of a planetary Hexarch.

Sharing the same space as Enyalios made Tritogenes's more relaxed robe seem even more plain—not that he particularly cared. Enyalios had, as always, meticulously done his hair and makeup for maximum effect. Even for an informal, if late, breakfast, he looked ready to stride into the Council chambers. Of course, when that time came, Enyalios would likely aim to be even fancier.

Eurybia, as the ostensible host of their impromptu get-together, rose to greet him. She wore a much newer robe than either of the other Hexarchs, stiff satin dyed in the bright purple of current fashions. It shimmered with a rainbow of embroidery that, when she moved, managed to outshine even Enyalios's garment. She wore it well, however, without the ostentatious air that a less self-assured person would have given off in such bright clothing.

Like Tritogenes, Enyalios wore an older style robe, dark purple with bronze-colored designs that created a rather somber, reserved look. His attention that morning had been on the choice of jewelry and the complex designs in his hair.

Tritogenes's robe was of a simpler fabric than either of theirs, but had been covered in much brighter embroidery than Enyalios's. His was also a mere four years old, much newer than the one Enyalios wore. Tritogenes knew Enyalios's robe had to be at least twenty years old, and he suspected some of his jewelry was even older.

He also left his hair plain, tying it back at the nape of his neck with a simple velvet ribbon. Let Eurybia make of that what she would, he thought.

She turned a broad, bright smile on Tritogenes as he approached the table. An inhabitant of Old Earth might have guessed Eurybia's age at thirty-six or thirty-seven, but she was in fact well over ninety years of age, three decades older than Tritogenes himself. Unlike First Lord Enyalios, whose decadent lifestyle and additional decade of life had brought some wear to the edges of his eyes and mouth, and peppered his once-black hair with gray, she still looked to be in her prime.

Her waist-length hair had been carefully braided into a pattern that depicted the double-helix of DNA. From a distance, he thought she had foregone more complicated makeup that morning, but up close he found the opposite to be true. Complex geometric shapes adorned her cheeks in a shade just barely darker than her own skin, emphasizing her thin face.

Still smiling, Eurybia extended a hand for Tritogenes to shake, taking the role of the social senior. He let it slide; she *was* his senior in experience, after all.

Enyalios remained seated, and Tritogenes greeted him first with a respectful nod while he was still a step away from Eurybia. A flicker of annoyance crossed Eurybia's face, but nothing more. His greeting to Enyalios only lasted a few seconds and he turned back to Eurybia with a smile he tried very hard to produce genuinely. He extended a hand and they clasped arms just past the wrist, shook once, and parted.

"First Lord Eurybia," he said. "Did you sleep well?"

She nodded, absently wiping at her forehead. "As well as could be expected on such a humid planet."

Enyalios laughed. "Now you know how I felt when I visited Kokkinos."

"My planet, First Lord, is dry. We have none of," she waved a hand toward the nearby waterfall, "that."

"I know. Why do you think I don't like it?"

She sat, motioning for Tritogenes to do the same. "I assumed it was because you had no sense of culture."

"I'm sure last night did away with that assumption," he retorted with a bemused smile.

Eurybia returned the smile, then morphed it into a smirk. "It did not."

"First Lords, please," Tritogenes said, holding up both hands. "Can we all agree on something, for once?"

274

Eurybia raised an eyebrow. "What do you propose?"

Tritogenes laughed. "Instead of arguing about humidity—which, by the way, *Limani* is the planet with the ideal humidity—let us agree that our planets are all nicer than cold places like Dasos or Kipos."

Eurybia raised a glass of some orange drink. "Hear, hear!"

A Second Lord came to take their food orders, and Tritogenes's drink order, then attempted to vanish with minimal attempt at conversation.

"One moment," Enyalios said, pitching his voice to carry.

The Second stopped mid-stride, apparently petrified with sudden fear. He turned, hands at his side in a relaxed posture that was almost believable.

"First Lord?" he asked.

"What's your name?"

"Lykourgos, sir. Thi—Second Lord Lykourgos."

Enyalios smiled, amusement radiating from his posture. "When was the Elevation?"

"Three weeks ago, First Lord."

Enyalios pantomimed applause, knowing it would not carry above the noise. "If I may pry," he said, and Tritogenes stifled a laugh, "what did you do?"

Now, the man truly relaxed as a smile of relief passed across his face. "Violin, First Lord. Second Lord Cassandra sponsored me. After the performance at Evander Hall last month, she said it was time."

"I saw that concert," Enyalios said. His voice was relaxed, conversational, but Tritogenes saw the new Second Lord stiffen. "You had the solo, then?"

"Yes, First Lord."

Enyalios nodded. "Then it's an Elevation well deserved."

"Thank you, First Lord."

Once their server was out of earshot, which did not require very much distance at all given the proximity and volume of the nearby waterfall, Tritogenes leaned forward and placed his elbows on the table.

"Enough distraction," Eurybia said.

"Agreed," Tritogenes interjected, speaking quickly enough to cut her off before she could begin her own line of questioning. He placed the same sort of affectations on his voice that he would have used when interviewing a prospective actor for his opera house. "So, First Lord Eurybia. We haven't heard much about your part of the Project on Limani. What can you tell me about it?"

She smiled, disarming. "You'll have to find out at the Council meeting."

"Come now," Enyalios protested. "Everyone's projects are public knowledge at this point."

Eurybia raised an eyebrow and turned that inquisitive expression toward Tritogenes. "Everyone?"

He nodded. "Of course."

Her smile never faltered. "That," she said, "is new."

Tritogenes resisted the urge to frown. He knew she was baiting him, but it would take something a lot less obvious than that to draw him out. "Not at all. In fact there was significant media coverage when I adapted Aphelion to serve as my Titan's training ground. I might understand if you missed that, however. You've been quite busy, after all."

She smiled, perfunctory. There was nothing genuine about it, and for someone with the iron control over her emotions that Eurybia had, letting him see that meant the gesture was deliberate.

"We have all been 'quite busy,'" she replied, mimicking his intonations exactly.

Enyalios made a show of leaning back in his chair to the point that Tritogenes expected him to cross his feet on the edge of the table. He cleared his throat equally dramatically. "Why *are* you here, First Lord?"

Tritogenes's comm flashed a single holographic light over his left hand. Normal messages blinked blue on his system, while high-priority messages either showed as green or red depending on their subject and who the sender was. Every one of the Hexarchs had a similar system, and as sure as he was that some of them bothered to memorize everyone else's color codes, he was even more sure that most did what he did and changed those codes at regular intervals.

This message came in with a green flash, and so he opened a single-sided holo to read it. The screen actually showed several messages, most from Philip and a single one from Hyperion. He opened that one first, revealing a short note agreeing to his proposition and implying that the meeting would be a feast.

The messages from Philip he opened and scanned in more detail. The first contained information about the Titans. Philip apparently realized Eurybia was here on Katarraktes—Hexarch movements were never secret—and forwarded what he had. He focused on the information about Eurybia's Titan, a man named Panatakis. In a few moments he had a few useful facts to throw out at her to test her reactions. If she was going to poke at Aphelion and his part of the Project, he would do the same thing.

Second were the numbers he asked for about his opera house. When the time came, those would be useful. Tritogenes manually moved those over to a readily accessible notes file under just enough layers that it would look like he did not have them already ready to display, but not so many that it would take a while to find the data. That way he could seem prepared without coming across to the others as being overeager.

They all played that delicate balancing act, and the social consequences for failure to handle things the right way were something Tritogenes learned early on in his career as a Hexarch.

The final message was much shorter, containing no additional data beyond the reply itself. "I haven't heard of any group by that name, but I can pay special attention for it. While I do, you ponder the potential symbolism behind such a name. It may be that you come across information before I do."

Oblivious, or at least pretending to be so, to Tritogenes as he checked his messages, Eurybia directed her reply solely at Enyalios. "I have not been away from Kokkinos in some time, and I was visiting some of my

277

holdings among the iron mines in the First Belt. Katarraktes lay between those mines and the capital, and I thought I would pay a visit to my dear friend First Lord Enyalios."

Enyalios laughed. "'Dear Friend,' you say? This is news to me!"

Mock affronted, Eurybia replied, "it shouldn't be!"

Amid continued laughter, Enyalios replied, "it's the superlative you threw in there that's giving me pause. I didn't think you were 'dear friends' with anyone but Aegesander."

Tritogenes shut off his holo and looked up in time to see Eurybia's face darken for a fleeting moment. When it passed, she placed a bright smile in its place. "If you must know the real reason I'm here, Aegesander needed my help."

Tritogenes stared at her for a moment, parsing the myriad potential social interactions that could have led to that, then the thousand ways in which either party could leverage her actions on Katarraktes for political capital.

A young, orange-robed Fifth Lord chose that particular lull in the conversation to approach the table with their drinks. The Hawk and Arrow's house dish was a type of crepe, and each of them ordered a plate with different fruit spreads. The Fifth Lord took a moment to assign the proper plate to the proper seat, doing so without, Tritogenes noticed, having to ask who each plate belonged to. The drinks were simpler, strong espresso for each of them and refills for whatever juice they had already been drinking.

The Fifth Lord then nodded politely to the Hexarchs and wordlessly excused himself. Tritogenes smiled, letting the other two see it. He suspected that young man would tell all his friends from school about how he personally served breakfast to not just one, but *three* Hexarchs today. The Ten Thousand knew Tritogenes would have done the same thing in his place. If memory served, he actually had done so in his youth.

"I remember when you were that age, Tritogenes," Eurybia mused. "Don't you, Enyalios?"

The latter Hexarch laughed, but shook his head. "I don't think I ever met Tritogenes until he was an adult."

"I was never that starry-eyed," Tritogenes protested.

Eurybia laughed. "No, I don't think you were. Even as a teenager, you had quite the opinion of yourself."

Tritogenes smiled and made a broad gesture with both hands that indicated his companion Hexarchs and his own purple robe. "And look where it got me!"

"I have to give you that, yes." Eurybia sighed, allowing her demeanor to change entirely. Stress showed now in her posture, as did as strange sort of guilt.

She was entirely too chameleon-like, Tritogenes thought. Even for someone who grew up in the world of actors and opera singers, Eurybia's ability to conceal her thoughts and emotions was impressive. It made working with her very difficult, though working with her mining conglomerate allowed Tritogenes to save a great deal of cost on several projects, Aphelion included. Despite that, he never felt entirely at ease around her, even when she was being nice like this. The feeling that she was hiding something never quite went away.

But, he thought with a smile that carefully did not reach his face, they were all hiding things in some way or another.

Eurybia picked up her espresso cup. Straight-sided, the white ceramic had been carefully hand-painted with floral motifs. Hers was primarily red, roses and azaleas, from what Tritogenes could see. He picked his own up, blue and purple and decorated with hydrangeas and hyacinths, and raised it in salute. Enyalios did likewise, raising a cup of brown ceramic painted with white moonflowers.

"Exquisite," she said, taking the cup away from her lips.

"Thank you," Enyalios replied. "I'll pass your thanks on to the staff."

"Do so." Over the rim of her cup, she smiled at Tritogenes. "To get back to the subject at hand: before you arrived, Tritogenes, First Lord Enyalios was telling me about the success he's had with Project Titan."

The look that he passed to Tritogenes told the other Hexarch that, in fact, had not been the subject of conversation previously. Nevertheless, he carried on with with gusto. "As I was saying, Second Lord Daniel has been spending more and more time synced up with the Aegis system. Presently, he can manage six hours before mental fatigue sets in. Perhaps twice that when his grasp of the armor's sleep functions gets better."

"And you feel this armor is up to the task?" she asked.

He nodded once. Enyalios made a show of reaching for his plate of crepes, slicing off a piece, and taking a bite before replying. "In trials, the current iteration of the Aegis system has proven able to stand up to multiple strong blows from enraged gigas with little to no damage."

Eurybia raised an eyebrow. "Current iteration, First Lord?"

"Indeed."

A ghost of a smile, one very different from the friendly expressions she showed before, passed across her face. "I hope the expense of multiple iterations of the Project has not put too much strain on your holdings. I would hate to see Hermes's efficiency suffer."

Enyalios barely suppressed the wave of annoyance that threatened to sweep across his face. From his seat, Tritogenes saw the corner of his mouth twitch once, but if Eurybia noticed, she failed to react.

It was not the first time Eurybia had brought up financial concerns with Enyalios, whose Hermes Corporation served much of the binary, including Eurybia's own planet of Kokkinos. Her mining conglomerate had to rely on his ships for much of their transport, a fact about which she had been unhappy since Tritogenes was a mere Second Lord.

Tritogenes bit back the retort on the tip of his tongue. He wanted to ask why she simply did not use Aegesander's merchant fleet. He owned the largest fleet by number and second largest fleet by firepower in the entire binary.

Enyalios's reply was as fast as it was short. "My shipping services have been unaffected, I assure you."

"Excellent," she drawled.

Something in her tone set off Tritogenes's "bullshit detector," as Pallasophia referred to his bullheaded tendency to forget the social niceties of being a Hexarch. "Has the Project been such a strain on First Lord Aegesander that his ships are unable to meet your increased demand, Eurybia?"

She scowled, plain and obvious. "I'm not going to use my working relationship with Aegesander as a crutch, Tritogenes."

Now, Enyalios frowned. Eurybia broke the veneer of politeness over their conversation, and he fell right in line. "But you *will* come to me asking for increased space aboard Hermes's ships for a paltry increase in price."

"Exactly."

Enyalios's eyes narrowed. "Why?"

She leaned forward, fixing him with an intense stare for a moment before dropping back into her seat. "Gods between, Enyalios, you're never this easy. I feel like I'm arguing with *Tritogenes*!"

"Hey!"

"Do you really want to know why I came here?"

"Did I ask?"

She nodded. "Aegesander has both raised costs for space aboard his ships and decreased their availability. He says he's re-arming as many as he can before the Titans depart for the mastigas battleship."

Enyalios crossed his arms and nodded, both annoyed and pleased in the same paradoxical moment. Doing that meant Aegesander was taking his commitment to the assault seriously, more seriously than he had at the start of the Project, anyway. On the short term, however, it put his own ships into a tight spot when it came to shipping cargo.

"So can you do it?"

Despite his attempt to conceal it, Tritogenes's face twisted into an open-mouth look of shock for a moment. Asking directly like that was a serious breach of social convention that leveled a rather substantial insult at Enyalios. In effect, by *asking* rather than simply stating what she

281

needed and offering a trade or payment, she called into question his ability to do it at all.

The insult did not go unnoticed, either. Enyalios's face pinched in and darkened as he mulled over the sudden shift in the conversation.

To his own surprise, Tritogenes put a rein on his emotions first. He raised his espresso cup to his lips and sipped in deliberate mimicry of the gesture Eurybia made earlier. "Have your own efforts proved a strain on your own finances, First Lord Eurybia?"

She turned slightly in her chair, a movement given away more by the rustle of her robes and the leather of the chair than any real change in her position. Her face showed an impassive mask that suddenly blossomed into a wide, and very fake, smile. "On the contrary, my dear Tritogenes. Thanks to the Project, every one of my industries are doing quite well. Raw materials and metals are in demand more now than they ever have been and my vineyards, well," she laughed, "last night's festivities should tell you how *that* business is going!"

"Of course," he replied, nodding agreement.

"And people always want entertainment, don't they?" Enyalios saluted Tritogenes with a forkful of crepe.

He laughed, raising his espresso cup in a return salute. "That they do."

Eurybia smiled, predatory and hawkish. Tritogenes had a sudden feeling that, whatever game she was playing, she was about to spring the final part of it. "The Project has been difficult for us all. Most of all you, I imagine."

He raised an eyebrow at her.

Eurybia took that as a sign to continue. "We are worried about you, Tritogenes. Your clothes are old, reflecting old accomplishments. Have you stumbled upon hardship, perhaps?"

"We have all stumbled upon hardship," he replied. His smile was thin and never touched his eyes. "I have made many sacrifices for Project

282

Titan, as have you, I trust. Tell me, what has come out of that facility on Kokkinos's second moon?"

Eurybia's face twitched with surprise, confirming Tritogenes's suspicions that she thought no one knew about the little building sitting in the shadow of a volcano. Thanks to Philip, he knew it existed, but nothing more.

"You will meet Second Lord Panatakis on the Council floor," she said simply. "Other information is, as our dear Katarraktean Hexarch said earlier, publicly available. Until then, let us say my research into cybernetics has been..." She paused, smiled. "Fruitful."

"Cybernetics?" Tritogenes asked, not bothering to conceal his surprise. Philip's information had mentioned that her Titan had some sort of sensory tech, but little else. Her secrecy, it seemed, was almost as good as his.

Growing up, he read stories about humans enhanced with implanted technology. They would crop up here and there in the histories, or what remained of them at any rate. Sometimes the stories were good, but Technocrat science had so far been unable to unravel the process in any meaningful way.

After a moment, he nodded in open appreciation. "That explains the secrecy."

"Speaking of secrecy, what *are* you bringing to the Project? You have withheld much from previous Council sessions. I trust you will not continue that trend now that we approach zero hour?"

"Of course not. My Titan will join me at Prosgeiosi in time to meet the rest of the Hexarchs, I assure you."

"Your Titan does not have a name?" Eurybia inquired.

"She does. She would also prefer it if I kept it a secret until the meeting."

Enyalios was his friend, but the odds of him not having listening devices scattered around the area were somewhere well below zero. Tritogenes would have, and had, done the same thing in his place. It was all part of the game the Hexarchs played with one another and they all knew it. Until he figured out how to integrate his Champion into Technocrat society, he wanted to make sure people knew as little about her as possible.

Privately, he was afraid of what they would do if the learned the lengths to which he had gone to achieve success in his branch of the Project. Too many died over the past five years, and their eyes haunted his dreams even still. Despite that, he would do it all again if it meant producing his Champion and preventing another planetary slaughter like Kipos.

Eurybia eyed him distrustfully for a moment, then replied with a slight smile and a shrug. "As you will." A moment passed, during which she finished one of her crepes, and she turned to Enyalios again. "First Lord, it occurs to me that it might be more economical to travel together to Prosgeiosi."

That, Tritogenes realized, was the rest of her game that morning. Another insult to Enyalios, another implication that his ships were substandard and unsuited to the task of ferrying him to the capital and back. He had to admit he admired her creativity. For Enyalios to refuse her offer would have been an even bigger insult to her than she gave to him by making the offer in the first place. Now, Tritogenes suspected he had been caught in the same Byzantine plan.

Enyalios's eyebrows rose. "Together?"

She nodded, but before she could speak, Tritogenes opened his mouth to speak. As her offer had been directed at Enyalios and not him, he could reject it without turning the whole complicated matter into another insult. "I would not want to leave my own ship here, First Lord."

"Perhaps," she said with a smile. "But Prosgeiosi's landing queue has developed a reputation lately for unconscionable backups. Being so busy, First Lord Tritogenes, you may have missed the upswing in traffic at the capital over the last year or so. One ship would fit into the queue more easily than three."

"And you propose to use your personal liner?" Enyalios asked. Tritogenes noticed that he had, very carefully, set his espresso cup back on its little saucer.

"I ferried a group of inspectors out to the mining complex on Cetus-A-Seven before coming here," she said. Her voice was carefully neutral. "So I find myself with several staterooms available aboard the *Akoni*. I would appreciate if you joined me."

Tritogenes found himself nodding almost involuntarily. With that phrasing, she removed the insult and turned the whole thing into a favor they could do for her. Refusing this would be an even bigger slight against Eurybia now.

Enyalios seemed to have put things together about the same time Tritogenes did. The muscle of his jaw tightened and loosened several times before he answered. "Your offer is a generous one, First Lord Eurybia. When do you want to leave?"

"Soon," she replied. "With your leave, First Lord Enyalios, I will go make the arrangements aboard the *Akoni*."

He nodded. "I will comm you when we have packed. At your leisure, First Lord."

She stood, adjusted her robes, and made a show of finishing the last of her still-warm espresso. "First Lords," she said with a nod before turning to leave. She stopped, turned back and added, "oh, First Lord Tritogenes. There is one other matter. I fear First Lord Hyperion may be sick. He declined my offer of an audience on my way to the belt. You correspond often with him, yes?" Before he could agree, she continued, "inquire after his health, please. I would consider it a personal favor."

Tritogenes nodded once, slowly. Hyperion had always been a supporter and patron of his before Ophion took him under his proverbial wing. Even after, he maintained an affable relationship with the centenarian. For the last twenty-five years Hyperion had also, quite publicly, refused to meet with either Eurybia or Aegesander in private.

"I will speak to him," was all the promise Tritogenes would make.

Eurybia nodded, apparently pleased with that answer, and turned again to depart.

Tritogenes and Enyalios watched her walk away. Once she was safely out of earshot, a fairly short distance given the roar of the hundred-meter waterfall less than half a kilometer away, Enyalios spoke up. "You're aware of the insult she threw at us with that offer, right, Tritogenes?"

He nodded. "Very much so. I'm afraid she played us quite well this morning, my friend."

Enyalios shrugged. "Such things happen. Besides, it's only fair after what she gave me last night."

"Oh?"

"That party was quite public and, despite her remarks this morning, she said a great many flattering things about Katarraktes and its arts. I imagine those remarks will make planetary news just after we depart."

Tritogenes grinned. "Well played."

Enyalios hummed. "She comes through this area of the system often, yet this is one of a very few times she came to my planet directly. Aegesander comes and goes..."

"As he does from all our worlds," Tritogenes interrupted.

"...but never Eurybia. One wonders what her actual reason for coming here was."

"Perhaps Aegesander sent her," Tritogenes offered.

Enyalios laughed. "He's a crafty old man, Aegesander, but I don't think he would stoop to something that petty."

"You're probably right," Tritogenes said, then rose. "At any rate, I'm going to return to my suite and pack."

Enyalios did as well, waving a payment into the cafe's system. "A wise decision. Eurybia will be quite cross if we're late. Before we depart, however, while we still have privacy, I would like to discuss at length the plans to entertain your, ah, 'guest.'"

Chapter 16

Victoria pointed at the door ahead of them with the end of her rifle. The door was exactly like it had been when she left this area the first time, but now with the aid of the lights Eleni restored, Victoria could more clearly see what it had originally looked like before the mastigas destroyed it.

On one side of the door a sign had been painted on the wall. Once vivid red with black block lettering, the colors were faded and large chunks of the stone had been smashed away. Now, thanks to the mastigas, the message read "A/T/O/IZ/D /E/SO//E/ ON/Y." The left side of the door was bare except for a series of small holes, much too small for the mastigas to have put them there.

"They're in there."

Pallasophia nodded. She said nothing, but motioned the rest of the team forward.

"She's right," Photeos supplied. "The dirt is heavier here, and the mastigas are easier to track. Nearly every set of fresh footprints leads through that door."

"How many?"

Photeos shook his head. "I'm sorry, Lochagos. When they get to the door, it's hard to tell them apart. My best guess is, 'many.'"

"This is the only door on this floor into or out of that room," Pallasophia said. "There is, or was, a clean room on the other side, but I suspect it's destroyed now."

Despite, or perhaps because of, the burning feeling in her nerves, Victoria laughed. "If it wasn't before, the fonias that jumped me made sure to smash whatever was left."

"Anything we should be aware of?" Stavros asked, gesturing to the door.

"The catwalks," Victoria replied. "They're going to attack from there."

"Impossible," Pallasophia argued. "The catwalks are inaccessible. The doors leading to them were welded shut during the Incident."

Victoria shook her head. "Impossible or not, several of them attacked from there."

"They could have climbed, Lochagos," Stavros offered.

"It's possible, but those catwalks are six meters up."

Victoria growled. "Again, impossible or not, that's what happened."

Pallasophia took a deep breath, then continued in a softer tone. "I apologize. I shouldn't doubt your experience."

"Thank you."

Pallasophia gestured to her soldiers, saying, "sweep the area. Make absolutely sure there's no chance of anything coming up behind us."

They nodded, saluted, and Photeos and Stavros moved off. Eleni stayed for a moment. "Lochagos," she said, "if you give me a few minutes, I can rig a motion sensor for this room. That way we'll at least have warning."

Pallasophia nodded. "Do so."

With a few moments of privacy, Pallasophia's posture changed momentarily. She stepped closer to Victoria, lowering her voice to a whisper just loud enough to be heard through the helmets.

"Are you alright?"

Victoria eyed her through her helmet. "Are you asking because of my injuries or because we're about to return to my birthplace?"

Rather than answer directly, Pallasophia said, "I won't presume to understand what you went through here."

Something in her tone, bitter regrets rising to the surface, made Victoria trust her just a little more. "I wouldn't ask you to, but I'm alright."

Pallasophia's hesitation before replying was obvious even through her mask. "Are you?"

"I was, quite literally, born to kill mastigas." She kept her voice at the same whisper, but let a hard edge creep in. "I'm not afraid of what we'll find on the other side of that door."

"But?"

She growled. This woman was damnably perceptive. Even Victoria had not known there was anything else to that thought until she asked. Her reply was slow and methodical as she carefully thought over every word. "If anything, what I'm afraid of is what we'll find when we're done."

Before either of them could say anything else, Eleni announced that her motion sensor was ready. Victoria's mind snapped back into combat focus, forgetting anything else she might have been planning to say. Instead, she started issuing orders to her team.

"Pallasophia and I are going in first. Stavros, Photeos, you follow right behind us and move out to the sides. Eleni, that sensor will alert you first. You watch our rear."

As she spoke, the sudden, and fundamental, shift in how she viewed these four Technocrats registered on her conscious mind. Victoria had no idea when that change happened, or even when she made the jump from distrust to trust, but it was there nonetheless. At least until the mastigas in the room beyond were dead, these people were as much hers as they had been Pallasophia's, or Photeos's before her.

For a moment no one moved, and Photeos started to argue, but Victoria was already in motion to the door. Pallasophia barked a simple, "you heard her!" and everyone sprang into motion.

Victoria reached out a hand and placed it on the door. With her other hand, she raised her rifle to her shoulder and flicked on the light. She left it, for the moment, angled down slightly so that it was out of her way, but immediately at hand. She rested her hand on the door handle for a half a second, then reached back to touch the baton hanging from her waist, the one she had taken from the mastigas gigas.

Behind her, a male voice muttered a quick prayer, but she was too focused on what lay ahead of them to identify it.

She pushed open the door and stepped through, again thankful for the work Eleni did. A single overhead light offered enough illumination that, with the team's combined weapon lights, Victoria could easily make out things around her.

With a smile no one saw, she told herself that things were already going better than they had the first time she went through this room. Now, if they got attacked, at least the piles of dirt and broken furniture would not be a hazard.

In the light, Victoria looked around, remembering the room as it felt in the dark. She overlayed that with how it now looked, and then visualized how it would have appeared before the mastigas trashed it. This was likely some type of waiting room, the voice of her memories told her, or perhaps a preliminary place where her predecessors should have been inspected by doctors.

At the far side of the room, the door stood open, spilling light into the darkness beyond. She remembered closing that door, but if the mastigas had indeed been gathering in the pod room, it made sense that they might leave it open to better watch for the humans' approach. Inside her helmet, Victoria grimaced as she realized their lights and noise already spoiled any chance they might have had to sneak up on the mastigas.

"They've got to know we're here," she said. "Watch overhead."

"You heard her," Photeos added quietly.

Victoria took a deep breath and motioned to Pallasophia. She counted down from three on her fingers before lunging into the room. She crouched low, sweeping the area with her rifle's light. Her other hand automatically went to her baton, bringing it up beside the lightweight rifle.

Thanks to the mastigas, the room that should have held the sleeping bodies of Victoria and the ninety-nine lives she dreamed about being was empty. It was not, however, quiet. Feet moved around and things popped and creaked, but none of them could get a clear line of sight on anything.

Someone behind her fired several rounds into the ceiling at an assailant that even Victoria had not seen, but stopped when Photeos snapped an order.

The passed by row after row of shells. The door was at what she considered the far end of the room, nearest the shell numbered "VI:I:T." From the other end, near her own shell, a voice came singing on the cool, damp air. Stavros started to comment, but a sharp, wordless growl of rebuke from Victoria stopped him.

"Victoria," it sang. "Vic. Tor. Ia. Vict. Ori. Ah."

Slowly, she led the team past the line of shells, growling an order to stay quiet every time one of them commented on them. Their lights never found anything, but the sounds of movements never ceased, and the voice at the other end continued repeating her name.

She almost stopped as they passed her shell with the inscription on the side from which she had taken her name. Without that little string of characters, her name would have still been "Number One Hundred," the thought of which sent an empty chill down her spine. That was not a name, it was a curse.

A few meters away, something shifted and creaked. Victoria spun and raised her rifle. Half a second later, the others did so as well. Four

291

cones of light shot off in different directions as they searched for the source of the sound.

After a moment, her attention fell on the heavy table with the thick, black top she used for shelter against those first gigas. One of the earliest memories that she could reliably say belonged to her was of those terror-filled moments. Naked and and confused, she stood up to the gigas and killed the monsters before they could kill her. Every second, every step of that fight had been etched into her brain.

Which explained why Victoria immediately knew that particular table was not in the same spot. It sat in a corner, wedged there with the thick top facing out. She leveled her rifle at it with programmed precision.

"No attack," hissed a voice from the far side of the heavy table. "No kill, you. Stand now, I. Speak, we?"

"Don't shoot," Victoria whispered as the others turned and aimed at that spot. The rifles they all carried could have penetrated that table with deadly precision, yet Victoria was curious.

"Are you insane?" Photeos retorted. His tone was hot, but he kept his voice nearly as quiet as Victoria had.

"I might be," Victoria admitted, "but I want to find out what's going on first."

"Don't shoot until Victoria orders you to," Pallasophia whispered.

"As you say, Lochagos." Photeos was not happy, but his tone indicated that he would obey her order.

"Stand up," Victoria ordered. "We won't shoot."

A fishbelly white face slowly appeared over the edge of the upturned table. Three brilliant green eyes regarded the five soldiers with wary interest. The neck supporting the bulbous head was thick and muscular, but the body to which it was connected seemed like it would have been better suited to a malnourished child. Two long arms ending in bony hands came up, raised in the air in mimicry of surrender, while a much smaller pair of arms stayed clutched close to its pale chest.

292

The sophont stared at each of them in turn, regarding them with a mixture of curiosity, fear, and revulsion. A hole opened in Victoria's gut as the temperature in the room seemed to plummet to something approaching that of deep space. Beside her, she could almost feel Pallasophia radiating hot tension.

"Who are you?" Victoria demanded.

Water washed across rocks as it spoke, wet and gritty. "Have no name, I. Victoria are, you."

"How do you know my name?"

"Big ones, gigas. Speak, they."

Victoria's mind reeled. Never in her time in these lower levels of the facility, the place she regarded as the labyrinth, had anything other than the sophont truly conversed with her. Even then, all it really did was try to dishearten her in a last-ditch effort to get her lost in the maze of corridors. It failed, and she killed it. She knew it was dead because she had removed the damnable thing's head from its body.

"Pallasophia," she hissed.

"I see it," she whispered back. "Looks like our theory was right, after all. Gods between, but I wish it wasn't."

To the sophont, Victoria said, "the gigas told you who I am?"

"Yes. Spoke, they, I. Killed many, you. Killed elite, you," the sophont hissed in its strange rhythm.

"So why shouldn't I kill you?" Victoria demanded.

"Answers want, I. Truth seek, you."

"Not good enough," Victoria said, tensing her hand on the rifle's grip.

The sophont held up its larger hands, hurrying through its words. "Speak now, I. Of you, only stories know, I. Not yet made, I, when killed elite, you."

"What do you mean, 'made?'" Stavros demanded. His rifle drooped and his posture seemed more like a man taking notes in a lecture than a soldier.

"Little ones, mikros, grow, they. Become sophont, even become elite, they. Hid from killer, I. Speak with you now must, I. *Survive* must, I."

"Why?" Victoria demanded. "The other sophont and every damned mastigas I encountered down here tried to kill me on sight."

"Few left, us. Survive want, us. Trapped were."

"Don't listen to it," Photeos hissed. "A sophont will tell you anything to get you to let it live."

Victoria ignored him. "The other sophont said that as soon as it escaped, it was going to kill everyone here."

"Yes," the sophont agreed. "Said that, it. Wanted that, it. Do not want that, I. Freedom want, I."

"Photeos is right. We have more information than we had before, but we still have a mission to carry out. And that," Pallasophia nodded once in the direction of the sophont, "is still a mastigas."

"You," Victoria said, ignoring her as well. "What will you do if we let you go free?"

"Leave, we. Return to ship, we. No kill you, we." For a moment, its face changed. The three hairless brows pinched together in a look Victoria would have called confusion on a human face. "Not *want* to return to ship, I, but must. Calls, ship. Call, they. Return must, I."

"Ship?" Victoria whispered, turning her head slightly toward Pallasophia.

"There's a huge ship sitting somewhere at the edges of the binary where they keep coming from. We've found it, but haven't been able to do anything about it. If this thing leaves here, it will take information about Project Titan with it," Photeos replied.

Victoria nodded. "One more question."

"Alright."

To the sophont, she demanded, "why do you kill us?"

The sophont made a face of disgust. The reaction looked immediate, involuntary, as though the very conception of humanity revolted it. It seemed to be choosing its words carefully, as though struggling against powerful emotions. "Hate, we. Understand not, I, but hate, we. Kill must. Speak of revenge, gigas."

"Then I can't let you leave."

"Must escape, I! Freedom, must have, I! Hate, I!" it bellowed.

As it yelled, the catwalks above the room creaked with dozens of bodies shifting around. The sophont's smaller pair of arms uncurled, revealing something small and metallic in one hand, which it pointed at Victoria faster than she could react. The dull cylinder barked and pain blossomed in her right shoulder.

In the heartbeat following the shot, the other four humans poured a dozen bullets into the sophont, splattering the wall behind it with bright blood.

Half a second after that, several pairs of feet hit the floor as mastigas sprang from the catwalks above them. Victoria jumped to the side as a gigas crashed down in the exact spot she had been standing.

The gigas opened its mouth. In a voice that sounded like the deep maw of an earthquake given life, it bellowed.

"HATE! KILL!"

***

Victoria's shoulder burned. Whatever the sophont hit her with did not seem to have done much damage—she could still move the arm, after all—but the dull ache warned her the shot did more than just bruise.

The nearest gigas turned toward her and slammed a fist into the floor. The spike on its rod shattered the tiles underneath, sending a cloud of dust and ceramic debris into the air.

Victoria took several quick steps backward, putting as much distance as she could between herself and the gigas's crushing strength. She stopped after a second and a half, not wanting to take too much time and risk the giant's attention turning toward her team instead.

She raised her rifle to her shoulder and spared a quick glance around the room. Less than ten seconds had passed since the sophont's death.

Pallasophia and Photeos stood nearly shoulder-to-shoulder, raising their rifles as though in slow motion. Eleni stood by herself, sweeping the muzzle of her rifle back and forth. Victoria at first thought she was unable to fix on a single target amid the milling chaos, but a half-second's consideration, watching the diminutive woman's movements, told her that Eleni was calmer than that and likely assessing the situation just like she was. She could not see Stavros—a fact which concerned her.

"Pallas! Teos!" Victoria snapped. Her brain automatically truncated their names into something she could snap out as a command. She gestured to largest group of fonias. "Deal with that group! Don't let them surround you!"

Photeos tensed, seemed ready to argue, then turned toward the mastigas. Pallasophia, either more willing to follow Victoria's orders or simply already thinking the same thing, fired a short burst into the close-packed mastigas. Photeos followed suit a moment later.

Victoria snapped another order. "Ele! Find Stavros!"

Eleni nodded. Her attention turned to the flank of the group of mastigas approaching Pallasophia and Photeos. She let off a series shots, one round at a time, as she moved away. From where Victoria was standing, it seemed as though each bullet found its mark in the skull of a mastigas.

Orders given, Victoria planted her rear foot and fixed her attention on the lead gigas. One had turned into two, but that meant two fewer to threaten her team. Four of them jumped from the catwalk, however, and Victoria knew she needed to resolve this fight as soon as possible.

She dropped her short rifle's front sight over the nearest monster's chest in a move that was both comfortable and unfamiliar. Her finger tightened on her rifle's trigger as the gigas swiped at her. She stepped back, aim never wavering, and squeezed the trigger the rest of the way. Three bullets exited the muzzle in a single brilliant flash and slammed into the lead gigas.

The giant's shoulder erupted in a brief spray of blood so red it looked cartoonish. Victoria knew that blood all too well. It covered her skin for days early on and some of it remained even after she made her first set of clothes. Some still coated her side where she used the burning stuff to seal the wound left by the elite's sword.

The first gigas stumbled, never actually losing footing. The second stepped around it, swinging the metal spike clutched in its fist. Victoria lunged backward, firing. Her shots went wide, but the gigas's automatic jerk backward gave her the space she needed.

She looked around the room again, searching for the two frustratingly absent gigas. Eleni had replaced Photeos at Pallasophia's side. The two of them were walking shots across the front of the mastigas horde, but too few of them fell at a time. The little knife-wielders were getting closer by the moment, using their own dead as cover.

At the far side of the room, she saw Stavros sprinting past an approaching group of mikros, firing as he went. Photeos, halfway between him and the spot where Pallasophia and Eleni stood rooted, moved toward him at a more controlled pace.

Stavros passed Photeos as their paired gunfire dropped several of the mikros on the spot. Two broke away from the group, chasing Photeos, while the last three continued toward Stavros. One immediately flew backwards, propelled by a burst of gunfire. The others lunged at him, clinging and dragging him to the floor.

Photeos body checked one of the mikros, knocking it out of the way, and shot the second in the stomach as he turned in place. Above the sounds of combat, Victoria thought she heard him say, "don't panic!"

She then lost sight of them as a gigas interposed itself. For a moment, she wondered if the giant was actively trying to separate her from the other four. None of the gigas she fought before had used anything resembling tactics, yet now these two seemed to be doing exactly that.

In fact, none of the mastigas assailing them acted quite like they had before. She had watched unguided mastigas attack one another, or at least get in each other's way, more than once. The only differences were the sophont and the sheer number of mastigas present. Experience taught her that they did not get smarter with more of them in one place, which only left one option: something the sophont had done had improved their ability to coordinate, and done so to potentially deadly effect.

An idle thought crossed her brain: so this was the monster Tritogenes brought into the facility. Victoria would have words with the Hexarch when they met, and as the heated things she wanted to say to him rushed to the surface, her focus crystallized on the two gigas in front of her.

Both gigas streamed bright blood from over a dozen bullet wounds each. They moved slower now, and one seemed to be favoring one arm over the other, but neither had actually stopped by the time Victoria realized she was running out of space. A quick look around the room told her that her instincts were right: the pair of gigas were pushing her away from the others, maneuvering so that they were always between Victoria and her team.

The nearer of the two gigas swung its fist at her and Victoria jumped backward again. There was no parrying or blocking the force that the gigas could put into a simple attack like that. That left only dodging, which, as she noticed a moment before, she was quickly running out of room to do.

She stopped and fired again as the second gigas attacked. At least one of her shots hit it in the hand, and it roared and drew back, coating her visor with a spray of bright red. In the half-second between that moment and when she was able to wipe it clear, the first gigas attacked again.

The blow took her in the midsection and Victoria crumpled and flew across the room like a doll. She went some three or four meters through the air before hitting the wall with an impact that drove the air from her lungs. She bounced and fell to the floor amid the clatter of broken tile.

When injured, humans naturally fell into one of two categories. The first coddle the wound, curl up around it and protect the ache from the world. That sort of person would have paid more attention to the pain, probably checked for broken ribs, or at the very least been distracted by the sudden blaze of agony in their core.

The second sort of person would fight harder when tired or hurt. To that sort of person, an injury was simply another source of adrenaline, more fuel for the fire. That is, assuming they even registered the injury at all.

Victoria belonged in the second category. Somewhere, she was dimly aware that her ribs were screaming, her abs were on fire, and her spine felt like *it* had taken the brunt of the gigas's attack. Those notions never formed clearly enough to be considered thoughts, because one overriding thought screamed in her brain: KILL.

In a flash, she took in the battlefield with crystal clarity. Her adrenaline-pumped senses worked with a sharpness she had only experienced during her fight with the four-armed elite.

To her right, across the room, Stavros and Photeos faced a crawling horde of mastigas that refused to go down. Bodies littered the floor, and the two soldiers swayed on their feet. Stavros's uniform and armor had been ripped and torn, and he streamed blood from a dozen places. Photeos howled like a madman, wordless screams of bloodthirst rising above even the gunfire.

To her left, Pallasophia and Eleni were nearly buried under mastigas. The line between living and dead blurred and ten or twelve of them still moved and lashed out. Pallasophia favored her left side, using only that hand to aim and fire her backup pistol. Her right arm hung limp at her side. Eleni stood a step ahead of her, leaning heavily on one leg. Her other foot stood in a dark pool of human blood.

Victoria processed all of that in the space between two rapid-fire heartbeats, then turned her attention to her own fight. Directly in front of her, the further gigas held its wounded hand in a tight fist that leaked blood. Its brief retreat meant that, for a few seconds, she was only fighting one of the resilient giants. She flicked the selector switch on the side of her rifle, taking advantage of her unnatural knowledge and letting her fingers operate on instinct.

The first gigas attacked, swinging down hard. The blow, had it connected, would have hit ten times harder than the one that threw her into the wall, probably hard enough to kill her on the spot. She, however, was not there. Rather than dodging away, Victoria lunged forward and with just enough of an angle to avoid the potentially fatal blow.

She contorted her body into a twist a gymnast would have envied and jammed the barrel of her short rifle into the underside of the gigas's jaw. Her heart thudded once before her rifle roared with all of the rage she felt inside. The hail of bullets ripped the monster's skull apart like a saw that only stopped when the magazine clicked empty.

Victoria sprang out of her crouch, ignoring the protests that came from her ribs and core muscles. Before the mastigas could fall, she grabbed it, sinking her fingers tightly into the dense, black fabric of its clothes. In a single motion, she hauled herself aloft, climbing up to the collapsing giant's shoulders and then dropping down the other side.

The gigas slumped against her. Victoria dropped the magazine from her rifle, inserted a new one from the bandolier given to her during one of their earlier rest stops. She chambered a round, and braced her shoulders against its massive back. The other one swatted at her. It missed as Victoria jumped away, sending the corpse of its dead comrade to the side.

For half a second, the other gigas's attention was on the dead one as it stepped around the fallen corpse. That was all Victoria needed. Her rifle remained in automatic mode, and she held the trigger down for two solid seconds. What was left of the gigas's torso when the gun clicked empty and Victoria released the trigger was unidentifiable.

She looked around again. Eleni and Photeos were nowhere to be seen, and Stavros had moved far into the shadows. He seemed to be wrestling with a lone fonias. Pallasophia stood alone, retreating from the few remaining fonias approaching her. She fired slowly, and Victoria wondered if she was running out of ammunition.

One of the fonias lunged, hitting Pallasophia in the stomach with his shoulder. She fell to one knee, struggling against the thing for a moment before firing three rounds through its torso. It fell to the side as the others approached.

She shot the next nearest mastigas twice in the head with her pistol, dropping it, before its slide locked open, empty. Victoria crossed the meters between them with a handful of fast, bounding lunges, slamming into the nearest fonias with her shoulder. She grabbed it around the head with her free hand and snapped its neck.

Pallasophia scrambled for a fresh magazine with fingers that refused to do their job. Without thinking, Victoria unslung her rifle and held it out to her. Pallasophia took it without protest and Victoria knelt to draw her daggers from their sheaths on her calves. Those daggers, the ones that she had taken from fonias just like these on that first day of her life, glinted in the light.

Victoria dove into the writhing mass of fonias and mikros, slashing violently. Less than a half-dozen of them remained, all injured. She struck with one dagger in the same motion as she parried with the other. Another step, and she dodged violently to the side, burying both knives indiscriminately in whatever mastigas was unlucky enough to find itself within her reach.

Against the guns, the mastigas had been hiding behind their own dead. Against a whirlwind of death in the midst, however, the remaining number fell rapidly. Victoria ripped through them like the proverbial hot knife through butter, carving her way from end to end of the shrinking horde.

Some part of her mind knew that some of the blood soaking her clothes and turning the floor slick and treacherous had to be her own. Her entire body hurt. She ached and her muscles burned and stung a hundred different ways. There were simply too many mastigas for even

301

her combat skills to overwhelm with complete safety. She felt the cold edges of knives and the hot rip of claws as she went, but the mastigas had to die.

Again, the same thought from before roared through her brain, but now it was tempered with the scream from the fight the day before.

KILL.

PROTECT.

She slipped in the mingling of human and mastigas blood. Despite her reflexes, her bare feet simply failed to find purchase on the slick tile and she hit the floor hard. Her hip hit first, followed by a shoulder, and one of her knives went skittering away. Before she could move, a mikros jumped on her, latching its long, spindly arms onto her shoulders.

The mikros tore at her face and throat with its claws, but failed to find a solid grip. Victoria lurched and twisted, throwing the little mastigas off balance just long enough to get out from under it. In a flash, she was on top, single remaining dagger in her dominant hand. A swipe of her arm drew the blade across the mikros's forearm and it hissed, flailing at her with the other hand. She ignored it as it beat on the side of her head, instead shattering the things faceplate with the heavy pommel of the dagger.

With a sharp exhalation of breath that might have been a scream, she drove the blunt end of the dagger through the opening in the thing's helmet. The first blow crushed its nose; the second shattered the bones around one eye. By the sixth impact, the mikros had stopped moving. She struck it three more times before a sharp pain in her leg took her attention.

Another mikros sank its long nails into her calf. She twisted, roared something incoherent, and slashed across its throat with the blade of the dagger. She kicked it away and rose as her instincts forced her to take stock of the scene around her.

Before she could do that, Pallasophia yelled from behind her. "Down!"

In the corner of her vision, something shifted, something big.

Victoria obeyed automatically, dropping flat to the floor in a pool of blood. A fonias slashed at her thigh as she dropped, painful but nothing that would incapacitate her any time soon.

On the floor, she rolled and wrapped her legs around that same fonias, pulling it to the ground with her. It ended up on top of her and raised its own knives to strike. She buried hers into one of its wrists and left it there. With the other hand, she grabbed the thing's other wrist and twisted that knife out of its hand. Heedless of it cutting into her palm as she held it by the blade, she slashed the tip of the dagger across the fonias's throat.

A curtain of red blood splashed across her face, stinging her cuts and scrapes as something immense sailed through the air above her. A dim part of her brain recognized it as the table the sophont had been hiding behind. That table had been easily two meters long or longer with a dense top.

The table crashed to the ground with a titanic thud that shook the floor, splintering and shattering into a cloud of wood and stone and dust.

The fonias continued to scrabble for her neck, despite the blood pouring from its own slit throat. She shoved it away, inadvertently throwing it against the knives of the one behind it. A burst of gunfire ripped through both of them.

Victoria stood. The last two gigas towered over the body of the sophont, standing where the massive table had been moments before. Pallasophia knelt behind her, bracing Victoria's rifle on her knee. Photeos was out of sight, as was Stavros. Eleni was running toward the massive table. Numerous mastigas legs and arms stuck out from underneath it, pinned between its titanic weight and Victoria's own pod.

A hail of bullets from the shadows told her where the missing soldiers likely were. Only a few of the bullets hit their targets, but it was enough to distract the two remaining gigas. Behind her, Pallasophia emptied the rest of the rifle's magazine into the two giants.

Against multiple sources of gunfire, the first gigas went down quickly. Victoria caught sight of Stavros as he limped into view. He held his rifle loosely, somewhere between his shoulder and hip in a stance that looked like an attempt at proper form done with arms that simply could not stand up to the weight anymore.

More shots came from Victoria's left as Eleni returned her attention to the mastigas and unloaded an entire clip in inaccurate, if devastating, automatic fire.

Victoria, now lacking a ranged weapon of her own, watched as speckles of red appeared on the wall behind the last gigas. It turned, sheltering his face from the incoming torrent of bullets long enough to pick up a chair and hurl it in Victoria's general direction. She threw herself sideways and the heavy metal chair missed her almost entirely. Despite the attempt at dodging, it slammed into her ankle, hard. The impact threw that leg backward and turned her evasion into a sloppy fall.

Victoria rolled, came upright, and then immediately went down again as her ankle refused to support her weight. Rather than fight it, she tucked that leg under her hips and went down again. As the gigas fell, she came back to her feet, avoiding putting weight on that leg as much as she could.

Eerie, terrifying quiet fell as gun after gun went silent. Victoria heard as much as felt her pulse hammering in her chest and ears. As quiet descended, so did the stinging pain of her wounds. Her head swam in the deafening silence as her ears rang with the echoes of a thousand gunshots.

Behind her, Pallasophia rose to her feet. Now that the fighting seemed to be over, she avoided using her right side entirely. Stavros stood across the room, streaming blood, but still on his feet. He held a quick heal dispenser in one hand. The light atop the little capsule indicated that it was empty. With fast, jerky movements, he swept his rifle's light across the room's darkest corners, making sure nothing else lurked there.

Eleni, somehow the least injured of them all, levered at the gigas-thrown table with a long pipe, trying in vain to move the heavy piece of furniture. She paid the rest of them no attention.

Victoria withdrew her own vial of quick heal from her pocket. She spread single-area doses on the worst of her wounds, emptying the device entirely. Without no conscious thought, she withdrew a second vial, dialed it to full strength and emptied the container into her mouth.

A welcome mixture of relief, numbness, and tingling set in across her entire body. In moments, the pain itself was gone. Her injuries persisted; even the accelerated healing from the chemicals in the little egg-shaped thing could only do so much so quickly.

"Gods between us," Eleni muttered. Her voice barely made it through the ringing in Victoria's ears, but when it did, the tone froze her blood.

Victoria turned to see Eleni throwing the body of a fonias aside. Stavros was one step away from her. Despite being barely able to walk himself, he dragged one of the smaller mikros away from the pile. Both of the mastigas had been crushed by the heavy laboratory table. Their helmets, and the skulls inside, were shattered and flat. Limbs bent in sickening directions.

Eleni's face was still shrouded by her helmet, but Victoria could see a little sliver of skin between it and the woman's collar. Perhaps it was the contrast between her skin and the dark uniform, but she looked bone-white.

Victoria almost asked what shocked her when her eyes fell on the object at her feet. Eleni knelt before a pair of boots, twisted and mangled like the mastigas she had tossed aside. One foot pointed to the side, but the spur of bone sticking out of the top of the boot sent a clear message. The other foot was crushed completely, folded back on itself.

They were not mastigas shoes.

She crossed the room as quickly as her ankle would let her. The pain was already gone thanks to the powerful chemicals in the quick heal, but the joint still lacked the ability to support weight. Without the pain itself to warn her, Victoria found herself stumbling constantly as that foot refused to function for more than a second.

Eleni unbuckled her helmet and dropped it. The cable on the back kept it attached to her backpack, but it hung loose and forgotten. Victoria's initial impression had been right; Eleni's face was a deathly shade of white.

Victoria dropped heavily down beside her, landing hard on the muscle of her hips as her ankle gave one last protest and buckled. She sat in silence for a moment until Stavros and Pallasophia joined them.

"I'm sorry," Victoria said after another moment. Her voice was quiet and scratchy, like she had been screaming and never realized it. The previous day, she would not have imagined caring so deeply about the loss of one of their team.

Yesterday, they had not been "her" team.

Eleni flinched, then, "you did everything you could. I know that." She laughed, but the sound was hollow. "I'm not some holo-drama soldier, ready to fly off the handle as soon as someone gets killed. It hurts, yeah, and Lochias Photeos was a good CO, but we all knew the risks coming down here."

Victoria nodded slowly. "I understand."

"Thanks."

"This is the second to last level," Pallasophia announced. The apparent non sequitur drew both Eleni and Victoria's attention. She tried and failed to get her holoprojector to work, presumably to display the map, but it had been destroyed in the fight. After a moment, she said, "we come back for his body, to *all* their bodies, after we sweep the last floor."

"There won't be anything down there." Victoria felt it in her bones, somehow. She then pointed upward. "Or there. They were all here, and now they're all dead."

Pallasophia turned, regarding her with curiosity. "Have can you be sure?"

Victoria glanced at the sophont, buried under the bodies of two gigas. One of its stick-thin limbs stuck out to the side, as though it had been scrabbling to free itself.

"I'm not sure. I just know we're alone now," she admitted after a moment.

Eleni rose to her feet. "Intuition?"

"Perhaps," Victoria said.

Eleni gestured to where Photeos's body lay. Her voice was mostly calm, tinged with its fair share of tension, but no one would have accused her of being irrational or hysterical. Angry, perhaps, but it was controlled. "That's where our intuition would have led, so you'll forgive me if I don't trust yours."

"That could have been any of us."

Pallasophia gestured to the room around them. "None of us ever expected any of this."

"That reminds me." Victoria wheeled around and faced the Second Lord. "How in the hell did you not know the mikros grew into sophonts?"

"I have no answer for you," Pallasophia said, voice dark. She spoke formally, a stark contrast in comparison to Victoria's demands. "Rest assured, I will be asking some pointed questions at the next Council meeting. Stavros, record everything we learned here."

"Understood."

Victoria paced away from the three surviving Technocrats. She faced the sophont, staring down at its corpse. Up close, she could see the similarities between it and the mikros—and between it, the mikros, and the elite.

She continued looking at the dead mastigas as she spoke. "As to why I think this was all of the mastigas. There was a certain logic to what they did here. They drew us in, separated us, and did their damned best to kill us all. That's not the sort of thing that happens by chance.

"I fought them when 'chance' was all they had to work with." She was pacing now. "Random encounters in the halls and rooms. Those were like encountering wild animals. Angry, territorial, brutish. These," she jabbed and angry finger at the veritable mountain of corpses, "fought with a unified purpose. To kill us all."

Victoria pointed now toward the sophont's corpse. "*That* was the difference." She turned in place, nearly falling as she placed weight on her damaged ankle, and approached the Technocrats again. "So there might be a few left, ones that didn't get 'the message,' but they're going to be upstairs, between us and the exit."

"I suspect you're right," Pallasophia said. "But first, we need to get out of this room and find somewhere we can rest."

Chapter 17

First Lord Hyperion stared out his office window at the ocean beyond. Twenty-one generations of Pterygan Hexarchs saw that same view, plus or minus a few hundred meters of shoreline. He supposed that some descendant of his would eventually have to abandon the office, but until the sea swallowed the rest of this headland, he supposed it would do just fine. Besides, it would not be his problem at that point.

He inhaled a deep lungful of salt air, relishing the atmosphere that permeated his planet. With his windows shut, the sounds of the waves never reached his ears, but nothing in the palace could successfully keep out the smell of the ocean. It was an old smell, one that told a story of his planet's great age.

That was just as well, he thought. After spending ninety-five years working in the same office, it was only fitting that it smell like the rest of the palace. Some of the awards and small items decorating the office were even older than his claim on Pteryga's Hexarchate; some even predated his own life. Here and there mementos belonging to his predecessor, First Lord Asphaleia, and even some that came from *her* Hexarch, littered the walls.

In fact, Hyperion knew that if we opened the right boxes or moved the proper things, he could uncover everything from medals and trinkets to the elevation paperwork belonging to Pteryga's Hexarchs for hundreds of years. If he was being completely honest with himself, which only the privacy of his office really allowed, he would much rather spend some time working to see what pieces of the distant past he could uncover.

It was certainly preferable to dealing with the present, as the beep from his work desk reminded him.

The alert sounded again and Hyperion grumbled under his breath. There were very few people in the binary who could truly get under his skin, but the Hexarch of Dasos was one of them. Aegesander and he, at one point, had been close friends and co-workers, but a variety of things over the years had driven them apart.

Hyperion preferred not to dwell on those things, but he also learned from them. Long-range comms were the only way he would meet with Aegesander anymore. Both men knew he had no evidence for his suspicions, but that changed nothing.

He crossed the spacious office to the door and locked it. Unlike many other Hexarchs, he did not rely directly on human security. No one waited on the other side of secret doors to rush to his aid if something happened, nor did they keep a sniper's watch on his windows just in case something suspicious happened.

By contrast, his office's security was provided by much more basic means—the men and women who made up his security force patrolled the area around his little building, and the stone making up his walls was a thin veneer atop starship alloy plating that stood for a thousand years. Nothing would ever get close enough to his office to hurt him and First Lord Hyperion could still maintain his privacy.

That privacy had caused no end of rumors, especially since the deaths of Meriones and Ophion. Both of them had been close friends of Hyperion's for some time, and their deaths hit the Hexarch hard and made him rethink his approach to security. Rather than add more guards,

Hyperion reinforced the building's armor and eliminated the human element entirely.

Both men died within a decade of the Mastigas's arrival. Hyperion knew no connection existed there—until they hit Kipos twenty-five years after their arrival, the mastigas never attacked anything outside the fringes of the binary—but that did not stop him from enacting tighter security.

Very few people, such as his former pupil Tritogenes, merited entrance into his private office. Hyperion conducted most of his business in one of two different places as a result. First, highly public areas such as the Council chamber, or other, similar, if smaller, places with an audience in attendance. The other was via holo, as yet another impatient beep from his desk reminded him.

With the door securely locked, Hyperion returned to his desk in time for another beep from his comm equipment to remind him once again of the call waiting for him.

Hyperion smoothed an errant hair from his long, white beard. It had an unfortunate tendency to bristle in Pteryga's humid air, and he usually kept such things pinned down with a set of six rubies twined into the coarse hair. Today was an exception, however, and there was little he could do beyond straightening it.

Drawing himself up taller and gazing down at the visual pickup where it sat at chin-level, he reached out and finally accepted the call.

In a moment, his holographic workspace vanished. Replacing it was a projected bust of First Lord Aegesander. The projection's eyes lined up exactly with Hyperion's own camera, allowing him to treat those with whom he met as though they were actually in the room. It also had the effect of forcing him to look down slightly, emphasizing his already impressive height and build.

Aegesander smiled, creating an odd effect against the crescent moon motif that dominated one half of his face. He then bowed formally, causing the projection to partially drop out of Hyperion's view. When he returned, the smile had vanished, replaced with a stern look which was itself covered over by another smile.

"Good day, my friend," Aegesander began. "Have I caught you at a bad time?"

Hyperion smiled and shook his head. He knew Aegesander would see exactly how fake his smile was, but after so many years, Hyperion cared little for that particular talent of his. More to the point. Aegesander was making no effort to project any sort of authenticity in his own facial expressions.

That told Hyperion a few things, first and most important among them was that Aegesander was as alone as he was. If any of his subordinates were around, his fellow Hexarch would certainly have put more effort into making himself seem genuine.

Hyperion allowed his smile to fade, relaxing his face and letting his neutral expression convey his actual feelings. His tone, however, remained genial. "Of course not. I was simply taking a few minutes for myself to appreciate the ocean."

Aegesander's false smile never wavered. "Your palace does have a rather pleasant view of the ocean," he said, waited a moment, then added, "at least from what I remember."

"It has been some time since you've visited my planet, hasn't it?"

Aegesander nodded sadly. "Twenty years."

"You're not forbidden from setting foot on Pteryga, Aegesander."

Aegesander raised an eyebrow. "So you say."

"So I say."

Aegesander laughed. "Am I to believe that if I were to land on Pteryga that you would not have me followed, shepherded here and there by your guards, and denied access to your palace?"

"I've told you for years, Aegesander, that you're not forbidden from my planet. We're both Hexarchs."

"Only forbidden from your presence."

Hyperion frowned. "Aegesander, if you contacted me simply to berate me for refusing to allow you into my presence alone, I've got better things to do. You know as well as I do that you're not the only one."

"Yes," Aegesander grated. "Eurybia, who I should note you *have* had removed from your palace, is also forbidden from being alone with you."

Hyperion glared. "She threatened you as well as me."

"And that particular incident was dealt with many years ago." The fake smile returned. "We've even become friends."

"How you managed that, I'll never understand."

Aegesander's face closed off for a moment. "I managed it because *Eurybia* is not an unreasonable person."

Anger flared up somewhere deep inside Hyperion. He knew he was not being unreasonable. He knew someone killed Meriones and Ophion, even if he could not prove who that someone was. Limiting access to his person to those he knew he could trust beyond a shadow of a doubt was the only logical outcome.

He stared at the holo of Aegesander's thin face, stroking his beard absently as he did so. It only took a moment for him to regain control over his emotions. During that moment, however, he thought strongly about ending the conversation right there, but that would give Aegesander more satisfaction than Hyperion thought he deserved.

"Let us start again. What can I do for you, Aegesander?"

Aegesander smiled, genuine this time. Hyperion was sure he thought he won their little sparring match. They never had these arguments, not these specific ones, when others could overhear and so Hyperion did not care whether Aegesander thought he won or lost.

"My friend, I simply wanted to discuss Project Titan. Eurybia tells me she met with Enyalios and Tritogenes yesterday. Second Lords Panatakis and Helena are already on Prosgeiosi and Daniel will be arriving on Eurybia's ship."

Hyperion kept his expression carefully neutral, filing that information away. Tritogenes and Enyalios, especially the former of the two, would not have gone with her without some serious social maneuvering. He was actually rather impressed she managed to pull that off and made a mental note to speak to Tritogenes about it.

Hyperion nodded. "I understand from your press releases that Helena is a cyborg?"

Aegesander nodded. An expression Hyperion could not read passed over his face for a moment, then he smiled. This one was genuine, if somewhat stressed in strange ways around the edges. "Second Lord Helena has shown a proficiency with computer systems that outstrips any un-augmented technician I have on staff."

"Impressive. How long did it take to develop the implants so that her body didn't reject them?"

Aegesander shook his head. "Longer than I would have liked, but fortunately Helena made great strides since then. She has also proven herself to be a capable combatant, which I admit I did not expect."

"Why is that?"

"Before the implants, Helena showed little interest in hand-to-hand combat. Since then, however, she's discovered a love for it."

Hyperion considered that for a moment. He knew a few things about what Tritogenes did at Aphelion, but his former pupil learned Hyperion's own preferences for security rather well and kept a tight lid on information flow. All he knew about Aphelion had been from Tritogenes himself, and that was limited to three areas: genetic engineering, memory learning, and the Incident.

After a few moments, Hyperion nodded. "If she's as skilled as you say, is it possible that she downloaded combat data to her implants and learned from that?"

"Perhaps," Aegesander replied. "Actually, no, not perhaps. I suspect that's exactly what happened. Hyperion, her abilities are actually quite impressive and, between us, frightening."

314

That stopped Hyperion cold. For Aegesander to admit something like that, even in private, especially to him, was a surprise. Aegesander's people respected him, but "vulnerable" was not exactly a word anyone would have used to describe him.

However, Hyperion was not going to let the moment pass. "Frightening?"

Aegesander nodded. "Yes. Her mind works in strange ways now."

"Why are you telling me this?"

Aegesander sighed. "Because, Hyperion. I'm worried I made another mistake."

"Project Titan was not a mistake."

"And yet we never did anything about the mastigas until Tritogenes stepped up."

"You and Enyalios know better than most how bad those early years were."

Aegesander's face darkened. When the mastigas arrived thirty years ago, there was no warning. They came out of the stars, destroying everything in their path, and for years none of the Hexarchs even knew anything organic lived aboard that massive battleship. At that point, Hexarch Enyalios was Second Lord Enyalios, sworn in service to First Lord Meriones, but when military action truly began against the mastigas, he and Aegesander led the charge.

The losses among their people and military over the next thirty years had been incalculable, yet the Technocracy never slowed its pace. By and large, they simply removed their presence from the system's outer rim, leaving it to the mastigas and the Technocrat military, whose standing orders were to "stop their advance and protect the civilians of the binary."

So it went until the day the mastigas hit Kipos, and First Lord Diomedes committed suicide out of shame and guilt. They had been repelled, but only after killing millions and destroying much of the garden-like planet's infrastructure.

Hyperion knew that guilt all too well, as, apparently, did Aegesander. When the mastigas hit Kipos, he and Dasos's Hexarch had long since stopped regular communication. This conversation was a good step forward, however.

After a moment, the dark cloud over Aegesander's face cleared. "Hyperion," he said, them breathed. "Project Titan must succeed. You know that as well as I do. The mastigas cannot be allowed to attack another planet. They must be *eradicated*."

Hyperion nodded. He understood the fear all too well. Diomedes had been a personal friend. "Yes," he said, then repeated himself. "Yes, my friend."

Aegesander smiled, but the dark cloud seemed to return. "I knew you would understand. My friend."

Hyperion spread his hands in a gesture of acceptance. "Of course. We made a mistake once. Not again."

Aegesander nodded. "Yes, and Diomedes paid the price for our inaction."

Hyperion allowed a smile, a genuine smile to spread across his face. "And to think, you and Enyalios voted against Tritogenes's elevation."

A ghost of a smile flitted across Aegesander's face. "Another mistake I am now trying to atone for. But tell me, are the news reports about your Titan accurate?"

Hyperion nodded, then shrugged. He laughed. "Most of them. Tabloids will report whatever sells copy."

"Of course." Aegesander nodded, then, "of course."

"Korakti has held three different planetary championships," he said, ticking them off on his fingers. "One for wrestling, where she was champion for six years, and another for open-form combat, where she held the title for nine years straight. She was also the planet's champion marksman for three years. Not three consecutive years, though."

"That's an impressive resume for someone so young."

Hyperion laughed. "As it happens, Korakti enlisted in the Pterygan military when she was young. *Very* young."

To Hyperion's surprise, Aegesander laughed. "That would explain a few things, yes. Tell me, when do you plan to bring her to Prosgeiosi?"

"Perhaps in two or three days. She wants to have an exposition fight before her training is officially over."

"Broadcast, I hope?"

Hyperion's smiled turned into a grin. "Of course."

"Once you arrive, I would very much like to see your Titan against Helena. I suspect that would be an interesting match."

"I agree," Hyperion said. "But now I must be going. Work calls my name again."

"Of course. Thank you for taking the time to speak with me."

Hyperion nodded. "Of course. Perhaps..." Hyperion hesitated.

"Yes?"

"Perhaps we can put the past away."

Aegesander shook his head. "The past will never truly leave us, Hyperion. The most we can do is make the best future for ourselves that we can."

"Very true," Hyperion agreed. He took a deep breath before continuing. "When I come to Prosgeiosi, perhaps we can meet over drinks."

Aegesander nodded. "Yes," he said. "Perhaps we can."

***

The challenge had been public, and open. When Second Lord Korakti awoke that morning, she knew the lines would be very long indeed, but this was to be her final exhibition before officially meeting the other Titans and training with them. As a result, a great many people expressed an interest in fighting her, despite the steep registration fee.

Looking at the list that morning, Korakti had a single thought that overrode everything else: that was a *lot* of people. Even in the largest planetary tournaments, she only really expected to fight a dozen people spaced out over the entire day. This was vastly different, and Korakti wiped sweat from her face as she prepared to face down her thirty-third, and final, challenger for the day.

The crowd outside cheered, giving her a measure of energy. That— and the knowledge that food, a hot bath and a long nap awaited her after she was finished—drove her to finish the fight. Fortunately, her challenger elected to make this fight one with swords. Her aching muscles could not have cared one way or the other, but her dwindling energy reserves were quite happy to have a weapon in hand. The stop-and-go of a sword fight was much easier to manage compared to the constant demands of a wrestling match.

She sat out of sight of the audience as the arena's announcer finished introducing her challenger. Most of his words washed right over Korakti without her hearing them. At that moment, it was not that she did not care about her opponent, but rather that she was taking every spare moment to rest. She would pay attention to important things, her support staff coming with water or small bits of food, or her name being called, but that was the extent of it.

While he spoke at length about her opponent's achievements, Korakti mentally reviewed her day so far. Out of thirty two people, she had beaten twenty-nine. Loses were expected, even for a someone with her win/loss record, perhaps especially for someone with that record. Most wanted to wrestle her, that was what she was best known for, after all, and of those twenty matches, she won nineteen. Seven challenged her to point boxing, four of which she won, and two to competitive target shooting. Those, she won handily.

Interestingly, this was to be her only sword match of the day, which was why Korakti had it scheduled for last. It would make the crowd happy to see something flashy for the final match, and, unless she was mistaken, she knew her opponent.

Finally, the announcer called her name and she pushed herself to her feet. Gathering her mask under one arm and her fencing saber under the other, Korakti took one final moment to purge her mind of fatigue. Her body could be tired for all she cared, but as long as she could keep her mind alert and awake, she would be fine.

Again, she reminded herself, she could rest afterward.

Drawing herself fully upright, Korakti strode into the arena amid the cheers of the crowd. She had taken special care during her last break to make herself presentable to them. Her combat robe, itself such a part of her image that she based part of her fighting style around its swirling patterns and shrouding layers, was of a blue so dark it looked black from a distance. It also did not show sweat, no matter how damp. Likewise, she was careful to dry her skin and calm her breathing. Her hair, at least, was kept short in a military cut and took practically no time to dry.

All in all, when she stepped back into the arena, she looked as fresh as she did before her first fight. That attention to detail helped her win more than one tournament in the past as her outward calm convinced her opponent she had more energy to spare than she really did.

The cheering of the crowd continued to buoy her spirits, but Korakti did not let it show on her face or in her body language. With what she knew would appear to be singular purpose, she crossed the arena to her opponent. Despite that show, her eyes darted around, watching the assembled mass of people to gauge their reactions.

Hyperion himself sat in the highest box opposite where she now stood. Despite being scarcely more than a centimeter tall from that distance, his very presence seemed to tower over those around him. His chair sat just a little taller than the others in his box, and the box itself had been installed half a meter higher than any other. It was a subtle difference, but the effect it created was anything but.

She stopped in the center of the arena, finally taking her eyes off her opponent. Over her career as a professional fighter, and even moreso as Pteryga's Titan, Korakti spent a lot of time with her Hexarch. Even across the distance that separated them, she felt she could read his body language. He radiated pride and she knew his sapphire blue eyes were fixed on her.

He nodded once, at that distance more a movement of his great, snowy beard than anything else, and Korakti felt a sudden surge of energy. Hyperion, elder of the Council and a man she viewed as a grandfather, chose *her*.

This fight would be easy.

She returned his acknowledgment, sending another roar through the crowd as hundreds of people, all convinced she nodded to them specifically, rose and cheered.

To her opponent, Korakti gave a smile. She shifted her sword to her other hand, holding it with the same arm that held her mask, and offered her empty hand to her opponent.

"Hello, Sotiria."

Sotiria took Korakti's arm and they clasped hands just above the wrist. From a distance, the two of them might have been sisters who pursued radically different hobbies. Where Korakti had the blocky torso of a traditional wrestler who optimized her physique to dominate her opponent on the ground, Sotiria was tall and thin with arms and legs that looked like they should have been doing flips on a balance beam.

The similarities were in their height and faces. They looked one another directly in the eyes, staring out of eerily similar square-jawed faces.

Sotiria also wore a more traditional duelist's robe. Rather than reaching the ankles or even the floor as most everyday clothing did, her duelist's robe barely brushed her knees. The top half of her robe was actually a separate padded jacket with hidden plates protecting her throat and joints. Despite its outward appearance, Korakti's robe sported similar internal pieces.

Sotiria smiled and released Korakti's hand. "When I heard our fight was going to be last, I was afraid you would be too tired to carry on."

Korakti laughed and slapped Sotiria lightly on the shoulder. "And leave Prosgeiosi's champion fencer with a bad fight? Never!"

"That's what I was hoping you would say, old friend. Now, are you ready to lose?"

Korakti smirked. "Have you taken to talking to yourself, Tiri?"

She laughed, but did not have a chance to reply as the announcer instructed them to take their places.

Korakti and Sotiria retreated away from one another, pointedly not turning their backs to one another out of respect. Overhead, the announcer was explaining the rules to the crowd, but Korakti tuned him out. She set the rules for the day's matches and did not need to be reminded that this final fight was going to be what was still called a "first blood" match.

The announcer finally finished and led the fencers through the ceremonial opening of the match. Korakti raised her sword's hilt to eye level, then flourished it through the air in a motion that ended in a deep bow from the hips.

Sotiria's salute did not end in a bow, but rather a dip of her knees. The effect was the same, however.

She then dropped her mask over her head while her opponent did the same thing. Korakti then raised her saber, waiting for the booming call that would come next. That one, she thought, was actually worth paying attention to.

"Fencers ready?" demanded the announcer. A moment passed, the last chance for either of them to request another few moments to adjust something or to back out, and the booming voice commanded them to, "Fence!"

Korakti sprang forward. Sotiria's strength came from her reach and flexibility, both of which augmented the long rapier in her hands quite well. Her own saber was a good thirty centimeters shorter, which put the burden of offense on Korakti.

Their blades clashed multiple times as she tried to press in closer. Korakti would beat the rapier's blade away and step closer only to find Sotiria had faded backward and returned the weapon's point to center.

Unfortunately, Korakti did not count on fatigue setting in as quickly as it did. Sotiria's defensive style demanded a lot of energy to fight, energy that she simply did not have. With each exchange of blades, Korakti felt her form slipping and her reactions lagging behind.

A minute passed and she backed off. Despite several engagements, neither of them managed to hit the other yet. That, at least, was good, Korakti reasoned.

They circled one another, weapons probing against out of distance targets. Sotiria had boundless energy on Korakti's good days, and while this was a good day, it was also the tail end of a good day. The more they played, the closer she could feel Sotiria's point coming.

That gave her just one chance to make things work and Korakti took her eyes off Sotiria's hand. She needed the fast-twitch reflexes of peripheral vision now, not the analytical ability that came from focus.

Their blades touched. She beat the rapier aside. Reflexes spoke to reflexes now. Inside her own fencing mask, Korakti was not watching anything. Her eyes were wide, taking in her surroundings on a subconscious level. She knew from Sotiria's movements that she was doing the same thing. If they could have seen one another's faces, neither would have been looking anywhere near the other's eyes.

The rapier probed forward, closer now. The ring of steel shuddered through her hand, transmitted through her bones as much as through the air to her ears.

Korakti allowed the sword to creep in. She beat at it again, readying another cut. She slashed the air in front of her, short of her target, but the movement prevented Sotiria from bringing the rapier on target again.

She shuffled forward. The blades met again, rapier pushing forward with opposition. She felt the control over her saber being pulled away by the other blade.

Korakti's hand twitched forward and her sword shuddered as the blade clashed against Sotiria's guard. The rapier shifted, rising, pushing her saber away and then pulling free.

Sotiria twisted to the side, neatly pirouetting away, as her rapier blade traversed a wide circle. Korakti was inside her reach now, forcing her to twist even further and shuffle step backward as she tried to bring the long weapon on target. As she did so, her saber slipped in, point forward.

Sotiria was not there. Her hand swatted Korakti's saber aside. She pivoted, turned her sword, and brought it down in a cut against Korakti's shoulder.

Exactly as Korakti wanted her to. She lunged forward, blade outstretched backward, and seized Sotiria's sword arm at the wrist. Korakti pivoted, twisting, pulling the other woman off balance, and struck her in the side of the head with her saber.

"Halt!" demanded the booming voice of the announcer.

They froze, disentangled, and stepped away. As the announcer described the action, Korakti and Sotiria removed their masks.

Extending her hand, amid deep lungfuls of air as she struggled to catch her breath, Korakti said, "you nearly had me several times!"

Sotiria stepped forward so they they stood nearly shoulder to shoulder. As the crowd's cheering grew louder, it became hard for them to hear one another. "Trust me, I know! I'm kicking myself for not taking a few of those openings."

"Next time, yeah?"

Sotiria clapped Korakti on the shoulder. "Definitely. Now," she gestured to the cheering crowd and waved.

Now that the fight was over, Korakti played to the crowd, smiling and waving. She turned in a circle waving to the crowd. Now that her fights were over, she challenged the crowd.

Loud as her tired throat could mange, she yelled. "IS THERE ANYONE ELSE?"

A moment passed before a murmur shot through the crowd like electricity, and it fell silent in moments.

Korakti, confused, scanned the crowd for a moment before turning around the rest of the way. Tired as she was, she did not have the control to keep her jaw from falling open slightly as the unexpected sight.

Not only had Hyperion risen to his feet, but the Hexarch was making his way through the crowd to ground level. People parted before him like grain.

At the edge of the arena, a hand gesture from Hyperion prompted the staff to open the gate. They did not question him. He stepped through and nodded to Korakti who, out of reflex, nodded in return despite her confusion.

A moment passed and Hyperion explained without words what he was doing. With both hands he took hold of two different edges of his purple Hexarch's robe and tugged. With a flourish, he removed it, swirling the brilliant purple fabric through the air like a cape before letting it fall to the ground.

Standing there in an unadorned, gray wrestler's singlet, Korakti was struck by her Hexarch's presence in a way she never had been before. The act of disrobing added several centimeters to Hyperion's apparent height, then a deep breath and a roll of his shoulders made him seem taller still. Korakti might have been used to his presence, but she had never seen him quite so imposing.

Even the announcer fell silent, which told her Hyperion might have planned this, but no one else knew. Wordlessly, the Hexarch of Pteryga nodded to her again and strode forward.

She laughed to herself, careful not to let it show on her face. This, she thought, was a challenge from which she could not afford to back down. She exchanged a glance with Sotiria, then handed her mask, sword, and gloves to the other woman who took them out of the arena and to Korakti's locker room.

When she turned back, Hyperion's towering, imperious visage waited for her. His voice was warm and so at odds with his presence that it was almost jarring. "What rules would you like to use, my Titan?"

Korakti did not even have to think. "Submission," she replied, then, "with striking."

Hyperion nodded and backed away, going directly to the starting point marked out on the arena floor. No one in the audience said a word and electric tension hung in the air as he waited for her.

Korakti came to her staring point and they exchanged two gestures. First a mutual bow, one which Korakti was shocked to see Hyperion returned with equal depth, then a simple head nod of acknowledgment.

She assumed a ready stance, both feet forward and wide with her arms close in and torso inclined forward. Hyperion, by contrast, remained upright, but sank deep into a pugilist's guard. He extended one fist, keeping the other in close.

The muscles on his arms stood out like steel cables.

"Shit!" Korakti exclaimed as Hyperion shot forward faster than anyone his age should have been able to move.

She blocked the first punch, a jab delivered with his outstretched arm, but the second punch struck her in the stomach. Powered by a rotation of Hyperion's torso, it staggered her backward, a momentary opening of which the Hexarch quickly took advantage.

Another blow struck her, then a third, before Korakti got her balance again. She blocked the fourth punch, then darted backward away from a kick aimed at her side.

When Hyperion came forward again, she was ready. They traded punches, kicks, and blocks for a full twenty seconds before her fist found his face. Somewhere past his bushy beard was a jaw of steel, but her strike still knocked his head backward.

Korakti was not about to apologize for punching her Hexarch in the face.

Her followup strike took Hyperion in the stomach and he doubled over, but as he rose his elbow struck her in the side of the head. The heel of his hand followed, and he immediately chased it with another palm-heel strike with the other hand.

Hyperion grabbed her with both hands, one under her shoulder and the other on one wrist. In a single fluid movement, his feet shot in and he threw her smoothly to the ground. Under the rules, a throw was not enough to win, and so Hyperion followed her to the ground, seeking the pin that would finish things.

Korakti bucked as he landed, then rolled to one side, escaping. Before Hyperion could do anything else, she rose to her feet. He followed a moment later, springing up with his head tucked under one elbow, shielding his face from the obvious counter, even though it never came.

They traded several more strikes, all blocked, before Korakti stepped in for a throw. She planted, twisted, and suddenly Hyperion was simply *not there*. With a single twitched movement, he escaped her throw and reversed it.

Korakti fell, toppled at the knee, but as she did so, she threw out an arm that wrapped around Hyperion's own knees. She rolled hard, pulling him down as well, then continued until she came out on top.

Hyperion bucked, but she shifted forward. With one arm she swept his hands upward, and with the other delivered an open hand smack to the ground next to Hyperion's head.

A trickle of red from a busted lip stained his white beard and Hyperion smiled. A moment passed and that smile turned into a laugh as Korakti stood. She offered him a hand up, but for several moments, it seemed Hyperion was content to lay there and laugh as though losing was the most entertaining thing in the world to him.

Finally, he accepted her help up and patted her on the shoulder. "Well done, Titan of Pteryga. Well done, indeed."

Chapter 18

Pallasophia's team—no, she corrected herself, Victoria's team—camped in a nearby room to tend to their wounds. Two kept watch while the other two worked. Victoria and Pallasophia stood guard first, saying only the minimum needed to convey whatever information was necessary at that moment.

When Eleni and Stavros, both haggard and hollow-eyed, came to trade places, Victoria went to the back of the room, trusting Pallasophia to follow. Thoughts, few of them pleasant, boiled in her brain. The things she had to say, if she said them at all, were for the ears of this facility's ostensible commander and no one else's.

First, she had a job to do. "You first," Victoria ordered.

"I'm going to need help. My right arm." She gestured with the left at the makeshift sling and bloody bandage around her right arm.

Victoria followed Pallasophia's instructions, acting more as a pair of functional hands than anything. First, she removed the Lochagos's uniform jacket, then the blood-soaked shirt beneath. Blood dripped in dark red rivulets from a deep gash in her arm, and the right side of her rib cage and her entire right upper arm were purple with bruising.

With Victoria's help, she first covered the cuts and gashes with quick heal, using the thick, surface-application version of the liquid. Pallasophia explained that it also functioned as a sort of bandage itself when it dried, sealing and protecting the wound with minimal scarring.

She massaged another dose into Pallasophia's bruised ribs, then checked her arm. To Victoria's surprise, Pallasophia did not cry out when she probed her arm. The bone there was clearly broken, however, and Pallasophia was on the verge of explaining how to set a broken bone when Victoria interrupted her.

"I know. I've done it before," she said. "Or I dreamed about doing it. Other hands and other bodies. This will hurt."

"I know."

Victoria braced both herself and Pallasophia, then with a single sharp jerk, tugged the broken pieces of her arm bone back into place. The Lochagos grunted and sweat sprang out on her suddenly pale face, but still she did not scream.

Victoria nodded in satisfaction. Even some of her own past selves had not possessed such an iron will.

Before the bone could shift again, and working under instructions she did not need that were given through Pallasophia's clenched teeth, Victoria wrapped her arm with a long strip of sticky, beige fabric. According to the instructions she was being given, it would start to harden in moments, fully immobilizing the arm within minutes.

"With quick heal and regular doctor visits, it should be healed in a few days," she added. With a pointed stare at Victoria, she added, "your turn."

"I'll be fine."

"You're injured."

"None of my bones are broken and none of the cuts are deep enough to be life threatening."

"How can you tell?"

Victoria glared, but it softened in a moment. "I remember how a great many life-*ending* injuries feel."

"You took the time to treat your wounds before," Pallasophia offered, carefully dropping to the floor with her legs crossed. "What's different now?"

Victoria joined her, moving slowly as her muscles took advantage of the current rest period and started to ache. She repeated the question in her head several times before saying, "I'm not sure."

"Is it privacy?"

Victoria shook her head. "No. It's..." She reached for the right words, struggling to say her thoughts out loud. Finally, she said, "my wounds are trivial. Myrto, Photeos, they're dead. You've got broken and bruised bones. I don't know how bad Stavros and Eleni are, but they don't look good."

"All of us got hurt," Pallasophia countered.

Victoria laughed. "Me? I have some cuts and bruises. Keep your trauma supplies for the ones who need it. I'll be fine with quick heal."

"What about the bullet?"

Victoria withdrew a small bundle wrapped in bloody cloth from inside her mastigas-fabric shirt. She held it up like it was a winning playing card before handing it over.

Pallasophia's eyes went wide. "You removed it yourself?"

Victoria shrugged. "It was easy enough. I have knives. The quick heal helped some, though, so thank you for that."

"You... dug it out yourself?"

Victoria nodded.

"When?"

A shrug. "Right after the fight, before the adrenaline faded and I remembered how to feel pain."

"Why keep it?"

"The same reason I'm keeping the elite's sword. It's a," she paused, smiled. "Souvenir."

"At least let me look at your shoulder."

"No."

"And if I insist?"

"You're in no position to insist."

"No," she admitted, "I'm not. But no matter how much better you came out of that fight than I or anyone else did, you're still injured."

"Yes."

Pallasophia's voice changed, hardening and taking on more of the true tones of command. "Then let me look at it, and your side."

Victoria sat for a moment before nodding once. "There's nothing you can do for my side anymore. The quick heal sealed the wound already. But..." She took a deep breath, then let it out all at once. "Yes, check my shoulder if it makes you feel better."

She undid the fabric ties that held her shirt closed and peeled the tight fabric back away from her shoulder. The wound itself was ugly, bloody, and the marks from Victoria's own knife as she dug the bullet out were obvious.

Pallasophia frowned, but refrained from commenting on it directly. Instead, she said in a somewhat detached tone, "this will hurt."

It did. In fact, as Pallasophia probed the wound, her fingers caused pain far in excess of the bullet itself. Burning agony flared there, eclipsing every other pain in her body for several seconds. Fortunately, those several seconds was all she needed to confirm that the wound was clean, and Pallasophia emptied an entire ampule of quick heal into ugly, torn flesh of her shoulder.

Warmth, pleasant this time, spread outward from her injury. Pallasophia handed the bloody bundle containing the sophont's bullet back to Victoria, who tucked it inside her shirt again.

Pallasophia sat back and waited a moment before withdrawing another of the dispensers and drinking a double oral dose. She smiled, a little giddy around the edges as the endorphin rush from the medicine hit. "You'd make a good commander," she said, then, "no, you *made* a good commander today."

Victoria's face tightened into an angry frown. In her head, she demanded to know how Pallasophia dared to say that. Instead, she said, "two people died."

Her face fell. "Two, yes. But you saved three of us."

"I did what I had to to survive."

"And I'm alive because of it," Pallasophia said. A moment passed and she reached into a pocket with her left hand. Out of it, she withdrew a small device. "Here, I thought you might want to see this."

She handed it over, and Victoria took it gingerly with both hands. It was a gun, at least in the most literal sense of the term. One end was dominated by a hollow tube wrapped in polished copper wire. The other end was gently curved and sat awkwardly in her human hands. The sophont's hands were longer and thinner and probably wrapped comfortably around the elongated shape. A battery protruded from one end.

Despite only having seen a flash of it before, the thing was etched into her brain after the firefight earlier. "This is the gun the sophont used?"

"It's not actually a gun," Pallasophia said. "At least not in the conventional sense. See that wire? It's a magnetic accelerator."

Victoria aimed the thing at a wall and pulled the trigger. It clicked, but nothing happened. She looked it over again, removing the battery. Past the battery was a nest of wires and small cylindrical objects. It was hard to tell, but it looked like the wires ran from the battery connector to the bare copper wrapped around the tube.

Pallasophia continued. "As to where it came from, the only explanation I can give is that the sophont made it."

"You said they were locked down here, locked in with me, with no high-tech weapons of any sort. That's why they all came at me with knives and clubs," Victoria accused. Despite the anger slowly bubbling to the surface, she kept her voice quiet, reminding herself of her earlier decision to keep this conversation between the two of them.

"That's true. May I?" Pallasophia extended her hand and Victoria passed the gun back to her. "This tube looks like a piece of pipe, probably ripped from any one of a thousand conduits. The wire and battery could have come from anywhere here."

"And the bullet," Victoria added, "was just a chunk of metal."

Pallasophia's next words were quiet, almost so soft that Victoria herself could not hear them. "In any event, I'm pleased you survived."

In a flash, the anger that had been bubbling beneath the surface ever since the mastigas killed Second Lord Myrto all came out. It was quiet, contained, but Victoria's words still hissed and spat like fire. "You're glad your *weapon* survived."

Pallasophia stared for a moment before looking away. She worked her jaw muscles for a second longer before saying, "yes."

"I must have been very expensive."

Pallasophia did not look her in the eyes. "Yes."

Victoria growled deep in her throat. "Nothing else to add?"

"No."

"Damn you, say something else!"

"What do you want me to say? I condemned ninety-nine good men and women, to say nothing of the dozens we lost in the Incident, to death just to produce you. That is a cost far in excess of any material or financial loss we might have taken."

Victoria regarded her for a long moment. Like her honesty when they first met, it seemed to her that the Second Lord was being genuine. In a strange way, that honesty disarmed much of Victoria's anger. "There is more that you're not telling me, isn't there?"

After a minute of silence, Pallasophia finally said, "there is. I started to tell you earlier, but didn't get through it all. Let me start again. The mastigas appeared at the outer edges of our system thirty years ago..."

She proceeded to give a summarized version of the last three decades. Mastigas had raided the outer settlements and facilities indiscriminately. They would hit a factory just as soon as a mine or a colony. Their very unpredictability, she explained, had been one of the hardest things to fight.

Early on, the death toll had been immense, hard to even calculate. The Technocrat military attacked the mastigas battleship, a massive vessel parked two weeks' travel beyond even Aphelion and defended by devastating missiles. One way or another, the mastigas won every engagement. After the first few years, the Technocrats pulled back and simply evacuated the outer edge of the system.

Then the day came when the mastigas ventured into the inner system. In hushed tones and with few words, she explained that millions died in the first few days.

"Project Titan followed almost directly after that attack, and now here you are."

"You're talking like I'm the subject of a prophecy."

"To a lot of people, you are. Project Titan was envisioned as a way to create the perfect soldier, six of them, to lead an assault on the mastigas directly.

"So yes," she continued, "I was concerned that we would lose our investment. You represent the hope of billions, Victoria. But I was also concerned that I would lose you, a flesh-and-blood human being."

Victoria folded her arms across her chest. "Then I need to know everything you know about them. Not just you personally, but I need access to every scrap of information your government has on these things. Because you clearly did not expect," she pointed to the sophont's gun, forgotten on the ground, "that."

Pallasophia looked back down at the gun. Wondering aloud, she said, "if they could build guns, why did they only build the one, and why only now?"

"Maybe this sophont was smarter than the other one?" Victoria offered.

"Perhaps. Hell," she let out a bitter laugh, "we didn't even know the mikros could, I don't know, 'morph' into sophonts."

Victoria spoke slowly, articulating thoughts as they came to her. "What if the two of them wanted radically different things?"

"What do you mean?"

Victoria explained how the first sophont had drawn her through the labyrinth of corridors, taunted her, then said, "this one didn't do that. It tried to reason with us."

Pallasophia's voice was like iron. "It tried to trick us."

"Probably," Victoria agreed, "but how could it trick us if it didn't understand how to adapt to what we might have wanted or been willing to offer?"

Pallasophia fell silent for another long minute. Tension hung in the air. Across the room, she could see Eleni and Stavros standing in silence. One side of her face was covered with a smear of quick heal and one arm hung in a sling inside her uniform jacket, strapped to her chest. Stavros looked, on the surface, better, but only because Victoria knew most of his wounds were on his torso, covered up by bandages and his jacket. They did not look directly at one another, despite guarding the same door.

"If I ask you something," Victoria ventured, "will you promise me, on your *life,* that you'll be honest?"

Pallasophia's expression wavered between concerned, frightened, and open. Finally she nodded once. She said nothing, instead waiting on Victoria to continue.

"These memories I have, these skills. I know you did that. I know it kept me alive but I need to know how much of my mind is really me." She paused for a moment, growled from somewhere deep in her throat, and continued. "When I started giving orders earlier, is that something you programmed me to do?"

334

Pallasophia looked back at her. For half a second, her face was hard, accusatory. That passed in a moment, replaced by the same serene concern she had shown earlier. "Some things cannot be... programmed. We only gave you knowledge. Your skill is yours alone."

"That's something, at least," Victoria replied. She was not sure whether she felt grateful for that knowledge or if it only served to put her more ill at ease. Perhaps, she thought, it was a little of both.

"I will say this, though. I will bring this matter before the Council of Hexarchs myself and demand a formal accounting for the gaps in our knowledge base."

"I would bring the matter before First Lord Tritogenes before you address the Council," Victoria said. Her voice was tight as she continued. "If he knew and still did not provide us with the information, a 'formal accounting' will be the least of his concerns."

"I suspect, no, I know Tritogenes had no idea that the mastigas could do some of these things. I know him too well for him to hide knowledge like that from me."

Victoria nodded. "Good. Because if Tritogenes or the Hexarchs fucked us over deliberately, I will not hesitate to do the job they designed and *built* me for."

Pallasophia jumped at the venom Victoria poured into the word "built." She started to say several things, but none of them actually came out. Finally, she repeated, "I trust him."

"And so far, I trust you," Victoria admitted after a moment. "You haven't lied to me that I can tell. If you trust him," she paused, "then, unless I have reason not to, I will as well."

Pallasophia's shoulders relaxed slightly. She still radiated tension, but it was less directed now. She stood. Louder, in a voice that carried across the room, she said, "start packing the gear. We're leaving."

The response from the two surviving soldiers was immediate, despite their obvious fatigue. "Yes, Lochagos."

***

335

Several uneventful hours later, Pallasophia stepped into the private wing of Aphelion's hospital. Automated systems would alert the doctor of her arrival in due time.

Victoria, masked once more, entered directly behind her. The door closed behind them. The workroom beyond was silent; the workers had been momentarily sent elsewhere before their arrival. Victoria's presence was hardly a secret to the facility's staff, though she was still considered classified information. Right then, what they really wanted to avoid was a throng of curious questions and onlookers.

They stood in the little room reserved for Pallasophia and Tritogenes only for a few minutes. It was silent between them, but the tension from earlier never came back. Pallasophia stood near the door, in the direct line of sight for anyone coming through it. Victoria took a seat in a wooden chair with a plush crimson cushion. She tried, and failed, to suppress a sigh as she sank against the soft material.

Already, she thought, this place was more comfort than she had ever known.

Victoria waited patiently, watching as Pallasophia shifted uneasily from foot to foot. She had no desire to rush into the unknown, even in an allegedly safe place like this. So far, every "unknown" had tried to kill her.

More to the point, she had no idea what to do. Having her knives and baton close at hand helped calm her nerves, but the idea that nothing here would try and murder her was so alien to her thinking that it only served to put Victoria more on edge.

The door opened after a few minutes, admitting a woman that Victoria assumed was the doctor. She wore a vivid blue robe, a color that Victoria's mind identified as sapphire. It was covered with embroidery in various colors, primarily oranges and dark reds. Most prominent was a spiral wrapped around one arm which, the longer Victoria looked at it, seemed to contain endless levels of minute detail. Streaks of silver stood out in her otherwise short, reddish brown hair.

"Ah, Second Lord Pallasophia," she said smiling. "It's been some time since I have seen you in here. What seems to be the trouble?"

Pallasophia smiled in return. The cuts and bruises from their fight with the mastigas were obvious, especially the particularly vivid contusion on her left cheekbone and the cast Victoria helped to wrap around her arm. Victoria noticed an unusual tension in her posture that was not quite fear. Rather, she seemed somehow uneasy. "I'm fine, Second Lord Iro, despite appearances. I'm here to introduce you to an unexpected visitor."

Doctor Iro's eyes finally made it past Pallasophia's ripped and torn uniform and hastily-treated wounds and settled on the black suited figure in the corner. An unusual mixture of fear, shock, and joy passed across her features as she looked from the top of Victoria's head to the floor and back.

"Sweet Lady Lovelace," she muttered, "you did it."

Pallasophia took a small step toward the door, putting the other Second Lord and Victoria directly opposite one another. "Doctor Iro, allow me to introduce Victoria."

"Victoria," the doctor repeated, sounding it out and seeming to roll it around in her head for a moment.

"Allow me to leave you, then. I'll give you some privacy, doctor. Victoria, I'll have your things sent to your room." Pallasophia nodded once and left the room.

"Doctor Iro," Victoria enunciated.

She jumped, then suppressed her shock with a laugh.

"What is it?"

"I suppose I didn't expect you to be able to talk," she admitted.

Victoria cocked her head to one side. That, she thought, was an oddly specific preconception to have. The team of soldiers who came to rescue her had not expressed such doubts. If they possessed them, they either kept them to themselves or worked them out before coming to answer her challenge.

Of course, the doctor did not exude the same sort of lethal air the soldiers did. Victoria supposed it made sense, relying on the encyclopedic definition of "doctor" her brain called up on demand despite never hearing the word before. Doctors healed; soldiers fought.

She did seem confident, however. Whether that was in her own ability—her voluminous robes made it hard to judge her physique—or if she simply placed her trust in Pallasophia's hands, Victoria could not yet tell.

"I'm going to assume, given how you reacted, that you know who I am."

Iro nodded. "We used to call you 'The Champion' back when you were only a hypothetical." She shook her head. "I'm sorry, that must have sounded heartless."

Rather than reply, Victoria continued watching the doctor through her tinted visor.

After a moment, Iro continued. "Anyway, to answer your actual question, yes. After the Incident, I voiced my dissent. I said that we ought to assault the lower levels and bring you, and the others with you, out of there and continue the Project properly.

"I was overruled."

"I see."

"Pallasophia is not a bad woman," she said quickly. "She..."

Victoria interrupted. "She explained the urgency of my, ah, existence to me already."

Iro's face darkened a bit. "Then you understand why we did the things we did."

"Understand, yes. Accept? I haven't decided."

"I can't blame you."

Victoria shifted in her chair. "Pallasophia said you were a Second Lord. I assume you're equal to her in rank?"

"In rank, yes, but she was also Aphelion's facilities manager. Ultimately, she was senior to everyone except Tritogenes himself."

"The Hexarch."

Iro smiled. "Yes. You learned a lot from those soldiers."

"I already knew a great deal. As a doctor, I assume you had a hand in that, so I suppose I have you to thank for the knowledge that saved my life."

"Pallasophia invented the process. I merely oversaw its implementation. Though, now I admit your presence puts me ill at ease."

"Why? From the sounds of it, you should be celebrating." Victoria made a derisive snort. "Your 'Champion' is alive."

"Your survival down there," she made a vague gesture toward the floor, "is proof that this Project was worth all of the time, all the *lives*, we put into it."

"Do you know how many deaths went into my..." Victoria stopped as she searched for the words she wanted. Finally, she settled on, "my engineering?"

"Many," Doctor Iro replied. Her voice was flat, face neutral. If she felt the same sting Victoria did, she hid it well. "Pallasophia was often upset by the measures she took to ensure this Project's success."

"'Upset?'" Victoria echoed, derision in her voice.

"Yes. It weighed heavily on her soul—on Tritogenes as well. The cost in lives brought her much," Iro paused, "frustration is not the proper word, because it ran deeper than that, yet sorrow is also not quite right. My job here was not just as a medical doctor, but also as councilor for them. I share that responsibility with Second Lord Philip, who resides in Tritogenes's palace on Limani."

"I see. I notice you're not using their ranks," Victoria observed.

Iro shook her head and smiled. "No, I find that such formalities tend to interfere with my duties as a doctor. You don't seem to put much stock in it, either."

Victoria nodded once. "I've been bathing in mastigas blood for days, doctor. Formality isn't in the picture."

The doctor nodded once. "That must have been difficult."

Coming from the wrong person, or delivered by the right person in the wrong way, that line might have seemed judgmental. Victoria felt a brief, involuntary bristling along her spine, but Iro's gentle demeanor put her concerns to rest.

Victoria nodded once, but her actual reply was a dismissive shrug a moment later. "That place was my definition of 'normal,' doctor."

Iro's eyes were sad for a moment before she looked away to busy herself looking for something in a drawer. "I suppose that would make things worse."

Victoria watched her withdraw things from first one drawer, then another before speaking again. "You're awfully comfortable around someone who killed a mastigas elite with her bare hands."

"I am not a mastigas," Iro replied. Her lips quirked momentarily into the barest of smiles.

"No," Victoria countered, "humans are significantly easier to deal with than mastigas."

Iro turned, a strange sort of smile on her face. "Yes, but you've got no reason to kill me, do you?"

"Do I?"

The doctor clasped her hands behind her back and turned to face Victoria. Her voice was firm, but level when she said, "you do not."

Victoria felt some of her tension easing. Early on, she learned to tell when the smaller varieties of mastigas were angry or simply scared. The difference was important, as she quickly figured out. The angry ones were predictable. The scared ones were not, and no amount of experience gave her the knowledge of how to accurately prepare for them.

The soldiers had been scared at first. She supposed she could not blame them. She did greet them with a man-height sword before overpowering and disarming the entire team. As they grew more comfortable, their behavior around her grew less erratic as well.

With this doctor already exuding that level of comfort, or at least confidence, Victoria felt more at ease than she had in some time. She wondered to herself if this was what "safety" felt like.

Victoria uncrossed her arms and sank back into the chair slightly. "What sort of tests are you going to run?"

"Tests?" Iro raised one eyebrow.

"I assume that's why I'm here."

"You're here, my dear Champion, because you've been wounded in your brave struggle for survival."

Inside her helmet, Victoria narrowed her eyes slightly. Her posture never changed. "And none of my blood or tissue will find its way into your machines?"

Iro chuckled to herself. "Pallasophia said you were perceptive."

"I imagine it's why I'm still alive."

"One reason, yes." Iro smiled. "Yes, I will be running tests on you as well, simple ones. I'll check your blood for pathogens or signs that your body might have been damaged in ways beyond obvious wounds. Organ damage, or poison, for instance."

"I would know if I've been poisoned," Victoria said. She crossed one ankle over the opposite knee. "I remember dying from several kinds."

"You remember," Iro said, then frowned. She spoke quietly, more to herself than Victoria, it seemed. "Yes, I suppose you would. I warned Pallasophia against using such vivid memories."

Victoria hummed, but said nothing. That statement alone conveyed a lot of information. She would never know how many nightmares she might have avoided, sleep interrupted by cold sweat and the memory of vomiting to death, if she had simply been educated with simple facts to identify poisons.

On the other hand, she reasoned, playing devil's advocate with herself, would such bland thoughts have had as much impact as the memory of feeling cold as her muscles liquefied because she drank from the wrong water source?

341

She shook off the memories and the fog that came with them. "Yes. I remember a great many things that never happened to me."

Iro seemed visibly shaken by that particular revelation and so Victoria decided not to press any more. "Well," the Doctor said, "for even a cursory inspection of your wounds, I have to ask if you would remove your helmet and clothing."

Victoria considered that for a moment. Around the soldiers, she did little more than take off her helmet. Despite that, Iro's examination room, and the doctor herself, radiated a feeling of safety.

After a moment, she said, "I'm going to keep my weapons nearby."

Iro's face brightened with a momentary smile. "Of course."

Victoria undid the strap under her chin and slipped the stolen mastigas helmet over her head. The sudden increase in light dazzled her eyes, and she shrank backward with her hands up in an automatic defensive reflex. The room might not have been quite as bright as the elite's arena, but it was brighter than anything else down there.

After a moment, when her vision cleared, she realized Doctor Iro was staring. The expression on her face was strange, different from what it had been before she removed the helmet, and Victoria struggled to comprehend the emotions beneath it. She thought for a moment that, despite her previous calm, the doctor actually looked somewhat frightened now.

No, she realized, not frightened—awed. If that was the case, Victoria thought she ought to try Iro's own trick against her.

She made a little half smile, hoping it seemed genuine. "Don't tell me there's something wrong with my face."

"No," Iro replied, after a moment. A smile crept across her face and she let out a small laugh. Her shoulders relaxed slightly. "No, there's nothing wrong with your face. It is simply that, behind that mask, you could have been anyone. You could even have been..."

"One of them?"

342

Iro let out a sigh. "Yes," she admitted. "Given your clothing and weapons, that thought crossed my mind, as did the idea that Tritogenes might have given up and ordered Project Titan to create an android instead."

"Would that be possible?"

Iro shook her head, but said, "ordinarily I would say no, as it's never been done before, but neither have you."

"Trust me, if I was a robot, there wouldn't be nearly as much of my blood staining the floor down there as there is."

"And now here you sit."

"And here I sit. So, what tests do you have to run?"

"Nothing invasive, I assure you. I need to run a few blood tests and scans. Check your hormone levels and..."

She continued explaining what was going to happen, but Victoria's mind had not been shaped for medical science and she quickly lost track of the procedures and tests. She simply nodded along, comforted in the knowledge that none of them would be as painful as a mastigas blade.

She concluded with, "first, however, we need to actually treat your wounds. Quick heal can only do so much."

Victoria nodded and began the process of removing her handmade clothing. The black garment was festooned with ties holding various overlapping layers together, ties that took some time to knot or, as she needed to do at the moment, unknot. Iro stood nearby, close enough to help if Victoria asked, but never once reached for anything.

Completely undoing the ties was difficult enough as her aching muscles and joints fought her. Much worse was the sensation of her flesh being pulled as the tattered pieces of fabric unstuck themselves from her wounds. It took more time than she thought it should have, but Victoria kept herself calm by counting breaths, happy that Iro did not offer to help.

Finally, the outer layers were off. Underneath them was the bandage she used to bind her chest. Like her outer layers, it was made of stolen mastigas fabric. The bandages underneath that, like those wrapped around her arms and legs, were from Pallasophia's medical field kit and were soaked with a mixture of her blood, mastigas blood, and the residue of quick heal.

Iro's eyes grew progressively wider as Victoria removed bandage after bandage. Scars stood out against her skin, some white, some pink, and some still the curious red they turned after coming in contact with mastigas blood.

Victoria carefully laid her clothes in the chair she had been occupying. The bandages from the soldiers' kit, she placed in a box for biological waste provided by the doctor.

Iro grew more comfortable, more clinical as well, as she inspected Victoria's wounds. She came to the deep gash in her side from the elite's sword and asked, "who did this?"

"The elite."

Iro chuckled. "No, I mean the stitching."

"I did that myself."

Iro hummed. "With your permission, I'd like to remove these stitches, clean, and re-close it myself."

"'My permission?'" Victoria echoed. Out of everything she experienced since encountering Pallasophia and her team of soldiers, that simple statement jarred her more than anything else.

Iro nodded. "I'm a doctor, not a jailer. I won't do anything without a patient's permission."

"Even if the Hexarch orders it?"

"A doctor has certain privileges that supersede rank. Regardless, may I?"

Victoria nodded, and Iro went to work. She numbed the area, a sensation Victoria found profoundly strange, removed the thread she had sewn there, and washed the cut.

"You used mastigas blood on this." It was not a question.

"Yes. I knew about it from... another life."

"I see."

"That idea bothers you, doesn't it?"

Iro continued looking at her work stitching Victoria's side up. Her voice was suddenly formal. "As I said before, I objected on an ethical basis to the manner in which this Project was carried out. That, however, is the past. I could no more change it than I could have fought that elite myself."

After another two hours, Doctor Iro pronounced her wounds as cleaned and cared for as they could be. She provided Victoria with a simple, gray hospital gown. Her clothing and weapons—aside from a single fonias knife she insisted on strapping to her bare calf despite Iro's assurances that she did not need it—now resided in a large bag slung over her shoulder.

As she escorted Victoria back to the waiting room, Iro reminded her that she had only cleaned Victoria's wounds and impressed upon her the necessity for bathing as soon as she was able to remove the rest of the dirt and blood. She also promised to tell her everything the tests found, and to explain, if necessary, what any of it meant.

"One final thing," Iro said. "We will most likely want to schedule several more appointments over the coming weeks to monitor your vital signs and other important factors."

Victoria nodded. "I understand."

Pallasophia was waiting for them. She wore a blue robe like the doctor's, but of a different shade and with different embroidery. The bruises and cuts still stood out on her face, but she looked like she had washed and cleaned her own wounds as well. She too stared when she saw Victoria without her helmet on.

Iro smiled. "Hello again, Pallasophia."

The other Second Lord shook off her surprise and stood. "How is she?"

"Excellent health, despite her wounds. Perhaps in better health than anyone else I have ever seen."

Pallasophia nodded, then turned to Victoria. "Good. I'm sure you want to sleep. If you'll follow me, I'll escort you to my suite here."

"Your suite?"

"Yes. I have a private kitchen and dining room and several guest rooms."

Victoria nodded slowly. If the guest rooms were as comfortable as the chairs in Iro's examination room, she supposed she could do worse. More importantly, she still had her knives and baton.

"Thank you, doctor," Pallasophia said, and turned to leave.

"Go with the suns, Victoria," Iro said, inclining her head slightly.

Victoria paused, turned back to where Iro stood watching the two of them and nodded in return. Unsure of what she was supposed to say in return, or even if there was a proper reply, she said, "you too, doctor."

Epilogue

Later that evening, a man in an yellow robe met with a woman in green. They stood just inside one of the smaller embarkation areas adjacent to the main landing pad atop the Aphelion's roof. Shuttles came and went every so often up there and it was always milling with people, so the two of them went entirely unnoticed.

A shuttle roared nearby, loud even through the walls.

"You are certain?" she asked.

The man nodded. "Fourth Lord Markos confirmed it himself."

"And you trust him?"

"I have no reason not to. He said that Second Lord Glaukos was very reverent in her presence."

"Did either of them address this woman by name or title?"

"No, Third Lord," he replied. The two of them had never used names, only the ranks that were obvious by their robes.

"And yet you are sure?"

"I am, Third Lord. Markos said she was not in the system registry, and the only people who would be missing from the system are criminals, those religious fools from Prosgeiosi, and..."

"And," the Third Lord Finished, "someone who was born at this facility."

"My thoughts exactly, Third Lord."

"I assume you have proof to back up your claims?" she asked.

The Fourth Lord nodded. "I do." He produced a small holodrive from the folds of his robe and held it out. It glittered with the same sort of artwork and decoration that covered everything else around them, perfectly unremarkable.

The Third Lord pocketed the holodrive with a swift, but unhurried, motion.

"That contains the few images that Fourth Lord Markos was able to capture as well as the biometric data the passive scanners were able to measure through her armor."

"Armor?" The Third Lord asked, raising an eyebrow.

He nodded. "Yes, Third Lord. Fourth Lord Markos said that her armor looked to be mastigas in origin."

"Fascinating."

"My thoughts as well."

"You have done well, Fourth Lord," she said after a moment's consideration. "I will arrange to have the payments made as discreetly as possible."

"Thank you, Third Lord."

"I should be thanking you, Fourth Lord. It is not often I get to bring such news to the First Lord. My Hexarch will be pleased to have a leg up on Tritogenes when the time comes."

"Go with the suns, Third Lord."

"Go with the suns, Fourth Lord," she said, and turned. "I must be off. My ship will be leaving very soon."

AUTHOR'S NOTES

The story that would eventually become *Scourge of Gods* started out as two separate writing projects. I'll explain what one of them was in the notes of volume 3, I think. Even going into what that idea was would result in a number of spoilers for volumes 2 and 3, so it'll remain a mystery.

The one I *will* talk about now goes back to the age-old divide among writers between people who plan their stories and people who just "wing it." I've always been the latter, what we call a "pantser," because we write "by the seat of our pants," but I wanted to see if I could take that one step further.

So, when I started writing *Scourge*, then simply titled "Arena Story," I did so with zero plan at all. I had a single image: a shadowy figure watching a monster prowl an arena, grumbling about how "none of them are good enough" before the hero/heroine arrived to kill the monster. That was it. I had no idea if the figure was good, evil, or something in between. That figure ended up being Tritogenes, so make your own moral judgements.

Likewise, nothing about the Technocracy was ever planned. It all flowed organically through the first draft. Later revisions would clean things up, but the initial pieces of Technocrat culture and symbolism are essentially exactly as they came to me. Even "Hexarch" was an idea fleshed out after the term came about—I wrote "Hexarch" and then had to figure out what the hell that actually was.

What resulted was a single 170k novel. When every beta reader agreed that they wanted more, I sat down to break it apart and re-write it. That resulted in what you have now: three 109k (roughly) novels. It's still Victoria's story, but we get a lot more of the rest of the world, and I think that was a change for the better.

The expansion allowed me to show more about the other Titans, the Hexarchs, and even the world itself. I got to explore *how* the world functioned and why, and what sort of customs and art these people have. When it was all said and done, *Born in Darkness* was roughly 50% original draft and 50% new material.

Ultimately, I had a lot of fun writing this story, and the cast and worlds are some of my favorite so far. I feel like I say that about every story, but in this case it's *actually* true.

I chose, again, to center the story around a female hero, a female *super*hero in this case, because I feel the world could use more of them. I see what those kinds of characters mean to people close to me, and I think, "yes. More of that."

Special thanks to my father, John Farmer, and to Don Church, both of whom convinced me to re-write the story as a trilogy. Jason McTeer, William Wagers, and Alyssa Underwood also deserve a ton of thanks for being excellent editors and sticking it out with me.

Additional thanks to: Rick Lowden, Mike Huddleston, Ashley Ward, Steve and Diane Mitchell, Becky Spain-Kaiser, Jacob Forbes, Heather Green, Beth Davis, Kaycee Dortch, Will Nunn, Jan Parks, Sarah Phillips, and Susan and John Farmer

ABOUT THE AUTHOR

Born to geeky parents and raised on a diet of Star Trek and Babylon 5, Thomas started writing at an early age, working his way through fanfictions of all types. For good or ill, a lot of that early work has been lost.

Writing occupied much of his spare time throughout school and the years after, eventually culminating in an ostensible *magnum opus* he calls the "Chronicles of St. Michael." To this date, those stories still reek of many "early writer" problems, but he promises they will, one day, see the light of publication.

What can you expect next? Odds are, the next project is going to be the sequel to "The Week the World Ended," but the title is, for now, a secret.

He also hosts a podcast (internet radio show, when he's feeling fancy) called "Authors in Abstract." As of this book, the show is well into its second season. You can listen to the podcast on a variety of platforms, or by going directly to www.authorsinabstract.com

When his hands aren't full with books, reading or writing, he fills them with swords. Four nights a week, as of this publication anyway, he teaches historic fencing, also called HEMA (Historic European Martial Arts) as one of the head coaches of the Knoxville Academy of the Blade (www.facebook.com/KABFencing)

He lives with his wife, Stephanie, their three cats, lizard, and snake.

www.ingramcontent.com/pod-product-compliance
Lightning Source LLC
Chambersburg PA
CBHW051326250626
47155CB00007B/2476